Silent Strike

A TROY STOKER, M.D. PSYCHIATRY THRILLER

DR. FRANCIS BANDETTINI
MATT NILSEN

Naoband, LLC
Baltic, South Dakota

To Naomi

To Julie

First Naoband, LLC paperback edition March 2019

This book is a work of fiction. Any references to historical events, real people, or real places are used fictitiously. Other names, characters, places, and events are products of the authors' imaginations, and any resemblance to actual events or places or persons living or dead is entirely coincidental.

ISBN: 0-578-47752-1
ISBN-13: 978-0-578-47752-7

Visit TroyStokerMD.com

@TroyStokerMD

 facebook.com/TroyStokerMD

Sometimes life is suffering. But how we endure the suffering can fulfill a grand life.
                    - Dr. Francis Bandettini

ACKNOWLEDGMENTS

We express appreciation to Naomi Bandettini for her edits and insights. Thank you, Alicia Colon, for your review, valuable critique, and keen insight. Adam Nilsen provided some early pushback that helped us to sharpen characters and the storyline. Jennifer Schovaers exposed a few myopias and connected numerous dots. Dr. Dave Auch for his military and historical insight. Kris Small taught us about HALO jumping. Richard Iverson, MD, introduced us to the Balamuthia mandrillaris amoeba. There are also numerous other friends in the military and civilian life, along with new acquaintances, who have provided keen insight but must remain anonymous. We owe you our sincere gratitude.

Dr. Bandettini wishes to thank his patients for providing him always with a continuing learning experience. As he wishes to express, "It is my deepest hope that in my continued working with all of you who may read this book that we all come to realize that we are really helping each other in this journey through life."

CHAPTER 1

Black Rock City, Nevada

For once, hijab wrapped around her face, she blended in with these Americans. Almost all the infidels around her shrouded their faces, thanks to the wind and sand. The lead engineer from CoolSolar kept a low profile while setting up for the big event, without averting her eyes and attention from her task in this holy cause. With one day remaining before the Burning Man Festival, carpenters, technicians, and stagehands worked at a feverish pace to make everything just right—or as perfect as it had to be for this hedonist event. Today the Iranian engineer would fit in just fine. With the unforgiving dry wind kicking up the desert sand, her hijab just seemed like a ubiquitous piece of apparel to prevent sand from entering her eyes, ears, mouth, and nose. Many other workers were wearing dust protecting goggles and face coverings—with no modest intent.

Tomorrow they arrive, Roya thought, *scorning modesty and celebrating debauchery. Now and then exclaiming some platitude of empty reverence to the trendy mother-earth goddess, Gaia, in the middle of the Nevada desert.* "A false goddess that demands nothing of her worshipers."

CoolSolar was providing a simple solution to help attendees cool off in the summer heat. Roya, a quiet, submissive mechanical engineer, was erecting a large mist machine powered by solar panels. The powers that be at Burning Man had assigned CoolSolar a prime location, along the road that traveled through the middle of the festival. In an area called the Six O'clock Sector, burners could linger to cool down. Tomorrow this high-volume corridor would team with people living the rapturous fantasy of radical self-expression.

The CoolSolar engineer set up the system with efficient precision. Her boss had walked her through more than a dozen drills when he taught her to assemble it in a Chicago warehouse. Like clockwork, she connected the structure, tubes, solar panels, water pump, and mist sprayers. And now, this humble woman from Iran was ready for the real attack. While the assault would be potent, this strike was also a dress rehearsal for greater silent ambushes to come. Broadway musicals had dress rehearsals. Sports teams had preseason games. And, Roya's cell had the Burning Man attack. The dress rehearsals and games meant something, but not as much as the events to follow.

The most critical action was adding an amoeba-infested solution to the water tanks without infecting herself. For Roya, the engineer with laser focus, discipline, and radicalized passion, this would be a gratifying moment. She had been loyal to the Shiite cause since her childhood. Her mist system would send the water-droplet-bound amoebas into the air. Most of the pathogens would fall to the ground and perish. But, those amoebas that implanted into humans would wreak havoc on their central nervous systems.

"An ideal target." That's how, Nikolas, the attack's mastermind described the event to Roya during their last rehearsal in Chicago. "This Burning Man Festival is perfect, with these American heathens at their height of debauchery in the middle of the Nevada desert. Local law enforcement will never detect the attack. They'll already be stretched too thin by the sudden influx of non-conformity. In silence, the wrath of Allah will afflict these devils for weeks before their symptoms ever appear," the man from the Middle East preached.

But why was the man's name Greek? Roya wondered. Even more peculiar, this person named Nikolas lived in America as a successful businessman. When Roya arrived in America, she started out working in his Chicago hotel—an ignoble role for an engineer. Nikolas, under a directive from Iran's Ministry of Intelligence and Security, invited her to also work on his other projects, like CoolSolar. As a hotel worker, American law enforcement would never suspect her as a potent jihadist. Because she was female, the Middle Eastern men in the cell would never suspect her skill and intelligence as an engineer. No leaks. Because only Nikolas would know what she was up to.

"Our silent Burning Man attack will afflict thousands," Roya had replied. She almost never interjected her thoughts when talking to Nikolas. But, the attack on Burning Man was the culminating incursion. Expressing her fervor was appropriate. "When our scourge, at last, appears among these godless whores—weeks after their pagan desert ritual—the upheaval will horrify every American heart. Hospitals across America will reach a slow, inescapable boil of sickness and death."

The man smiled and exclaimed, "Says the Koran, 'And whoever disbelieves, I will grant him enjoyment for a short while, then I will drive him to the chastisement of the fire; and it is an evil destination.' The prophet foretold this day! This Burning Man is the fire; and we shall provide the chastisement. What is the weapon that will chastise the heathens?"

Roya paused for a moment to make sure this was not a rhetorical question—that the man with the Greek name, in fact, expected her to answer the question. When he did not answer his own question, Roya proceeded. "Weeks after the fire of Burning Man, the chastisement, cited in the Holy Koran, is a one-celled organism. These organisms will bury themselves into the matter of the infidels' brains. It is the amoeba, Balamuthia mandrillaris."

"Yes! It is all so clear. This festival, it is indeed an evil destination. Can you envision another place on earth more depraved? And, this attack is just the beginning. Soon the masses will weep."

Two years ago, Nikolas started a business that appeared harmless on the surface, CoolSolar. But, he had apocalyptic intent. During the summer, the new firm would set up solar-powered mist machines at events such as outdoor concerts. CoolSolar provided these services for free under the guise of promoting the firm's new solar-powered technology. Until now, the mist only contained harmless water.

Tomorrow, when the outside temperature reached eighty-three degrees, Roya would exercise great caution as she poured gallons of an amoeba-rich solution into the mist system's water tank. She would then walk far away and be careful not to return for a few hours. "Avoid any risk of infection," Nikolas had warned her. "We need you for the duration of the war."

Roya was willing to die. As an Iranian spy, no one frightened her. Her fear was reserved for Allah. She had many battles to fight, as the person in charge of ramping up CoolSolar's amoeba attack operations. And, she wanted to see the day—to experience the moment—when Sharia would rule America. She envisioned a future when she could wear her hijab in good company—when all women would cease revealing too much of their faces, hair, necks, and arms.

Nevertheless, I must focus on the here and now; and my job in this battle is critical, she thought.

So, she had driven a large pickup truck, pulling a sizable cargo trailer, from Chicago to the Black Rock Desert of Nevada. She transported the solution containing gallons of the Balamuthia amoeba-infected water, stored at a perfect temperature. And now, as she finished testing the mist system, she could, at long last, rest. It was time for her to pitch her tent a good distance from the Six O'clock Sector and wait for night to fall. Rest was critical. Over the next few weeks, she would need all her strength. Burning Man was just the first silent volley in the war that would bring down the Great Satan. Roya still had so much work with dozens of other attacks.

CHAPTER 2

Near Chihuahua, Mexico

With one quick step Stoker won the bet. As much as he loved his adrenalin rush, he loved the feeling that Rivera was watching from below cursing the devil while watching Stoker fall through the sky. He had learned some things during his training much quicker than Rivera would ever admit to him. Stoker bet Rivera he could solo HALO parachute within two jumps.

Damn that Stoker, Rivera thought as he watched from the desert floor. *He's won this ridiculous bet.* Rivera would never admit it to Stoker, but his friend was indeed an exceptional man. But, Rivera knew that Stoker had a tremendous ability to surpass physical and mental limits as he had seen while training this thirty-three-year-old man.

HALO jumping from 13,500 feet, Troy Stoker activated his chute at a mere 2,500 feet. It was on the low side, especially for his first jump solo; but he wanted to give Rivera a little rush. The adrenalin surge from the fall collided with 102-degree fury as the Mexican desert swiftly rose to meet him. Troy Stoker, a soldier and psychiatrist, was completing special operator training. With this continued parachute descent toward the desert floor, he ticked off the last of his specialized training exercises.

He knew why life was taking him in a new direction. Stoker had learned a lot in his service of humanity as a physician. But, he could see how his country would also utilize his unique skills. Rivera once told him he had the *cojones* for this new position. Stoker took that as a compliment. And, here he was, just a few miles outside of the Mexican border town of Chihuahua.

As he descended under canopy, he checked his chute. Finding it square, stable, and steerable, he turned his attention to surveying the terrain below. Stoker sensed a little surprise when he saw a group of men who appeared to be of Middle Eastern descent. They seemed to be running in formation some distance ahead of him, jogging in a synchronized military cadence. Had the runners looked back, the blinding sun may or may not have obscured their view of

Stoker suspended from his chute. He angled away and increased his vertical airspeed by grabbing his front risers and pulling the lines to his chest. Missing his anticipated landing zone was a deliberate decision. He needed a rapid descent to get him to the desert floor where the enemy could not detect him.

After landing, Stoker packed and stashed the parachute and started tracking the men. Stoker used his radio to call Rivera. "Alpha Bravo Two, this is Medic Alpha One. We might have an interesting situation here. Will explain later after a sitrep in thirty. Over. Over."

Sitrep was short for a situation report, which Stoker would provide once he knew more about the out-of-place runners. He assessed the situation as he ran behind them. Making mental notes on these tangos, he followed and surveilled for two miles. When he got back on the radio with Rivera he had insights to share.

"This is Medic Alpha One reporting approximately ten to fifteen possible tangos running in formation, in what appears to be training exercises approximately three clicks north of my position. Over."

There was a small crackling silence, and Rivera got on, seemingly upset. "What the hell are you doing, Stoker? Over."

"Colonel Rivera, I see ten to fifteen tangos, about two clicks north of my position." Stoker said, "Over. Over."

"What the hell are you talking about? Tangos? What's going on? Over."

Stoker frowned, and with some exasperation, thought about how he would reply. "Rivera, I'm on a training mission. And, if I'm going to train, I'm going to start tracking these boys. You know, those Shiites we've been watching." Then he let his irritation crackle through the radio. "You can track me, and I'll track them! How about that? Over."

"If this is some type of joke?" Rivera asked. "You almost killed yourself waiting to pull your pins at that low altitude! The CYPRES unit almost activated your reserve chute for you. Over."

"I'll explain later." With his sixty-pound pack, Stoker ran for an additional hour. He kept pace with the group while maintaining a one to two-mile distance. Every twenty minutes, they stopped to participate in different combat exercises. The group commenced their run again and again after each objective was met.

By default, this chance encounter with these Iranians,

Lebanese, and Yemenis preempted Stoker's training. Circumstances catapulted him into this real mission. These enemies had been training here in the Mexican desert. And, they were days away from slipping into the United States and joining a cell of like-minded Shiites.

After a few more miles, their leader stopped the men and drilled them in battlefield hand signals and communication. Stoker crept closer. But, the sparse desert vegetation, mostly parched creosote bushes and an occasional tumbleweed, offered him limited camouflage. Finding an observation point around an outcropping of rocks, he decided two hundred yards was about the right distance to avoid detection.

Dr. Stoker took a keen interest in the body language of the leader as well as the men he commanded. This gave Stoker some important clues as to how these men operated as a group. He noticed four stars on the leader's shoulder epaulets. "A *sarvan*," Stoker said under his breath, whispering the Farsi word for captain. At a clinic in Chihuahua, he had treated some of these men. Stoker looked on as the *sarvan*, whom he had also seen as a patient in a brief visit, issued orders to these hardscrabble men in a language Stoker easily recognized. Instead of the staccato sounds of Mexican Spanish, he heard an idiom, Farsi, which flowed between smoother sounds. To Stoker, the language spoken in Iran sounded like some of the Eastern Block languages, with a few additional guttural tones and soft hisses.

This group, mostly composed of Iranians, was a band of new arrivals to the Mexican frontier, and Stoker was one member of a team paying attention to the radicals. The CIA needed help. The agency was over concentrating its assets and operatives in North Korea and Syria. Russia was also requiring more intelligence assets. Perhaps a mistake in Stoker's estimation. However, the nation of Iran, with its eighty-one million inhabitants, had significant resources now. But, the country's leaders, the ayatollahs, were motivated by a divine mandate to conquer and convert the world. The grand prize was the United States of America, The Great Satan. For more than thirty years, the ayatollahs carefully built sleeper cells in many parts of the United States. So, with his new team, *Espada Rápida*, Stoker would continue to watch this group of Shiites as they staged and trained. Here they were, just 200 miles south of the U.S.-Mexico border—foolish audacity! Stoker and the *Espada Rápida* team would report their ongoing intelligence gathering to the three alphabet agencies. The FBI's Joint Terrorism Taskforce had shown an acute interest in this battalion of mostly Iranians. The moment these aspiring terrorists crossed the border, the FBI was ready to track them and further infiltrate their network. As a physician, Stoker had treated many of these Muslim extremists in a clinic he and Rivera set up in Mexico as an intel gathering mission. He worked side by side with Dr. Errol Rivera. They both posed as physicians sympathetic to radical Islamic terrorists. As they had cared for their injuries, viruses, colds, and sexually transmitted diseases, they learned valuable bits of intelligence.

For the present situation, Stoker knew he had to stay hidden. Dehydration was his greatest enemy. He ran out of water an hour ago. With his high intensity running, he was starting to feel more than thirst. His abdominal and leg muscles were cramping from the heat and from lactic acid buildup. He felt nausea and a headache coming on, and then a wave of fatigue.

As Stoker was watching the tangos at their next stop, the rookie combatants engaged each other in simulated hand-to-hand combat. This group was different from other trainees he had seen in previous weeks. Their lackluster engagement was appalling by Stoker's military standards. These men would never survive unarmed combat. They showed no psychological evidence of focused aggression, grit, or anger. Their caliber of boldness felt like a bad handshake. Perhaps it was the heat. They practiced disarming gun-toting enemies. Their awkwardness with this drill was embarrassing, perhaps even to the men, Stoker thought. He wondered why this group was allowed to perform at such a low standard.

On an order from the *sarvan*, the combatants drank water. They gulped from large canteens. Stoker winced in envy. His parched throat burned. But, he had taken control of his mind, blocking his thirst. He was still walking and functioning. He had a radio, and he wasn't concerned. His body would let him know when he was in danger, and he would take heed soon enough.

The *sarvan* removed six daggers from his backpack. He gathered the men around in a half-circle and gave a brief demonstration. Looking toward a man to his right, he gestured for the man to attack him. His opponent accepted the challenge, and they sparred. The trainee was putting forth such halfhearted effort that the *sarvan* took his knife and stabbed the man perfectly between his second and third cervical vertebrae, which effectively gave this person a hangman's break and a rapid disconnection between his brain and his body. The others were horrified, and Stoker even was surprised. This man disconnected this young soldier's brain from the rest of his body and was leaving him in the sand to suffer. The *sarvan* walked over to the man, stood over him with two feet, looked at his head whose eyes were slowly closing and before he died he said something about wanting rest. He moved in closer. "Now you will have rest." He spat at him. "May Allah take your soul to hell! Your fellow soldiers now understand how serious our *jihad* is and how hard we must work—the great suffering we must endure to earn paradise."

Stoker hastily chose a large rock to conceal himself. He crawled his way back behind this perfect observation area. Stoker witnessed almost thirty minutes of sparring with the training daggers. Now, their motivation renewed by a jolt of fear, the men trained with increased intensity.

Stoker heard a noise behind him. Instinctively he flinched and pushed himself away from the disturbance. A rattlesnake came out from the cover of the rock and coiled. Stoker flinched away from the snake. Through the lens of a nine-power rifle scope, a Persian eye caught the sudden movement. After a hurried shout, two of his comrades picked up automatic rifles and started running toward Stoker and aiming in an undisciplined fashion. It was most likely a combination of fear and bloodlust that was directed toward Stoker. He was exhausted. He felt thirsty. But, his senses were awakened. In an evolutionary sense, his ancient human DNA evolved over millennia and was always helpful in a fight or flight situation. Stoker revived instantly. A surge of adrenaline and glucose flowed into his bloodstream.

Instinctively, Stoker dove back behind the rock and landed on his stomach. A steady barrage of bullets pierced the air around him. A shockwave of pain seared his right forearm. Stoker looked up just in time to see the rattlesnake coiled, ready to strike a second time. Before Stoker could pull his arm away, the snake pierced his flesh again. He yanked his burning limb away from the reptile and rolled to safety, exposing himself briefly to the gunmen. There was only one place that was safe from gunfire, and it sheltered the lethal viper.

Time slowed. Fractional seconds expanded to slow motion in Stoker's brain. Stoker, genetically blessed with lightning-fast reflexes, enabled his training to take over. He reached for his Kimber 1911 Gold Match II and aimed the .45 caliber hollow point projectile into the snake's shadowed lair. Stoker had laser-like focus with weapons. One bullet flew past Stoker's ear with a supersonic crack, but his serenity only grew deeper. He pulled the trigger once, firing at a vague shadowed outline of the rattlesnake. Then, Stoker took a flying leap toward the rattlesnake's lair. His impact with the ground shocked him, but the realization that the snake must be under his hardened pectoral muscles was evident. He thought to himself, *wait until I tell Rivera about this one.*

More enemy bullets flew around him. Time sped up, and the burning in his forearm almost overwhelmed him in his weakened state.

Sitting up now with his spine pressing against the rock, he quickly inventoried his situation. "I'm breathing," he said aloud to himself. "I'm not bleeding." He needed to quickly tourniquet his arm until he reached safety. He had no idea how long it would be, hoping it was quick enough. He pulled off his belt, which luckily was the kind that had no holes, but rather ratchets. Stoker immediately and entirely restricted the circulation in his arm. He could stop the blood flow for forty to fifty-five minutes with no damage. It would be better than dying.

The volley of bullets continued to fly around him. Excruciating pain enveloped him. Dozens of rounds had already ricocheted off the rock. His enemy's lack of training was evident. They were wasting ammo. As far as he knew, he had fired one bullet and he had twelve more to go with one spare clip. He could hear the enemy getting closer. And so, Stoker used valuable moments to listen and wait as the men were taking turns providing cover fire and then advancing. He estimated they were a hundred yards away. Volleys of rounds continued. There was some concern about ricochet, but he did not believe he was in a line of fire—yet. His instincts could not be ignored. He had to live. But to live he had to kill. *I am the predator. They are the prey.*

Reaching for his utility belt, he grabbed a grenade and waited. When the time was right, Stoker, with searing pain in his arm, pulled the pin and threw the grenade. It made its mark. The gunfire ceased as he heard frantic cries. The men recognized fate. Stoker positioned himself right against the rock and looked down at the dead viper and said, "Damn you," as he felt the report and the concussion of the grenade. The rock's protection and the distance from the explosion spared him from any damage. The assailants weren't so lucky.

Stoker looked out from behind the rock. He thought to himself, *Now is the time to go after those bastards.* In a full sprint, he used precious seconds afforded after the grenade to reach a sandstone ledge. He jumped out and found three bloodied men on the ground. He didn't feel that they could provide any information. He did not want them to suffer. He put two quick bullets into each man's brain. These choices might have been difficult at one time, but they were easy now—almost a little too easy. Stoker had one thing on his mind, survival.

He drew his FN Five-Seven pistol from his right leg holster. This was Stoker's choice for accuracy and distance. He loved the boat-tail bullets that filled his twenty-round clip. This gun was essentially a rifle with armor-piercing bullets—in his hand. He raised his weapon to his side and took a few moments. Stoker heard no footsteps. He quickly counted the bodies—or what he could make out of the grenade-mangled bodies. There were between thirteen and fifteen dead men.

So much for my training! he thought. Stoker had risen to the occasion. It felt oddly automatic. However, there were still enemies missing! The group's *sarvan* escaped the grenade blast and fell back. Stoker scanned the horizon, and with his laser-targeting monocular he found his man at about eight hundred yards. This leader knew he had to die. But, so soon? He was looking for the army that killed his men.

Stoker really didn't have much time. The best outcome would be to discourage the *sarvan* from pursuing him. However, intelligence obtained from this man would be inherently useful. After scanning the horizon again, Stoker saw the battle-hardened officer taking cover behind some of the scant creosote bushes. Since most of the trainees were dead, Stoker decided to do something else seemingly outside of the military training box. He took aim at a patch of sand close to the *sarvan's* hiding spot. He compensated for elevation and squeezed the trigger. Stoker was a dead eye with an FN Five & Seven. He could hit a melon at a thousand yards, if he knew the approximate wind speed and humidity. The bullet threw up a puff of sand. After adjusting a few degrees, he pulled the trigger again. The second shot found its intended mark about two feet away from the officer. Stoker wanted to try to take him alive, but it was becoming increasingly difficult.

The *sarvan* emerged with fury from his insufficient cover, firing a standard AK-47, bullets spraying wildly. He didn't stand a chance at hitting Stoker. Even with his position compromised, Stoker still liked his options. He took a moment to survey the terrain behind him for avenues of retreat.

The volley stopped. Stoker knew the man was turning the banana clip around, so he popped up and laid down three shots of fire from his Five & Seven. The first one made sand fly up just to the right of the Iranian's foot. The second one landed just to the left. The third blew into his right shin and shattered his tibia. The officer hit the ground hard, screaming in agony.

With his foe immobilized, Stoker left his cover and started moving toward the *sarvan*. As Stoker approached the injured man, the Iranian reached for his AK-47. As he tried to raise his barrel, Stoker landed a round just to his right side and then immediately to his left. His stunning accuracy sent a message to the enemy. Stoker could kill him if he wanted. The message sunk in. The Iranian realized he was up against a formidable foe. Stoker gained another thirty yards, all the while watching his adversary writhing in the sand.

He ejected his clip and popped in a new mag in less than two seconds. His adrenaline rush was wearing off. It had saved his life. Now the realization of his exhaustion and dehydration was starting to set in. He wanted to vomit. As Stoker was closing in, he decided that he didn't want to be shot at anymore. He shot at the man's right arm and hit it. Then, he aimed at the man's left shoulder hitting it square in the socket. At fifty yards, he was very accurate. Stoker intended to prevent the *sarvan* from his continued shooting. The man's trainees were dead, and the leader was lying in the desert with some possible critical information.

Stoker realized that his energy levels were waning. His dehydration was a great concern. He forced himself to draw in two deep breaths. As Stoker reached the *sarvan*, another wannabe soldier jumped out. Only a few feet away, the man attempted to stab Stoker with a dagger. Stoker immediately blocked the weapon and quickly broke the man's jaw with a right elbow strike. As the stunned man started to fall to the ground, Stoker reached to his left side, grabbed his K-bar knife, and slit the man's throat. Stoker realized this was almost an instinctive response. It was either kill or be killed. Black and white.

The *sarvan* was stunned at Stoker's intensity and ferocity. This single American took out his entire group. The leader's right arm would not respond, and his left was barely functioning. Stoker kicked his gun away, searched him for other weapons, and asked the man a question in Farsi. "What are you doing here in Mexico?"

The terrorist couldn't answer. He was so thunder-struck and shaken that one man had killed all his men—and he also spoke Farsi! As he resigned himself to Stoker, he looked up, and there seemed to be a strange looking bird appearing in the sky. He felt as if he were dying.

There was a roaring wind of turbines, steel, and sand that enveloped Troy Stoker and the dying man. The *sarvan* became fearful as the helicopter descended. It gracefully tilted forward and descended sharply creating a small sandstorm. With a banking turn, the helicopter circled to Stoker's left and came around. The bleeding man looked up and began shaking with fear. This was like no helicopter he had ever seen. He'd lost a lot of blood. Perhaps that was why he was hallucinating about this strange bird in the sky. And, this powerful man—perhaps an American—was now taking his hand and speaking in his own tongue of Farsi. The powerful man said to him, "Why are you here?" The man was so stunned he couldn't answer. He said again, "Why are you here?"

The Iranian noticed he was getting medical attention for his arm and shoulder from some strange people in black. It all felt very surreal to him. *Why were this infidel and these secretive people helping me?* They seemed to be coming out of nowhere. The *sarvan* was shaking, not only from shock, but also from intense fear and misunderstanding of who these people were.

Soldiers filed out of the helicopter to help Stoker with the injured captive. Even with his uncontrollable short, panting breath and searing pain from the rattlesnake bite, a brief smile of relief broke through Stoker's grimace. As Stoker stood, he realized that the Iranian was now in shock. He would have to be interrogated later.

Stoker remembered an experience a few months before when this elite group of hand-picked warriors landed on a frozen pond in South Dakota to help him. Together, they detained the man responsible for the attempted murder of one of his patients and the kidnapping of his wife. This was Troy Stoker, M.D.'s new band of brothers. The *Espada Rápida* team was there to extract their newest and probably most gifted recruit.

Thanks to Stoker's past military experience and his friendship with Errol Rivera, he had been invited into the private military fraternity. *Espada Rápida* took on special missions to protect and defend the United States. The low-profile, high-impact missions were less visible but essential in the ongoing war against terrorism and corruption. *Espada Rápida*'s association with the FBI Joint Terrorism Taskforce put them on the front lines of challenging missions—the kind that rarely made it into the news.

Three warriors fanned out from the helicopter to form a perimeter around the landing site and to monitor what appeared to be the remains of combatants. Two other warriors jumped out and started running toward their wounded teammate. "Troy, are you injured?" the warrior known as Z asked with urgency in his voice. "Yes," Stoker frowned as he answered gruffly. "But, I think the score is oh, I don't know, fifteen of them against one of me. And, I'm thirsty. Can I have some water?"

Z removed a water bottle from his pack and shoved it toward Stoker. "Drink this first eight ounces slow and easy, Troy. Those are Rivera's orders. He doesn't want you throwing up in his helicopter. You're severely dehydrated, so we'll give you fluids through an I.V."

With his one good hand and every bit of quivering energy he had, Stoker squeezed the bottle. In seconds, he drank all the water. Z opened another bottle and poured the water over Stoker's head. "Thank you," Stoker said as he reached for yet another bottle and took a swig. The relief was amazing. However, the pain from the snakebite interrupted the moment of renewal and demanded attention.

"My arm." Stoker winced as he held it up. It was swelling noticeably. "I think we should treat this."

Z looked at Stoker's injury and made a sour face. "Whoa! If

that hurts half as bad as that looks—"

"Yeah, and it's my left arm."

Z turned and spoke into the radio headset affixed to his ear. "Colonel Rivera, LZ is clear. We need your doctor hands out here with Stoker. And, could you bring whatever you need to treat a bad-ass snakebite for this badass out here?"

The helicopter door popped open and out jumped Errol Rivera. Warrior, helicopter pilot, colonel, and physician. He was also the original leader of *Espada Rápida*, which means "swift sword" in the language of his home country, Cuba, which he fled as a young man. He ran toward Stoker and Z.

"What's going on, *amigo*? Why are you the one having all the fun?" Rivera asked as he fell to his knees beside the prone Stoker.

"Oh, these damn snake bites, they're just a pain in the ass," Stoker grunted in pain as he knelt and elevated his arm. "They burn like hell. I'm sure that rattler envenomed me, and I need to get to a hospital to patch me up."

Rivera responded. "My gosh, Stoker! You descended so quickly on your HALO jump. I guess winning the bet was not enough for you? But, I know why you missed your designated landing
site—"

"I had to change my designated landing site," replied Stoker, "because I didn't want those tangos getting a look at me."

"Now I understand why you radioed," Rivera said. "I was just giving you a hard time. I know you were onto some tangos, but I had no idea you had to fight a small war singlehandedly. I'm sorry we weren't there to help you. But, you've turned into a real badass."

Stoker responded to Rivera. "No, you've turned me into a survivor. I didn't have a choice. But, I spent a lot of effort trying to keep that one guy alive for you." Stoker pointed at the injured Iranian and frowned." I'm assuming he's the leader." Then Stoker pointed in a different direction and asked, "See that boulder? You'll see dozens of bullet marks on one side and a dead bloody snake on the other that yours truly jumped on."

Rivera said, "Well that's one way to kill it."

"No, no," Stoker replied. "I shot it first."

"Well, that's another way to kill it I guess."

Rivera turned and ordered one of the soldiers. "Grab a plastic bag, and get what's left of that snake. The head and tail are the most important parts." Rivera turned to Z. "And, you get to help me with Troy. This snake bite could be serious."

Rivera unzipped two medical bags. "Okay, Z," Rivera said as he examined Stoker's snakebite. "See the red line around the fang marks?" Rivera removed a Sharpie from one of the bags. "Take this indelible pen and draw a line around the border where Troy's skin is starting to turn a bright, beefy red." Rivera gently elevated Stoker's arm to shoulder height. Stoker winced and let out a grunt. "By drawing the line," Rivera continued, "we're documenting how the skin cellulitis damage advances. Every ten minutes we assess the swelling again and draw a new border. But if it doesn't advance, we don't draw over the same line. Got that?" Z nodded as he carefully held up Stoker's arm as he began to draw the outlines of Stoker's swollen snakebite.

"Just a reminder that I know how to treat snake bites," Stoker noted. "Next on the agenda is pain medication. Just get me some Tylenol. I don't want any of that morphine or other opioid crap. We're in the Mexican desert, and I need to be alert, especially around you guys."

"I'm terribly ignoring your pain," Rivera replied. "I'm worried about getting you rehydrated, but gradually. I'm starting an I.V.; you need more than just clear water. Then we're going to get you back to the field hospital. That Mossad doctor has a lot of experience administering snake antivenin. He's done it many times."

"We'll make sure Allie knows you didn't take the easy way out with the opioids," Z chided. Allie Stoker was Troy's wife, and she had an incredible tolerance for pain. Avoiding pain medications became somewhat of a competition between Dr. Stoker and his wife.

Rivera removed a pair of scissors from the medical bag. "Let me get to your good arm here, Troy." In mere seconds Rivera had cut away the sleeve of Stoker's desert camouflage shirt. Then he looked at Z. "With Stoker being so dehydrated," he said, "why don't you help me get an I.V. started on him?"

"Sure thing," Z said. "You're a big doc, and I'm a techie. I love medical stuff, but I'm all thumbs."

"Oh, just get the I.V. set up, I'll do the tricky stuff," Rivera said. "Just find one good vein just below Stoker's elbow—one that sticks out—and then pull some Betadine out of the medical bag and start cleaning and sterilizing the skin around the vein. A diameter of two to three inches should do."

Z reached into the medical bag and started to rummage around. "Betadine. Betadine. Where's the Betadine?"

"They're little white packets," Stoker coached through his pain-clenched teeth. "Here do you want me to do it?"

"Okay, here they are." Z tore a packet open. He removed the iodine drenched gauze and started to scrub. Rivera reached into his bag and removed an I.V. kit. In two minutes, Rivera had the I.V. inserted into Stoker's arm. He adjusted the drip to infuse the proper amount of saline into his friend. Stoker felt some relief after approximately two to three minutes. "Wow, I love I.V.'s; they're wonderful! And, I'd like some more water too, thank you."

"I've got the snake," a warrior named Jessica said as she came running back carrying a bag filled with serpent scraps. She was a new *Espada Rápida* warrior. Z was also her new boyfriend.

"Let me take a look," Rivera said. He reached over and spilled the contents of the bag onto a sterilized cloth. Then in a tone of open mockery, he said, "Let's see what the mighty snake slayer, Troy Stoker, has defeated today."

Stoker cocked his head to the side and smiled with a wince that acknowledged Rivera's sarcasm. "I'm sure you'll keep mocking me about the rattlesnake. When you're done entertaining all of us, come help me treat this arm."

Rivera was quite concerned but didn't want to show it. Stoker's condition looked serious. "All right, mister big-shot psychiatrist. I'm sorry I hurt your feelings. Just let me know when you're done using your therapy techniques, or whatever the hell they are." Rivera was still mocking him as he bent down toward the snake remains. "I only have a limited amount of humor skills. If you strip me of mockery and some occasional cynicism, what am I left with?"

"Touché, Rivera," Stoker said. "And I have one for you! What would a psychiatrist be without therapy?"

"A neurologist," Jessica interjected.

They all laughed. Rivera picked up the dead snake's head. His jovial demeanor changed to a serious frown. "Whoa, Troy. Look what we have here. You tangled with a nasty rattlesnake here, *amigo*. And, I just want to let you know, I've been concerned, but now I'm very concerned."

"What is it?" Jessica asked.

Rivera started to speak as if he were a ringside boxing announcer. "In this corner at six feet two inches, one hundred and eighty-five pounds of pure muscle, . . . Troy Stoker, M.D."

"Okay, just get on with it," Stoker said. "What kind of rattlesnake is it?"

CHAPTER 3

South of Istanbul, Turkey

As he stood at the helm of his sixty-four-foot sailboat, the wind whipped at Nikolas Antoniou's cheeks and blew surf from lightly salted waters of Turkey's inland Sea of Marmara. Circumstances of his life excluded him from seeing his wife and children for months at a time. He was missing all those special moments and events in their lives, being always absent from the day-to-day life and challenges of his sons and daughters. But, missing big events was no matter to him. The ayatollahs had spoken, all those years ago. And, he was so close to fulfilling his mandate.

Today he concluded the short, strange visit with his family. It was always odd visiting people on house arrest. The separation started with a flight from Jubail, Saudi Arabia to Istanbul, Turkey. Then a short taxi ride took him to Viaport Marina, where his yacht, The Winds of Athens, was anchored. Now the air currents had swept him a short three nautical miles away from Istanbul into the Sea of Marmara.

His life was full of opportunity with his education, a vibrant family, and wealth. The ayatollahs and an Iranian trust organization called a bonyad had given him venture capital and control. Control was everything. He was the master puppeteer. His wealth and holdings were his stage. Employees were his serfs. He further leveraged his power by shrouding his evil with a cloak of Islamic religiosity. Today, he was returning to his business empire based in the land of the Great Satan, the idolatrous wasteland called America.

With the lights of Istanbul diminishing behind him, Nikolas set the boat's autopilot. He had never been "touched by poverty" as the Koran suggested. Quite the contrary. He had known decades of vast wealth. The Iranian bonyad supported his business ventures and provided him with more fortune than he could've ever imagined. At the outset, the bonyad that employed him was set up as an Iranian-government-sponsored charitable trust. But the organization soon lost its benevolent bearing and deviated into a loosely controlled, slushy investment fund. Since his childhood, the bonyad had groomed him as a business mogul while the government taught him spycraft. The director, the bonyad's foremost authority, arrayed Nikolas with opportunity and training in his youth. After he finished MBA school, the bonyad gave him responsibility and capital. By the time he turned thirty, the bonyad was supplying him with almost endless financial resources. Any new venture or business acquisition Nikolas recommended from his office in Chicago received instant funding.

Yet, there was an implied debt. His family was the collateral. And the director had explained, in stark terms, how the debt must be satisfied. In theory, once Nikolas's grand plan afflicted the Great Satan, his family would go free. But for now, his family would continue to live and exist under house arrest on the eastern coast of Saudi Arabia.

Over time, family had become even less important to Nikolas. In his barbarous, cold, and calculating mind, his wife and children had always been important, but as props, PR propaganda, or pawns. However, because of the attacks Nikolas was soon to unleash on America, he did not know what would then become his family's future. Would accomplishing his mission reunite him with his family or put more distance between them? He might even have to make his wife and children a casualty of his dread scourge.

As a psychopath, having his family under house arrest in Saudi Arabia offered little motivation. He craved power, control, and praise of the ayatollahs in Iran. A sentiment of sadistic anticipation accompanied his every waking moment, soon expecting the coming day when Americans would suffer long, protracted fear, pain, and sorrow.

Every four months he made this pilgrimage for a visit to the eastern shore of Saudi Arabia. His sailboat always arrived and departed from a different port in Turkey. Most people would revel in the sailing experience and its accompanying beauty and serenity. For Nikolas, sailing was a necessary evil that helped him slip undetected between the Middle East and the western world. Sailing took time away from harnessing biology and economics to build lethal weapons that would bring the opulent West to its knees.

With a slight adjustment to The Winds of Athens's mainsail, he exploited the wind and optimized the laws of physics to propel his yacht west. Scanning the horizon, he saw no other vessels jockeying to intercept his intended course. He trimmed the sails, and soon his sailboat was traveling at five knots—a crawl in terms of modern speeds. He would soon fire up the boat's diesel motor and double his velocity.

As he was evaluating fickle changes in the wind, the alarm on his wristwatch chimed. It was time to pray. Had he been at work, with his many other Muslim brothers, he would've paid the alarm heed and prepared for prayers. The appearance of devotion was an important pretense Nikolas maintained before his trusted employees. But, on the open sea, he had no need to keep up the charade.

For this trip, Nikolas's plan took him through Istanbul. But, he always varied his routes as a safeguard. He had reasons to hide his world travels from American officials as well as watchful eyes from the Sunni Muslim world. He sailed into or out of different ports in Turkey. Often, Nikolas anchored in the touristy yacht clubs to give the impression he was a leisure traveler from Greece. Without fail, he would complete the necessary paperwork with Turkey's Ministry of Customs and Trade before he put to sea, always declaring his travel rationale as pleasure.

Nikolas Antoniou wore a Greek name. But, his name was a fabrication. His bloodlines consisted of thousands of years of Persian heritage. The government of Iran conspired to change his identity when he was thirteen years old. Academic tests identified him as an outlier. He showed a special aptitude for strategic thinking, and he was a leader. He exploited manipulation, cruelty, and violence to maintain the seldom-challenged alpha status amongst his peers. Test results revealed some innate promise as a scientist. In due course, a Greek double agent facilitated the metamorphosis of a young Iranian psychopath into Nikolas Antoniou, Iranian sleeper agent. His handlers also created the appearance of family history with two substantial real estate transactions, conducted in the names of his fictitious parents. In Greece, he enrolled in a prominent international school, paid for by funds his bonyad laundered through various Mediterranean interests.

Nikolas dominated the Greek language, excelled at school, and thrived in social circles. When he was accepted at Cambridge University, the government of Iran was thrilled to arrange secret financing of any and all expenses. Nikolas knew all too well who was paying for his education. He looked forward to the day when everything he was learning would make him a powerful hero in his secret motherland.

It was a mandate, not a choice. He was ordered to major in biology and economics. The ayatollahs and the director had a plan for him. Earning an MBA from the University of Chicago was a critical milestone in the plan. His mission was clear: He would be Iran's secret captain of industry in America. Nikolas needed little mentoring to access Iran's secret capital to build large enterprises. Large enough to develop and hide, within the United States, the weapons to bring down the West.

Like a puppeteer, Nikolas had his marionettes—his employees. As a psychopath, he craved the sensation of control. The euphoria of seeing thousands of people doing his bidding, around the clock. He created a grand commercial stage, through several business ventures. But soon, a few of his chosen marionettes would leap off his commercial stage. These actors would slink onto a hidden stage of guerrilla warfare. They would afflict millions of Americans.

Nikolas set the boat's autopilot and gave one last scan of the horizon before him. Then he stepped below deck. Nikolas reached for the microwave oven in the galley. He never used this device to prepare food. He pressed some buttons as if he were programming the microwave. But, Nikolas was, in reality, entering an access code that activated a compact screen. As he had done many times before, Nikolas looked at the small display and held his eyes steady. The screen scanned his left retina. The device detected the eye indeed belonged to the correct person. He heard a click, and the microwave's control panel slid downward, exposing a small, waterproof safe secreted inside the microwave. Nikolas extracted a small device, a Raspberry Pi computer. Alone this device was almost useless. But, when he connected it to a mouse, keyboard, and large display, this computer became the window to his business and terror enterprises. As the CEO over a few companies, this small computer linked him into the information he needed to run the companies and hide his terroristic plans within the businesses. He had been out of touch with his accountants, lawyers, and scientists for a few days while traveling in Saudi Arabia. It was critical to avoid communicating about his Chicago dealings while he was in Saudi Arabia. American intelligence did not have to play by the same rules in Saudi Arabia, so Nikolas elected not to play at all while he was there.

Now, he was on his way back to America. This time he would, at long last, carry out a plan that would dwarf all other terrorist attacks on the West. In America, his Greek identity was a perfect cover. When Nikolas Antoniou introduced himself as a businessman from Greece, Americans perceived him as European. To further convince people of his status as a European, he would speak with a masquerade of enthusiasm for his sailboat adventures throughout Europe. He would refer to his home in Athens. The people he did business with never imagined Nikolas Antoniou was orchestrating large-scale jihad on the United States.

With his computer, he delved back into the world of documents, reports, emails, and plans. His subordinates had done a reasonable job of moving the attacks forward. But there was one effort that earned his praise. "At last!" he exclaimed aloud when he read about the mist machines at the Burning Man Festival. "The ayatollahs will soon see the seeds of jihad blooming. Let's see how well our soldier-engineer executes in the real world." He examined nine pictures the engineer, Roya, had included in the email. There, in the middle of the Nevada desert, sat the CoolSolar misting machine. Roya's setup was perfect.

Despite his excitement over deploying the Balamuthia amoeba in the desert of Nevada, Nikolas had many other matters to attend to as the sailboat's autopilot navigated him toward the Dardanelles. This thirty-eight-mile strait of water would lead him out of Turkish waters and into the Aegean Sea, his gateway back to Greece.

Nikolas Antoniou quickly glanced at some other reports and documents. But, he was not interested in sales reports, financial ratios, and measures of commerce. At this critical juncture in his mandate as an Iranian operative, he was obsessed with the reports from his laboratories. These biological workshops, secreted deep in the basements of his legitimate hotel, were incubating the amoeba as well as multiplying a bacterium. Each pathogen had a separate mission. But, Nikolas would arrange their incubation timelines to confuse the United States populous, the government, and the healthcare system. He would infuse panic into all Americans—a long, protracted dread and anxiety. Very different from the ragtag terrorism of hasty bullets and bombs.

Amoebas were the simplest of pathogens, but very deadly. There was not much a scientist could do—or needed to do—to alter these elementary organisms and their lethality. But bacteria, on the other hand, these microscopic creatures were complex and easily modifiable. Scientists around the world were starting to tap into the genetic programming that could weaponize simple bacteria into virulent killers. And, Nikolas and his team of genetic biologists had modified one of the most common. People who ingested their bioengineered *Campylobacter jejuni* bacteria stood a fifty percent chance of suffering a long and dreadful disease. While rarely lethal, the illness subjected its victims to months of misery.

On his computer screen, Nikolas scoured a document that reported the results of a small trial of the bacteria on a group of unsuspecting, voiceless human subjects in Chihuahua, Mexico. "Wow," he said softly. "A fifty-two percent infection rate. Sick people filled up the ICU and much of the medical floor." The trial was exceeding expectations. The report concluded with an over-zealous recommendation. The scientists universally agreed this bacterium was ready—as a weapon. More importantly, the scientists expressed their willingness to enter the front lines of a silent strike the Americans would never see coming.

As Nikolas was working, a new email arrived. "Damnit!" he yelled as he smashed his fists on the table. He quickly read an email from this Roya woman he had come to trust. She reported their new team of his biologists would not be sneaking into the United States from Mexico. They had just been massacred in the Mexican desert. Nobody knew who carried out the violence.

With so little time before the next attack on American soil, Nikolas did not have time to re-start the process of smuggling another team of scientists through Mexico and into the United States. There was no time to find out who perpetrated this attack. He shot back an email instructing Roya to train more of the foot soldiers in some of the simple biological tasks. She would have to assume almost all the intellectual responsibilities and delegate the rote and mundane tasks to the men of lower rank. If any man had a problem reporting to a woman, Nikolas informed her that he would promptly adjust his insolence. Using a woman for this strike was a stroke of genius. Even the Americans could not imagine a powerful female in an informal Muslim hierarchy.

Nikolas shut down the computer. He returned the small but powerful device to the safe disguised as a microwave oven. Then he retrieved a simple piece of paper from a slim drawer in the boat's rich wooden paneling. On the paper, he scribbled a few lines. Then he flipped open a small compartment, which revealed a fax machine.

While this telephone-based technology was rarely in use in the business environment anymore, fax machines still had their place amongst mariners. They served well for sharing weather and other sailing related information transmitted over long-range radio bands or satellite phone signals. Nikolas fed the document into the machine, entered a memorized phone number, and pushed the send button. His message was encrypted by the fax machine and transmitted back to Chicago.

After a brief scan, the machine spat the original document back out to him. It was done. He had just issued the order for the second stage of attacks to begin. This wave would take the bacteria, so well-proven in the Chihuahua trial, and disburse it to large groups of unsuspecting Americans. It was a brilliantly timed sequel to the amoeba attacks that had started with Burning Man.

Nikolas took the document and stepped up the companion ladder that would lead him topside. Once on the boat's deck, he carefully rolled the paper into a scroll. A verse from the Koran came to his mind—one he assumed his attack would fulfill. "And remember the Day when We shall roll up the heavens like a scroll rolled up for books, as We began the first creation, We shall repeat it, it is a promise binding upon Us. Truly, We shall do it." Then he allowed the small scroll to fall into the vastness of the salty sea. He watched it languish for a moment on top of the water and then vanish into the vessel's wake.

Within moments the small scroll was forgotten. The winds were kicking up, and Nikolas saw a cloud formation before him that forewarned a fresh breeze, or perhaps even a thrilling gale. He was ready. He needed the challenge of the storm—the only time he enjoyed sailing. Nikolas needed to harness tempestuous velocity and anger and tame it into propelling his fine vessel toward Greece with haste.

He disabled the autopilot, trimmed the sails, and assumed the helm of his boat. Feeling the wind against his skin, Nikolas instinctively knew every adjustment to make to the ship's wheel and sails. He allowed the boat to lean slightly to the right as wind, sails, and hull came into perfect balance. Within thirty minutes, the clouds enveloped him. A light rain turned into a downpour, and a severe gale became his opponent. The waves crashed over the bow of his magnificent vessel. The thrill of battling a powerful storm made Nikolas Antoniou feel truly alive. For the next three hours, the mariner tamed the storm and made it his servant, allowing him to travel at a remarkable pace across the Sea of Marmara.

As the storm abated so did his adrenaline. He felt weary as his drenched clothing hung from his body. Weariness overtook him, and he felt the desire to sleep. He set the boat's autopilot and went below deck to change into clean, dry clothing. A few minutes later he emerged back topside to make some final course calculations. As he turned and surveyed the sea to his starboard, the serenity vanished.

"Attention, The Winds of Athens," came a stern voice through a megaphone, startling Nikolas to his core. But, his spy training had taught him to restrain his natural reactions when something surprised him. He harnessed the wave of panic and capitalized on his surging adrenaline. "This is the Turkish Navy. Prepared to be boarded."

He considered the possibility that the Turkish Navy might find his computer, access it, and unravel his war plans. But months ago, he had enacted a scheme to misdirect them.

"Halt right there! Don't move." Nikolas stopped in his tracks and gently raised his hands so they could see he was not armed. He was surprised to see the approaching vessel was also a sailboat, a speedy catamaran. He estimated the length at fifty feet. The Turkish Navy had used wind power to sneak up on him undetected. A surprise indeed.

As the Turkish catamaran came alongside The Wind of Athens, three sailors jumped aboard and pointed at Nikolas. "Why do you look so fearful?" one of the sailors asked him in Turkish.

"We Europeans sometimes watch movies Muslims find offensive, even you more secular Turks." Nikolas's response was one he had practiced many times in his mind. The movies were countermeasures he wanted the sailors to find instead of his computer. Furthermore, the DVDs were palpable items that easily satisfied the confiscation reflex, which some law enforcement personnel seemed to possess in abundance.

"But, are you not Muslim? You speak Turkish so well."

"Yes. But, I am a conflicted Muslim. I observe my daily prayers; but I also possess the heart of a European, which leads me to sin. I occasionally drink alcohol, and I have some on board. I also watch some popular European movies. They are beautiful and deeply meaningful. The one in my DVD player right now is Scandinavian. It won many awards. There are love scenes, which many Muslims would deem forbidden."

"We must search your boat," a sailor declared.

Nikolas Antoniou said nothing, and he was careful not to make a hand gesture or other motion that would indicate his consent. But, the sailors weren't concerned about consent. They were the law on this stretch of water.

The Turkish men were orderly as they passed through the hatch and down the companion ladder into the sailboat's saloon, bringing Nikolas with them. Two men rifled through cupboards, drawers, and closets. One man opened the microwave. He closed it once he found it empty. One sailor discovered the collection of DVDs—the European movies. "We will confiscate these."

Nikolas did his best to look disappointed. He even faked a stammer. "That—that is my prized collection of some of the finest European films," he lied. He was pleased they were confiscating the distraction and falling for the countermeasure. He was occasionally boarded by the Turkish or Lebanese navy. If his boat had been free of infractions, the searchers would just search deeper. If he spoon-fed them easy violations, they would issue their citations, collect their fines, and move on. "These films. They mean so much to me. I beg of you."

"The Republic of Turkey does not forbid all pornography," the sailor continued. But, it does forbid unnatural pornography. We will cross reference these titles with our database. Leave us your address in Greece, and we shall endeavor to return the movies we judge acceptable. We must also collect one thousand lira, for postage."

Postage, Nikolas thought. A subtle bribe request. He liked the suggestion. "Just one moment." He stepped into the stateroom, slid open a wall panel, and revealed a safe. He quickly entered the combination and opened the safe. This too was all according to his contingency plans. This safe contained money for such an inconvenience as this. "I have the *postage* money right here." He handed one man 1,000 lira. The Turkish sailor could not contain his smile. The other men looked on with envy, which concerned Nikolas. He did not want the sailors who remained unpaid to search for additional infractions. "And just in case you should lose that cash to a particularly violent storm, here is a little insurance." Nikolas gave the other men 1,000 lira each. The jealousy vanished; now everyone was happy. Nikolas felt profound relief. Certainly, the movies would also be divided amongst the men, not cross-referenced to a database. They would never be returned. *Such a small bootie for these pirates*, thought the Iranian spy disguised as a Greek. *If only they knew the riches and secrets hidden within The Winds of Athens.*

"Well, sir, see that you do not return to Turkey with this salacious material again." The sailor's voice was stern.

"Oh yes," Nikolas said. "Once you return my precious movies to me, they shall remain in Greece. I apologize for my error in judgment." Nikolas noticed they gave no thought to writing down his address in Athens. They didn't even ask his name, insist on inspecting his passport or inquire about the travel documents he had filed with their country's Ministry of Customs and Trade.

"We must ask you, what is your destination?"

"Athens."

"Is that your final destination."

"Yes," Nikolas lied. "Athens is my home. I must return to my responsibilities." It was true he had a beautiful home in Athens. But, he would only stay there for a matter of hours before he boarded a plane for Chicago.

"Very well. You may continue on your journey."

Nikolas surveyed the catamaran. The ship was entirely out of place in a naval fleet. "How did the catamaran come to be part of your fleet?"

"This sir, is a product of the biggest criminal arrest on Turkish seas. We confiscated this catamaran when we arrested a Russian mobster. He used it to run drugs and weapons. It also has a sad history of human trafficking. I've never looked a more vicious, well-financed criminal in the eye before."

Sounds like a small-time criminal to me, Nikolas thought as he wished the sailors safe passage. *If they only knew what my eyes will soon behold.*

Nikolas watched the catamaran sail away. Then he fired up the diesel engine and sailed at twelve knots through the Dardanelles Straits and into the Aegean Sea. Nikolas again accessed his microwave oven safe. There, he secreted away his Iranian passport—a document that had never seen the light of day in the Western world. He removed his Greek passport and slipped it into his pants pocket. This small ceremony completed the transition from Iranian traveler to Iranian operative—functioning under a Greek identity in the United States of America.

At the helm of his ship, he sailed over the blue waters of the Aegean Sea. He would leave The Winds of Athens, and his Iranian passport, in Athens. A direct flight would soon have him back in Chicago turning billions of Iranian investment dollars into a silent jihad against the disbelievers.

CHAPTER 4

Near Chihuahua, Mexico

Rivera continued his boxing announcer imitation as he described the rattlesnake. "In this corner at three feet, four inches long, ... Crotalus scutulatus."

"A Mojave rattler?" Stoker asked.

"This baby's indeed a Mojave," Rivera confirmed. "Let's get you to the field hospital right away. We're not messing around out here in the Mexican desert. The Mojave's several times more toxic than other rattlesnakes. We're throwing out the textbook and treating you aggressively."

"Bring it on," Stoker said with his eyes squinting in reaction to the pain. He cradled his injured arm next to his chest.

"I'm sorry about your snake bite. But, your injury does help us, in a way," Rivera said. "You just opened a window of opportunity."

That hospital, here in Chihuahua," Stoker said. The one we need to check out.

"You've seen the intel," Rivera said. There's some weird stuff going on in that hospital. And, your injury gives us a perfect excuse to visit. It gets our foot in the door. Now, let's get moving."

Stoker pushed himself up into a standing position and held his snake-bitten arm against his abdomen. Then he winced as he stooped to grab his backpack and turned toward the helicopter. "What is this window of opportunity?" Jessica asked.

"There's an outbreak in a Chihuahua hospital," Rivera said. "And we need to look into it. We heard about it from an asset who's working as a nurse on the hospital's medical floor. Her story seemed far-fetched. But, when we verified it with a second nurse, we decided it was time to investigate it. Stoker's going to get admitted there. *Hospital de Los Santos* is the name of the facility. Using his hacker skills, Z verified the outbreak rumor."

"Give me the latest details about this disease outbreak in this *Hospital de Los Santos*," Stoker said. The pain of holding his arm in one position became overwhelming. Again, he jostled his shoulder with an instinctive twitch.

"Oh no, I'm not going to tell you what I think's going on. Let's see if you can figure out what's going on there," Rivera said. "Hey, can you please do your best to exhibit symptoms that get you admitted to the medical floor? That's where all the action will be."

"Sure, Rivera. No problem." Stoker was closing his eyes now. Between comments, pain pursed his lips. "When I get to the hospital, I'll give them my two cents worth of what I think is going on with my symptoms. I'll fake some severe pain in my right, lower quadrant."

"Don't overdo it, buddy. I don't want you to land in the ICU."

"Let's get going," Stoker said, "The pain in my arm's getting nasty."

"If it's getting nasty for you, the pain would be excruciating for mere mortals."

"Whatever, Rivera. Let's quit the chit-chat and go. I'm not interested in bucket kicking today."

Stoker, Rivera, Jessica, and Z all climbed in the helicopter. Above the whirring of the blades, Stoker yelled out. "What is this beast of a gunship, Rivera? It's not American."

Rivera smiled his infectious toothy Cuban grin. "No *Comrade*! It's Russian. She's a Mil Mi-24."

"How did you get your hands on a Russian gunship?" Stoker asked as he winced and climbed into the helicopter in one fluid motion.

"It was a trade."

"Okay, I don't feel like guessing." Stoker leaned against the seat, winced his eyes closed, and gritted his teeth. "What did you trade?"

Z interjected a quick answer. "For our services to the American government, we were allowed to purchase this from some Russian friends. This is it in a nutshell. *Espada Rápida* did a little intelligence gathering that would've been illegal for OGAs."

"What? The OGA?" Jessica asked.

Stoker interjected. "Other government agencies."

"Okay, I get it."

Z continued with the story. "We had a deal, and the Russian president kept his end of the bargain.

"So, this Russian behemoth was part of the deal?" Stoker asked.

"Yes, *amigo*," Rivera responded. "I was also motivated to get involved, thanks to a phone call from a friend on the Senate Select Committee on Intelligence."

Rivera took a quick look at Stoker's bite wound before he buckled in. "At the hospital in Chihuahua, we'll admit you under a fake identity so we can all remain anonymous. I'll come up with a good name."

"All right then. Get me to the field hospital!" Stoker said. "The sooner you can take off, the better. This snakebite makes my arm feel like it's on fire. It's a bitch."

"You've got it," a pilot responded as he flipped a few more switches and controlled the throttle.

"I always look forward to seeing new places," Stoker said with blatant cynicism in his tone. "Chihuahua, Mexico here we come."

The Mil Mi-24 took off and ascended into the Mexican sky. The pilot radioed the field hospital and informed them of his intent to land there. Rivera continued treating Stoker. Z used the permanent marker to draw another outline on Stoker's arm, documenting the advancing redness and underlying cell damage. Rivera jotted some quick medical notes on a pad of paper about Stoker's vital signs and fluid intake.

For the next few minutes, the helicopter flew over the Mexican desert landscape. Stoker kept his eyes closed as he supported his elevated arm. The burning pain from the venom sinking deeper into his tissues forced his facial muscles into a bitter wince. With an I.V. dripping vital fluids into Stoker's bloodstream, Rivera kept a vigilant watch over his friend, colleague—and now patient. As a colonel and a doctor, Rivera was supposed to possess an acquired tolerance for others' pain. But, the best he could do was mask his distress with humor. Seeing a devoted friend in pain brought back a flood of memories from wars, overt and covert, when the pain of blood brothers once seared his soul and almost snuffed out his will to live.

CHAPTER 5

Temporary Special Operator Base Camp
Near Chihuahua, Mexico

"There he goes," said one of the U.S. Army Night Stalkers. "That phenom physician, Stoker, just pulled off his first solo HALO dive, and after just one training jump." These elite Army aviators had been training in Mexico with Stoker all week. Also joining the team were CIA operatives, agents from the FBI's Joint Terrorism Task Force, some Navy SEALS, and a few of Israel's elite special operators. This multi-organization task force was on maneuvers tailored to address the threat from a group of rogue Iranians and other Shiites staging and training in Mexico.

Just eight days earlier, these elite teams descended upon a few acres in this sparse desert. They set up a small field hospital, which primarily served as the classroom for training by battle-hardened trauma surgeons from the Israeli Mossad. Doctors from the Army and Navy joined Drs. Stoker and Rivera as they immersed themselves in the practical desert warfare medical experience.

For a week, these teams also conducted extensive training in *Krav Maga*, marksmanship, parachuting, and the Farsi language. They focused on preparing to combat radicals inside the United States and along its borders. Survival training prepared the men for the warm deserts and cold semi-arid terrain that made up most of Iran, Lebanon, Iraq, and Yemen—countries with sizable Shiite populations. On day six, the teams went out and did some snooping and pooping on a group of would-be terrorists. With binoculars and parabolic microphones, they spied on this cell of Shiites who were training in the Mexican desert with the intent of sneaking into the United States and joining sleeper cells. They overheard their conversations, filled with the hateful rhetoric of radical men hoping to achieve jihad on the streets of America. The not-so-covert training camps were out in the desert, a few miles from the city of

Chihuahua.

"That shrink's got some balls," commented a CIA agent. "He ran at the front of the pack on our training run yesterday."

Another Night stalker commented on how Stoker trounced a Mossad instructor in hand-to-hand combat and had one of the best shooting scores with his .45 caliber 1911.

"I'm no psychiatrist, but it sounds like somebody's been repressing his inner soldier."

The elite operators' laughter was cut short as they continued to monitor Stoker's descent.

"He's falling through about 3,000 feet. He'll have to open his chute pretty quick here."

"There he goes. Chute deployed at 2,500 feet. That's pushing it."

The men watched as Stoker floated toward the desert floor. When he made a sudden course change, the always cool special operators let it play out. They shared the instinct—the intuition most elite soldiers are born with. Training perfected the sense. If Stoker needed to alter the game plan, these elite warriors trusted there was a reason.

To their left, they heard Rivera barking orders as he and the *Espada Rápida* team ran toward a hanger. The sound of rotors spinning up caught everyone's attention. A few seconds later, the strange helicopter emerged from the hangar and took off.

"What's going on?" one of the Army Night Stalkers asked.

"Let's find out," another man replied as he squelched his radio. The men overheard the transmissions between Stoker and Rivera. They listened to Stoker's report about the group of Shiites. "Those tangos are way out of their normal territory."

A few minutes later they heard Rivera calling through the radio. The *Espada Rápida* team was about to land. Awestruck, they learned Stoker had wiped out the enemy. They heard the snake bite news. Without even waiting for orders, the two men sprinted for the field hospital. They notified the Israeli Mossad doctor and assembled a team.

"This is Alpha Bravo Two," came the voice of Dr. Rivera. "Stoker's bit by a nasty-ass snake. He needs some attention ASAP."

"The team is already assembled," said a radio operator. "How far out are you, Alpha Bravo Two?"

"About seven minutes."

"Roger that. We're ready."

Right on schedule, Rivera's Russian helicopter landed back at the training base. As the rotors powered down, Stoker exited the aircraft under his own power. Z carried Stoker's backpack. Jessica carried his I.V. Bag. They walked the 200 yards to the field hospital.

"Right over here, Dr. Stoker," said the Israeli physician, as he motioned for Stoker to climb onto the treatment table. "Let me see the snakebite. I've treated hundreds of them."

Stoker sat down and held out his arm for the doctor to see. "It was a Mojave rattlesnake."

"A very venomous rattlesnake here in North America," said the Mossad doctor. "But, your Mojave rattler is, at best, a somewhat lethal snake when compared to the vipers, cobras, and asps of the Middle East. I think you're going to be just fine."

The Israeli doctor enlisted Rivera's help. Together they mixed four vials of antivenin in a bag of normal saline. Using an infusion pump, the doctors set the antivenin and saline to infuse through Stoker's IV. "I'm going to infuse this over the next hour. After that, we'll repeat additional doses for the next day or so."

"Right," Stoker said. "Sometimes it takes hours for the effects of the rattlesnake venom to kick in. Let's flow it slow and steady."

Rivera chimed in. "I agree with slow and steady. But, we need to move this treatment to a hospital in Chihuahua."

"I agree," Stoker said. "I've been enlisted as a spy and guinea pig in this spontaneous new operation."

"Yes, you have. We're going to get you into *Hospital de Los Santos*'s medical ward so we can verify reports we've heard."

"Well, there's a history of antivenin causing allergic reactions," Stoker said. "So, if it will speed my hospital admission along, let me roleplay an allergic reaction. I'll be convincing enough to land me in a hospital bed."

"Let's see some of that psychodrama in the ER," Rivera said. Stoker often used a technique called psychodrama in his psychiatry practice. He, his patients, or groups would act out different scenarios. It allowed participants to process feelings, explore the meanings of their emotions, and recognize flawed thinking. And while Rivera was misusing the term psychodrama, he was tapping into one of Stoker's strengths. Troy Stoker, M.D. was a convincing actor—a handy skill for this spontaneous snoop at the hospital.

"I can act out that allergic reaction," Stoker said. "Shortness of breath will be easy. But, I can't fake hives and swelling."

The Israeli doctor interrupted. "For now, let's concentrate on getting these first vials of antivenin into you without an *authentic* allergic reaction. Then we can see about transferring you to the hospital in Chihuahua to carry out your covert operation."

"Infiltrating a hospital may not seem like much fun to a Mossad veteran like you," Stoker said.

"You would be surprised how many of my missions were underwhelming, Dr. Stoker. Most spy work is low-risk and low-excitement. No matter the level of intrigue, good espionage is just about reporting an accurate and useful story. Only sometimes are the stories also entertaining, or better yet, dangerous."

"Stoker got a little spoiled," Rivera said. "The first time we ever worked together—last winter—our work included car chases, fights, kidnapping—"

Stoker interrupted. "In total disclosure, my wife was kidnapped. But, we also kidnapped the South Dakota Attorney General and flew him across state lines."

"So, you're a felon now?" the Mossad doctor asked with a tinge of humor in his voice.

"No comment," Stoker said.

"Sometimes getting the job done requires some high crimes," the Mossad doctor said. "Most of my work now is in medicine. But, I sure miss those days. The days when I too roved about the globe as a government-sponsored felon."

With the antivenin infusing into Stoker, Rivera called an ambulance company to arrange Stoker's transportation to *Hospital de Los Santos* in Chihuahua. When the paramedics arrived, Rivera explained the snake bite. After he exaggerated Stoker's dehydration and fabricated a story about Stoker showing possible signs of an allergic reaction, they loaded their new patient into the ambulance. Rivera climbed inside the ambulance and recommended an oxygen mask, claiming that Stoker had experienced some shortness of breath. As a prop, the oxygen mask indeed helped Stoker appear more acute.

After a short ride, the ambulance pulled up to the emergency room doors of a four-story hospital. The two-man crew removed Stoker from the ambulance and wheeled him into the emergency room, where a triage nurse met them. She began to examine Stoker and ask him questions.

Then the acting really started. "How do you say shortness of breath in Spanish?" he asked Rivera.

"*Dificultad para respirar,*" Rivera responded. When the triage nurse and orderlies heard Rivera's response, they frowned in unison and fast-tracked Stoker into a treatment room. A moment later one of the emergency room attending physicians arrived. Rivera introduced Stoker with an alias. "This is my friend, Rand Paul." Stoker worked very hard to avoid laughing or smiling at the name Rivera chose. He did not expect his friend to use the name of an American politician. But he was not surprised Rivera would interject flippant humor into a serious moment.

Rivera switched to Spanish and gave the doctor a complete report. Stoker understood occasional words and phrases. However, in another of his life paradoxes, Stoker had been working so hard on learning Farsi, he had not studied Spanish during his time in Mexico.

The doctor ordered a nurse to continue infusing saline through Stoker's I.V. He requested labs and ordered a second round of antivenin. This time, he specified and even slower drop-by-drop infusion, through a slow IV over three hours. Then he turned and addressed Stoker in English. "You've done an excellent job treating the rattlesnake bite. The wound and damage from the venom are minor concerns at this point. I'm more concerned about managing a potential allergic reaction. I'm also considering your infection risk. Let's admit you to the medical ward, at least overnight. We'll administer some I.V. antibiotics and consider more doses of antivenin. How is your pain level, Mr. Paul?"

Again, Stoker tried not to laugh at his false name. "Horrific, doctor. But, let's avoid any opiate-based pain management. I can manage with ibuprofen and acetaminophen."

"Very well," replied the ER doctor. "I suspect the worst of the pain is over. If your symptoms act up, please inform a nurse."

"You don't need to worry about Mr. Paul's willingness to complain," Rivera replied in Spanish. "He never has trouble making sure he gets the attention he wants."

The ER doctor smiled. "Let's get him admitted and see if he

can get some rest." He made a quick exit, and the nurse remained to carry out his orders. A few minutes later a phlebotomist appeared and drew three vials of blood from Stoker. By now all the excitement and adrenaline had worn off.

"Hey Rivera," Stoker said. "This is the most comfortable bed I've been in for days. I hope you don't mind if I get some shuteye?"

"Of course not," Rivera said. "I'm going to go find out how to make payment arrangements."

Within seconds Troy Stoker, M.D., was snoozing. His time in the military and a psychiatry residency taught him to get sleep whenever and wherever the opportunity arose.

When an orderly came to wheel him up to the medicine ward, Stoker awoke. After an elevator ride and a few turns through the hallway, he entered the floor. Stoker noticed he was one of about three dozen patients sharing the same large room. He felt a little intrigue being a patient on a hospital ward, instead of on a floor with individual rooms. Stoker also noticed how soon a meal arrived. The scent of the food reawakened his voracious hunger. *Fighting off serpent venom and cleaning up on terrorists turns a no-nonsense soldier into a ravenous warrior,* Stoker thought.

Truth be told, he had eaten nothing during the previous ten hours of survival training, enemy tracking, combat, and fending off venom. Stoker only recognized half of the food on his tray; but he ate it all. He never thought he would be so grateful to eat hospital food—in a foreign country.

After his meal, he embraced his exhaustion and fell into a deep sleep.

CHAPTER 6

Chihuahua, Mexico

"*Señor* Paul?"

Stoker awoke. He didn't recognize the voice. But he had adjusted to his temporary name, Rand Paul. When Stoker opened his eyes, a woman stood before him.

"My name is Valentina," she said in passable but heavily accented English, "and I need to draw more blood. May I please see your arm?"

Stoker held out his unbitten arm, and the phlebotomist started to clean the skin with alcohol. Stoker noticed a mask covering this woman's mouth and nose. It was not the typical disposable mask. This mask was a heavier-duty particulate respiratory mask, which seemed excessive for the task of drawing blood. Then he looked at her gown, and it appeared to be a gown a doctor or nurse would wear in surgery. She was also double-gloved with thick surgical gloves. It seemed like an extraordinary level of precaution for routine blood draws.

"And after your snakebite, a meager blood draw should not bother you at all."

Valentina's extra protective clothing and gear piqued Stoker's curiosity, and he paid little attention to the needle puncturing his skin and extracting his blood into tubes.

"Valentina, can I ask you a question?" Stoker inquired. "I'm not from your country, so I think you may be able to enlighten me."

"Of course, Mr. Paul. What is it you would like to know?"

"In my country, someone performing surgery would wear the protective gear you're wearing," Stoker said. "You have two pairs of gloves on, and your gown seems more protective than I would expect for a phlebotomist on a medical floor. Are you taking extra precautions?"

"You are very aware, *Señor* Paul. This is not our regular personal protective equipment for phlebotomy work."

"So why the added safeguards against infection?"

She hesitated. Then she looked around to see if any of the

other hospital employees or patients were close enough to overhear. Outside the sun was setting, and orange rays of light bathed much of the medical ward through the westward-facing ribbon window. The nurses on the floor worked out of earshot. The bed to Stoker's left was empty. The man in the bed to his right was asleep. "There are two things I can tell you. First, we are not quite sure what is happening, yet. This protective equipment is just an extra precaution. And second, the hospital administrators have ordered us to say nothing about the matter."

"Is there some strange hospital-acquired infection cropping up here?"

"I'm surprised a lawyer from your fancy Las Vegas would ask such a question, Mr. Paul. Have you worked in the medical field?"

"Yes. Quite a bit. But, is there an outbreak in this hospital?"

Valentina was silent, and she directed all her attention to filling a second vacuum tube with blood from a vein in Stoker's muscular forearm. As the test tube filled with blood, she answered his question. "I'm sorry, Mister Paul. I can say little more on the matter. But, I can tell you, I believe you are safe. Patients have not picked up and infection while *in* the hospital. They arrive with it. And, if you keep your eyes open, you just might figure a few things out."

"Thank you, Valentina. My eyes will be open, and my mouth shut."

She finished the blood draw. "Thank you, Mr. Paul. I hope your recovery is rapid." Stoker sensed the flavor of the Spanish language when she rolled the *r* in rapid.

"When will my lab results be available?" Stoker asked.

"It depends. Our lab slows down at night. I imagine your results will be available in about five hours." With a soft pat on Stoker's arm, Valentina left his bedside and moved down the ward in search of her next patient. As Stoker looked down the line of patients, he observed most of them were asleep. To his surprise, some patients were on ventilators. *Why aren't ventilator patients in the ICU?* he wondered. There were at least six ventilated patients he could see.

As Stoker continued to survey the scene, a nurse entered the ward and rushed down the corridor in his direction. She was about to hurry past him when he interrupted her.

"Excuse me," Stoker asked. The nurse stopped, turned toward him, and smiled. But, her smile could not hide the stress she emanated.

"Yes, *Señor* Paul. How may I help you?"

"Do you often have patients on ventilators on your general medical floor? When I've visited hospitals in other countries, ventilated patients are treated in an intensive care unit."

"It's curious how you, a lawyer from Las Vegas, seem to know so much about how hospitals operate, *Señor* Paul. Have you worked in the medical field?"

Stoker was surprised a second person would question his knowledge of hospitals based on his supposed profession as a lawyer. "As a matter of fact, I have done a fair amount of hospital-related work." Stoker paused for a moment to gauge her reaction. "Are vents the norm on the hospital floor, or do you prefer to treat those patients in the ICU?"

Her response felt abrupt. "Sometimes our ICUs fill up, and we have to bring a ventilated patient onto the regular medical floor."

Stoker decided to use one of his psychiatric skills. Instead of taking his turn in the conversation and responding, he remained silent. By allowing a vacuum in the discussion, he created some social discomfort and provoked the nurse to fill the void by speaking again. She may even divulge a few forbidden facts. Stoker, ever the master of non-verbal communication, slowly nodded his head.

"And well," the nurse pressed forward, hesitating and lowering her voice. "I'm concerned about our current situation. Our patient load has never been like this." Stoker remained silent but leaned forward and directed all his attention toward her. His non-verbal gesture ensured the nurse that her American patient was giving her his full attention. "Right now, we have too many patients on ventilators. But, that's all I can say. That's about all I know."

"I respect your situation," Stoker said. "When you lack concrete information, it's best to limit what you say. So, let me ask you a question that is general knowledge. How many beds are there in the hospital's intensive care units?"

"Our medical ICU has fourteen beds, and our surgical and trauma ICU has twelve. They are all full, so we get the overflow."

From a few beds down, a distressed and weary voice called

out. "*Enfermera, por favor*," A patient was calling for the nurse's attention.

"He needs you," Stoker said. "Don't worry. You and your colleagues will find the answers you need to do your miraculous work."

The mention of miracles made the nurse smile. "I can only pray." The nurse walked toward the patient.

Stoker looked down the length of the hospital ward and further inventoried his fellow patients. He could see far enough to count twenty-one other patients, before the menagerie of equipment, nurses, and patients blended to block his view of the rest of the floor. But, there were more patients and ventilators beyond Stoker's line of sight. His curiosity grew deeper. He thought about standing up and going for a walk down the hall to get a better count of patients—especially those on ventilators. *But, if there's a dangerous infection in this hospital*, he thought, *I should keep my distance.*

Stoker relaxed his neck and allowed his head a gradual descent to the pillow. Then he closed his eyes for a moment. The serenity permitted him to clear his mind and relax. Before even a minute passed, Stoker realized he was bored. "This is the first time I've been bored in years," he said out loud to himself. He considered how to pass the time as he recovered. The first thought that came to mind was to email his wife, Allie. He sat up and looked around the hospital ward. *Good luck finding a computer, Mr. Paul*, Stoker thought. Watching TV was out of the question since he couldn't understand much Spanish. He looked around for something to read. He longed to read a medical journal—in English, Farsi, or Spanish. But, none were to be had. It occurred to Stoker that boredom was more taxing on him than the rattlesnake bite. *At least the snakebite invigorated my mind, tapped into my intellect and survival instinct,* he thought. *Not a bad adrenaline rush.*

Stoker looked around, seeking to glean clues about this mystery from the people around him. Most of the patients were asleep. Many of those who were awake appeared bewildered, as if they were in some type of inattentive fog. In contrast, the nurses and other hospital personnel were working at a rigorous pace. Stoker's psychiatric intuition detected clue after clue indicating the dreadful levels of anxiety the staff members were suffering. The patients' needs were overwhelming them—even more than usual.

Stoker made a conscious decision to be a low-maintenance patient. Closing his eyes, he laid back. He willed his mind to relax. Then he chose to fall asleep. It was a short nap, with scant glints of distorted dream moments. Rivera's voice woke him. Jessica, Z's girlfriend, accompanied him. "We got Z off to Burning Man."

"His Bohemian bash in the Nevada desert?" Stoker replied.

"It was not his choice for the venue," Jessica commented. "He's going to Burning Man to support a good friend getting married there."

"How come you didn't go to Burning Man with him?" Stoker asked.

"We've only been together for a few months," Jessica responded. "Going to a wedding together might freak Z out."

"I think it would freak *you* out, too," Rivera responded. "The whole idea of Burning Man reminds me of a twenty-first century Woodstock."

"And, by the way," Jessica said, "the intel on the Burning Man Festival says the intention of the participants is the pure temporary subversion of authority as well as the throwing off of cultural norms."

"You have intel on Burning Man?" Stoker asked.

"Some paranoid kooky bureaucrat at Homeland Security was worried the event was a precursor to a rebellion against the government," Jessica explained. "In true government form, someone hired consultants to provide an analysis and recommendations."

"And what were the findings?" Stoker asked.

"Infiltration by Islamic radicals is a minuscule probability," Rivera interjected. "Right-wing militias will also stay away. It's not their cup of tea—with the lack of guns and Bibles to cling to. Z's greatest security risk at Burning Man is acquiring a sexually transmitted disease."

"He wouldn't dare!" Jessica interjected. "He knows I'd punch him in the gut." Jessica was a martial arts enthusiast. She often shot Z harmless knuckle jabs to his abs as part of their banter.

Stoker changed the subject. "Hey, Rivera. Let me tell you what I'm noticing on this floor. There are a few things that stand out."

Stoker turned his head and gazed down the hospital ward. "I'm wondering why there are so many patients on ventilators? And, why aren't they in the ICU instead?"

"It must be a Mexico thing," Rivera said. "That's just the way they do things here, I suspect."

"One of the nurses enlightened me," Stoker said. "Like most hospitals around the world, their practice is to treat ventilator patients in the ICUs. When the ICUs are full, they send a ventilator patient or two to the medical floor."

Rivera turned and made a gesturing glance down the medical floor. "But, that's not a patient or two. There are a bunch of people on ventilators down there." Rivera took a few slow steps further into the ward as he surveyed the scene. Then his footsteps became more deliberate. Soon he disappeared into the sea of patients, beds, nurses, ventilators, and other equipment.

A minute later, Stoker and Jessica saw Rivera returning. As he approached, he held up a can of Coke to make it appear as if he had accomplished his mission to find his friend a drink. "Here you go, Mr. Paul. I found a drink for my thirsty *amigo*." He also brought three surgical masks.

Stoker took the Coke and went along with Rivera's acting. "Thank you. These medications make me extra thirsty."

Rivera grabbed a chair and pulled it up right next to Stoker. When Rivera was confident Stoker and Jessica were the only people who could see his face, his expression changed from jovial to serious. "There are eleven patients on vents—"

Stoker interrupted him. "And, the staff's double-gloving and wearing extreme personal protective equipment."

Rivera handed Stoker and Jessica each a surgical mask and then put one on himself. Stoker followed Rivera's example; there was no need to explain why. Rivera continued talking, a little muffled by the mask. "It's as if there's some infectious outbreak. I'm sorry if I landed you in a hospital housing a raging epidemic, Stoker."

"It's too soon to tell what's going on here," Stoker replied. "But, I asked my phlebotomist and one of the nurses about the double gloving and personal protective equipment. Their words and body language told me something's not quite right. And, their bosses have ordered them silent. Who can tell us what's going on?"

"Nobody's going to tell us," Rivera said. "Hospitals become tight-lipped about these situations."

"The situations that can damage their reputations," Jessica interjected.

"We've got an enigma and no other volunteers to solve it," Stoker said.

"What's your intuition telling you, Troy?" Rivera asked.

"The same thing yours is telling you. There's something wrong around here. Something very wrong." Stoker thought for a moment. A wry smile graced his face. "I've got an idea."

Rivera's somber look flashed to a countenance of curiosity and excitement. "What're you thinking, buddy. I like it when you get your ideas."

"Yes, you *are* an adrenaline junkie, Rivera. And, this idea may just give one of your constant cravings a fix." Stoker sat up higher in his bed and leaned in a little closer to Rivera. "According to the phlebotomist, the lab here slows down at night. I'm not sure exactly what that means. But, if we can get into the lab and look at specimens and paperwork, I bet we can find out what the dirty little secret is."

"Either we get into the lab, or we kidnap and torture one of the pathologists," Rivera said with a smirk. "I'm sure we can make a pathologist sing in five minutes or less."

"Sounds like a fascinating clandestine exercise," Stoker said. "I hope you're joking. Can you imagine the international incident waterboarding a doctor would cause?"

"The adrenaline rush would be profound," Rivera said. "Your plan to infiltrate the lab is more appropriate. And yes, I was only joking. It amuses me when your shrink skills can't pick up on my sarcasm."

Stoker became serious. "Listen, Rivera. It amuses me—no it concerns me—how you hide your deep-seated desires behind sarcasm. There's therapy for that. I think I just spared an innocent pathologist a world of hurt."

"Hey, *amigo*. I'm cool. Chill out, *Señor* Paul." Rivera said. "I know I've got some ghosts and goblins in my head. I can't help it sometimes. Instead of all this psychoanalysis, let's spend our time figuring out why all these people are sick with the same symptoms. Now, how should we break into this lab?"

"How about we wait until there's nobody there?" responded Stoker. "Then, we pick the lock?" Rivera started to respond, but

Stoker cut him off. "It's not elegant or badass, but I think it'll work."

"Truth be told, I like your idea," Rivera said. "But remember, *amigo*, we're in Mexico. Like most other countries in the world, a little grease money can get us through any door."

"Touché," Stoker replied. "I often neglect your cosmopolitan solutions when we're out on our worldwide magical mystery tours. Let's find someone to bribe—for the good of dozens of patients in *Hospital de Los Santos*."

"Alright," Rivera said. "I'll come back to visit in a few minutes. We can work on getting access to the lab, once the night sets in and the hospital settles down."

"For the next little while," Stoker said, "I'll do as much observing as I can. I'll give you a sitrep a little later."

"Sounds good," Rivera said. "Try stretching your legs. Something tells me walking's going to be a prerequisite for tonight's mission." Then Rivera stood up and motioned for Jessica to follow him. "Let's get you out of here, Jessica. If Stoker and I are going to break some rules, I need to get you away from the troublemaking."

Jessica smiled and followed Rivera from the medical floor. "Bailing my superiors out of a Mexican jail just went on my bucket list."

CHAPTER 7

Black Rock City, Nevada

The sun was setting over the Nevada desert. Z stood with about a hundred wedding guests on the dry, parched ground. For almost a mile the high desert sand nursed no trees, flowers, birds, or mammals. The uproar from the Burning Man Festival raged to their west.

Z watched his friend make marriage vows with a stunning woman. The preacher took the groom's hand and the bride's hand and brought them together. The couple's chosen vows were powerful in their simplicity.

As dusk yielded to darkness, the wedding party moved to a large tent. All the guests joined the couple in a celebration and meal. The menu featured fare from the Mediterranean. The earthy, rich flavors pacified a primeval appetite within Z as he dined on vegetables, roast lamb, hummus, and fruit. The caterers provided warm pita bread in abundance. He reached into his pocket and switched off his phone. Setting aside cares he had not abandoned for years, he decided to savor this one moment.

After the wedding party diminished, Z walked alone over the barren desert back toward the Burning Man Festival. As he approached the outskirts of the temporary metropolis, he absorbed the creativity, energy, and expression. He passed the temporary structure labeled Arctica, where volunteers sold ice. Z realized he needed to hydrate and cool off a little. His training in the Mexican desert had acclimatized him to operating under duress in the heat. But, he still needed to pay attention to his hydration, no matter which desert, jungle, or arid plateau he occupied. So, after buying some ice, he sucked on one piece, while he used another piece to rub on his face, neck, and head. *Sublime*, he thought.

Z continued to walk amongst the camps, art installations, parties, villages, and countless other fascinations. There were more than 50,000 people present. He came upon a giant geodesic dome, most of which was covered by white cloth. But, there were a few clear windows. Inside he saw revelers dancing while millions of feathers were blown about by powerful fans. The phenomenon was fascinating to watch from outside the dome. But, Z disliked the idea of stepping into the chaos. He turned and walked in another direction. As he passed a giant statue representing a frog, he felt a gentle mist cross his face. Much like the ice, this mist had been a refreshing contrast to the desert heat. So, he turned a bit to his right and sensed the location of the mist's source. A system of tubing delivered a refreshing vapor to the throngs crowding the thoroughfare. Z walked a few paces and allowed the moist fog to envelop him. He welcomed the cold humidity. And, he was in good company. It was a favorite spot for revelers to linger and cool off.

As Z breathed, he inhaled minuscule water droplets and hundreds of thousands of Balamuthia mandrillaris amoebas. They were finding a warm, moist home in the mucous membranes of his nose and sinus cavities. Other amoebas moved into his bronchia and lungs. Then some amoebas entered Z's blood stream.

A few minutes later, thousands of amoebas crossed Z's blood-brain barrier. There they found their hospitable, warm home and began to eat, grow, and infect. In this case, they found an ideal host in Z.

After a couple of hours of drifting through Burning Man, Z sensed a subtle wind shift. The Sierra Nevada mountains surrendered a cool, mountain-scented wisp, which intermingled with the dry desert currents and triggered contented drowsiness in his soul. Z returned to his tent. But before he fell asleep, he switched his phone back on again. Among his texts, there was a message from Stoker informing him a private jet would pick Z up in the morning. He needed to be at the Black Rock City Municipal Airport at 0700 hours.

Things must be getting serious in Mexico, Z thought. Then he laid down for the night and fell into a deep sleep. By lunchtime the next day, he would be back in Chihuahua, Mexico, clueless he was incubating the deadly amoebas.

• • •

At Sioux Falls Regional Airport, Allie Stoker boarded a nonstop flight to Chicago. She would spend the next two weeks designing the interior of a new high-rise office building. But, she was also excited about running a half marathon this upcoming weekend. In the best shape of her life, Allie was confident she would shatter her personal best time for the thirteen-point-one-mile event.

As she took her seat aboard the 737, she sat next to a woman who was eager to strike up a conversation. "What takes you to Chicago?" she asked.

"I'm doing some design work for a construction project there," Allie answered before asking, "Is Chicago your final destination?"

"Yes. I'm going home to sleep for twelve to sixteen hours. Then, I'm back to work tomorrow."

"Tough travels?" Allie asked.

"Not really. My fatigue is secondary to the amazing time I had during two days at Burning Man."

Allie smiled. "Wow! I'll have to tell my husband I met a burner. I keep trying to cajole him into taking me—at least for a day or two."

"Oh," responded the woman with enthusiasm. "I bet you'd love it. There's something for everyone. Unless that *something* is sleep. There's very little of that."

"I suspect air conditioning is in short supply, too," Allie joked.

"Yes, but so is clothing. There *is* an abundance of sunscreen."

Allie laughed. She shared a few more minutes of conversation with her fellow passenger about the Burning Man experience before fatigue overtook the woman. Ninety minutes later, Allie Stoker deplaned, claimed her luggage, and walked out to the curb. She caught an Uber to her hotel. When Allie walked up to the registration desk, the smiling clerk greeted her with a warm, "Welcome to downtown Chicago."

CHAPTER 8

Chihuahua, Mexico

Stoker had been walking up and down the main corridor of the medical floor when his dinner tray arrived. The woman delivering the meal did not speak English, so Stoker thanked her in Spanish and began to eat. An aged man in the bed next to him seemed to awaken, as if by instinct, when his meal arrived.

"*Buenas tardes*," Stoker greeted him when the man glanced over at him. With a weak voice, the patient returned the greeting. Stoker could tell the man did not have the strength to maintain a conversation. So, he watched the old patient eat. The meal his neighbor had was different. The patient was eating soup at a snail's pace. It consisted of chicken broth and rice. He also had mashed potatoes, pureed chicken, and some yams—an easy-to-swallow meal. In contrast, Stoker's dinner included a chicken drumstick, vegetables, boiled potatoes, and some bread.

Stoker took a few bites of his meal. Then he decided to make up an excuse to walk around. He wanted to observe the other patients' food. So, Stoker stood. Then he started to make his way down the corridor at a casual pace. As he passed other patients, he noticed about half of the patients had the same meal he just ate. But, the other half of the patients were relegated the easy-to-swallow soup, pureed chicken, mashed potatoes, and yams. During his military years and psychiatry residency, Stoker had walked down hospital wards many times; and this moment evoked emotions of the past. He recalled hundreds of his patients in hospitals in the former Yugoslavia, Jamaica, Guatemala, and other countries. Stoker had treated patients suffering from countless infections, injuries, and syndromes. As a psychiatrist, he also worked to relieve patients when they agonized through fatigue, PTSD, dissociative states, and many other behavioral illnesses exacerbated by stress and their environment. War and strife always introduced tragedy as well as trauma.

Now here he was in Chihuahua, Mexico. Stoker noticed the people with the easy-to-swallow meals also exhibited signs of muscle weakness and fatigue. As he observed, Dr. Stoker noted how these weary patients also struggled to respond to conversations with the nurses, dietary staff, and other hospital workers.

"May I help you *Señor* Paul?" one of the nurses asked. Stoker discerned that she appeared stressed and overworked. "Why are you loitering way down on this end of the floor?"

"I'm just on my way to the bathroom," Stoker replied as he continued walking down the hospital ward at a languid pace. "Recovering from that snakebite has sucked away all of my energy." She accepted his half-truth.

Stoker was taking his time, analyzing each patient he passed. By the time he reached the bathroom, he'd observed a few more patients on ventilators. And, most of the patients on this ward had very similar symptoms.

On Stoker's return trip to his bed, he walked back at a sluggish pace. At one point, he decided to do a little experiment. Stoker identified one of the patients who appeared to suffer from the common illness on the floor. As he walked by the man, he gave his bed a sharp bump. "*Lo siento, Señor*," Stoker said apologizing for his sham clumsiness. He expected the patient to react with a startled jump. Instead, the man responded by whispering back an inaudible comment. Stoker tried the experiment a few seconds later with another patient. Again, the patient exhibited almost no reaction to the jolt. *What's causing this muted central nervous system response?* Stoker wondered.

As he arrived back at his bed, Stoker turned and looked down the corridor again. One of the nurses was instructing a middle-aged woman to take a deep breath and blow into a tube attached to a simple spirometry device. When she exhaled into the machine, her puff would propel a little ball up into a cylinder. The patient exhibited poor results, as her earnest huffs and puffs barely propelled the ball up the cylinder at all. Something was weakening her breathing muscles.

Stoker watched the nurse administer the spirometry test to about a dozen of the patients. As he ate his dinner, he made a mental note of their poor results and compromised breathing. Now, Stoker felt near perfect confidence many patients on the floor were suffering from the same condition. The evidence screamed epidemic.

"Hey, *Señor* Paul." Thanks to his concentration on the

patients surrounding him, Stoker failed to notice Rivera walking onto the busy hospital ward. "How's that arm of yours doing?"

"Now that's an interesting question. I'm so distracted by the spectacle on this floor that I've neglected my own recovery."

"What did you notice, Stoker?" Rivera asked as he set down a backpack he had in tow. It was full of survival and tactical gear.

"See the stressed-out nurse over there? She's administered spirometry tests on a bunch of patients."

"They're worried about pulmonary insufficiency," Rivera commented.

"Right," Stoker said. "Couple that with a bunch of patients on vents, and that's enough to get a couple of doctors curious."

"What else should make us curious?"

"The patients who share this congruency of symptoms also show obvious signs of weakness. I mean, they can use their arms, although with some weakness. But it appears their legs are even weaker than their arms. Nobody's walking around."

"Now that you mention it, the nurses' aides are going crazy with bedpan duty," Rivera interjected. "Many of these people cannot stand up to go to the bathroom on their own."

"Bingo, Dr. Rivera," Stoker said. "I knew there was a reason I brought you along on these crazy missions. Let's keep watching."

A couple of years ago, when Rivera was first getting to know Stoker, he spotted Stoker's remarkable observation skills. His almost superpowers of perception and intuition made Stoker a formidable asset on the *Espada Rápida* team.

"It might be time to meet a few of these patients," Rivera said. "Let's get to know our new *amigos* and memorize a few of their names. Will you watch my backpack?"

"With that beast of a bag, you're prepared for anything. I'm always happy to support a good Boy Scout."

Rivera put on a surgical mask and walked toward a man who was struggling to find the strength to feed himself. In his native Spanish, he asked the patient, "Can I get you some water? I just happened to notice the nurses are running around crazy this evening. Are you thirsty?"

The man nodded and whispered, "*Gracias*."

Sit up straight. Put your chin down. Now you're a chicken. When you swallow, move your neck back like a chicken clucking."

The man made the odd movement as he swallowed. But, his face registered a new level of satisfaction. "My mom always told me not to be chicken," the patient whispered. "This is one time I will disobey her; may she rest in peace."

"It will be our little secret," Rivera said. A surgical mask covered his mouth, but his smile was evident in his eyes.

"The man thanked Rivera with a stammer. Who taught you that?" he whispered. "Are you a doctor?"

Rivera dodged the question. "I've just had to take care of some people I love during challenging times."

For the next twenty minutes, Rivera went down the hospital ward asking select patients if he could help them drink. Stoker watched his friend, the man who had become a doctor to atone for his barbarous military past in the jungles of Central America. He could see, as he had witnessed dozens of times before, Rivera relished the opportunity to care for people. In an instant, he set aside the tough exterior of a soldier and exercised deep, sincere compassion. Even though this group of patients was suffering from some facial paralysis, the thoughtful Dr. Rivera could still make them smile. He even elicited laughter from a few. Not only had Rivera cared for a dozen strangers in a Mexican hospital today, but he had also comforted their souls.

Rivera made his way back to Stoker's bed. "The old medical school skill, observational assistance, is such a powerful tool for us doctors. A large percentage of those weakened patients also show dysarthria. I've been hearing Spanish sounds since the moment I emerged from the womb in Cuba. These patients struggle to pronounce every syllable emerging from their lips. So, let's just call this a made-up name, non-running man syndrome. What's our list of symptoms so far for potential differential diagnosis?" Rivera asked.

"Well, before you go making the list, look at that technician over there. She's performing yet another nerve conduction study—I count at least five so far. I think that's an EMG machine."

"Look at that," Rivera said. "You're right. She's got electrodes on the patient's thumb. They're testing nerve reflexes. That's interesting."

"She's also doing the needle EMG on the elbow," Stoker interjected.

"This could be significant for the diagnosis. Let's watch and see who gets nerve conduction studies."

"We already know the answer," Stoker said. "It will be all the weakened, immobile patients. The ones who fit your non-running man syndrome profile. The same individuals who also got the spirometry tests."

"Why don't you just eat some of your dinner," Rivera said. "We can pretend to be chatting while we observe what's going on."

Stoker took a bite. "Even from here, I can see that patient's having a poor response to the nerve conduction study. His fingers aren't twitching as they should be."

"You're right," Rivera said. "Let's see what happens with the next patient." Stoker and Rivera continued to watch. Stoker ate another bite here and there. Over the next few minutes, the technician administered the study to the patients who fit the profile Stoker and Rivera had observed—the patients who were weak, stoic, and unable to walk.

"The patients are not doing so well with the EMG study," Stoker pointed out. "It's time for you and me to get back to making that list of symptoms. There's a lot of uniformity here."

"First, and most alarming, is the number of patients on ventilators or receiving the spirometry tests," Rivera said. "People with this syndrome are having trouble breathing or need machines to breathe for them."

"Add in the fact they have a lot of muscle weakness," Stoker interjected. "They have some upper-body strength, but their lower bodies are compromised to the point they can't walk."

"Throw in the difficulty swallowing, and I can think of quite a few conditions and diseases that fit these patients' profiles so far," Rivera said. "We're both leaning toward a neurological diagnosis, because of the nerve conductions studies. The fact that the hospital staff is treating it as if it is contagious helps us rule out quite of few of those, however."

"Yes, I thought I had it figured out," Stoker said. "I'm curious how it spreads and how contagious it could be. We need more data."

"That's okay," Rivera said. "Let's get our hands on the lab results and medical records. It would help if we could perform physical examinations, but I think that would blow your cover, *Señor* Paul, the lawyer."

"I'm starting to feel better," Stoker said. "It's time for me to get up and walk around. A rehabilitation walk—say down to the lab and back—would be the perfect therapy."

Rivera's eyes filled with mischief. "You know how I love snooping," he whispered. "While a hospital lab is not the greatest reconnaissance challenge, I'll take my undercover rush wherever I can get it."

Stoker started to stand up, but Rivera put his hand on Stoker's shoulder and sat him back down. "Not so fast there, *amigo*. Remember, you're supposed to be injured and afflicted."

Slower on the second attempt to stand, Stoker pushed himself to the edge of the bed, and rose to his feet. He tried to contort his face a little and make it look like standing was painful. "How's that for frail?"

"Much better," Rivera replied. "Thanks for acting the part of a sick man. Just make sure to look downward as we walk through the halls. Your eyes are so excited and animated, anyone who makes eye contact with you will sense your enthusiasm. You'll give us away and get us busted on a simple lab infiltration."

"The surgical mask will hide my evil grin," Stoker said. "I'll work on toning down the intensity in my eyeballs."

CHAPTER 9

Chihuahua, Mexico

Breaking into the hospital lab was a simple matter. Stoker and Rivera found a janitor who wanted to make fifty dollars. Learning their way around this lab was also easy. Stoker and Rivera had memorized the names of many patients they suspected of suffering from the mystery they dubbed non-running man syndrome. They found the lab reports among the paper records, and Rivera navigated the Spanish. "Look at these results. This patient, Mr. Flores, had a spinal tap. And, there's evidence of elevated protein in his cerebral-spinal fluid. But, there's not a substantial increase in white blood cells."

Both doctors looked at each other. "Guillain-Barre," they said in unison.

"Are there any abnormal liver function tests?" Stoker asked.

"Yes, his LFTs are elevated. But take a look at this report on his blood culture."

Stoker looked at the report. "The culture grew Campylobacter jejuni! I don't need to be fluent in Spanish to read that." Campylobacter jejuni, or CJ, was a common bacterium, responsible for most instances of food poisoning. It was also responsible for roughly twenty percent of Guillain-Barre cases in the United States, and perhaps in Mexico.

"That confirms our suspicions. Mr. Flores is suffering from Guillain-Barre syndrome. What about patient Rosarita Gomez?"

Rivera thumbed through more paperwork. "Yes, here we go. Ditto for Ms. Gomez. A spinal tap with protein in her cerebral spinal fluid, and her blood culture grew Campylobacter jejuni."

"We've got twenty or more people testing positive for CJ who display significant motor paralysis of the larger muscles, to the point they can't walk. Then we saw hospital personnel conducting spirometry and nerve conduction studies. The hospital is overwhelmed with patients on ventilators. And, now we find the spinal tap and blood culture results for two patients that point to Guillain-Barre—a non-contagious disease, I might add."

"I can't think of anything else," Stoker interjected. "If Guillain-Barre is the culprit, I have no idea why the staff was wearing extra protective equipment. Let's check on the rest of these patients' lab results."

"We know what we'll find. Abnormal protein in the cerebral-spinal fluid as well as the Campylobacter bacteria in their blood. But, we still need to do our due diligence and look at all the data."

Stoker and Rivera went through everyone on their list. The results they saw left them with little doubt the patients were all battling Guillain-Barre syndrome, a rare disease that often paralyzed its victims for a few weeks to months. "So why, in a city of this size, do all of these people suffer from this rather rare disease?" Rivera asked.

Stoker thought for a moment. "More than twenty people have it at the same time—and that's just in this single hospital. The whole city of Chihuahua should see less than twenty cases in a whole year." Stoker started to lay the lab results out on a counter. "Can you take pictures of these documents, Rivera? We may need this evidence to get people to listen back at home."

Rivera took out his smartphone and started taking pictures as he commented. "Here's the good and the bad. There's a good chance, with the right support, ninety-five percent of these people will live. The bad question is, do they have enough ventilators in *Hospital de Los Santos* to support all of these people if they continue to have an epidemic?"

"We'll never know," Stoker said. "And, even if we did, we could not do anything about it right now. Our pressing priority is getting out of here with enough evidence to persuade the right authorities to look into this phenomenon."

Rivera continued taking pictures of the lab results. Stoker returned the reports to the right folders, binders, or filing cabinets.

"And why would they be having an epidemic of this particular disease?" Rivera asked. "The odds of a Guillain-Barre epidemic of this magnitude—well, it's just not something that would happen naturally. Something's going on here."

"My intuition tells me it's human-made," Stoker said.

"So, *amigo*, what else is your big right brain telling you?" Rivera asked.

Stoker stopped organizing the paperwork for a moment. He furrowed his forehead and frowned. "Genetics. Someone's manipulating the damned genetics."

CHAPTER 10

Chicago, Illinois

Nikolas Antoniou chose Chicago as his base of operation, all those years ago, for two reasons. First, the Ayatollahs had ordered him to select a large Midwestern city. Second, Lake Michigan offered plenty of sailing. Yachtsman was part of the persona Nikolas had projected over the many years he'd been laying the groundwork for his silent terror attack on a vast scale. In conversations, he claimed sailing was his refuge from the pressures of running his hotel and other ventures. But, business deadlines and economic strains didn't bother him. Those troubles stood no comparison to the threat of Middle Eastern terrorist maniacs, driven by a mandate from Allah, making demands with impossible timetables.

Today Nikolas sailed due north on a beautiful sixty-four-foot yacht over the waters of Lake Michigan. This vessel was quite similar to The Winds of Athens sailboat he'd left in Greece. The breezes were a little lighter than he would've liked. His vessel's velocity vacillated between three and four knots. It was silent and peaceful—experiences his psyche could not appreciate. He could not recognize beautiful aesthetics or participate in meaningful relationships. Yet, with some effort, his dispassionate brain could contrive fake emotions—an exercise he had to engage in dozens of times each day as he helped lead and pace conversations. It took strenuous effort and immense focus for his frigid dark mind to fabricate false empathy, passion, enthusiasm, or warmth in interactions with all people.

After two hours of sailing, Nikolas anchored his boat a mile offshore from Northwestern University. He set up a robust unidirectional Wi-Fi transceiver and directed it toward the school. Then Nikolas went below deck and connected to a Wi-Fi hotspot at Northwestern University. Using different hardware and software to encrypt his data, he masked his computer's location and I.P. address.

At 10:30 am sharp, Nikolas joined a teleconference. A man he had known since his youth issued a curt greeting. His bonyad director, Alireza Pour-Mohammadi, always treated Nikolas as subservient. But today, the director started the meeting by expressing blatant hostility toward the agent he had mentored and buried so deep in America. One of Nikolas's counterparts from Iran's Ministry of Intelligence and Security joined the teleconference from Nassau, Bahamas. The director greeted the man in the Bahamas with some level of warmth. Then a man, who was not Iranian, joined the teleconference from his location in Asia. "Let us begin," stated the director. "We must be direct in addressing our most frustrating constraint. Nikolas, why are there not yet thousands suffering from your diseases in the streets of America?"

"We accomplished our first attack, my Sayid," Nikolas explained. "We used the amoeba at this barbaric festival, Burning Man."

"So why is nobody dying or suffering?" the director asked with a venomous tone. "I think your attack has failed!"

"My Sayid, It takes four weeks or longer for symptoms to appear. As we speak, there are thousands of American devils incubating these amoebas. In a month, doctors will start seeing these cases. In two months, the amoeba, Balamuthia mandrillaris, will create death and chaos in America's homes, clinics, hospitals, and workplaces."

"And there is another germ—or whatever you call it—you will be releasing soon. Report on that."

"Yes, I issued the order to begin disbursing the bacteria. The teams are staging as we speak. The germ is one of the most common bacteria in the world. Again, its name is Campylobacter jejuni. Millions upon millions of people are infected with it each year. They experience diarrhea for a few days. But we've made our version much more potent. About half of the people infected with our Campylobacter bacteria will develop the miserable Guillain-Barre syndrome, thanks to the genetic modifications we've done."

"This Guillain-Barre, it is the disease that paralyzes people so they cannot breathe?"

"Yes. But, victims do get better after months. We will infect millions of people—and at about the same time, America will start to grapple with the amoeba Balamuthia. The hospitals will be overwhelmed just when they are reeling from the amoeba. Most of these Campylobacter patients who get Guillain-Barre will need ventilators to breathe for them. A medical study published in 2010 estimates there are, at most, 161,000 ventilators in the United States. If a million people need those ventilators, and there is just a fraction of the demanded ventilators available, our little germs will break down the medical system. Americans will perish at the hands of an illness that rarely kills its victims—as long as they have access to a ventilator."

Then the man in the Bahamas broke into the conversation. "Why do we need two germs, when one suffices?"

"Many of the initial symptoms are similar," Nikolas responded. He chose to contrive some fake emotions as if he was excited and optimistic. Nikolas added energy to his voice and mannerisms. He knew it would help his bonyad director feel some enthusiasm for the biological attack and its violent elegance. "Both pathogens' symptoms steer doctors toward a neurological diagnosis. At first, the consequences from the bacteria will start to show up as Guillain-Barre syndrome. Doctors will start getting alerts about the epidemic from the CDC, which will condition them to be on the lookout for it. Only days into this conditioning, patients will start showing up with the amoeba infection. Just enough people will be misdiagnosed with Guillain-Barre because the symptoms are so similar. They'll get the wrong treatments for a few days as the amoeba continues to eat away at their brain. After many deaths, doctors will discover there is a second epidemic—a very lethal epidemic. They'll be behind the eight ball with thousands of patients—who are also candidates for ventilators.

"Yes, this delay will kill many people. But more important, it will terrorize *everyone*. The American media will report on this phenomenon and make it even larger than it is. Americans will feel a deep lapse of confidence in their medical system and their government. For Americans, this triggers horror in their news-cycle-hypnotized satanic minds. Their medical system is both their Mecca and Medina."

Nikolas's counterpart in the Bahamas finished the thought. "Because they are so focused on this amoeba you call Balamuthia, the Americans will fail to see this other bacterium, Campylobacter jejuni?"

"Yes, at least in many cases for a few initial days or weeks. This will further amplify the confusion and terror. That is the beauty of attacking with the amoeba Balamuthia mandrillaris first, and then following up with the genetically modified bacteria, Campylobacter jejuni. It will take them a few weeks to figure out the Campylobacter jejuni is weaponized. By then, America will be using every single ventilator and trying to figure out how to keep millions of paralyzed people breathing."

"Once they have it all figured out," asked the bonyad director, "for how many weeks will they be testing people for two different pathogens?"

"The Campylobacter bacteria will begin to subside within about ninety days. But the Balamuthia amoeba will be a longer, slower burn. There will be a consistent number of cases for about six months before it starts to taper. But, I imagine doctors' offices and emergency rooms will be screening for both pathogens for at least eight months. It will be a long, tiring terror."

"It's brilliant," the man in the Bahamas said. "Americans expect bombs and the type of terror that occupies a few days in their news-cycle-conditioned mentality. Eight months of wide-scale, slow, protracted terror will be hell on Earth. I shall relish every moment as I witness the hand of Allah across the land!"

The director, Alireza Pour-Mohammadi, interrupted his enthusiasm. "But, I for one do not like this timeline! My patience has worn thin with these many years—almost two decades now— of incubating bacteria and amoebas and storing them in the basement of your hotel. While I see your vision, I am not as optimistic as your counterpart in the Bahamas. Right now, it's a pipe dream. I need results. I need sick, dying Americans. I need hospitals bursting at the seams. I need families begging for their loved one to have access to a ventilator. I want fights in the streets of America as brother rises up against brother and neighbor against neighbor. The irony of it all. It is Allah who gives the Ruh-Allah, or the breath of life. And here, these Americans will be begging for a false, mechanical breath of life while ignoring the true source of life!"

Nikolas stared up at the monitor before him. His enthusiasm for the majesty of his biological attack plan had not diminished during Pour-Mohammadi's speech. His response was simple. "You shall have your wish. In days we shall release the Campylobacter jejuni bacteria."

"No!" the director responded. "You will attack now. Your elegant timing is an unnecessary extravagance. You will unleash our fury now. We do not have the luxury of timing. We have two other attacks from your colleagues in the Bahamas and Asia. Their attacks are the death blow calamities. Your germs will terrorize all; but when it comes to death, they are just a harbinger of what will be."

"Yes, my Sayid," Nikolas replied. He did not dare argue with Pour-Mohammadi face to face. Nor did he need to.

"For your sake, and the sake of your loved ones under our constant watch and protection in Saudi Arabia, you had better be right. I need millions of infections. If your silent army of billions upon billions of germs fails, you, your wife, and your children all become useless to us. Dead weight, which we would need to shed."

Nikolas chose to say no more, hoping the director would move onto the additional business at hand.

"Now we shall discuss the final judgment. It will hit the Great Satan and turn their hearts to the East, to Mecca," Pour-Mohammadi said.

"Have you taken possession of the cruise ship?" the director asked the man in Nassau.

"The boat is now in our possession. Last night we readied some of the hardware we will need. Tonight, we will finish loading our cargo from the Bahamas.

"The benign materials that are easy to disguise." The director clarified.

"Yes, the delivery we acquire off the coast of Belize will include the important elements."

Until now, the man in Asia had been silent. "And what does your timeline look like for you to arrive in Belize and acquire those materials?" His tone was urgent. "We have fallen behind schedule, you know. People here in Asia are starting to doubt us."

"Give us two months," the man in the Bahamas said.

"Can you buy us two more months?" the director asked the man in Asia.

"Concrete data and plans will help me. While logic is not the primary criteria for making choices here, showing actual progress and a firm timeline will offset the mixture of mysticism and emotion that drives decisions here."

"If Nikolas does his job right," the bonyad director said with anger in his voice, "the headlines will be full of outcry about the sick, suffering, and dead in America. We will have a proverbial hurricane of cloud cover."

"So, it's all resting on you, Nikolas," the man in Asia said. It was a taunt more than a comment.

Nikolas felt something inside of him trigger. He sensed beads of perspiration developing on his temples. Profuse moisture wet his armpits. He hoped the others in the teleconference could not see his forehead glistening with sweat. With a herculean effort, he relaxed his face. Injecting a hint of false bravado and an abundance of insincere piety into his voice he spoke. "I am honored to have such a *holy* responsibility on this the dawn of our greatest hour."

Pour-Mohammadi spoke. "May your responsibility lead to happiness and prosperity for your fine family." Then he ended the teleconference, and the screen went black.

Nikolas closed the cheap notebook computer he had been using and took it with him onto the deck of the sailboat. He let the device slip out of his hands and fall into the depths of Lake Michigan. If anyone ever attempted to associate today's conference call with a computer MAC address, they may uncover the MAC address. But, they would never find the computer.

CHAPTER 11

Chihuahua, Mexico

Within a few minutes, Stoker and Rivera took more than a hundred pictures of lab reports.

"There's got to be more to this epidemic," Stoker said. His investigative intensity was peaking. "Somewhere in this laboratory, there's documentation or some other clue about why this cluster of people has the same illness. For some reason, someone wanted all these people to get Guillain-Barre at the same time."

Then, without notice, they heard a key in the door. Stoker and Rivera had nowhere to hide when a lab technician entered the room. "Who are you? What are you doing here?" the man said in stern, punctuated Spanish. He was wearing typical hospital scrubs.

"The door was open," Rivera lied, also speaking Spanish. "I'm Doctor Hernandez, and this is my colleague Dr. Gunter. He's a neurologist from Germany. I am an epidemiologist from Mexico City. We've been friends for years. We both did our residencies at the same school." Rivera was convincing as he contrived a cover story. Stoker noticed how easily he improvised, how practiced he was as a deceiver. "Dr. Gunter has always had a special interest in Guillain-Barre syndrome. And of course, my curiosity is always piqued whenever potential clusters of illness occur anywhere in Mexico."

The lab technician eyed Stoker and Rivera warily. "So why did you need to come into our lab—and without advanced notice or an invitation?"

"Well, I heard you had a unique cluster of Guillain-Barre syndrome cases here. The rumors always get to me before the actual statistics do. In any case, I called Dr. Gunter, and he flew out only eighteen short hours ago. He has a very limited window of opportunity. So, what can you show us?"

"I know nothing of a Guillain-Barre epidemic. I'm sorry you have come all this way, and in such haste. The rumors are false."

"Look. We've already toured through your hospital." This part of Rivera's story was true. But, he quickly resumed the fabrication. "We rounded on many of those patients with the attending physicians here. There are more than twenty cases of Guillain-Barre syndrome in *Hospital de Los Santos*."

"I have strict instructions from administration to avoid discussing information with people I recognize as outsiders. If you would like access to my laboratory data, you must be properly introduced by our medical director or administration. Now I'm instructing you to leave this lab."

"Listen, my friend," Rivera said. "Earlier today, one of your hospital administrators introduced us to all the doctors and nurses in your intensive care unit and on your medical floor." Rivera's fictional stories grew and grew. Ironically, they sounded ever more believable. "We're sorry they've not provided the proper introduction or communication to you here in the lab. I assure you. It was only an oversight." Rivera removed two crisp one-hundred-dollar bills from his back pocket and laid them on the countertop to the side of the lab technician. "We just need a few minutes of your expertise and access to some of your data."

"You can keep your money," replied the technician. "Now get out of my lab."

Rivera placed 800 additional dollars on the countertop.

"Take your dirty money and leave right now."

Stoker, ever the analyst of human behavior, observed how the man's body language had just shifted from resolute to potentially violent.

"What's really going on here?" Rivera asked. "Nobody refuses $1,000 for a little lab data."

The lab technician's reply was wordless and swift. He reached his hand back under his scrubs into the small of his back. In one fluid motion, he withdrew a small knife and thrust it toward Rivera's torso.

The man never knew what hit him. Stoker's straight punch landed squarely on the lab technician's cheekbone, violently snapping his head to the side and sending the lab technician sprawling to the floor unconscious.

"Oh man!" Rivera complained. "I was looking forward to a good brawl, and you had to go and wreck it."

Stoker laughed. "Only Errol Rivera would ever complain about an *amigo* saving his life."

Rivera stepped over to the lab technician and rolled him onto his back. "You didn't save my life. I was milliseconds away from blocking his stab." He found the man's pulse.

Stoker bent over him, pushed his eyelids up one at a time, and checked his pupils. "No, I clobbered this guy in the head before you could block it. And, that guy had some training. That was a well-executed move, not a desperate slash attempt."

"If you would've let me block his well-executed move," Rivera continued, "I could've subdued the guy."

"And then what?" Stoker asked. "Interrogate him for hours here in the lab without anybody noticing?"

"It would've been a very short interrogation," Rivera insisted.

"Let's wait for him to return to consciousness."

"No longer an option," Rivera said. "You've left too much evidence on his cheekbone."

Rivera reached around to the only pocket in the unconscious man's scrub pants and pulled out his phone. "Here's our canary in the coal mine. When people start texting him." He pushed the phone's home button. The screen reported it was locked, which was no surprise.

Stoker grabbed the unconscious man's hand and pressed his index finger against the button. But, there was no response. "This phone's touch ID isn't active. We need the passcode."

"I'm not surprised," Rivera answered. "As much as I want to know what's on his phone, we're not going to figure it out right now. The best thing we can do is to bring the phone with us. When this guy eventually remote wipes it, we'll know he's awake, and his people are onto us. Again, our canary in this coal mine. We've got to get out of here. This guy spoke excellent Spanish—for an Iranian."

"His body language and gestures were definitely not what I've observed in most Mexican men. But, how do you know he's an Iranian?"

"His Spanish accent was close to perfect. I sensed some slight variations that reminded me of other Spanish-speaking people from the Middle East. Someday I'll tell you a story about working with lots of Arabs and Iranians who had dominated Spanish. It involved an undercover operation with oil in Venezuela."

"And how Hugo Chavez got cancer?"

"That wasn't me! Let's get that straight right now. What did Z tell you?"

"Touchy, touchy, Rivera," Stoker said. "Relax man. That was just humor. I joked myself right into a coincidence that struck a raw nerve with you. Z and I never discussed the subject."

"There are no coincidences," Rivera responded. "Like us interacting with so many Shiites here in Chihuahua. And now, bumping into an Iranian who knows how to run a lab, just 230 miles south of the border."

"Yes, about him. He didn't take your money. So, we can conclude the security of his operation is certainly much more valuable to him than a healthy sum of cash."

"It's evident working as a Mexican lab technician is not his highest priority. Keeping a big secret was. That's why we need to get out of here, Troy. He is hiding a lot of information, including his true identity. Our safety is critical to unraveling this mystery. If we're dead, so is any chance of putting this puzzle together."

"When he comes to, he'll immediately communicate with his superiors. We're marked men. They don't know who we are, but they'll assume we know a lot about their little secret."

Stoker and Rivera dragged the lab technician into a closet and removed his scrub top. Stoker reached into Rivera's large backpack. He removed some zip ties and fastened them around the man's wrists and ankles. "Let's make this look like a robbery," Rivera said.

"You mean, instead of the inception of an international conflict between an extremist pocket of radical Shiites and Americans, on Mexican soil?"

"Exactly. The conflict is happening. But, we don't want these would-be terrorists to know just how much we're learning about them. This needs to look like a robbery. They probably won't report any of this to the police. But if they do, this robbery scenario is a gift for the extremists. These terrorists don't want to tell the Mexican police what's really going on here."

Stoker and Rivera finished binding the lab technician's wrists and ankles. "It will take him a few minutes to get himself untied," Stoker said. "He'll kick through that door in about thirty seconds."

"But the dark, cramped space in the closet will slow him down a few more minutes," Rivera responded. "Let's make it harder for him to turn on the light." Rivera took a quick picture of the knocked-out lab tech then flipped off the light switch in the closet. After rolling his shoulders forward twice, Rivera made a fist, smirked, and delivered a roundhouse punch to the drywall next to the light switch. The drywall caved in. With his other hand, he grabbed the light switch plate and yanked it out of the wall, with disconnected wires trailing. "Now it will take him way longer than thirty seconds." Rivera smiled at Stoker. "Besides doing a little demolition was very therapeutic. So, Stoker, How do you like that aggressive therapy?"

"No, we call it aggression therapy. But with you, it's *regression* therapy. You've now reverted to the ripe old age of nineteen again. I'm detecting very pronounced role confusion issues with you, Rivera."

"Well thank you very much. When I was nineteen, I was a boxer in the Army hoping to fly helicopters."

We don't have much time," Stoker said pointing toward a counter on the other side of the lab. "But I think we should use two minutes to collect any these patients' blood specimens we can."

Rivera stepped quickly in the direction of the refrigerators that held the blood specimens. "Good idea. These must have recently arrived. Grab any names you're familiar with."

Out of instinct, Stoker and Rivera put on surgical gloves and started sifting through the various tubes of blood. They found specimens that belonged to patients they knew to be battling Guillain-Barre syndrome. Carefully but quickly, the doctors wrapped the test tubes and other samples in paper towels to protect them from breaking. Then they put them in a box they located at the end of one of the counters.

"*Vamanos*," Rivera said gesturing with his head toward the door. Rivera grabbed his survival and tactical backpack and the lab technician's phone. Stoker took the box containing the many blood samples, and they exited the lab and started walking down the corridor. As they neared a door to a stairwell, the lab technician's phone vibrated in Rivera's pocket.

"Look at this," Rivera said showing the phone to Stoker. Even though the phone was locked, alerts still appeared on the screen. This alert announced a text.

"It's in Farsi," Stoker replied. "It's just a friend checking in, asking if the lab tech guy saw a recent soccer match."

"I wish we could answer," Rivera said." We might be able to capture a clue or two."

"It's moments like this when we really need Z," Stoker said. "It seems like you can get ahold of FBI agents anywhere; but where's a good hacker when you need to crack a smartphone?"

Rivera slipped the phone back into his pocket. "We'll have to do our best as active listeners. That's one of your shrink skills, right?"

"Speaking of doctor skills, I think I need a good internal medicine physician to discharge me from this hospital."

"You're in luck," Rivera replied. "Mr. Paul, by the power vested in me by my long-expired Mexican medical license, I hereby discharge you from this fine medical institution. I further stipulate that remaining here would be deadly, given the trouble you've managed to get yourself into—again. You stand a better chance dancing with a snake again."

Stoker laughed as he opened the door to the stairwell and waived Rivera through. "Thank you, Doctor. You're a fine internist." Stoker and Rivera scaled the stairs and came to the hospital's main floor. They followed the signs to the hospital's main entrance and exited into the warm night air of Chihuahua, Mexico. They made a beeline for the closest grocery store.

"We need to keep these lab samples fresh. Let's pick up Ziplock bags and some ice. I also need some tinfoil for a little experiment with this phone."

It was a quick trip to the store. In and out in about five minutes. As they started to check out, the lab tech's cell phone vibrated again in Rivera's pocket. "It looks like this friend really wants to talk about soccer. He's asking the same question. Did he see the soccer match earlier today?"

By the time they had the Ziplock bags and tinfoil in hand, the friend had texted about the soccer game one more time. "This time the friend is almost demanding to know about our sleeping friend's opinion of the game."

"Soccer is only a code," Stoker said. "Whoever is texting the lab tech is actually requesting a status report."

While walking out of the store, another text came in. "Now the friend's demanding to know the score. I'm sure that's an escalation code. It's as if they're saying, 'We think you're in trouble.

Respond now, or we'll assuming something's wrong and come rescue you.'"

"Let's put some distance between the hospital and us."

"Better yet, let's gather more information before we get out of town. We've got some samples to analyze, and I think we can work on this puzzle better from the safe and objective viewpoint of Fort Sam Houston."

"We'll also have access to a good laboratory there."

Rivera hailed a taxi. "Where to?" the driver asked.

"Take us to the hottest nightspot in town. Where do you recommend?"

"That would be *La Sotolería*."

Stoker only understood a little of the conversation in Spanish.

"A little sotol sounds perfect," Rivera said referring to the locally distilled spirits. But tonight, he would not be drinking any. He needed perfect clarity. "Take us to *La Sotolería*."

The driver sped away. "It's not for everyone. But it may be entertaining for your American friend. A local novelty a lot of the clubs will sell by request, we call it the *soltol* with a snake."

Rivera allowed himself a hearty laugh.

"It's so good to hear you belly laugh," Stoker said. "It's a strong indicator you're not a psychopath. But, I didn't pick up on your conversation in Spanish. What did he say?"

"He says they have great drinks with snakes in them!"

"Hey! Aversion therapy. Bring it on, Rivera!" Stoker leaned up to the taxi driver, and in broken Spanish, he said, "Take us to the snakes." Then he held his bandaged arm forward to show the taxi driver. He could not figure out how to explain that his arm injury was a snake bite, so he just used his other hand to gesture and imitate a snake biting his injured arm. The taxi driver understood him instantly, and the realization a snake had recently bitten Stoker made him uncomfortable.

"It was a Mojave," Rivera said. The driver winced. "My friend likes your entertainment suggestion. He wants to confront his fears. But I won't let him drown his sorrows."

The driver made a brief artificial smile and then decided to direct his attention to navigating traffic.

Rivera sent a text to his helicopter co-pilot ordering him to take the team to the helicopter and be on alert. The lab tech's cell phone was receiving texts every thirty to sixty seconds asking him to report the score on a soccer game. "I suspect someone is tracking this phone's position at this point. Fortunately for us, we can choose when we want to be tracked and when we do not want to." Rivera removed the aluminum foil from a grocery bag, tore three pieces from the foil roll, and wrapped the foil around the cell phone. "There we go. Radio silence." Three layers of foil were enough to block any signals to or from the cell phone. If somebody was tracking the cell phone, they just lost their trace.

When they arrived at *La Sotolería*, Rivera paid the driver the taxi fare in pesos. Then he gave him fifty American dollars and instructed him to wait. "We may be a little while. And, when we come out of that bar, we may be in a huge hurry. When we jump in the car, just go! We'll give you instructions once we're moving."

Stoker and Rivera entered one of Chihuahua's hottest night spots. "Do you happen to have a table for five? One where we can be facing the door that also sits right next to a wall?" Rivera asked the host. After a ten-minute wait, Stoker and Rivera were led to a table that allowed them to see every person who entered the establishment. Rivera hid his backpack under the table. They ordered appetizers and Cokes for four people. Having food for four people made it appear they were part of a larger group—a hoax that would prove helpful in a few minutes. They chose appetizers because they wanted the food to be served quickly. When the food arrived Stoker and Rivera started to eat.

Rivera removed the lab tech's cell phone and unwrapped the phone from its tinfoil cocoon. "Let's give them thirty seconds of insight into this phone's whereabouts." Then he flagged down their server. "Can we have two of those bottles of *soltol*? One with the viper inside, but the other with no snake? And, four glasses if you please? We have friends joining us." After the server stepped away to fulfill Rivera's request, he wrapped the phone in the foil again.

A minute later the server brought the bottles. "We're doctors, and we may need to leave quickly. We're on call this evening." Rivera said. Then he handed her ten twenty-dollar bills. "I just want to make sure the tab is settled if we have to rush out of here." The server smiled. "And might I borrow a pair of tongs? You know, the metallic type chefs often use with the hinge at the back? I know it's a strange request." The server had no problem accommodating the strange request after the large tip she had just received.

Rivera poured *soltol* into four glasses, but he did not fill them completely. He wanted to enhance the illusion that a few good men accompanied him. "I need to get this snake out of this other bottle."

"I think I see where you're going with this. I'll handle the snake extraction," Stoker said, "as soon as the waitress brings those tongs you requested." A minute later, the waitress brought the tongs. Stoker took them and the bottle and made his way toward the restroom. He stepped into the bathroom and dumped the *soltol* into the toilet, leaving just the snake in the bottle. Then he smashed the bottle on the inside of the garbage can and used the tongs to fish the dead rattlesnake out of the garbage can. Stoker rinsed off a few glass shards in the sink. Holding the snake behind his back, Stoker returned to the table. "Here you go, Rivera," as he handed off the rattlesnake carcass and tongs discretely.

Rivera draped the serpent over his leg and covered it with a napkin. Then he unwrapped the cell phone from the tin foil. "Let's see who our friends are."

He removed a .22 pistol from an ankle holster and handed it to Stoker. "I need you to find a place where you can shoot out the light above our table." Rivera directed his eyes to the lamp about six feet above their heads.

"You've got it," Stoker said. "You'll need a moment of darkness—some time for their eyes to adjust to the surprise. Now let's see who comes through that door with the wrong body language."

Stoker walked toward the bathrooms and found the perfect spot. He could see the door, he could see Rivera's table, and any shot he took would fly upward into wood paneling or drywall and be highly unlikely to endanger anyone.

As the two men watched the door, groups of people entered. Sometimes a lone person would enter. Everyone's body language was relaxed. People were coming to *La Sotolería* to have fun. Twelve minutes after Rivera had let the phone be tracked again, two men passed through the door. Their faces were grave, their strides purposeful, and their spines held their shoulders high at alert. These men ignored the hostess and started looking around *La Sotolería*, heads panning and eyes darting in all directions.

Rivera held up the cell phone. When he caught the attention

of one of the men he just put a big exaggerated smile on his face and pointed toward the cell phone in an animated style. The men moved quickly toward his table, closing in on him aggressively. Rivera took two bold strides toward them and elected to speak first in Farsi. "If you value your mission."

One of the men was stunned, and the words in Farsi stopped him in his tracks. Rivera then chose Spanish. "If you value the mission." The second man halted his advance. Rivera held up his own phone displaying a picture of the lab tech he had snapped. The tech's eyes were closed, and the injury to his cheek from Stoker's blow was apparent. "Tell me about the soccer match," Rivera said in Farsi and then Spanish. "Please take a seat and enjoy some *soltol* with me. Wasn't that some great *fútbol*?"

The men refused to sit. "Give us the phone!" This man was Iranian. Yet, he chose to speak in Spanish.

"Good Spanish," Rivera said. "You still have some work to do on your accent. Let's practice. Do you know where your lab tech friend is?" Rivera jiggled the phone again for emphasis. The men did not answer. But, they could not hide their surprise. It was apparent nobody had gone to the hospital to check on him. Hence, Rivera could bluff, and pretend the lab tech was his hostage. "This man is not just an expendable soldier. He's key to the biology of your whole operation. I am suggesting an exchange." Rivera paused. "Now sit down if you want to see this mission through and get your man back."

The men stood resolutely. "What do you want?" This time the man from Mexico was taking the initiative. "We have no time for games."

"I want you to sit down right now. My boys have the advantage over you." Then a gunshot rang out and the light bulb above their heads shattered. The Iranian responded by ducking into a partial crouch. The Mexican fell to the ground and reached for his pistol. The other bar patrons went silent. One woman shrieked.

Then Stoker threw six glasses to the floor. "I am so sorry. Oh, *lo siento*," Stoker proclaimed with a drunken Texas drawl in his voice. That was all my fault. *Mia culpa, amigos*."

While a gun going off in a Mexican bar was a rarity, a drunk American was all the explanation people needed. *La Sotoleria* eventually roared back to life in a few seconds.

Now the two men were sufficiently frozen by the control and confusion. They felt threatened by the sudden darkness. And, it was apparent their foe was not alone. They had no idea how many men they were up against.

"Now have a seat boys," Rivera snarled. "Do you want to drink, or do you want to talk?" The men slowly slid into the table where Rivera stood. Rivera bellowed out to the bar patrons in Spanish, "I apologize for my crazy American friend. Drinks for everyone!" The crowd roared their approval, and Rivera held up his hand and signaled for the waitress. She approached quickly, and he slid her nine hundred more dollars.

Turning his attention toward his two adversaries, Rivera sized up the Iranian and guessed he was talking to someone who had some authority. He knew more about the grand Mexico Guillain-Barre syndrome plan than the lab tech had. The hair on the Iranian's temples was starting to gray. The man had not overreacted to the gunshot. Rivera concluded he was a trained and experienced operator.

"Let's get right to the point. I want to give you back your lab tech. He's an asset, but not worth all the strings he has attached. I must assign people to guard him. I have to feed him and take care of him. Returning him would be better for everyone."

"What do you want in return?" the Iranian asked.

"Why do twenty or more people have Guillain-Barre syndrome?"

"I know little about this. Yes, I have heard about this concentration of cases from one of my sources. But, this source also tells me Mexico is a place where these little epidemics can arise. One little germ travels fast. This one happens to cause this disease you speak of with the French name.

Rivera leaned over the table and changed his voice to a menacing half whisper. "I don't tolerate lies, half lies, omissions, or deceptions. Then he let slow, sinister grin grace his face. "Don't look down."

The wise Iranian held Rivera's gaze. But, this aspiring Mexican mercenary was not battle hardened. He could not resist looking down, which was precisely what Rivera wanted him to do. The shock of seeing a rattlesnake just inches from his manhood caused the Mexican to flinch and move his chair sideways three inches.

"Now look," Rivera whispered as he glanced downward with his eyes. The Iranian made a situational awareness decision and looked down to understand what had unhinged his *amigo*. He didn't flinch as he saw the head of a rattlesnake undulating between his legs. Battle and experience had seasoned this man. He kept his cool.

"Say hello to my little friend." Rivera was holding the dead snake with the tongs under the table. With a subtle wave of his wrist, he made the snake undulate. "Who is making these people sick?" Rivera demanded. "I don't know where this snake will strike, but let's hope it's your thighs."

The Iranian's face went ashen. It was too dark in the bar to recognize the serpent was dead. The tell-tale sign of a rattle would have been obscured by the cacophony of dozens of surrounding conversations. A bead of sweat appeared on the Iranians forehead.

Rivera growled. "I have more snakes, I have more guns, and I have more men with me here in this noisy *cantina*. And by the way, your lab tech feels your pain," Rivera bluffed. He loved fabricating deceptions. "We're holding him, and we're extracting good intel from him. Only complete, truthful answers can save him, *amigo*. Only complete, truthful answers can save you. Now, who's doing this?"

With all the concentration on the snake, neither the Iranian nor the Mexican had noticed how Stoker had inched his way back toward the table. He was now sitting in a chair almost within earshot.

The Iranian continued. "We are a medical team doing work on Guillain-Barre syndrome."

"With Campylobacter jejuni," Rivera interjected.

The Iranian was stunned. This man sitting before him, threatening him with a rattlesnake, knew more than he could've ever imagined. He was trapped. And, trying to deceive would only entangle and endanger him more. "This group of people. They are test subjects, guinea pigs if you will. They should all survive. We came to an, well, an agreement, with *Hospital de Los Santos* to admit these patients early and put them on ventilators when they needed it."

"You said when they needed it, not if they needed it," Rivera interjected. But many Guillain-Barre patients never need ventilators. Your statement implied all patients would need ventilators. Why?"

Now the Iranian had many beads of sweat forming on his

forehead. *How does this man know so much?* he thought. "This is a very potent strain of Campylobacter jejuni. From what I understand, the subsequent Guillain-Barre disease is much more likely to occur."

"How did it get so potent?" Rivera asked.

"You must forgive me." The Iranian's voice trembled a bit. "I'm not a scientist. I'm a soldier. I don't know the words to explain exactly. I just know our scientists have somehow manipulated Campylobacter jejuni to be stronger and more effective. Most of the people who drink the water we laced with our Campylobacter jejuni end up developing the subsequent Guillain-Barre."

Stoker had moved to an empty table just behind the Iranian and the Mexican. He could pick up bits of the conversation—enough to understand the potency of the germs they were dealing with. He could also see this revelation was angering Rivera to an extreme. He was struggling to control himself from instigating immediate and violent retribution.

"Then tell us, why are nurses and the hospital employees double gloving and wearing such extreme protective equipment?"

"Because they do not know the patients have Guillain-Barre. They only know there is a little epidemic. We've coerced the doctors into telling them it is a new syndrome, perhaps yet to be discovered. As a result, many of them are taking extreme precautions."

Rivera was a phenomenal interrogator. He could grab onto a single word or phrase and use it to open up a subject like a clam. "You just said, '*our* scientists.' Then you said, '*we* laced' and '*we* coerced.' Who is the 'our' and 'we' you speak of?" The Iranian hesitated, so Rivera whispered. "I really hope it's not a testicle this viper nails."

The Iranian grabbed the table, leaped up, and flipped it toward Rivera, fully expecting to be bitten by the snake in the process. Rivera sidestepped the table and swung with a roundhouse punch. The Iranian was more concerned about the rattlesnake, making him inattentive to Rivera's fist. It landed squarely on the Iranian's jaw, stunning him and causing him to spin 180 degrees. Rivera then attacked him from behind and wrestled the Iranian into a sleeper hold.

The Mexican reached for his pistol, but he never had a chance to grasp it before a mighty tackling body blow from Troy Stoker whiplashed his neck and took him to the ground. Stoker rose up into a kneeling position above the man and cocked his fist back. But the Mexican was gasping for breath and would need no additional thrashing thanks to a few broken ribs and a herniated disk in his neck. Stoker and Rivera frisked the men. They were each carrying two pistols. "These are ours now," Stoker said. Then he picked up the dead snake and wrapped it loosely around the dazed Iranian's neck.

Most of the crowd had retreated from the chaos. But, some of the crowd had gathered around to enjoy the short skirmish. Rivera held up his hands to show that the fighting had ceased. In Spanish, he addressed the crowd. "I am sorry you had to see that. We're doctors, and these men followed us from the hospital and attempted to rob us." Rivera slowly turned toward the door, and Stoker followed his lead. "They used that dead snake to threaten us. We're sorry about the commotion and damage. Now, will you please call an ambulance?" *La Sotolería's* manager emerged from the sea of onlookers. Rivera handed him 500 dollars and instructed the manager to send the Iranian and the Mexican to *Hospital de Los Santos*. "I will call ahead. I know the emergency room physician on duty. I'll tell him what happened and exactly how to care for these men. I will also arrange for the police to meet them there."

The Iranian was still too dazed to realize he would be going to the hospital that was the epicenter of the Guillain-Barre epidemic. The Mexican understood right away. The pain in his eyes was displaced by the sheer terror of landing in the middle of an epidemic he little understood. "No!" he gasped. While his voice was barely audible, his desperation came through loud and clear. He started pleading to be taken to another hospital, hastily naming almost a dozen alternatives.

Stoker frisked each mans' pockets once again to find car keys. He found them in the Mexican's pocket. Then Stoker picked up the box containing the lab samples. Rivera still had the cell phone they had taken from the lab tech and his survival and tactical backpack. Pushing their way through the crowd, they dashed out the front door into the night and sprinted for the waiting taxi.

"Send the taxi away," Stoker shouted to Rivera as they ran. "I got some keys to a new car."

"Excellent!" Rivera exclaimed. "You are really a natural at all of this tenacious stuff we have to do. And you don't even seem to think of the possibility you're on the verge of committing grand theft auto in Mexico." Rivera smacked the taxi's hood and told the driver he was free to leave.

Stoker smiled as he said, "I wonder how an American psychiatrist would do in a Mexican prison?" He pressed the unlock button on the car key. They didn't hear a horn, chirp, or the sound of a car unlocking. "I'm doing a seemingly wrong thing, but for all the right reasons. I think a Mexican jury may see that even more clearly than an American jury."

"You're right about that, *amigo*," Rivera responded. "You gringos tend to see things in black and white."

Stoker pushed the unlock button again. They heard the distinct clicking of door releasing, and they turned in the general direction of the sound. He pushed the button another time, and they were able to identify a white Dodge Ram 3500 pickup truck. "Toss me those keys," Rivera said. "I'll drive. This is a great opportunity for you to get some practical experience with some of our cutting-edge weapons."

"Sounds good. Let's see if we have any other tools of the trade here in our new truck." The men jumped inside. Rivera started it, and they drove away. Stoker shook down the cabin. "There are no documents to tell us who this truck belongs to. But, the glove box contains some tire spikes, and a generation two Taurus 24/7 pistol, forty-five caliber."

"That's a beautiful gun, Troy. But *amigo*, I suspect my pistol and that *pistola* will be—"

Stoker finished his thought. "A lot less firepower than our next wave of attackers will have. We need to get creative. I love getting creative. What's in that bag of yours?"

The truck rapidly accelerated onto a highway heading out of town to the northwest. "Behind door number one? Open up my goody bag and check out the magnetic grenade."

Stoker opened the bag and removed it. He started to examine it closely.

"When the perfect moment comes, pull the safety pin, slam down the fuse, and toss it at your enemy's automobile." Rivera handed his phone to Stoker. "Text the helicopter crew. Have them get that bird in the air. We just need them to follow us and provide intel."

Stoker sent a message to the crew. The response was almost immediate.

Turn on your radio.

"Is there a radio in your mega backpack?"

"Side pocket. It should already be tuned to the correct channel."

Stoker took out the radio and powered it up.

"This is Medic Alpha Six," Stoker said. Do you copy?"

"Yes. Medic Alpha Six." The helicopter pilot responded. He reported the crew was already in the air. People at the airport had started coming around and asking questions about the Russian gunship. The helicopter had stuck out like a sore thumb in Mexico. With it getting dark, they started to sense vulnerability. So, they decided to get in the air.

"Are you ready to be our eye in the sky?" Stoker asked.

"Copy that," came the reply. "What's the plan?"

"We are headed out past the airport in a white Dodge Ram pickup truck. We're pretty sure we'll pick up a tail. We have the cell phone we lifted from a tango. We're pretty sure his friends are tracking us through that phone. We want to draw out the enemy. We need to figure out who they are."

"And you want us to watch your tail," said the pilot, "and tell you who shows up to this party?"

"Exactly. But, do not engage. We'll take care of confrontations here on the ground. And once we've dispensed of these radical thugs, we'll have you pick us up. It's time for us to get to a lab in Texas and work on unraveling a mystery."

"Sounds good. We're watching your six."

Stoker set the radio between him and Rivera and the two men drove down the highway toward the airport. Stoker studied a map of the area on Rivera's phone. "I'm looking for a secluded area, where it will be easy to see who follows us." As they passed the airport, Stoker made a recommendation. "In about three miles, let's turn off this highway to the left. That takes us up a road that goes into some farmlands. At night it should work great."

"You've got it."

Just before they made the turn, Rivera started to formulate a plan with Stoker. "We don't know how many people are coming, but they *will* have guns. I'm thinking AK-47s or Uzis. And, we must stay out of their range. But, we have to get close enough to somehow attach that magnetic grenade."

"If you're close enough to use the grenade, you're close enough to get shot a few dozen times," Stoker said. "I've got an idea. Let's allow these goons to close in on us. I know how we can work this." Stoker shared the plan. Rivera responded with a deviant smile. "I love it."

Stoker and Rivera turned off from the highway onto a dark paved road that passed through some green, irrigated farmlands. Rivera slowed the truck to twenty-five miles per hour. Then he radioed the helicopter team with his position.

"We see you on infrared," the pilot said. "We're seven thousand feet above you."

Five minutes later the helicopter pilot radioed back. "There's a motorcycle bogey who turned off the highway. He's about two miles behind you."

Rivera slowed to fifteen miles per hour.

Three minutes later the pilot radioed in again. "The motorcycle stopped. And there are two more pickup trucks about four clicks behind the motorcycle. Each with two men in the truck bed. They turned down your same road. Let's see if they rendezvous with the motorcycle."

After Stoker and Rivera had traveled another few minutes, Stoker instructed Rivera. "Pull over about halfway through the next curve. It's a bit of a tight corner. Turn the truck perpendicular to the road. Instant roadblock a few meters into a blind turn."

The pilot's voice came over the radio. "The motorcycle and two trucks are coming your way. They're all on the same team of tangos, and they're moving fast. Those guys in the truck beds have some big guns propped on top of the roof of the pickup truck. There's some serious firepower."

As Rivera turned the truck perpendicular to the road and stopped, he responded. "Roger that."

Stoker got out of the truck and removed the magnetic grenade from his pants pocket, examined it closely, and rehearsed the steps in his mind. This was a new weapon for him. And, getting a detail wrong could cost him limb or life. After satisfying his inquisitiveness, he put the grenade back in his pocket. Then he jumped into the cabin, picked up the radio, and issued instructions to the helicopter. "About three seconds after we engage these guys, you will swoop in behind us. We need bright lights shining in their eyes."

"You've got it, Stoker," the pilot responded. "Do not engage. Just help them see the light of day!"

"Exactly."

"Getting into position now. At their current pace, the tangos are about thirty seconds away. But the motorcycle is hanging back about a quarter mile."

"Let's plan on a rendezvous and pick up about 200 yards down this road behind us."

"Copy that. Tangos fifteen seconds away."

"Enjoy the show!" Stoker said as he dropped the radio microphone and turned to Rivera. They could hear the hum of the trucks closing in on them.

Stoker yelled at Rivera and pointed to the side of the road. "Take your backpack and the box of lab specimens, and go crouch down over there! I'll have a new weapon in your hand in a few seconds. Rivera dove to one side of the road and Stoker dove to the other. Their only shroud was darkness. The trucks barely slowed to come around the corner. Stoker and Rivera saw headlights.

Stoker jumped up into the headlights and caught the attention of the two gunners standing in the bed of the first truck. They never had a chance to aim their guns or pull the trigger. At the same moment, the driver perceived how he was about to t-bone the white Dodge Ram 3500 pickup truck blocking the road before him. The driver slammed on his brakes and careened toward the roadblock. The second truck didn't have time to respond. Just as the first truck collided with the Dodge Ram, the second truck rear-ended the front vehicle and sent it smashing into the truck that was blocking the dirt road. The men positioned as gunners in the back of the trucks flew forward through the air, and so did their weapons. Stoker sprang for one of the guns, as it slid over the dusty gravel road. He picked it up, instantly transforming from the hunted to the hunter.

"Now Rivera!" Stoker yelled as he tossed the newly acquired weapon to Rivera. Errol Rivera sprang from the shadows. He caught the gun, positioned it against his shoulder and laid down thirty rounds of suppressive fire. Stoker dove for another automatic rifle and retrieved it, as he barrel rolled back to the side of the road. He too laid down suppressive fire. Then the furious sounds of helicopter rotors and a marvelous flood of light illuminated the crash before them. Three gunners had been ejected forward from their trucks and were wriggling on the ground, trying to make sense of the impact, the light, the sounds, and the pain. One of the gunners was unconscious. Stoker kicked all the rifles away from the men who had been so intent on murder just moments before. Rivera grabbed the drivers and yanked them out of the trucks. They went willingly and walked fifteen yards beyond the front of the accident. Rivera ordered them to kneel on the ground and put their hands behind their heads.

Rivera used hand signals to communicate with the helicopter. In response, it ascended to an overhead position but continued illuminating them. Then Stoker and Rivera dragged the four gunners and laid them in front of the drivers. The three conscious gunners were in shock from their cuts, bruises, fractures, and concussions. They squirmed on the ground moaning and bleeding. Stoker checked for a pulse on the unconscious man. "This guy's dead," he told Rivera in English.

Rivera recognized that the drivers were Iranian, and he blitzed them with harsh interrogations in Farsi. Compelled by blows from the butt of his rifle, the drivers did not hesitate to confirm they were indeed Iranian. The gunmen were Mexicans. One of the Iranian drivers was wearing hospital scrubs, and Rivera singled him out assuming he might know more about what was going on at the hospital. The next question came in Spanish so everyone could understand. "Where did the CJ bacteria come from?"

The middle eastern man in scrubs answered in passable Spanish. "From a lab you idiot. It's not hard to multiply bacteria."

"Isn't that sweet," Rivera said. "Well, Congratulations! You've just won a trip to Saudi Arabia, where our Wahabi allies will pump every last bit of information out of you." The Iranian man tried to look smug. But, he could not shroud the fear from his eyes. "As much as I want to spill your entrails onto the Mexican desert, I know you have some crucial intelligence. The kind that will take some time to extract. But, let's find out how much you'll tell us right now."

Rivera bound the Iranian's wrists behind his back with zip ties. Then he secured his ankles. After rolling him onto his stomach, Rivera grabbed the back of his head by his hair and repeatedly shoved his face into the dusty sand. As the Iranian held his breath, his nose smacked against the dirt. The cartilage in his nose crunched. Then a cascade of tears, blood, and snot gushed. Waves of pain reverberated through the Iranian's head. Still, he continued to hold his breath while Rivera taunted him with questions. "Where did this bacterium come from?" The Iranian refused to answer, but his lungs started to burn as he starved for oxygen. Rivera went silent as he gripped the back of his head and shoved it into the dirt with every ounce of force he could muster. The Iranian trembled with horrified anticipation. *This guy's just a maniac*, he thought. His gasping reflex screamed to override his will to hold his breath.

A primal reflex overwhelmed him and the Iranian inhaled. But, his lungs rejected the cloud of dust and sand that rushed in. He panicked, writhing on the ground as his body's multiple breathing and coughing reflexes battled each other in a maddening conflict between craving oxygen and rejecting dust and sand.

Rivera was yelling. "Let me repeat the question. Where did the bacteria Campylobacter jejuni come from? What's its source country?"

"Iran!" the man spat out between horrendous coughing fits. His craving for oxygen turned his muddy, blood-covered lips blue.

"Who's in charge?"

"I don't know!" He could barely get the hoarse words out between gasps.

"How could you not know? Who's your boss? Tell me, or you're eating more dust."

"They do not tell us. There is a system. A courier drops off an overnight package with instructions and money. We never meet with anyone. Occasionally we get a phone call or a text. But, we have no idea who it is. We've run this whole operation in this manner."

Rivera lifted the man's head from the dirt, giving him some hope and allowing his breathing to recover a little. "Let's pretend I believe you, which I don't. Anyway, who sent you down here? Who got you into Mexico?"

"A laboratory sciences professor. He told me I had been assigned a three-month internship at a hospital in Mexico, working in the lab. That was six months ago. He handed me a letter, on official government letterhead, that gave me three mandates. First, I was to learn Spanish. Second, I was to conduct the test of this CJ bacteria strain. Third, I was to ensure the hospital administrators had any funds and resources they needed to make this test happen."

"Who signed the letter?"

"No one person signed it. It was by order of the Ministry of Science Research and Technology."

It was Stoker's turn to contribute to the interrogations, and he turned to the men from Mexico lying on the ground injured. "Okay, now it's your turn, *amigos*. How did you get involved in this whole debacle at the hospital?"

One of the men spoke up and explained through a pained voice. "At first these men from the Middle East introduced their activities as a clinical trial, you know, legitimate research. They paid us well—both formally and informally. By the time we figured out what was really going on—that they were testing a Campylobacter jejuni weapon—they knew the names of our wives, children, parents, brothers, sisters, aunts, uncles, grandparents, neighbors, and friends. As long as we stayed silent and kept the science experiment moving forward, our families and friends were fine, and the money kept flowing."

"Then why do you dare talk now?" Rivera asked.

The man looked up, and tears began flowing down his face. His hands shook. Stoker answered the question. "We took advantage during your moment of trauma and shock. For a moment, your lips were temporarily loose. With all the excitement, your mind was too overwhelmed to weigh the consequences. You're weighing the consequences now, and you're realizing the magnitude of what you just divulged."

"Who is 'they?'" Rivera asked. But it was too late. The man started to shake. Rivera knew he would say no more.

But Stoker was undeterred. He took the grenade out of his pocket, pulled the pin and tossed it toward the truck at the back of the pileup. "Sounds like we need more shock!"

The grenade landed in the bed of the badly damaged pickup truck and attached to the metal. Stoker and Rivera dove for cover.

The report of the grenade was furious, tearing into the truck's gas tank and creating a hot, smoky secondary explosion. Stoker lined up the five surviving men across the road from oldest to youngest. He knelt and went nose to nose with the oldest man. He had plenty of gray in his hair and stale beer on his breath. In his broken Spanish Stoker boldly asked, "Who is your contact with the people who are paying you?"

The man was silent. Rivera repeated the question in Spanish.

"*Nunca jamas*." The man said it with conviction. He had just told Stoker and Rivera he would never tell them what they wanted to know.

Stoker took the rifle, pointed it between the man's eyes and pulled the trigger. His body toppled to the ground and convulsed briefly. Stoker moved onto the next oldest man. "Who is your contact? Who's paying you, and what in the hell is going on in that hospital?"

All at once, the four remaining men started talking. Rivera interceded and directed the conversation. Over the next few minutes, they shared all the information they knew. Their faces were twisted with horror and their hands convulsed in anxiety. One of the men provided snippets of details between the ebbs and flows of hyperventilation. Another man cried. Stoker and Rivera learned how two Middle Eastern men, a laboratory technician, and a "money man," had been calling the shots and paying. Stoker showed them the picture of the lab technician on his phone. Two men affirmed he was the lab technician they had worked with. The man Rivera had confronted at the *soltol* bar in downtown Chihuahua fit the description of the money man.

With the fire from the explosion dying down, Rivera stood up and announced to the men that their ordeal was mostly over. "My *amigo* and I are family men. We can imagine the fear you are living right now. We promise to work in a way that no harm will come to your family. Right now, we do not plan to involve the authorities." Rivera stroked his chin thoughtful for effect.

"This is a perilous situation," he continued. "Mexico has been attacked by a bioweapon, and the United States is about to be attacked. We want to treat you humanely and provide some protection for your families. The best thing we can do for you and your families is to take you into custody and blow up these trucks. If you are missing, the Iranians who are holding your families hostage may assume you perished here, at least for a few days. If they think their secrets went to the grave with you, they will be less inclined to harm the people you love."

Rivera and Stoker gathered all the cell phones from the men and tossed them onto the smashed trucks. Rivera marched the men a little further down the dirt road. Then he gave the helicopter a signal. Stoker took out another grenade and some paracord from Rivera's backpack. He attached a 100-foot length of the paracord to the explosive's pin and magnetically fastened the grenade to the middle truck. He backed the line 100 feet away from the truck, pulled the pin, and sprinted down the road toward Rivera and the men they had just captured. Seconds later, the grenade exploded, and the ground rocked underneath their feet.

Two minutes later, with the glow of the trucks still burning in the background the helicopter landed. Stoker handed the box of lab specimens to Jessica as he climbed aboard. "Put this someplace where it will stay cool." Then he gave the Iranians' phones to her. "Get these to Z to see what data and intel he can pull off of them when he gets back from Burning Man."

Stoker and Rivera chose seats next to each other and strapped in as the helicopter ascended. Stoker removed the lab technician's phone from his pocket. "Look at this." He pointed to the phone. "It's been wiped."

"No surprise there. It would've provided us with way too much intel." Then Rivera held up the phone he had just taken from the Iranian driver wearing scrubs. "I need a faraday bag for this cell phone. I know the code to unlock it. But we should unlock it underground where it cannot pick up a signal to wipe it. We'll have Z work his magic on it, once he's back from his Burning Man festivities."

"Where to Colonel?" the pilot called out.

"Fort Sam Houston. But before we go, what happened to the motorcyclist who was with these guys?"

"He hightailed it out of here," the pilot reported. "We've been watching him. He's already traveling south on the main highway out of town."

"My guess is he's not going to report back to headquarters for fear of the punishment that awaits after failing to eliminate us. His odds of survival are better on the run than they would be if he showed up after having failed," Stoker said.

"Mexico's got a lot of places for a motorcycle rider to disappear," Stoker said. "For a few weeks, anyway."

"Speaking of disappearing," Rivera said. "I think it's time for us to disappear from Mexico for a while. We need to let things cool down here for at least a week or two. We've committed more than a dozen felonies. We'll assign a team to clean up this mess."

Stoker smiled and yelled to the pilot. "Take us to Fort Sam Houston."

CHAPTER 12

Chicago, Illinois

Roya Elfar Shahin pushed her housekeeping cart down the main floor hallway of Chicago's celebrated Hotel Esatto. Just as she had done dozens of times before, she knocked on the men's restroom just outside the gift shop. "Housekeeping," she called as she opened the door a crack. Because it was two o'clock in the morning, nobody answered back. She wasn't surprised the bathroom was empty.

This hotel catered to business types, mostly aspiring moguls, who were likely to be asleep. It was not a party hotel. Hotel Esatto had a reputation amongst global executives as a place that took their guests' business as serious as the guests did. It catered to the type-A go-getters of the twenty-first century. The hotel's understated bar oddly closed at ten o'clock p.m. to downplay nightlife, partying, and other lures that suppressed focus and productivity in hard-driving executives.

In contrast, Hotel Esatto was a beehive of activity every morning. At 5:30 a.m. the gym was jam-packed with the impassioned aspiring financiers and moguls. The kitchen staff hustled to ensure the hotel's trademark complimentary fresh-squeezed tangerine juice flowed liberally, along with hearty Colombian coffee. Guests raved about healthy power breakfasts delivered to their tables within three minutes. Hotel Esatto understood the pace and intensity of business and commerce. Executive travelers were fiercely loyal to this unique property when they visited Chicago. And, there was a reason why Nikolas Antoniou wanted to attract some of America's most driven people. By attacking this group, he would deal a devastating blow to the American economy and psyche.

Roya entered the bathroom and paused. "Housekeeping," she announced once again, just to be sure she was entering an empty restroom. She walked all the way in and peaked under the stalls. "No feet," she whispered under her breath in her native tongue. She had just arrived from Reno last night, from this perverted Burning Man Festival. There she saw debauchery that certainly rivaled, if not exceeded, the lechery witnessed by Father Ibrahim in the city of Sodom. She prayed her silent assault in the desert of Nevada would yield the fruits of Allah's vengeance upon the decadent Westerners who were ripe for destruction.

With three squirts from a bottle of disinfectant, she quickly cleaned the toilets, sinks, and countertops. Then she wiped down the mirror and emptied the trash. For Roya, her housekeeping job was a cover. She was a soldier in a much higher cause. Her mundane bathroom cleaning task was actually a part of a greater mission, a preparation for a future day. She often prayed to Allah for this day.

From her housekeeping cart, she effortlessly removed a small stepladder and set it up against the wall. She ascended two steps to reach the plastic box affixed near the ceiling, a metered aerosol dispenser. The device emitted a puff of aromatic scent into the air every few minutes to keep the bathroom smelling fresh. She lifted the lid and unscrewed the small canister that was almost empty.

Metered aerosol mister systems had been the focus of her efforts during the last few months. She had perfected a method for delivering airborne bacteria from the canisters into the air. She had a knack for electronics, a fact Roya's test scores in Iran had corroborated as a young teenager. But, she came from a poor family that could not afford the schools to develop her abilities. However, thanks to a generous family friend—unknown to her, he was a bonyad director—Roya was offered a scholarship that allowed her to go to school at a university and study engineering. There she dominated computer programming, physics, circuitry, soldering, and the advanced science of volts, watts, and ohms. She also loved mechanical engineering. The wealthy friend and bonyad director further encouraged Roya to accept the mentorship of a mullah who exposed her to the true path of Islam. As a girl, her family and the local mosque had taught her the Koran. But in her youth, she quickly learned and embraced so many more teachings of Islam. The religion opened her heart and mind. Roya yearned to live Sharia law. The Twelfth Imam would soon arrive—he may already be amongst us. The Caliphate would arise to confront Israel, Europe, the United States, and the apostate Sunnis. Now was the time for Allah's power to go forth amongst the heathen nations. And Roya, with her training as an engineer, would strike an immense blow for Allah. And, these seemingly inconsequential aerosol misters would help her perpetrate a silent jihad for the glory of the Caliphate.

She quickly screwed a new canister into the dispenser and crawled down the ladder. She repeated this same bathroom cleaning ritual in nine other main-floor bathrooms on Hotel Esatto's main floor. Her canisters would soon infect hundreds of people on any given day when the time finally came. It would be weeks before anyone would figure out the source, these simple little bathroom canisters that kept America smelling like cherry, a tropical breeze, a lavender meadow, or a beautiful wooded forest.

But that's what these Americans did. They covered up their filth, waste, and excess. They used public relations to label bloody battles as mere skirmishes, economic exploitation as sanctions, and devout Muslims who lived the pure religion as extremists. But soon the day would come. Only last week, the preacher at her mosque referred contemptuously to the Jewish prophet Isaiah who wrote: ". . . instead of sweet smell there shall be stink; and instead of a girdle a rent; and instead of well-set hair baldness; and instead of a stomacher a girding of sackcloth; and burning instead of beauty."

"Baldness, sackcloth, and burning," she said aloud. Nobody was around to hear her words, to sense her zeal. "I shall pray to be a warrior for baldness, sackcloth, and burning."

Roya wheeled her housekeeping cart down through some service doors, then down a ramp that led to the hotel's massive laundry facilities. She stopped next to a nondescript door and looked around to make sure she was still alone. When she saw nobody else nearby, she removed a key from her sock and used it to open the unlabeled door. Hastily she pushed the cart through the door and closed it behind her. She walked twenty more paces to get to yet another door. This one led to a pre-clean room adjacent to a laboratory. To get through this door, she had to press her index finger on a fingerprint reader. Then she placed her eye in front of a retinal scan. Only two other people had access to this work area, Roya's lab.

When the door opened, she stepped into the pre-clean room. There she removed her housekeeping uniform and shoes. She stepped forward and put on a cleanroom suit. After punching in a long code on a keypad, she finally entered the clean room, Roya's lab. She had with her the empty canisters she had just removed from the bathrooms of Hotel Esatto.

Today would be the last time she would refill the canisters. After today, the activity of filling metered aerosol spray canisters would occur on a much larger scale, in a factory. Nikolas had purchased the whole factory. For the last year, the factory had functioned much as it did before coming under Nikolas's control. But, Roya had been instrumental in learning the details of running the factory. She was also ready to scale up production on a new process for filling the canisters—a process that would allow them to introduce the bacteria Campylobacter jejuni into the canisters.

Nikolas's scientists weaponized this particular strain of Campylobacter jejuni by manipulating the genes. It would affect the body different than the Balamuthia amoeba they released at Burning Man. But, there was a stroke of genius in this second biological attack wave. It would fool doctors and the Centers for Disease Control, at least for a few critical weeks. In these next vital weeks, when the timing was right, the doctors would be confused as to what they were treating.

Roya questioned, in the world of the Great Satan, why the Christians and Jews put so much faith in physicians? Placing extreme trust in doctors was wrong. Allah would prove their fallibility in the months to come.

Americans also unquestioningly believed the proclamations of this Centers for Disease Control in Atlanta, Georgia. Roya reflected on a strange phenomenon. Americans had turned their backs on their god—a god they claimed was infallible and almighty. Instead, they looked to the prophesies and prognoses of doctors, financial experts, attorneys, scientists, and executives. They even stooped low enough to revere the illusory and shameful behavior of actors, politicians, musicians, and journalists.

Roya affixed two of the empty canisters to a machine. With the simple push of a button, the cartridges received an infusion of a liquid laced with high doses of Campylobacter jejuni bacteria. When the canisters were full, she stowed them away in a refrigerator. With today's additions, her inventory contained ninety canisters. She was ready to unleash a terrible disease on some of the world's most evil people, Westerners. Removing these movers and shakers from the planet would ensure that jihad would not only be a jihad of blood and terror, it would also bring banks, companies, and markets to a standstill and freeze the very lifeblood of western society. Roya and

Nikolas were spending much their time and energy on weaponizing scented aerosol mist canisters at the newly acquired factory.

Roya finished her tasks with the canisters. After she left the clean room, she removed her biohazard suit just in time to hear the shrill whistling of her encrypted fax machine. Every so often she would receive instructions from Nikolas or Tehran via this almost outdated means of communication. These transmissions always looked as if they were weather reports. Weather reports were the disguise. The real message usually appeared at the bottom of the page as a cryptic handwritten note. In today's fax, the unimportant weather report was from an agricultural weather station in Thorup, Washington. The message, scribbled in Farsi at the bottom of the fax, was momentous. Roya's heart leaped when she read the news. It referenced a significant verse from the Koran. And then, it gave an order.

I will drive him to the chastisement of the fire.
Go forth and chastise!

The timing was perfect. In the next few days, the canister factory would ship the first truckloads of weaponized Campylobacter jejuni. Over the next few weeks, janitorial workers across America would install these. Soon businesses, hotels, factories, stores, and other buildings would dispense the Campylobacter bacterium—and the people would not know how they would become sick. But, here in her lab sat the canisters she would install in Hotel Esatto—a tactic for the later part of their plan. After a time, Nikolas would bid a permanent adieu to Hotel Esatto.

CHAPTER 13

Galveston, Texas

Tropical Solace had the perfect name for a cruise ship—way back in 1991. Back then, she had been one of the most popular boats on the sea, proudly sailing to the larger ports and destinations in the Caribbean and Mexico. But eventually, grander and more luxurious ships came on the scene. Tropical Solace couldn't compete with vessels featuring waterparks, ice skating rinks, and surfing simulators.

In 2012 a relatively new cruise line, owned by one of Nikolas Antoniou's shell companies, purchased Tropical Solace and updated her with a zip line and climbing wall. But, by now Tropical Solace could only compete on price and party. Nikolas's marketing gurus promoted "booze cruise" itineraries to target audiences who wanted the full Margaritaville experience. Now, she had reached the end of her useful life. Today, she would set sail on one of her final excursions shuttling people for a six-night getaway to ports in Cancun, Mexico, Belize City, Belize, and Roatan, Honduras.

Four Iranian engineers were along for the excursion. Two carried forged passports that appeared to be from Jordan, while the other two had illegitimate Turkish passports. Their small, secretive mechanical engineering firm had worked on dozens of highly sensitive projects for the Iranian government. Like most assignments, this was a military contract with ties to Nikolas. But, the engineers knew nothing of Nikolas; and they took orders from a general they had never before worked with. The general had given them strict instructions to spend seventy to ninety percent of their time doing things tourists did on the ship. "If you can send me all the information I want by the second day, then you are free to take part in the debauchery. Eat what you would like, drink what you would like. But, I must warn you. Sex with loose western women is likely to come at a cost." The engineers had occasionally traveled outside of Iran. They did not need the general to explain the sexually transmitted diseases so common amongst the infidels.

The men with the Turkish passports made friends with one of

the ship's officers, the staff captain of the engine department, who was thrilled they were engineers. He gave them a tour of as many of the ship's systems as he could show off in two hours. The Iranian engineers recorded it all through small microphones. They had studied in-depth schematics of the boat before they departed on the cruise. Their job was to understand if there were any significant changes not represented in the original schematics. The most important task was to assess the status of the doors that opened from a large ballroom out onto the main deck of the boat. In a few weeks, they would be working on a secretive project aboard this very boat. They knew no additional details at this point. And, they were threatened with a torturous death if they revealed any plans or created any suspicions.

By the second night of the cruise, the engineers sent an encrypted email updating the general on the condition of Tropical Solace. The ballroom doors had been welded shut. But a cutting torch would let them disassemble the doors. They also recommended bringing a backup electrical system aboard. The electrical system on the ship had many potential fail points.

As soon as they hit the send button, the four men hastily exited the cabin. Two hours later, they had managed to neglect their daily prayers and commit a string of unlawful deeds. They had already consumed several shots of whiskey—a new experience for them. After gambling away a few thousand dollars on games, they barely understood, one of them withstood a sharp slap from a western woman the likes of which he would never understand. By midnight, the first engineer had thrown up, mostly over the railing into the sea. The second figured out blackjack and naively started counting cards. His winning streak got him ejected from the casino. Another of the men was back in his room watching erotic movies. He had no idea the cruise line was charging his credit card thirty dollars per video. The fourth man was on the bow of the ship charming a corpulent woman from New York who prided herself on being open-minded. For the rest of the trip, the Iranian men did a splendid job participating in all of the activities and entertainment tourists pursue on cruise ships.

The last night, during a drunken conversation in Farsi, they did call some attention to themselves as they swore they would defect from Iran when the ship landed back at the home port.

The next morning, all four had forgotten their oath. The men packed their suitcases and waited. The engineer who had spent much of the cruise with the muscular New York woman snuck away from the group. When the other three engineers finally found him, he was begging the woman to let him run away with her.

"Like two ships in the night, Honey," she responded. "It was fun, but now the trip is over. And, so is our little tryst."

"Tryst?" He was not familiar with the English word. "What is a tryst?"

"You know. A short little love affair where you both do a little giving—and a whole lot of taking."

When the man failed to understand, the New Yorker rolled her eyes, held up a hand, and backed away two steps. "Look, you're starting to creep me out here. Do I need to call the police when I get off the ship?"

"Come with us" his friends told him. "We will explain along the way. For now, it is enough to know she never cared for you. She used you." They disembarked and got into a taxi together. The other three men understood what their friend was feeling. They would not report the event to the general, and none of them would ever talk of the incident again. Nor would they ever experience anything like this. But, they had the memories. A few weeks later the fourth engineer would pick up his broken heart, visit a doctor under a fake name, and receive an antibiotic injection and oral medication to combat a raging case of gonorrhea.

CHAPTER 14

San Antonio, Texas

The Russian gunship descended out of the night sky and landed on the illuminated helipad at the Brooke Army Medical Center at Fort Sam Houston. Stoker and Rivera climbed out of the helicopter and walked briskly toward the building entrance with the blood samples from Mexico in tow. They stepped through an automatic sliding door and into a corridor that started snaking through the hospital. "Which way to the lab?" Stoker asked a nurse. Before the nurse could answer, a familiar voice spoke up behind them.

"As always, the lab's in the basement."

Stoker and Rivera turned around while Rivera chimed in. "There he is. The bohemian Burning Man beast."

"How was your existential miniature golfing in the dust bowl?" Stoker chided.

"You think you're funny, Stoker. But you're not too far off," Z responded. "This way to the lab," Z said with a gesture. He led them toward some elevators, which took them down to the basement.

"Welcome back, buddy," Rivera said.

When they arrived at the lab, the lab director greeted them. He was not a physician. But, he was accompanied by one—the hospital's chief of infectious disease. The doctor's body language and mannerisms projected hostility toward Stoker, Rivera, and Z.

"Well, my commanding officer informs me you have some blood samples that may test positive for Campylobacter jejuni," the lab director said.

"Yes," Stoker replied. "From some patients battling Guillain-Barre in a cluster in —."

The infectious disease doctor rudely interrupted. "I don't understand what all this hubbub's about. Campylobacter is one of the most common germs in the world. I'm certain Mexico is crawling with the stuff, as is the United States. I'm sure people get infected south of the border even more than we do here in the U.S. This is as ridiculous as being fascinated by the existence of water at a yacht race. And, I for one, do not appreciate being pulled away from pressing matters just because someone with rank and reputation—I'm referring to you Dr. Rivera—has a far-flung hunch about a wild epidemic in another country."

"Listen," Stoker said, raising his voice with a fusion of authority and indignation that surprised and impressed Rivera. "This is urgent. Are you willing to take a chance with this issue that could cost hundreds or thousands of American lives? Because if you're not, we'll take our results, and your apathy, up your chain of command."

The infectious disease doctor squirmed and said, "My work is constantly interrupted by military doctors showing up here, insisting I take a look at germs they consider unique and dangerous. It's almost always the same old germs behaving in the same old ways."

"Unique and dangerous," Rivera responded, "Your *work* doctor, is to listen to as many doctors from the field as you can. Because among the many false alarms, you'll find an occasional outlier. There's too much at stake for you to fail. Americans need you at your post, Soldier. You're a military physician, charged with detecting biological threats. If you don't help us, I will call the right generals, and they will remind you of your duty."

"I think we'd better look at these samples," the lab director said to the infectious disease doctor.

"Go right ahead," replied the doctor. "Knock yourselves out. Call me if you find an apocalypse under the microscope." The doctor turned and started to walk away. Then he yelled over his shoulder. "You won't call me."

"Right this way," the lab director said to his three visitors.

"To hell with this guy," Stoker said. "Let's make sure he gets stationed at the South Pole for the rest of his career."

"I can make it happen," Rivera said. "But, after we conclude our business with the reasonable people around here. Let's focus on getting these samples analyzed for now."

The lab director said nothing. He was not fond of the stubborn chief of infectious disease. And, he could not stop a broad smile from appearing on his face as Stoker and Rivera expressed their disapproval.

Rivera turned his head toward Stoker as the men walked

quickly down the hall. "I'm not used to you making offensive threats like that. You usually use one of your Jedi mind tricks."

"One psychiatric technique is exaggerating and bluffing," Stoker responded. "And, don't call my behavioral interventions Jedi mind tricks. I practice interpersonal excellence with a bold streak. Sometimes doctors need intervention, too."

Stoker, Rivera, and Z walked into the lab with the lab director. The lab director handed the box of specimens to a technician. "Let's start culturing these samples and see what grows." Then he spoke to his guests. "Why don't you come back in four days, and we'll look under the microscope to see what grows."

"We'll do it," Rivera replied. "But, my intuition is telling me this is big. An epidemic of Guillain-Barre syndrome is coming to the United States."

"We don't have four days to wait before we start notifying people," Stoker said. "I'm going to call the CDC right now and let people know what the test results are going to say. I'm also going to get some investigators from their Outbreak Response Team down to Chihuahua."

• • •

"There go the first ten thousand units," Roya Elfar Shahin said to Nikolas. A delivery truck pulled away from their factory. It was loaded with canisters to be installed into timed aerosol meters. These had large, active, and lethal colonies of Balamuthia mandrillaris amoebas living inside. Bathrooms across America in office buildings, malls, and hotels would become toxic over the next few weeks. Nobody would figure it out until it was too late for thousands of Americans.

"This shipment goes to Saint Louis," Nikolas said. "We also have shipments to Los Angeles, Houston, and Atlanta today. Tomorrow we have twenty orders to fill. It's amazing how orders shoot up when you reduce the price by forty percent." Nikolas was selling the canisters at break even. But, he was not in this venture to make money. He was using his MBA skills to bring down the capitalists. It was terror by merger and acquisition.

Roya felt the thrill of this next silent battle she was spearheading. She had barely slept during the last two days. Eating had been an inconvenience that interrupted the zeal she felt as she used that American phenomenon, the factory, to manufacture blood and horror.

Inside this new canister lived a biosphere. One Roya had helped to create. High concentrations of the amoeba waited within. At that very moment, these pathogens were ripe for planting themselves in moist noses, throats, ears, and lungs.

"*Allahu akbar*," Roya quietly whispered as she exited the factory before she went home to sleep.

• • •

Stoker and Rivera thanked the lab director and walked out into the hallway. "What connections do you have at the CDC?" Stoker asked Rivera.

"Despite years of military and medical work, I don't have many good connections at the CDC," Rivera said. "We'll have to work through a friend or two."

Stoker smiled. "Do you mean to tell me home-town psychiatrist, Troy Stoker, has a better connection at the CDC than the world gallivanting Colonel Doctor Errol Rivera?"

"Okay, Big Shot. Who do you know?"

"Let's call my former Baylor Medical School classmate, Susan Taggert. After completing her residency, she jumped into public health. Now she oversees a dozen Epidemic Intelligence Service Officers in the National Center for Infectious Diseases."

"Well, let's call her," Rivera said. "I suspect she can navigate the CDC better than we can. She knows who the bosses are."

Stoker and Rivera found an empty classroom at Brooke Army Medical Center. After calling the main number in Atlanta for the Centers for Disease Control, the receptionist connected them to Stoker's old medical school classmate.

"This is Dr. Taggert," she answered.

"Hi, Susan. It's Troy Stoker. And, I've got you on speaker phone with my colleagues, Dr. Errol Rivera and a guy named Z."

"Troy! Oh, it's so great to hear your voice. How are you? Why are you calling me? Wow, this is such a surprise. Wow, listen to me. I'm babbling. So, how are you? Are you in town?"

"It's good to talk to you, too, Susan. I promise we'll get caught up. But, my team and I are in a bit of a professional pickle here, and I think you could help."

"A public health nerd like me? What could I possibly do for a psychiatrist? Where is it your practice? Des Moines or someplace like that?"

"You were no nerd, Susan. You have never been, and you never will be. I'm practicing in South Dakota. But, let me throw you a twist. I think I found a horrific disease outbreak in Chihuahua, Mexico, which is on its way north. Dr. Rivera and I feel grave alarm. We think this disease could infect hundreds of thousands of Americans. Something is fishy with this vector. We'll have some answers after four days of incubation."

"Tell me everything, Troy. Give me all the facts."

"While traveling in Mexico, I was a patient on a medical floor in Chihuahua."

"South of the border, about 100 miles below El Paso," interjected Taggert. "I know the place you're talking about. Famous for their *soltol*. What were you doing in Chihuahua, Mexico?"

"It's a long story, which you won't believe anyway. And, how do you know about *soltol*?"

"Don't ask. It's a short story, and you would *not* believe it." Taggert kept dropping little flirtatious lines into the conversation. "Anyway, on with your story. We can drink later."

"On that medical floor, we witnessed more than a dozen patients exhibiting classic Guillain-Barre symptoms, ventilators and all. The ICU was overflowing with Guillain-Barre patients, too. Chihuahua is a city that should have less than a dozen cases in a year. I was seeing twice that many cases, at that single moment, and in just one hospital."

"Help me understand two things," she said. "First, there is already a lot of Campylobacter jejuni and diarrhea in Mexico. Subsequently, we could expect a high incidence of Guillain-Barre syndrome. I would not be surprised to hear of outbreaks in Mexico. Second, diagnosing Guillain-Barre syndrome would be difficult, I mean from your vantage point as a patient, in your hospital bed.

There's a lot you could observe. But you couldn't perform the tests and analyze the lab data when you're lying there, in your bed, being a patient."

"You're right. I would not usually diagnose Guillain-Barre syndrome from the vantage point of a patient. Dr. Rivera was there with me, and we gathered a lot of extra information."

Rivera chimed in and explained. "This group of patients received spirometry tests and nerve conduction studies. They exhibited muted central nervous system response and lower extremity weakness. These patients had a lot of trouble speaking, so obvious dysarthria. And we even substantiated that many patients had difficulty swallowing. But more importantly, we snuck a peek at some lab results. Elevated protein in their cerebral-spinal fluid, without a significant increase in their white blood cell counts."

"Any lab work?" Taggart asked.

"The cultures grew Campylobacter jejuni," Stoker said. "We brought some samples with us. The lab at Brooke Army Medical Center in Texas is growing cultures from those samples as we speak. But, there's something more."

"What?"

"To make this crazy story sound more outrageous, we, um." Stoker paused for a moment and chose his words carefully. "Let's just say we interviewed a few people familiar with the cases." He realized how Taggart, from her comfortable office at the Centers for Disease Control, may not approve of the interrogation techniques he had used to find out this information. "These people knew about the sick people, and they told us this was some twisted and depraved clinical trial. They informed us that these people had been infected deliberately. Some of our sources even speculated that this is weaponized bacteria."

Dr. Taggert remained silent for a moment. Then she broke into wild laughter. "Okay, you had me going there, Troy. Very good."

"What?" Stoker said. It was more of a statement than a question.

"My old med school flame calls me out of the blue and concocts a wild story that plays right into the hands of a public health wonk like me. Then you imply we should catch up and have a drink together, perhaps *soltol*."

"The drink was *not* my idea. You brought up the *soltol*. I never would suggest *soltol*. I have an aversion to the stuff—and all things viper."

"Oh, you're good. The psychiatrist, weaving his patients' paranoid stories in with my ever-vigilant epidemiological outlook. You really had me going there. You even concocted rough numbers on the incidence of Guillain-Barre syndrome. This prank took some effort. Bravo!"

Stoker was silent, hoping Taggert would realize he was not kidding. She didn't take the hint.

After a flirtatious laugh, Taggert said, "And, I loved every second of your little farce, Troy. Now when are you and I going to get that drink? You must be coming to Atlanta."

"No really, Susan. Where can I send you an encrypted email with a hundred plus pages of lab reports? This is a crazy story, but these results may convince you what I'm saying is true. I don't want to waste your time at work."

"Oh," Susan said as she paused for an uncomfortable moment. After a few quivers at the corner of her mouth, she frowned, realizing it was not a joke. "Damn you, Troy Stoker!" she finally replied. "You got my hopes up," Taggert said with embarrassment and disappointment in her voice. "I thought you *might* waste my time after work, perhaps on the weekend."

"Look, Susan," Stoker said. "I'm sorry for the confusion. I'm happily married, and I'm very focused on this outbreak in Mexico. So, we'll send those lab reports ASAP," Stoker said. "Also, it may help you to ask around and do some verifying to lend some credence to this out of the blue phone call. Check to see if some of your military contacts know my friend here, Colonel Errol Rivera. Associating his name with this data should add some weight to our story."

"Send us your lab reports, Troy. It feels like this conversation is fizzling, just like we did."

Stoker paused for a second to help calm the conversation. Then he spoke. "We fizzled because summer clinical rotations took us two thousand miles apart. What about you? Are you married?"

"I've never found the flame again, Troy."

As a psychiatrist, Stoker handled awkward moments all day long. He navigated them with ease. But, he'd been clumsy when he broke women's hearts. He was rugged and handsome, which attracted plenty of women to him superficially. Under the surface, he had off-the-charts intuitive and connective abilities. During medical school, Troy Stoker met hundreds of women in classrooms, bars, medical school study groups, clinical rotations, and at social events. Connecting with them came naturally. Without knowing it, short conversations with women, animated by his curious and intuitive nature, forged a mercurial emotional intimacy and attraction to him. Too often, however, it was only one way. His residency training disciplined the unparalleled empathic skills that made him a phenomenal psychiatrist. Nevertheless, there were still some landmines in the love battlefields of relationships he left behind a decade ago. Today he and Dr. Susan Taggert tripped one of those old landmines.

"You know Susan, those were good times. But, we're looking down the barrel at some horrific times. I need your help. Can you help me?"

"I'm happy to help," she replied.

Stoker got Taggert's email address and a password for unlocking the encryption. He ended the call by saying, "Call us back when you know something."

Stoker gave Rivera the email address for Dr. Taggert. "When you send her those files, don't tell her about the Shiites. Imagine if we had thrown the Middle Eastern intrigue into the conversation?"

"That she would not have believed," Rivera said. "She would've hung up on us." A sly smile appeared on Rivera's face. "Old med school flame?" Rivera chided Stoker as he removed a small laptop from his backpack. In a poor imitation of Dr. Taggert's voice, he mocked, "When are we going to get that drink?"

"Shut up and send the email."

"I will," Rivera replied. "But, while I'm online here, I think I'll find an online liquor store to send Dr. Taggert a bottle of *soltol*. But, I won't say who it's from."

Stoker ignored the wisecrack. He thought back to medical school. Susan Taggert had been his girlfriend for most of their second year. She was stunningly beautiful and brilliant. The relationship fizzled the summer before their third year when the Army shipped Stoker off to a summer rotation of military medical drills. Now, she was a memory. Psychiatrist Troy Stoker, a man who absorbed his patients' rawest feeling and most profound emotions, was strong enough to look into his own heart. Emotionally, intellectually, and even habitually, his wife Allie owned and occupied his whole heart. It was not a sappy relationship. It was a fun, rugged and adventuresome kind of love he had never experienced with Taggert or any other woman.

"I've got all of the pictures we took of the lab results. I rolled them into one pdf," Rivera said. "Attaching." He hit the return key with exaggerated emphasis. "Sending to the flirtatious Dr. Taggert."

Stoker crossed his arms and stared at Rivera while deep in thought.

"Your wheels are a turnin'," Rivera said. "What's going through that head now?"

"So, we have a four-day wait before we have results," Stoker said with contemplation. "I'm thinking about all the variables here. We are *not* going to just wait around for four days wasting time. Besides getting the CDC's wheels moving on this, what can we do to minimize the impact of this silent, invisible attack?" Then he answered his own question. "I think we need to get back down to Mexico and follow the next wave of would-be terrorists when they cross the border into the U.S. If we're going to thwart their progress, we need to find where they choose to end up in the States. Then we need to try and anticipate their next steps so we can interrupt their plan."

Stoker's phone rang. The caller ID told him the call came from Atlanta. "This is Dr. Stoker. You're on speaker, also with Dr. Rivera."

"Troy. This is Susan. You're on speaker phone with Dr. Kaitlyn Steele, the Director of the Office of Public Health Preparedness and Response."

"Thank you both for calling," Stoker said.

Director Steele took over the conversation. "So, Colonel Rivera, why does your name whip heads around faster than most generals' names?" Director Steele asked Rivera.

"Because I keep having all the adventures. I get stuff done. And, the generals are all chained to their desks. Now we've got something new to bring to your attention."

"We've seen the lab reports. Dr. Taggert briefed me. You've got our attention. You interviewed sources about the so-called clinical trials. How certain are you these people in Mexico have been infected deliberately?"

"A few sources familiar with these barbaric human experiments verified the deliberate criminal offenses. One was the Iranian financier. We invited him to a spontaneous meeting in a *soltol* bar in Chihuahua. The other sources were low-level types. But, we corroborated their stories."

"And you assert it has been weaponized?"

"One of the low-level sources who works in the hospital shared this theory with us. We have samples incubating. And, we'll have germs ready for analysis in four days. Then we can verify the issue of weaponization."

"And what were you two doing in Chihuahua, Mexico?" She asked.

"Training," Stoker said.

Rivera gave Stoker the thumbs up and said nothing.

After a few seconds of silence, Director Steele decided to pry. "What kind of training?"

"We're happy to share details of our training when we meet face to face," Stoker said. "But, our visit to the hospital was not part of any training. I needed treatment."

"For what?"

"A snake bite."

"Something tells me the snake bite had something to do with your training?"

"You're right," Stoker said. "Let's save the rest of that story and focus on some next steps with this Campylobacter jejuni bacteria and the Guillain-Barre syndrome it causes."

"Yes. Here's the plan," Director Steele said. "We'll have investigators in Chihuahua within forty-eight hours. I'll activate them today. We'll let you know what we learn. Can you send us your samples? We would love to look at this Campylobacter jejuni under our electron microscopes."

"Yes. We'll send you what we have," Stoker said. "What do we do now to contain this?"

"We'll determine the next step when our investigator reports from Mexico, and when we've been able to scrutinize your samples."

"What about ramping up communications to doctors and hospitals today, so they're prepared for this wave of disease? And, let's tell the right people in the military—let them know what's coming."

"It's premature because it's unconfirmed. This information could create panic. You need to trust me on this," Director Steele said. "I'm going to move this investigation along as fast as the data suggests we should. But, we're not going to get the military or medical community all excited about this until I've been able to corroborate your story and verify samples. If we start telling people, this will leak to the press.

"We agree. It is too early to get this into the hands of the mainstream media." Stoker said.

"The media may conjure up more hysteric harm than good," Steele said. "My next step would be asking my boss to notify the Joint Chiefs. And, that's only if and when this develops, as you presuppose."

"With all due respect, Director," Stoker said. "The implications of this bacteria are so huge that we need to get some big wheels in motion. We need to do it now."

"Let's at least convene a planning team," Rivera suggested. "We'll have representatives from the CDC, the military, and the American Medical Association. We need to prepare the hospital beds and medical equipment to handle this epidemic."

"What if American hospitals only have a fraction of the ventilators we need?" Stoker asked.

"No!" Suddenly Director Steele was adamant. "You're getting ahead of yourselves. Do *not* breathe a word of this to anybody," Steele insisted. "I don't have the authority to give you an order. But, I will find someone, in the next ten minutes, who can. Is that clear?"

Stoker responded calmly. "Look, Director. That choice is up to you. We don't want the media to get their hands on this either. But, we're not going to sit on this while the bureaucratic process takes its sweet time."

Stoker frowned while looking at Rivera. Then he made a cutting motion across his throat, signifying he was going to end the phone call. Rivera nodded his head in agreement. Then he pointed above his head. Stoker knew what he meant. It was time to go above her head.

"Thanks for your time, Director," Stoker said. "We'll share

additional information as it becomes available." Then Stoker ended the call.

"*Amigo*," Rivera said. "You handled that well. Just don't let this get to you. I'm going to speak to some old friends, not long forgotten. They'll cut through the red tape and get us to the Secretary of Homeland Security."

Stoker's face relaxed. An insubordinate, headstrong smile replaced the intensity. "The CDC may not want to get ahead of this. But we can still do our part by getting more information. Let's have Z work his hacker magic on the cell phones we retrieved in Mexico. Perhaps he can also do some digital snooping in *Hospital de Los Santos*'s computer systems. Let's get down to Mexico, follow the aspiring terrorists across the border, and see what additional evidence we can gather from these guys about the eminent disease outbreaks."

Rivera turned to Z. "I agree. Z, you have your orders. Get started right away. Let's also check in with a few military doctors and tell them what we see happening. We'll get their impressions. At least we can prime the pump that way."

"Let's get these samples to the CDC," Stoker said. "Anything to keep the momentum going."

"I'll have the base commander here at Fort Sam Houston arrange a transport flight," Rivera said. "Our samples will arrive at the CDC by three o'clock this afternoon."

Stoker steepled his fingers in front of his face. "Now, let's go leap over some bureaucratic heads!"

CHAPTER 15

Chicago, Illinois

His was a different kind of terror, a better brand of terror. Nikolas was not into the loud here-today-gone-tomorrow suicide bombings. He had committed for the long run. He wanted terror with staying power—the kind that required patience. Much like nurturing crops, investing money, or aging wine, in Nikolas's brand of terror, time amplified the magnitude of the results. This attack would be massive, by far the grandest and most violent to ever occur on American soil. Ironically, the weapons would be small, almost imperceptible. Silent.

The publicity CoolSolar received at Burning Man led to invitations to provide cooling services to other festivals. Electric Zoo NYC, KABOO Del Mar, and the Austin City Limits Music Festival were next on the company's calendar. But the High Life Music Festival, Bonnaroo, Lightning in a Bottle, Symbiosis, Wasteland Weekend, and dozens of other events would not happen until next year.

"Thanks to the excellent work our two pathogens are doing, next year these festivals won't happen," Nikolas pronounced in a comment to Roya. "They'll be canceled on account of terror! Cool Solar will complete its mission long before next spring. Let's sign the agreements to participate anyway."

CoolSolar also won a contract to set up their mist machines in the concessions areas for five NASCAR races remaining in the year. The firm booked booths at more than a dozen state fairs in September. The political season was in full swing. CoolSolar set up mist systems at many rallies for a few hotly contested Senate and House of Representative seats. Each event was a target, and the brain-eating amoeba Balamuthia mandrillaris would be the weapon. Democrat, Republican, Green Party, or unaffiliated, Nikolas didn't care. He just wanted victims—lots of them. The kinds of statistics that would be punctuated by the grave *basso profoundo* voices of newscasters on the evening news.

Cool Solar and Nikolas's other businesses were taking off. To the average businessperson, it would've been easy to envision years of profits. But all Nikolas Antoniou wanted was a few months of terror.

• • •

The popular new sandwich chain, Little Italy, had just been touted as one of the top up-and-coming American food franchises by the Wall Street Journal. The concept was a brainstorm of two twenty-something sisters in Dallas. They started a single sandwich shop with the slogan, "The savory way to eat right." It quickly gained a loyal following. That's when the business consultants started calling. More than a dozen franchising gurus were competing to help the sisters expand their business. And, four years after the sisters opened their first sandwich shop, they offered franchise rights to entrepreneurs all around the United States. But, the franchise rights had just one buyer. Almost overnight, Little Italy sandwich shops began springing up throughout the United States. A private equity firm, secretly controlled by Nikolas Antoniou, opened Little Italy shops in all 50 states. Thanks to his connections in the Shiite world, he never lacked funding for such crucial, target-rich ventures.

Every day, the lunch rush would fill 6,100 locations secretly controlled by Nikolas. According to the latest reports from the accountants, the shops fed more than a million people each day. As of today, none of these eager patrons would notice that their condiments were now tainted with an extremely virulent form of the bacteria Campylobacter jejuni. A light mist cooled the few hundred Little Italy locations that offered al fresco dining. The spray included Balamuthia mandrillaris amoebas. A person who wanted mustard, catsup, mayonnaise or other condiments would swallow a generous weaponized dose.

Because Nikolas's scientists manipulated this Campylobacter jejuni strain, the risks of contracting a dangerous infection were hair-raising. In a laboratory in Turkey, a team consisting of geneticists and microbiologists weaponized this common pathogen. First by transforming the outer coating of the bacteria to make it more virulent. But, their second step was the real stroke of evil genius.

They carefully manipulated the DNA to create the most potent outer coating molecules—the antigens the human immune system would attack. These deadly super bacteria would severely wound America. The tiny bacterial assailants would trigger an aggressive immune response—so aggressive it would turn the infidels' own immune systems against their nervous systems. When these Campylobacter jejuni germs infected victims, their bodies would launch a cascade of antibodies to respond and kill the threat. Unfortunately, billions of nerve cells would end up collateral damage in this biological war, when the antibodies would also attack neurons in the brain and spine. The ultimate result of this nerve damage was a disease called Guillain-Barre syndrome. Yes, America's health system was prepared to handle a few thousand cases of Guillain-Barre per year. It did so every year. But, American hospitals were not ready to handle millions of patients, most of whom would need ventilators to keep them alive through the most crucial weeks of the disease.

Much of that from a sandwich shop that started out as the savory way to eat right.

• • •

In outdoor shopping malls across America, cooling misters, built and maintained by CoolSolar, started popping up. Restaurants, zoos, amusement parks, and athletic arenas also hired the firm. Every day more than three million people chose to walk by a mist machine to catch a refreshing breeze. The cooling mist system CoolSolar set up along a stretch of the Hollywood Boulevard sidewalk was ostensibly a demonstration and good PR. The mist reached tens of thousands of people per day. Roya had mixed the amoeba *and* the bacteria together for the Californians. These people, who lived the epitome of the Great Satan lifestyle, deserved the opportunity to play host to both diseases.

The Baltimore Orioles were one of the hottest teams in baseball, so CoolSolar gladly cooled their fans as they entered and exited Camden Yards. Philadelphia tourists visiting the Liberty Bell and Independence Hall had the option of walking under misters to cool off. Walkers along Boston's freedom trail encountered two different amoeba-dispensing misters.

• • •

One of Nikolas's new companies had recently purchased three *indoor* water parks. The first one was in New Jersey, about twenty miles outside of New York City. The second was in Orange County, California, and the third was in a suburb of Dallas, Texas. During the two weeks leading up to Labor Day weekend, Nikolas's biologists reduced the chlorine content in the water that circulated through the pools and water slides to just two parts per million. Then they added billions of Balamuthia mandrillaris amoebas, which were hardy. The marketing departments advertised a special—daily admission was only $10 per family.

People came in droves. If visitors didn't want to cool off in the pools and water slides, they had the option of walking by mist machines set up by CoolSolar. If they got hungry, the water parks were offering special four-dollar Little Italy sandwiches. On Labor Day weekend these amusement parks were jam-packed. The water parks entertained more than 40,000 visitors. But, the season never ended for these indoor water parks. So, they would continue to introduce thousands of people per day to billions of lethal amoebas.

• • •

Little Italy sandwich shops considered it a great honor. The sandwich shops received an invitation to provide catering services to 120 special events for wounded and disabled United States servicemen and women around the country. Nikolas felt so honored; he offered the food for free. How ironic that secret Iranian money would fund the demise of so many who fought in Islamic countries. Little Italy would lose millions in the deal. But Nikolas would have the privilege of infecting tens of thousands of souls with savory sandwiches. "Whatever you need," Nikolas commented with enthusiasm when he committed to catering the events.

• • •

The late summer heat was their perfect backdrop for a silent attack. People walking along the Las Vegas strip loved the new mist machines. With temperatures consistently soaring well above 100 degrees, they would walk by the hotels and restaurants courteous enough to impart a merciful mist of water onto Sin City's vacationers. Today, technicians at CoolSolar would begin performing routine maintenance on dozens of misting systems within the city. During this fine-tuning, the technicians would attach a water bypass line to introduce fluid from a new source—an amoeba tainted one.

• • •

On the first day of the silent attack, the Benevolent Iranian Student League had more than 300 radicalized Muslim students in place working in the food-service industry throughout the United States. Some of the most accomplished students were working as prep cooks and chefs in hotels, making ready for large banquets. This sleeper cell was now active, and it quietly served Campylobacter jejuni-tainted food to hundreds of thousands of convention-goers each week. Of course, their employers, some of the most respected names in the hotel world, had no idea what was happening. In many cases, these employees had built up trust over two or three years.

The Benevolent Iranian Student League helped more than 300 radicalized Muslim students come to the United States to study by day and work in food services at night. Their handlers taught them everything they needed to know to help customs officials, employers, and neighbors find favor with these less-than-benevolent men and women. One of the rules participants had to swear to before they left their homelands for America was to keep secrets, at the peril of their lives. The second rule was to start working nights and weekends in the foodservice industry. They were rewarded financially if they eventually secured a job as a cook in a large hotel, convention center, or sports arena.

The Benevolent Iranian Student League started five years ago. Nikolas hired a man from Iran to start and operate this not-for-profit organization—sort of his own little American bonyad. Director Alireza Pour-Mohammadi funded the association immediately. Within ninety days, the first students—and future combatants—entered the United States under the pretext of education. Thanks to scholarships and travel stipends Nikolas provided, they could get here. By design, they had to work to pay for living expenses. Many of them started working in fast food. But, their diligence paid off, and they were able to apply for and get new jobs in kitchens that would serve large banquets and sporting events.

There were still some who worked in the ranks of fast food. They too would serve up Campylobacter jejuni to the infidels. But, it would be harder. In fast food, there was always a manager, supervisor, or coworker close by. In contrast, large banquet kitchens were busy producing huge, uniform meals. A member of the Benevolent Iranian Student League could easily taint ingredients hours before they were mixed, folded, kneaded, or whipped into the courses of a delightful meal.

• • •

Hookah vapor smoking's popularity was on the decline. Nikolas saw the downward trend in the market research his minions gathered. But, he could not overlook how effective hookah would be at infecting people with the amoeba Balamuthia mandrillaris. Nikolas's biologists estimated infection rates would reach eighty percent or better in people who inhaled infested hookah vapor.

Nikolas started a new company and hired a team to set up hookah lounges in fifteen cities. They often chose sites near universities, because it was popular among the college crowd. One of Nikolas's businesses analysts pointed out how these lounges would also tend to attract Muslims. "Acceptable collateral damage," Nikolas had to admit. "Most of them will be Sunnis anyway." Then he admonished them. "Never hesitate to offer specials on

LivingSocial or anyplace else you can promote our unique brand of Hookah."

• • •

Back in 2011 food trucks were emerging as one of the next big business crazes. Nikolas loved the trend, but not because the businesses performed well. Food trucks were another means of distributing bacteria and amoebas to thousands of people each day.

Nikolas was *not* interested in owning or operating food trucks. He was interested in making tainted products flow through the food trucks. So, he got the word out. Nikolas was involved in being an angel investor for food trucks. He started a small lending company to provide seed money for entrepreneurs who were starting their food trucks. He also steered the new truck owners toward a food supplier and distributor he owned. The quality of the food they supplied was excellent, and the prices and payment terms were surprisingly favorable. As of today, many of the foods and condiments would contain the weaponized Campylobacter jejuni bacteria.

He was currently financing hundreds of operating food trucks all over the country. Today alone, he estimated these little kitchens on wheels would expose more than 100,000 people to Campylobacter jejuni. Over the next thirty to sixty days, the food trucks would infect millions.

• • •

CoolSolar loved advertising with blimps at sporting events. They signed contracts to fly over college football games and participate in the celebration. When the home team ran onto the field, the blimp dropped confetti on the audience. When the home team scored a touchdown, again the confetti tumbled. These unique confetti were laced with microscopic dust. While the dust was too small for the human eye or nose to detect, the microparticles were the perfect size to house a potent colony of Campylobacter jejuni bacteria. It only took two or three particles landing in a drink or inhaled into the mouth of a cheering fan. A few days after the game, the fan would likely blame their raging stomachache on the stadium food. The confetti would never cross their mind.

• • •

Between football tailgating parties, marathons, triathlons, trade shows, parades, festivals, concerts, political rallies, and protests, Nikolas's businesses were reaching and infecting millions of people. But, he suspected tens of millions of his infections would cripple Americans with fear and overwhelm doctors' offices and hospitals. Many would be sick, but *everyone* would be terror-struck.

CHAPTER 16

Chicago, Illinois

Allie Stoker was making great time in today's half marathon. As the event snaked through the streets of Chicago, she took drinks of water and electrolyte-replacing sports drinks. Hundreds of volunteers provided the beverages along the trail. Passing mile marker six, she pushed herself even harder. Her goal for this race was simple—improve on last year's time. Within a few short minutes, she would reach the half-way point. Her body now screamed for calories. The sugar was her lifeblood as the miles clicked on.

• • •

It was almost too simple. Nikolas ordered the strike, and Roya carried it out. With the offer of double pay, Hotel Esatto recruited a team of employees to volunteer at the half marathon event for three hours on a Saturday morning. Roya asked marathon officials to assign her team to drink stations. Handing out tainted drinks to the runners along the path of the race was an effective way to spread the weaponized Campylobacter jejuni bacteria and continue the attack. Twenty Hotel Esatto employees were assigned to take care of four separate drink stops along the race route.

The volunteers performed basic tasks. They mixed up large pitchers of sports drink, poured the pitchers into cups, and kept a table filled with dozens of cups at any given moment. For ninety minutes they regularly prepared new batches of the sugary beverages. If nobody was looking, Roya included a small squirt of Campylobacter jejuni-infested water into the batch. She was able to contaminate most batches. Roya estimated more than 5,000 participants drank the bacteria, at least once.

As the last runners of the day passed by, she wondered how many other triathlons, marathons, and half marathons she could staff with volunteers over the next ninety days.

• • •

At mile marker nine, Allie reached for a cup of sports drink. She didn't notice the color, but the taste was citrus. As the seventy-eight-degree liquid passed down her throat and into her stomach, billions of Campylobacter jejuni bacteria entered her gastrointestinal system. Implanting themselves within her intestines, they set up shop and multiplied.

By the time Allie Stoker reached the last mile of her race, a colony of Campylobacter had reached critical mass in her blood. Her immune system was starting to rally and counterattack the bacterial onslaught.

When she finished the race, she rested briefly. Then she took a deep drink of a blue-colored sports drink and cooled down with a stretch. Dangerous bacteria were now invading her body, and she had no idea. Her immune system was producing antibodies with vigor. The battle against the Campylobacter jejuni bacteria was on— a clash the antibodies would win in the next five or six days. But, between now and then, she would experience a few days of upset stomach and cramps in her abdomen.

Subsequently, in a few weeks, Allie Stoker would most likely feel the effects of her immune system's attack on Campylobacter jejuni on her nervous system. And the symptoms would be long, debilitating, and miserable.

• • •

The CoolSolar team was in Southern California, planting the seeds of infectious terror at KAABOO Del Mar. The perfect weather made the misters unnecessary. But, a generous sponsorship allowed CoolSolar to run the water stations and contaminate the water.

Nikolas got a little creative for this event in California. Sure, Little Italy sandwich shops were there serving up apocalyptic disease. But, he was feeling the bloodlust. He wanted to do more damage—create more terror. So, Nikolas found out who two of the other food vendors would be. Then, he made generous offers to purchase the companies. The company owners enthusiastically accepted the proposals, and the bonyad financed the deal with equal zeal. Nikolas insisted on his newly acquired food service vendors preparing and serving food with condiments he supplied. Virtually every meal served at KAABOO Del Mar contained high Campylobacter jejuni bacterial counts.

CHAPTER 17

San Antonio, Texas

When Stoker's cell phone rang at five o'clock in the morning, it brought Stoker out of a deep sleep. His most recent slumbers had occurred in a tent in the Mexican desert and in the hospital in Chihuahua. Opening one eye, he frowned and reached for his phone. Somebody was interrupting the last thirty minutes of his prized night of comfortable sleep. In a gruff voice, he answered. "This better be my wife or parents. And, it better be urgent."

"Sorry, Dr. Stoker." It was the lab director at Brooke Army Medical Center. "What I've got to tell you is worth waking up for."

"You have results in less than four days?" Stoker asked.

"We do. That's the reason this call is urgent. Something strange is going on with your bacteria. Get over here right away. You're not going to believe what you see."

"I'll wake Dr. Rivera. We'll be right there."

At six a.m. Stoker and Rivera were sitting in the lab director's office. "These cultures have grown three times as fast as a normal Campylobacter culture," he explained. "We've confirmed your samples are indeed Campylobacter jejuni through our other assays. Now, we've even taken pictures through an electron microscope. The problem here is the way they're acting. Using genetic manipulation, someone has, without a doubt, created a weaponized version."

"So, what you're saying," Stoker said, "those super bacteria were weaponized to create a much higher incidence of Guillain-Barre syndrome, exactly like we saw in Mexico."

"It's obvious what is going on here," Rivera declared. "This is intended for the United States of America."

Z chimed in. "I'm running some numbers in my head. This is horrific in any scenario."

"There's no other reason why it was weaponized," Rivera continued. "People will get the diarrhea, but the antibodies will not attack much more than the Campylobacter jejuni to kill the bacteria. This is sinister—these *same* antibodies will maliciously attack the myelin sheath on its victims' nervous systems at a much higher rate."

"Therefore, the Guillain-Barre syndrome symptoms will appear at least a few days sooner," Stoker said.

"Campylobacter jejuni is a unique pathogen because it hits a few people twice," Rivera said. He was explaining to Z who lacked the clinical background of Stoker, Rivera, and the lab director. "The first time it gets you with an inconvenient case of diarrhea. If you're unlucky enough to get it a second time, the same bacteria that caused the diarrhea will stimulate the antibodies to cause the Guillain-Barre syndrome. After that, it's paralysis, ICU, and—."

"They end up on a ventilator," Z finished Rivera's thought.

"Exactly," Stoker said.

"I understand this atrocity," Z said. "Hospitals will overflow with hundreds of thousands of people, on ventilators breathing."

"The only redeeming factor is, with physical support, these people can survive," Stoker said. "Think of it this way. It reminds me of streptococcus infections that initially cause strep throat," Stoker said. "But, when a small minority of cases progresses on to rheumatic fever, patients experience heart valve damage."

Stoker turned to the lab director and asked, "Do you have any idea how many people could develop Guillain-Barre syndrome?" Then he stepped up to a microscope and looked at some of the samples from Mexico while he listened for an answer.

Rivera reframed Stoker's question. "What proportion of people infected with this strain the Campylobacter bacteria will develop Guillain-Barre?"

"I really have no idea," replied the lab director. "Until we find a cluster of people infected in the United States, we can only speculate. We just need to be ready to treat the symptoms aggressively until the body heals itself over a long period of time."

"Remarkable," Stoker said as he examined the bacteria cultures. I cannot believe the multiplication rate of this culture. It's grown so aggressively."

"That's not all," the lab director said. "We also performed agglutination on these cultures."

"To test for antibodies?" Stoker asked. "What did the titer look like?"

"It's about ten times higher than we would expect with Campylobacter."

"So, this strain of Campylobacter jejuni has an incredibly

high antigen level."

"We need to do a little more testing on some lab animals," the lab director said. "But, I'm apprehensive about this new version of an old germ—one somebody manipulated to amp up the antigens."

Z interjected a thought. "If I understand correctly, does all of your science speak about agglutination, titers, and more antigens equates to a more intense immune system response?"

"Possibly," replied the director. "Our animal tests will play your theory out. If you are correct, the animals' immune systems will mount a strong response."

"What you're saying is, this particular strain of the bacteria would be more likely to trigger Guillain-Barre syndrome," Z said.

"That's our working theory," the lab director responded. "We'll know when we see if the test animals develop Guillain-Barre syndrome. But, I'll go out on a limb here. I think a talented geneticist manipulated Campylobacter jejuni. Some scientist made if more virulent as well as more likely to cause Guillain-Barre syndrome. This is man-made."

"This is weaponized bacteria," Stoker said. "A brilliant, evil weapon. Part of the brilliance is the choice of Campylobacter jejuni. It can incubate quickly. It's contagious through food and ingestion. I can imagine dozen—no hundreds—of foods that can deliver the Campylobacter bacteria right into victims' stomachs and intestines. That's the dangerous part. It's so easy to deliver, in significant dosages, to millions of people. And, somebody from the Middle East is testing it out in Mexico."

"Only a hundred miles from the border with the United States," Rivera said turning directly to the lab director. "Obviously you're sending this data to the CDC?"

"Yes. As we speak, it's being done. I'm also sharing it with the Military Health System's Epidemiology and Analysis section. But, let me show you one more thing. We also did a separate culture of the Campylobacter, this time with minimal nutrients and with lower temperatures. These conditions resulted in the trophozoic phase of the bacteria. It's kind of like the cells curling up in a sort of protective shell."

"Like an armadillo curling up when it feels threatened," Stoker interjected.

"Yes. But, in this case, the cold and the absence of nutrition are the enemies. And these weaponized bacteria withstood incredible temperature variations with this hardened coating around it."

"And then, we put this Campylobacter jejuni in a culture that was good for growth. The bacteria grew faster than any previous Campylobacter jejuni culture has ever grown before."

"Okay, let me get this straight," Stoker said. "Number one, it's coating is even stronger in the trophozoic stage when the conditions are not ideal. Second, when the conditions are ideal, it grows much faster than any Campylobacter jejuni strain we know of. And third, it produces a stronger immune response and hence the possibility of Guillain-Barre syndrome skyrockets."

"So now, it can really attack the myelin sheath in a much more aggressive manner," Z said. Then he followed up with a question. "How complex is all of this genetic manipulation?"

"It's easier than you think," the lab directors said. "It's too easy. There are hundreds of scientists, around the world, with the skills to do this in a properly equipped laboratory."

"Can you provide us with a digital copy of all of the data you've shared with us?" Rivera asked.

"Certainly. Give me about three minutes," the lab director said. "But, promise me you'll work around our idiotic chief of infectious disease."

"Don't worry," Stoker said. "We'll go above his head. Then we'll explain how he opted out of participating in any of the discovery or analysis. Like I said, he was not at his post. In my judgment, he committed desertion as well as dereliction of duty."

Three minutes later Stoker, Rivera, and Z were leaving the hospital lab with a USB drive in Rivera's pocket containing all the different bacterial assays, for safe keeping. They drove to a small office building at Fort Sam Houston where Rivera sent an encrypted email to Director Steele at the CDC.

"Your medical school girlfriend Susan Taggert and that Director Steele may have to wake up and get serious when they see this data," Rivera said as he stood up from the computer. "I attached all the lab data. I'll be damned if this Guillain-Barre syndrome isn't more prevalent and virulent. But, how are dozens of people, in a Mexican community of eight hundred thousand people getting it? In a city the size of Chihuahua, there should be perhaps one or two cases at any given time. That's in the whole city. We counted more than a dozen people with the disease right there in that single hospital."

"And that's only one of the ten hospitals in Chihuahua," Stoker said. "I bet there are more cases—and more serious cases, thanks to the increased virulence. Also, we would typically expect to see less than twenty percent of the patients on a vent. But, we've got most of these patients on ventilators. It's like Guillain-Barre syndrome on steroids."

"You're right. And, we can't get the CDC to open their eyes."

Stoker stroked his chin in serious thought. "Hey Rivera, let's think about the big picture for a minute. On the one hand, we have a potential superbug brewing. On the other hand, we've got Iranian terrorists who'll be crossing the border any day and secretly entering America. We need to do an end-run around the CDC and get some people to start listening to us."

"I see where you're going," Rivera said. "You want to return to Mexico. We need to be there to watch the Iranians. And, we don't need to be in America to orchestrate an end run around the CDC about the weaponized Campylobacter jejuni."

"Yes," Stoker replied. "We can juggle both conundrums better from Mexico. Those Shiites are going to cross into the United States soon, and we need to be right there tracking them." Stoker furrowed his forehead. "Z, we need you to set up some cutting-edge surveillance on the Iranians. And, Rivera and I can contact each of the hospitals to see if there are even more patients suffering from Guillain-Barre right now."

Rivera looked Stoker in the eye. "Mexico, here we come."

"Let me call Allie and update her on our plans," Stoker said as he picked up his phone and dialed his wife."

When she answered, her voice was gloomy. "Hey, Troy."

"Allie. What's going on? You sound sick."

"I feel horrible. I'm stuck here in my Chicago hotel room with a monstrous stomachache. I'm not talking about the garden variety stomachache. This is the kind that feels like a perpetual cramp in your intestines, along with plenty of diarrhea."

It couldn't be possible, Stoker thought as he replied to his wife. "Allie, I'm really sorry. I was about to return to Mexico with Rivera. But, I'm going to jump on the next plane to Chicago and come take care of you."

"No. Don't come. By the time you get here, I bet I'll be feeling much better."

"Okay. You'll never catch me second guessing you—especially when you tell me not to take care of you." It was true. There were some occasions when Allie accepted his care. But, there were other times when she just needed her space while she recovered. It was a trait from her stoic Norwegian heritage. "I'll be heading back down to Mexico. But, when did this discomfort start?"

"I felt the first stomach cramps late yesterday. I thought I might just be slightly premenstrual."

"No. That's not it. You would be about two weeks early."

"Troy, darling. You know, almost as well as I, about my unpredictable cycle. Early or late by four days. That's just my norm. And, it's become worse—"

Stoker finished her thought. "Since you've been training harder."

Exactly.

"That's common for women runners who train as hard as you do," Stoker said. "What are your other symptoms?"

"I have a bit of a headache and a slight fever. I wonder if I have food poisoning?"

"What did you have to eat last night?"

"I didn't want to go out. I just wasn't hungry enough for a full meal. Instead, I ate a couple granola bars and an apple. Then I fell asleep."

"To me, it sounds like your basic viral gastroenteritis," Stoker said. Continue to rest and drink plenty of liquids. See if Room Service has Gatorade on their menu," he suggested. "Or Pepto-Bismol."

"That I can look into. Or, I'm sure the concierge or bell staff will fetch me some, in anticipation of a generous tip."

"If you were in Chihuahua, Mexico right now, I would be concerned that you have a bug called Campylobacter jejuni."

"What's that?"

"It's an extremely common bacterium all over the world. We stumbled upon a high concentration down there recently. I'll tell you the story back at home."

"Does this *campy* germ also exist in the United States?"

"Yes. It's responsible for a large percentage of gastroenteritis cases in the United States. It's a common bug that's been around for thousands of years.

"That's comforting," Allie said sarcastically. "And, it's ironic. You're the one spending all this time in Mexico, and I get Montezuma's Revenge."

"Trust me," Stoker said. "You don't want the bacteria they have going on in Mexico. It has been causing a lot more than diarrhea. It's also attacking their nervous system."

"Wow. That sounds serious. Does it kill people?"

"Not usually. We manage the patients' symptoms—some profound misery—for a few weeks. Then they come around and experience a slow recuperation."

"Speaking of coming around," Allie said in a foreboding tone, "I had better get off the phone in case Montezuma comes back around."

"Okay, Allie," Stoker said. "Can I make one more request?"

"Sure. What's that?"

"Here's the situation. Go to the closest emergency room and have a culture. Let's go find out what is causing this infection. On the off chance you have this Campylobacter jejuni, it would be better to treat this bacterium aggressively now. Do you understand?"

"Yes, Troy. You wouldn't ask if it wasn't even a possibility that I had the bug. The chances are small, but the consequences are huge. Do I just ask for a Campylobacter jejuni culture?"

"No. Just tell me which ER you're going to, and I'll call in the order. They'll take it from there."

Allie checked her phone to find the closest hospital. "How about I go to Northwestern Memorial?"

"Great," Stoker said. "They're a highly reputable academic medical center. They'll have a great lab."

"I'm on my way," Allie said.

"Hey, Allie. Thank you for doing this for me. I love you, and I know you're tough as nails."

"Thanks for caring enough to be a little worried. I love you, too Troy."

When the phone call ended, Stoker called the Northwestern Memorial emergency department and left orders with the triage team. Then he called the concierge at Allie's hotel. He gave the concierge a credit card number and asked him to arrange for Gatorade, Pepto-Bismol, and a new pair of pajamas in Allie's size to be delivered to her room. "If you can get it done in two hours, you can also charge a $100 tip on that card."

Twenty-four hours after Allie visited Northwestern Memorial Medical Center, the lab called Stoker with the results. She was positive for Campylobacter jejuni.

• • •

Over the Labor Day weekend, CoolSolar spent a very productive time spreading disease at the Electric Zoo Festival in New York. They set up the mist machine, but it was not so popular. Labor Day weekend temperatures in New York were not as hot as the temperatures in the Nevada desert at Burning Man. But, as generous corporate sponsors of the event, Cool Solar had the privilege of operating the water bottle refill stations. Thousands of gallons of water laced with Campylobacter jejuni bacteria flowed into the digestive systems of the 85,000 attendees.

Nikolas's biological terror reach was not only limited to the misters and water over this weekend in New York. Little Italy sandwich shops were also a big Electric Zoo sponsor. Throughout the event, they served more than 150,000 sandwiches. Most of the customers ordered mayo and an involuntary dose of Campylobacter jejuni. Nikolas's epidemiology consultant in Iran estimated the mist machine would lead to hundreds of Balamuthia mandrillaris amoeba infections. The water stations and sandwiches would lead to tens of thousands of cases of Guillain-Barre syndrome. Not bad for a weekend.

Chapter 18

Juarez, Mexico

Secretly crossing the border west of Juarez, Mexico was an arduous endeavor. Ten hours of darkness was about all the time the Iranian terrorists had to sneak up to the border, cross it, and then make enough progress into the United States to avoid detection. Even then, a border crossing was a high-stakes venture. Tonight, *Espada Rápida* was watching and waiting on both sides of the border—the same thing they had been doing for more than a week since Stoker, Rivera, and Z returned from Brooke Army Medical Center. Thanks to some audio and overhead surveillance, Stoker, Rivera, Z, and the rest of the team were ninety percent sure this was the chosen night for the would-be Shiite terrorists to enter the United States. They would travel on foot, under the guise of being Mexican emigrants. On the Mexico side of the border, Stoker and Z were on a stakeout of sorts. They were monitoring the terrorist compound with high-performance drones.

"You never told me much about your Burning Man experience?" Stoker asked Z. "Did you get to go on any free-spirited benders?"

"Contrary to what you think, most attendees were not frolicking in unrelenting hedonism. Sure, amongst tens of thousands of creative souls expressing their repressed selves, there was plenty of debauchery. But my experience at the wedding was refreshing. Soul cleansing if you will. The rest of it—the sights, sounds, the energy—was fun."

"I'm glad you got to recharge your batteries a bit with something a little different."

"Wow. Listen to me," Z said. "The mighty *Espada Rápida* warrior and techno-geek, talking about soul cleansing. I guess it's a given when you're stuck doing surveillance with a psychiatrist."

"Definitely an occupational hazard," Stoker joked. "Soon you'll be telling me about your childhood. And, I'll be hypnotizing you. You won't even know it."

"If you hypnotize me, I'll hack you. And, you'll absolutely

know it."

"You mean, I'll know who to blame when my 401k balance is only four hundred dollars?"

On the American side of the border, Rivera and Jessica waited at an airfield with the Russian gunship. There would be a natural handoff of responsibility at the border from Stoker and Z to Jessica and Rivera.

About an hour before sunset, Stoker and Z watched as a Ford Expedition pulled up to the home. A group of six fighters exited a house they'd been surveilling. The men loaded into an old Ford Expedition. Each carried backpacks. Stoker and Z suspected the packs contained the provisions necessary for their cross-border trip.

Z and Stoker landed the drone, jumped into an old jeep, and drove toward this home they had been watching. As they approached within fifty yards of the home, they pulled over and waited. The Expedition pulled out of the driveway and away from the house. Stoker and Z followed as the fanatics drove southeast, through the streets of the border city of Juarez. For a moment the Expedition slowed to a crawl as it passed an auto repair shop. Moments later a garage opened, and two pickup trucks exited and followed the Expedition. These two automobiles carried men, women, and children riding in the trucks' beds. Between the three vehicles, Stoker and Z counted at least twenty-two people in the convoy.

"This is the real thing," Z radioed to Rivera. "The Shiites also have a group of women and children with them, Mexican nationals. Putting them in a large familial group will improve their disguise."

"Decoys," Rivera said.

"Yes, sir. That's what we're thinking."

"We'll be tracking your every move," Rivera responded. "We're in the air, and we'll be watching from above."

"Okay, guys. These tangos are about to cross over into the United States," Stoker declared. "I'm getting the FBI on the line. The moment these guys cross the border, this surveillance needs their oversight."

After traveling for forty-five minutes, the convoy pulled onto a farm road and turned toward the Rio Grande. Stoker and Z remained at a distance. The three cars Stoker and Z had been following parked two hundred yards away from the river. The sun had just set, and the shadows were starting to overcome the light.

Z and Stoker parked their jeep in a cluster of trees about a quarter mile away from the radicals and Mexican families. On foot, they snuck up on the three vehicles and watched. There was no movement. Everything was as quiet as a night could be. The silence felt surreal. Stoker and Z waited undetected behind some vegetation, which grew reasonably well so close to the river. The terrorists stayed in their cars, and the Mexicans remained in the backs of the pickup trucks. Everyone just waited almost motionless. Over the next thirty minutes, darkness fell, and the stars came to life. The moon, in its waning crescent phase, offered a mere sliver of light in the cloudless sky.

Z and Stoker watched through infrared binoculars. The people in the beds of the trucks whispered occasionally. But then, as if by some unseen signal, the Mexican families started crawling out of the truck beds. They formed two groups. One group walked upriver forty yards, and another walked downriver for sixty yards. Stoker and Z did not dare follow them for fear of being detected by the Shiites. Just after the Mexicans had disappeared into the thick vegetation lining the river, two of the Expedition's doors, quietly opened. One by one, the six men rolled out and landed on the ground. They quickly crawled to the underbrush and disappeared toward the Rio Grande. The three automobiles started their engines and slowly rolled away with their lights off.

Now, with nobody within fifty yards of Stoker and Z, they dared whisper. "We've gotta see what's going on," Z said in a hushed tone. "Let me send a drone up. One with an infrared camera."

Z prepared the drone, manipulated a few buttons, and launched it quietly up into the air.

Over the radio, Rivera's voice came through to their earpieces. "Can you give me a sitrep?"

Stoker answered him in a whisper. "We've stopped pretty close to the Rio Grande, but everyone we were following has disappeared through the vegetation. We want to see how this all plays out, so we're sending up a drone."

"Let me know what you see," came Rivera's reply.

"Roger that."

Z fired up a tablet. The scene above the Rio Grande came into clear view. Thanks to the drone, they had a birds-eye view of the Shiite and Mexican groups. They could see the downriver group of Mexicans standing at the edge of the water. Then out of one corner of the screen, a raft rowed toward them and reached the shore where they waited.

The oarsman rowing this boat had been hired to meet them and ferry them to America. Immediately men, women, and children jumped into the raft and cast off, hoping not to touch Mexican soil again for a while.

When the boat reached the half-way point between the Mexican and American riverbanks, four spotlights lit up from the American side. In Spanish, a loud voice came over a bullhorn announcing the presence of the United States Border Patrol on the American side of the river. The voice from the bullhorn warned the crossers they would be detained if they tried to enter the United States of America.

But the soon-to-be emigrants knew the border patrol agents couldn't capture and detain all of them. Furthermore, the American side of the riverbank was full of lush sugar cane plants. Years ago, someone sympathetic to Mexican immigrants had planted the sugar cane there to make escaping through the foliage easier. The oarsman paddled on and approached a dark version of America's shining shores.

Two border patrol agents jumped out of hiding spots in the sugar cane just as the rowboat was about to make landfall. The experienced oarsman knew precisely what to do. He had helped hundreds of Mexicans cross these waters, and he had some tricks for the border patrol. With a few swift swipes of his paddle, he redirected the boat a little further downriver. The maneuver put fifteen yards of tall, thick sugar cane plants between the Mexicans and the border patrol agents.

The raft stopped abruptly as it slid up the riverbank. Via the drone's camera, Stoker and Z watched as Mexican men, women, and children jumped out of the boat. The emigrants grasped onto the sugar cane plants and pulled themselves up onto the shore. Then they began to run along the trails hundreds of their other compatriots had established as they sought for a better life.

One of the border patrol officers seemed to know these trails well. He ran through the sugar cane and intercepted a young man, who was carrying a young child in a colorful sling, and his wife. Their escape to a more prosperous life had ended.

Another border patrol agent nabbed a Mexican woman. Yet, of this first group, the border patrol managed to stop only four of the nine. The five Mexicans who escaped stood a good chance of making it to San Antonio, Dallas, or Houston and disappearing into the community.

Z zoomed the drone's camera out. The upriver group of Mexicans was now crossing the river in a raft. "We suspect these first two groups are the diversion," said Z to Stoker. "Let's see if we can find the tangos. That's who we really need to be tracking." Z made the drone descend to 300 feet, and the picture below the mini aircraft became much clearer. Huddled up in a patch of tall grass were the Shiites. They each had their backpacks on. But now, they were also wearing swim fins, masks, and goggles. "They're going to swim across after they've sacrificed the Mexicans."

Z zoomed out just in time to see the upstream raft landing on the shore. A border patrol SUV had just pulled up and was shining its lights on the newly arrived emigrants. The foot chase ensued, which gave the six Shiites the perfect moment to slip into the water. In a few seconds, they managed to swim across the river completely undetected. On the other side, they abandoned their masks, snorkels, and fins. Then they stepped three feet into the sugar cane before they squatted down and hid in the plants. There they waited quietly, listening to the border patrol agents while they situated the Mexicans they had captured into the back seats of their SUVs. Five minutes later, the border patrol agents used their spotlights to sweep the river and its banks. The Shiites were too deeply concealed in the sugar cane plants for the border patrol agents to detect them.

Satisfied with their spotlight sweep of the area, the border patrol jumped into their vehicles and drove away.

"The diversion worked," Z reported to Rivera over the radio. "All six of the tangos made it onto American soil. They're all yours."

"Roger that," came Rivera's voice in response. "We're about five thousand feet above you, and we're looking at them through our infrared now. But, can you get your annoying drone out of the way? It keeps blocking our view."

"Hey Rivera," Z said. "Don't disrespect the drone. It can get into some pretty tight spaces when you need it to."

"But right now, I need it out of my airspace."

Z hit a button, and the drone set an automatic flight path to return to Stoker and Z's location.

"With these tangos in America now, they are your responsibility, along with the FBI," Stoker radioed. "We'll cross the border legally and catch up with you ASAP."

Rivera and Jessica watched as the extremist Shiites—now illegal aliens in the United States—slowly climbed up the riverbank. Then they started to run in formation. They paid no mind to the crops in the farmers' fields as they jogged through acres of farmland. When they came across barbed wire and other obstacles, they overcame them with ease. It was apparent their training had anticipated these obstructions.

After three miles they stopped. These men from Lebanon, Yemen, and Iran were approaching some more significant roads, and they needed to remain undetected. The men huddled in the middle of a field planted with an ankle-high crop. Jessica and Rivera observed the men removing water and energy bars from their backpacks. One of them also removed a cell phone. After powering the device up, it appeared he was sending a text.

The group continued to wait while sipping on water and snacking. Then the man's phone lit up, and he paid attention to the message that appeared. He gave a command, and the men slung their backpacks on and started their jog through the fields again. This time their course was due north. When they reached a two-lane road, they turned and continued running down the road. When a car would approach, the men left the road and scrambled into the field beside them. They had no idea Rivera and his team were watching their every move from above.

After running an additional two miles, a car up ahead of them flashed its lights. This time the men did not exit the road, but they kept running. The vehicle, a black Chevrolet Suburban, slowed as they approached. Then it rolled to a stop twenty yards ahead of them. The men slowed to a walking pace, walked up to the car and casually got in.

"Hey Stoker and Z," Rivera called out over the radio. What's your location?"

"We came through at the Ysleta border crossing about five minutes ago," Stoker answered. "Can you give us a sitrep?"

"These Iranians just got picked up about four miles to your southeast. Why don't you jump on Highway 375 and travel west?

We'll do our best to navigate you toward them. They just climbed in a black Suburban with Texas plates. You'd better follow them for a while. Our bird will need to refuel."

"Roger that," Stoker said. "But where's the FBI?"

"The FBI is on their way. We just need to keep track of these guys. I bet the tangos jump on I-10. Let's see if they travel north or south."

A few minutes later, Stoker and Z arrived at I-10. "Do we go north or south, Rivera?"

"Give me a minute. They're approaching the exit a couple miles to the south of you."

"Roger that," Stoker said as he pulled the car over to wait.

A minute later Rivera's voice came through the earpiece. "They turned north, so give them two minutes to reach where you are. Then you can jump on the freeway and tail them."

Stoker pulled a bag out of the back seat. "Hey Z. If those terrorists are going to stay fueled and hydrated, so should we." We've got Gatorade, Coke, or V8 Fusion. What'll you have?"

"I packed my own poison," Z said as he pulled a liter of Mountain Dew out of his bag. "I'm ready for a long night of driving."

"Why don't you try to get some sleep?" Stoker said. "Then you can drive in a few hours. Save your caffeine for later."

Word came from the helicopter. The tangos in the Suburban were coming up on Stoker and Z in the jeep. Stoker pulled back onto the road and turned onto the entrance ramp to I-10. Z reclined his seat and closed his eyes. They merged onto the lightly traveled freeway and found themselves well behind the Suburban. "The license plate on their car is LS3-C4891," Stoker reported over the radio," They still appear to be headed back toward El Paso."

When the large SUV changed direction and continued its travels north into New Mexico, Stoker and Z followed. For the next few hours, they tracked the Suburban north on US Highway 54. Z slept. Stoker informed Rivera along the route.

"We'll fly about an hour ahead of you," Rivera radioed. "We'll rent a car. Then, we'll take our turn following them."

There wasn't much traffic on this highway as it meandered through a dark New Mexico night. Stoker elected to stay a mile behind the Suburban, which traveled at the speed limit.

Just after 3 o'clock in the morning, Rivera radioed Stoker. "We're coming up on your six. We're here to relieve you. And, you'll be meeting up with the FBI along the way."

"Thanks. I'll slow down so you can pass me. Z and I will stop for food and fuel."

A few minutes later, Rivera and another *Espada Rápida* warrior passed in a Chevrolet Impala. Stoker keyed the mic on his radio. "Hey *amigo*, how do we find these FBI guys?"

"Don't worry, Stoker. She'll find you."

Stoker pulled off at the next exit. There he fueled his car and bought some food. Z slept soundly. As he started accelerating the jeep up the onramp to get back on the freeway, his headlights illuminated a hitchhiker. Stoker gave no thought to picking up the straggler until the person held up a cardboard sign that read, "Mojave Stoker."

"Enough with the rattlesnake jokes, Rivera," Stoker muttered under his breath as he pulled over. Stoker unrolled the window.

As Rivera had hinted, the hitchhiker was a woman. "A Cuban doctor told me I could bum a ride from you."

"Jump in. But I must warn you, we're going to have trust issues. That Cuban doctor introduces me to a lot of shady characters."

The woman opened the jeep door. "I'm not going to lie to you, Stoker. I fit the bill." She pulled on the latch to move the seat forward so she could jump in the back seat. Z woke with a start, and his hand flew out in front of him just in time to save his face from smacking into the dashboard."

"Who's your friend?" the hitchhiker asked as she crawled through the small gap and into the back seat. Stoker laughed as Z's alertness went from sleep to enlivened, and his forehead pressed against the windshield."

"This is Z," Stoker said.

"You'll have to be a little more specific," she said. "Names are more than just a single letter."

"Good luck," Stoker said as he pushed Z back into sitting position and forced his seat back to normal. "Z does not do specific." Stoker reached across Z and pulled the door shut. He put the jeep into gear and started back up the freeway onramp.

"I'm Special Agent In Charge, Sarah Ahmadi, FBI JTTF."

"JTTF?" Stoker asked.

Z answered before Ahmadi could, with his eyes still closed. "Joint Terrorism Task Forces."

"How do you know about the Joint Terrorism Task Force?"

"No, it's not one task force. It is plural, task *forces*." His eyes were still closed and his head leaning against the jeep's window.

"Okay Grammar Girl. I didn't ask you to correct my English or even to define the JTTF. I asked you how you know about these JTTFs?"

"And there's an official reason I eluded your question about my name," Z responded. "Now let me sleep."

Ahmadi explained. "The Joint Terrorism Task Forces exist all around the United States. The FBI coordinates it, but our team members come from municipal law enforcement, Homeland Security, the TSA, military, and a handful of other organizations."

"The amoeba of the JTTF just swallows whomever it wants whenever it wants?" Stoker asked.

"We're not an amoeba. We're more like an immune system. We kick in and help out when the scourge rears its ugly head."

"I like your analogy," Stoker said. "Now that we're on American soil, I suspect the FBI will take over?"

"Oh no. You and Rivera are still in charge. You're in way too deep." Ahmadi said. "You, Doctor Stoker, are in the starting lineup now. You're leading and executing this mission through to the end. Welcome to the team."

"Rivera continues to lead," Z clarified while opening one eye. "But he keeps letting you be in charge, Stoker." Z closed his eye again. "You also overlooked one other impressive piece of information Agent Ahmadi shared with you."

"What's that?" Stoker asked.

"She is *Special* Agent In Charge," Z said. "She runs the whole task force."

"Does that mean, from the FBI's perspective, you're in charge of this whole 'Iranian bioterrorism coming in through Mexico' operation?" Stoker asked.

Z did not let her answer. "She's in charge of the whole Joint Terrorism Task Forces efforts—in the whole Universe."

"So, what are you doing here, following terrorists in the middle of the night? Shouldn't you be calling all the shots in a command center or something like that?"

"Usually, yes. But, some extenuating circumstances brought me into the field. And it feels great to be out of my office."

"What are the extenuating circumstances?"

"First, my intuition tells me this Iranian cell is a big deal. I think your team is onto something huge. Second, I heard the guy running this op—that would be you Stoker—is a natural leader and operator, who could use some training."

"So, you just turned over your responsibilities to your next in line and flew down here?"

"Not exactly. My boss, a deputy director, doesn't let me just take off on a hunch. I need some proof. You and Dr. Rivera have provided enough to set off hellacious alarm bells in my head. But, my deputy director in Washington D.C. is more jaded. He needs a bit more justification. Besides, my boss would want me to send agents to do the fieldwork, instead of getting out into the field myself.

"That's why I arranged to take off three days of personal time. I've spent the last 48 hours handing off my work to my next in line. Then I flew down here—on my own dime I might add."

"You took time off to come and do your job?" Stoker asked.

"Yes. And, Rivera tells me you're a psychiatrist. Does using personal time to go out and do field work make me crazy?"

"I don't know. I'm taking time off from being a psychiatrist to do fieldwork. Nobody's paying me. I'm not in a position to evaluate your situation objectively."

Ahmadi laughed. "I could get in a lot of trouble for pulling this little stunt—taking personal time off to follow a hunch and work in the field."

Z chimed in sarcastically. "Oh gosh! We don't like gritty people like you. That kind of out-of-the-box thinking's not going to work with us."

Stoker followed Z's lead and continued in the same sarcastic vein. "We don't play well with people who break the rules."

Ahmadi smiled. She picked up on the sarcasm. Her new acquaintances understood her well.

Z opened both of his eyes. "Welcome. You're going to like working with *Espada Rápida*," Z said.

"Well, let me validate your intuition a little more," Stoker said. "Let me tell you a story that starts in Chihuahua, Mexico."

"Sorry to burst your bubble," Ahmadi said. "But, I've heard about the Iranians training in Chihuahua. We've been watching them for a while.

"Do you know about the weaponized bacteria the Iranians likely tested on residents of Chihuahua."

"No. This is a new story for me. How did you hear it?"

"We lived it," Stoker said. "It all started with a training exercise just outside of Chihuahua a few days ago. And it ends with some lab data Z is going to email you right now."

Z used his phone to send the email, then he closed his eyes and started to fall back asleep. Over the next two hours, Stoker told Agent Ahmadi the story of discovering the patients suffering from Guillain-Barre syndrome in the hospital. He admitted to stealing the blood samples and results from the lab. He recounted the confrontations in *La Sotolería* and on the Mexican dirt road. Ahmadi had a lot of questions. Stoker answered each of them with precision and confidence. She was convinced.

"I'm looking at lab results from the Mexican blood samples, processed at Brooke Army Medical Center?" She was reading the email from Z on her iPad.

"That's right. You're not only seeing data confirming Campylobacter jejuni causing Guillain-Barre syndrome. You're seeing proof someone created bacteria—"

Ahmadi cut him off and finished his thought. "That's thousands of times more likely to give somebody Guillain-Barre syndrome. In other words, this is bioterrorism."

"Exactly. Most people survive the disease, but it's a long miserable recovery."

"That assumes there's a ventilator available to everyone with Guillain-Barre. But, how many ventilators and ICU beds are there in America?"

"I don't know. But, I suspect there would not be nearly enough."

"I'm no health care number cruncher," Ahmadi said. But, I'm guessing the next two or three months are going to bring millions of infections. Let's just guess it's two million people?"

"I think you're in the ballpark."

"Are there two million ventilators?"

"No way. And even if there were, most of the ventilators are already in use. They're mechanically breathing for patients with strokes, pneumonia, heart and lung conditions, drug overdoses, and brain and spine injuries. I bet there are 200,000 ventilators in America right now. That's a wild guess. 20,000 of them are available just in case there is an epidemic of Guillain-Barre syndrome or another disease."

"Who have you told about this?" Ahmadi asked.

"The CDC. They're looking into it—but too slowly, in my opinion. The lab at Brooke Army Medical Center also sent the data to the Military Health System's Epidemiology and Analysis section."

"Can I send this to the FBI Weapons of Mass Destruction Directorate?"

"Absolutely."

For the next twenty-nine hours, teams of *Espada Rápida* warriors and FBI agents, in a few different cars and aircraft, took turns following the Suburban as it crossed parts of New Mexico, Texas, Oklahoma, Kansas, and Missouri. The teams alternated as the lead car.

In the jeep, Stoker and Z learned about Sarah Ahmadi. She was born to first-generation Iranian immigrant parents. They named her Zahra, a common female name in Iran. She anglicized her name to Sarah after she finished high school.

Z and Stoker took advantage of Ahmadi's native Farsi fluency. They practiced speaking the language for hours as they drove.

"So why did you become a doctor?" Ahmadi asked Stoker as they were driving.

"I grew up in a family with some medical issues. When my parents were newlyweds, my dad was diagnosed with type 1 diabetes. He tried real hard to manage it, but he could not keep it in check. When I was a teenager, he was hospitalized nine different times. When I was seventeen, he had a stroke. As for my mom, she started having severe depression about a year after my little brother was born. When I was eighteen, a doctor finally figured out my mom had depression from a thyroid condition called Hashimoto's thyroiditis. A medication called Synthroid helped her depression and saved her a life of sluggishness and misery. After watching my parents, and learning so much about their conditions, I really wanted to be a doctor. With my dad on disability, my parents couldn't help me pay for college. But, the Army served a few purposes. First, I could get mountains of medical experience working as an Army medic. Second, the Army would help me pay for school. But, I was also an active and athletic soul. Getting paid to do pushups appealed to me. By the time I was nineteen, I was on maneuvers with paratroopers treating everything from bug bites to complex fractures and life-threatening injuries. After college and a couple of full-time years in the military, I entered medical school at Baylor. But, I didn't even consider psychiatry until my third year of medical school. During my psychiatry rotation, I was enthralled. I had a knack for psychiatry."

Every few hours, all the cars following the black Suburban fell back, and surveillance duties switched to an airplane or helicopter. In western Oklahoma, the Suburban stopped at a gas station. There, Z managed to place a tracking device under the Suburban without being detected. This would let the teams fall back and allow Z to monitor the enemy electronically. The tangos had no idea they were being observed and tracked.

A few times the terrorist Suburban doubled back to check for surveillance. They never detected their followers. In Missouri, the terrorists took a circuitous route through the backwoods. In two small towns, they even tried some rigorous maneuvers to trick and expose possible followers. But the tracking device had no trouble following the Suburban's crazy route.

The large SUV would pull over at an occasional gas station. Only two people would ever get out of the car at any single stop. They never stayed at a hotel to sleep. Stoker figured the terrorists were doing their sleeping in the car, much like he and his fellow warriors.

In St. Louis, Stoker parked the jeep and rented a sedan. He, Z, and Ahmadi were three miles behind the black Suburban when it arrived on the outskirts of Chicago.

Ahmadi was in the passenger's seat. Z had just awoken from a four-hour nap in the back seat. They followed the tangos for more than an hour before the Suburban exited the freeway. "Now this could get interesting," Z said. "Something tells me we're close to the hornet's nest."

"Chicago is a great place for a terror hornet's nest," Ahmadi said. "Anonymity and plenty of targets."

As they followed, Stoker called his wife, Allie. "Hey babe, how's your stomach feeling?"

"Four days symptom-free." Allie had suffered for five miserable days, all the while discouraging Stoker from flying to Chicago to take care of her. She thought she was out of the woods. But, she had no idea how much damage her immune system was doing to her nerves. "I missed a lot of work, so I've been catching up," Allie said. "What's your latest update—minus the top-secret stuff you can't tell me?"

"You'll never believe this."

"Your political views have shifted?" Allie teased.

"My news is not that incredible."

"Okay, what's the big reveal."

"I'm driving into the fine city of Chicago."

"Troy, you often impress me with your romantic side. But, something tells me this is more of a coincidence instead of a planned nostalgic gesture."

"It's a coincidence. But, I'm thrilled at the possibility of seeing you."

"What do you mean, possibility?"

"I'm on a journey, and I hope it ends in Chicago."

"Why is it a question mark?"

"It's a long story. But, let's just say some people who caught our attention in Mexico started driving north a couple days ago. But now, we're following them through a Chicago neighborhood."

The Suburban came to an abrupt stop. The right rear door opened, and a man emerged wearing a Chicago Cubs baseball hat and sunglasses. Stoker and Z watched as an Iranian man walked briskly down the sidewalk and disappeared into a train station.

"Gotta go," Stoker said to Allie. "The odds of us staying here just increased." Stoker ended the call.

"Should we follow him?" Z asked.

"No," Ahmadi suggested. "It's just one of the six. Let's stay with the majority."

Z radioed Rivera with a sitrep.

"Can you guys stay close?" Rivera asked. "Things get tricky in traffic like this."

"One of the tangos just exited the Suburban. It looks like he went and got on the L," Z said referring to Chicago's elevated train.

"We're about thirty yards behind you," Rivera answered. "If someone else exits that Suburban, Z will follow him."

"Roger that," Z said. "I'm always game to navigate a little urban sprawl. I'll call or text you with updates."

"We'll track your phone's GPS, too," Rivera said.

For the next few blocks of travel, they followed the Suburban. At an intersection, the light turned red, and the Suburban stopped. Suddenly a Yemeni man jumped out of the car and started walking briskly down the sidewalk.

Z reached for his door handle. "My turn."

"That guy's destination is probably the Archer L station a couple blocks over," Stoker said.

"No problem. I don't know Chicago so well. Thanks to my phone, I can navigate it like a boss." Z jumped out of the car and followed his target down the sidewalk.

The light turned green, and traffic moved forward. The Suburban accelerated quickly, but Stoker chose a slower pace and fell back another twenty yards. Sarah Ahmadi elected to stay in the back seat. Stoker caught a glimpse of the Suburban almost a block ahead of him. "Hey Rivera," he called into his radio. "How close are you to the Suburban and us?"

"I'm closer than you. I just passed you. I'm about five cars back from that Suburban. I'll take the lead."

Stoker and Ahmadi followed the Rivera team, as well as the Suburban, for ten more minutes. When the large SUV pulled into a four-story parking structure adjacent to a shopping mall, Rivera's voice came over the radio. "I'm not following them in there. It would be too easy for them to make us."

"I'll follow them on foot," came Jessica's voice over the radio. "If someone jumps out in the parking garage, I just might see them." Then Stoker watched Jessica jump out of the rental car. She flipped her hair back, put on her sunglasses, and started to walk nonchalantly toward the parking garage.

Stoker pulled over and decided to wait, just in case the Suburban exited from the garage. Rivera drove his rental car around the corner and watched the other side of the building. Ahmadi was listening to other FBI agents through an earpiece. "We've got two cars with agents circling," she explained.

Stoker's phone vibrated, and Z's phone number appeared on

the caller ID. "What's up Z?"

Z was breathing heavily. "This guy I'm following." Z paused to catch his breath for a moment. "He did *not* get on a train." Again, Z breathed for a few seconds. "These guys really like to run, because I'm following this guy down the street. Staying about forty yards behind him."

"You're running after him?"

"Yes."

"Why is that a problem? You're in great shape."

"Because he had shorts on under his pants. He stripped off his sweatpants in a park. And, the shoes he was wearing are running shoes."

"And you're wearing combat boots and jeans?"

"Exactly—skinny jeans."

Stoker's face winced. "Now that's going to chafe."

"Going to chafe?" Z replied with some indignation in his voice. "Oh no. This is not a future event." His voice was elevating. "The chaffing is happening *now*. Major chaffing!"

Stoker's empathy for Z's discomfort clashed with his desire to laugh at the unexpected chain of events. "Stay on that guy. I'll write you a prescription for some cream and a topical painkiller later. Then tonight, we can call your mommy. You can tell her all about it."

"Okay, Stoker. Now's *not* the time to play your reverse psychology mind tricks. I've got a country to save. In response to President Kennedy's question about what I can do for my country? I can chafe like hell as I run through the streets of Chicago." Then Z ended the call.

Finally, Stoker could laugh. "Hey Rivera," he said through the radio. "Z just called me."

"Really? What did he say?"

That guy he's following did *not* get on a train. He had running shorts on under his pants. He took off his pants in a park and started running as if he were just out for his daily jog."

"So, we've got a group of Shiite terrorists, Rivera said. "Two have broken off from the rest. We suspect one got on a train. Another arrives in Chicago and decides to go for a run? We are very close to the hornet's nest."

"Okay," Stoker said. "But, while we're waiting let me share one other part to this story."

"What's that?"

"Z is still chasing him."

Rivera emitted a short huffing laugh. "In combat boots and denim jeans, no less." Then he chuckled. "That's going to chafe like Richard Simmons working out in a wetsuit."

"On amphetamines," Stoker interjected.

"I think we may have another piece of the puzzle," Rivera said. "I've got another of our tangos exiting the parking garage on my side of the building. This one's on foot." Rivera paused for a moment. "And he's getting in a taxi."

After a brief crackle, Jessica's voice came over the radio. "I'm coming down the parking garage stairs quick. I never saw that guy in the parking garage. I'll be exiting out to the street in ten seconds."

"Hang back Jessica," Rivera said. "If you exit onto the street right now, they'll know you're following them."

"I'll follow the taxi," Rivera said. You go get in Stoker's car with him and Ahmadi. But, wait for that Suburban to come out of the garage before you make your move."

Rivera drove away, following fifty yards behind the taxi. Jessica jumped into the silver sedan. "What's next? Is someone going to jump on a bicycle?" she joked.

Stoker smiled. "After that, we'll have an Iranian riding a horse down the street."

"Then the horse just may be a Caspian," Ahmadi interjected from the back seat, taking advantage of the humor in the air. They were waiting for the Suburban to emerge, and the wit let them blow off some steam.

Jessica turned around and exchanged introductions with Sarah Ahmadi.

"Is Caspian a horse breed?"

"Yes. Caspians are small horses. Almost as small as ponies. They're popular in Iran."

"Explain to Jessica how you know so much about Iranian horses," Stoker suggested.

"My parents are Iranian, and we spoke Farsi in our home growing up. We remained in contact with our family in Iran. And, with the advent of social media, I'm in touch with my cousins, aunts, and uncles there more than ever. I even visited Iran during my college years."

"Did you like it?" Stoker asked.

"I loved the sights, the sounds—even the smells walking through the open-air markets. I love the people."

"I've never been to Iran," Stoker said, "but the Iranian people are a dynamic mixture of intelligence, strength, and warmth. I wish most Americans understood that."

"It's the leaders of Iran that get all the headlines," Ahmadi said. "The Ayatollahs oppress the people and do a lot of international saber rattling. They do not reflect the will of most of the people, who dream of a peaceful world."

Just then the Suburban came out of the parking garage. Stoker, Jessica, and Ahmadi followed. After a few turns on the streets of Chicago, the Suburban veered onto a freeway entrance ramp and accelerated quickly. It merged onto the freeway and promptly swerved over into the left passing lane. Then the Suburban sped up to eighty-five miles per hour.

"They're driving like maniacs to see if anyone is following them," Stoker said. I'm going to stay back and drive with traffic. We can rely on the tracker that Z placed at the gas station. Try to keep eyes on them as long as you can, Jessica."

"I've lost them," she said.

"Me too," Stoker admitted as he accelerated a little. "It's a good thing the tracker can keep track of a needle in a haystack."

But three minutes later, traffic on the freeway had slowed considerably. Stoker, Jessica, and Ahmadi were able to pull up ten cars behind the terrorists. After following for a little while, the Suburban left the freeway and drove into an older neighborhood. Suddenly, the large vehicle pulled over and parked. Four men jumped out of the car. They all departed in different directions.

"It looks like we've got four choices," Jessica said to Ahmadi. "Rivera taught us to always follow the toughest looking one." Jessica pointed at a guy with broad shoulders and a steely look. "There's my mark."

Ahmadi pointed at another of the men. "I'll follow him. I know that guy. He's an Iranian the FBI's been keeping tabs on for a couple of years. We'll just have to let the other two slip away." They let the terrorists get a little further down the sidewalk. Then Jessica and Ahmadi exited the rental car and casually walked down the sidewalk as if they didn't have a care in the world. Yet, the safety of the free world was riding on their shoulders.

CHAPTER 19

Chicago, Illinois

Roya waited a few blocks from Hotel Esatto, at a bus stop. She had no intention of boarding a bus. But, the location was ideal for the task at hand. She looked down at an iPad as if she were watching something amusing on it. She pretended to direct all her attention to the entertaining device.

"That's what these Americans do now," Nikolas had explained to her when he gave her the iPad. "They engage with their devices, staring endlessly into screens—so entertained they never consider the need for Allah in their lives."

In truth, Roya was watching an icon on a map, making its way closer and closer to her. They had attached a GPS tracker to each of their new men traveling from Iran via Mexico. In a few minutes, an Iranian combatant would arrive and complete his long journey to Chicago. The man had been instructed to watch for an Iranian woman wearing the hijab. He would recognize her because her dress would be green, the same green as the stripe atop the Iranian flag. And, her hijab would be the same color of red that graced the bottom color band on the flag. She wore this outfit to direct the men arriving at the Chicago safe house. When they recognized her, they were trained to ignore her and keep traveling down the street to a modest red brick building. They would enter and meet a security guard on the ground floor. They had strict instructions to tell the security guard they were here to see a Mr. Ramsey for a job interview. They were to speak Spanish. The security guard would ask them which position they were interviewing for. "Biohazard engineer," was always their answer.

From there, a secretary would emerge and accompany the man back to the supposed offices. But, this structure was not offices. The space was a very temporary safe house that would shelter the terrorists for a few hours. There they altered their identities, ate, and rested. Today, the Shiite men had accomplished a significant milestone. Now they were here, in position to execute a silent strike against the United States of America.

Roya watched the icon approaching on the iPad map she was monitoring. When he arrived, their eye contact was ever so brief, before the man disappeared into the red brick building. Roya was sure nobody was following this man. He had arrived by train and then walked the few blocks to the safe house. The next man would appear on foot, posing as a metropolitan jogger. Judging by his icon on the map, he was still more than three kilometers away.

Fifteen minutes later, she saw the runner from Yemen. The man was incredibly handsome. The defined musculature in his powerful legs caught her attention. *Never should good Muslim men be allowed to wear shorts—let alone such short ones*, she thought. Roya quickly toggled the iPad to the Koran and began reading passages to cleanse her mind of her lustful thoughts. When she eventually glanced up, their eyes met for that brief moment. Suddenly an infatuation besieged Roya. It was a forbidden lust she had never experienced. Yes, she had had a few crushes in her young life. But, this was a new depth of desire, to meet a man, to know his heart, and to share hers, in hopes they would intertwine in a holy union. Yes, that was it. Her thoughts assumed a pure, hallowed union. Her musings were not unclean after all. Perhaps it was the hand of Allah who prompted her desires. This unknown man, posing as a jogger, would undoubtedly feel something similar soon. Roya looked back at the iPad, but her mind was replaying the new memories of a man, who shared her convictions, running down a street in Chicago. She was so distracted by her passionate feelings she did not see Z who followed behind the man. Had she been paying attention, it would've been easy to notice him, in his military boots and jeans, also running down the streets of Chicago—a sight out of place in the summer heat. She sent a quick text to her bosses reporting how two men had arrived, and she had not seen anyone following them.

When Z saw the Yemeni enter the red brick building, he ducked around a corner where he bent over and gasped for breath. The skin on his inner thighs was past feeling. After a few seconds, his heart rate started to slow, and the burning in his lungs diminished. His thirst was overwhelming from the run, so he bought some Gatorade. Then he decided to find a place where he could watch the red brick building and the door where he had last seen the tango.

After considering a coffee shop, a pharmacy, and office building, he settled on a bookstore. He purchased a copy of the latest novel featuring the character Mitch Rapp. Then, he walked up the stairs to the second floor and began to look like he was reading the book. He had a good view of the door. And, for a few minutes, nobody entered or exited the building. He made mental notes about the people he saw on the street. Among the hundreds of individuals, Z noticed a young woman who was wearing a red hijab while she waited for a bus. He took out his cell phone and tapped out a message to Jessica, Rivera, Ahmadi, and Stoker.

> *My mark entered a building on State Street near cross street Elm Street. Surveilling from the bookstore on the second floor.*

A few seconds later his phone vibrated. He answered the incoming call. "Hello."

It was Rivera. "I'm following this taxi in a car, but I can't follow my mark and find you on a map. Can you help me navigate?"

"Sure," Z said. He spoke softly to avoid drawing attention to himself. "I'll reel you in. Where are you?"

"I'm on LaSalle Drive. I just crossed Huron Street."

"As the crow flies you're less than a half mile from me. I bet your taxi comes my way."

"Agreed," Rivera said. "Stay on the phone with me, and let's see what happens."

Z and Rivera kept talking as Rivera followed the taxi that had picked up the terrorist at the shopping mall. Rivera passed Superior Street and Chicago Avenue. "The taxi just pulled over. I think this guy's getting out."

"My bet is he's going to walk to this same red-brick building. Why don't you hang back and see if I'm right?"

"Okay. Keep your eyes open for this guy."

"I'll recognize him. He's one of the guys we've been watching for weeks."

Three minutes later, Z saw him. He came walking down State Street at a quick pace. From his birds-eye view, Z watched as the tango approached the red brick building. Just before he made it to the door, he noticed the man make brief eye contact with the woman at the bus stop. As the man walked through the door, Z turned to look at the young woman at the bus stop. There she sat, interacting with an iPad. *She's been sitting there for too long to be waiting for a bus*, he thought. She was part of the process of embedding these terrorists into a cell here in the United States. Z made a mental note to discover more about this puzzling woman.

While most special operators or soldiers would have their pants' pockets full of weapons, survival equipment, and first aid gear, Z was a technology enthusiast. His pockets contained digital antennas, a small iPad, power sources, and cables. Most importantly for this moment, he possessed a button-sized camera. The instant he activated this dime-sized high-tech device, it started transmitting audio and video to a cloud server.

Z attached the device to his left earlobe, so it looked like an earring. Then he walked downstairs, exited the bookstore, and made his way to the bus stop. There Z pretended to wait for a bus, while he looked at his phone. The camera hanging from his ear pointed at Roya. Z captured a few minutes of footage of her while two more busses passed. Z got a text from Jessica.

> *My mark just exited a train two blocks from your location.*

Z texted her back.

> *I'm @ bus stop. Hang back until I get on a bus. Then watch the woman in the red hijab. She's your new mark.*

A few minutes later, another Iranian man passed Roya. Z's camera captured their brief eye contact. Then he considered his situation and decided not to take any more chances and risk raising the woman's suspicion. He jumped on the next bus that passed. He rode it for two blocks before he exited and started backtracking.

From thirty yards away, Jessica now watched her mark, this Iranian woman with a red headscarf. Over twenty minutes, she saw three more terrorists arrive. They walked past the woman, made ever-so-brief eye contact, and entered the red brick building. After the last man arrived, Roya stood and started to walk away.

Jessica followed her from twenty yards. She picked up her phone and called Z, which helped her mix into the crowd of walkers, many of whom were also using their phones for any number of activities. When Z answered, Jessica told him what was going on.

"This woman and I are walking toward you, Z. Can you try to stay ahead of her?"

"Yes," Z replied. "Let's see where she goes."

Roya's pace picked up. Every thirty seconds she would stop and look over her shoulder. Jessica stayed well out of sight and remained undetected.

Z saw her coming down the sidewalk toward him. He picked up his pace and remained ahead of her by twenty to thirty yards until Roya suddenly changed course.

"Come back Z," Jessica said through the phone. "She just ducked into the gym you passed. I'll enter first in case I see her making a beeline for the dressing room."

"Yes," Z replied. "You get dressing room duty."

When Jessica entered the gym, she didn't see Roya, so she walked toward the central workout area. The next thing Jessica saw made her feel vulnerable. She had nowhere to hide. The gym's main wall was a huge mirror. It made it impossible for anyone entering the gym to go unnoticed.

Look natural, Jessica told herself as she walked toward the dressing rooms. She still had Z on the phone. "Hang back and don't hang up, Z. I'm going to leave us connected but put my phone in my pocket." As she walked, she used her peripheral vision to locate Roya. The Iranian woman was pretending to work out by lifting some light dumbbells. Jessica could not be sure, but she thought Roya was watching her. Jessica guessed this gym was probably a pre-planned location this woman had chosen, where it would be possible for people following her to walk into a trap of detection. This woman in the red hijab was surely observing everybody who walked through the door, memorizing their faces.

When Jessica got into the dressing room, she picked up her phone again and continued the conversation with Z. "I'm in the dressing room now. She's on the left-hand side of the gym lifting dumbbells. That whole wall is a huge mirror. If you enter, there will be nowhere to hide. She briefly noticed me, and she will see you."

"What do you want me to do?" Z asked.

"Wait outside. Be ready in case she leaves. You could follow her."

"Roger that," Z said.

Jessica waited for three more minutes. Then she walked out of the dressing room and walked over to the membership desk. She struck up a conversation with the person there under the pretenses of joining the gym. From her peripheral vision, Jessica noticed how Roya continued to monitor the door, the people in the gym, and her surroundings. When she felt somewhat reassured nobody had followed her, Roya put down the dumbbells and walked toward the back of the gym. She looked at a treadmill as if she was considering using it. But suddenly, she slipped through a door labeled "Employees Only."

Jessica felt conflicted. She didn't want to lose this mysterious woman wearing the hijab. But, she also knew it was more important to avoid detection. Jessica chose to let the mystery woman go. She picked up her phone again. "Z, she just went through an employee only door. I bet she's sneaking out the back."

"I'll see if I can find an alley to the back," he replied.

"I would not go down the alley."

"No," Z replied. "I'm just putting myself in position, in case she comes out an alley and onto the sidewalk again."

Jessica turned to the person at the membership desk. "Do you have a blank piece of paper?"

"Yes," said the gym employee as she removed a simple plain white piece of paper from a printer. She slid it to Jessica along with a pen.

"Thank you. I'm such a visual person. If I draw the gym, I'll understand it better." Jessica made a rough sketch of the gym. "I see the weights here and the cardio area over here. Do you have classes?"

"Yes," replied the employee. She pointed to a place on Jessica's rough building blueprint. Jessica filled it in and labeled it as a classroom.

"Now, I admit I'm a little obsessive-compulsive, but I'm kind of paranoid about fires, earthquakes, and other natural disasters. Where are your fire exits?"

The employee pointed to the main door and then a place representing the very back of the gym.

"In the event of a fire, do we go through those 'Employee Only' doors?"

"Yes, they lead to a back alleyway."

"And, where does it go?"

It will take you to the north or the south.

"Oh," Jessica replied. "Nothing to the east?"

"Not unless you plan to go through the back entrance of Hotel Esatto."

Jessica laughed. "I'm sure they would *really* love that." She had never heard of Hotel Esatto, but she pretended to be familiar with it. "Those Esatto people wouldn't like me trying to use that back door."

The gym employee smiled. "They're weird over there. There's a loading dock and employee entrance back there. And they have super tight security on that loading dock. A security guard behind a bullet-proof glass window monitors and controls all the comings and goings back there. We're all wondering why getting into the service entrance to Hotel Esatto is nearly an airport TSA experience."

"Just a second," Jessica said turning away. She picked up her phone and spoke to Z, who she had kept on the line.

"She's either leaving through an alley. It leads north or south. Behind this gym, there is a hotel. But, it sounds like the back entrance is kept very secure. I doubt she figured out a way to breach that hotel's security.

"I'll head north," Z said. Let's see if I can detect her coming out of the alley."

"I'll go south," Jessica said. "But, I'm going to remain well-hidden. If she sees me again, she and the other tangos would know somebody followed them all the way from Mexico.

"Don't worry, Jessica. I got some pictures of the woman. We'll find her again. Losing your mark isn't so bad nowadays. Thanks to technology, it's tough to stay lost."

• • •

Inside Hotel Esatto, Roya walked to the housekeeping

department. She felt satisfied nobody had followed the latest soldiers arriving from Mexico. How wrong she was. She had no idea she'd been tracked for about an hour now. Nor did she know she had also managed to slip away from her pursuers. Jessica had not registered in her mind as a person of concern.

Roya was thrilled. So many of her Iranian compatriots had finally made it to Chicago, along with some men from Yemen and Lebanon. This last group was a select group of technicians who just might help her scale her attacks, yet again.

Roya quickly changed into a kitchen uniform. Then she returned to the service hallways of Hotel Esatto and walked toward the kitchen. After cutting through a back corner of the kitchen, she walked to a loading dock, exited the hotel, and climbed into a catering van. Tonight, Hotel Esatto was catering a rehearsal dinner. Before she pulled away from the loading dock, she entered the location of the event into her phone's navigation app. The phone spoke to her in Farsi. Roya followed the directions, pulled out into Chicago's busy traffic, and blended in with the masses.

• • •

Agent Sarah Ahmadi leaped out of the car and followed the Iranian man. While she had never met him in person, she knew about this man, Yosef Ali Nazem. When she saw him emerge from the black Suburban, she immediately volunteered—no she insisted—on following him.

Homeland Security had been keeping tabs on him for more than two years, and she had reviewed his dossier. He had legally entered and exited Mexico and Iran many times over the last twenty-four months. Why Nazem chose to cross the U.S.-Mexico border illegally this time, with this group of men, was a mystery to Ahmadi. Sure, Agent Ahmadi had enough information on Nazem to arrest him immediately. She could detain him on the simple crime of illegal entry into the United States. But, arresting him would do more harm than good. If the FBI took him into custody, the rest of his network would notice. The other Shiites would likely respond by going deeper underground.

No, Ahmadi would follow the man. She would track him as far as she could. She would know where he went, expose his conspirators, and blow the lid off his center of operations.

Ahmadi followed Nazem on foot for about a mile, trailing from a distance of thirty yards. Then he entered the Cicero train station. Cautiously, Ahmadi ascended a few stairs onto the train platform while paying close attention to her phone. With a quick glance, she inventoried about twenty people, including Nazem, waiting for the train. She eased back behind the crowd, where she could continue to glance at him from time to time. Ahmadi had her cell phone at her side. For a brief moment, when he looked over his shoulder, she pointed the phone up a bit and snapped a quick photo. When the train arrived, Nazem jumped on quickly. Ahmadi entered the car behind him, but she kept her gaze on the platform. Suddenly, as the train's doors were about to close, Nazem jumped out of the train back onto the platform. He'd just used the train as a means of doubling back so he could identify who might be following him. Ahmadi fought her instincts to jump out of the train and expose herself as a tail. The doors closed, and the train pulled away. Yosef Ali Nazem's caution paid off as the FBI agent was whisked away on Chicago public transit.

Ahmadi texted Stoker and attached the image of Nazem.

I lost my guy at the Cicero train station. He jumped out of the train at the last second. Here's his picture. His name's Nazem.

A few seconds later came Stoker's reply.

The next train's in 8 minutes. I can make it.

Stoker followed his phone's voice prompts to the Cicero train station, where Nazem would be waiting to board a train for the second time. He parked a quarter mile away. A short jog got him there with two minutes before the train's departure. By the time he ascended the train platform, he heard the train approaching. The timing worked out well for Stoker. He merely slipped in behind people who were starting to inch toward the train tracks. He had not yet spotted Nazem, so he decided to stroll toward the front end of the platform. As the train pulled up, Stoker pretended to pay slight attention to lining up with the location where a door may stop. Using his peripheral vision, he caught a glimpse of Nazem about fifteen feet away. But, he never turned toward the Iranian or looked at him directly.

When the train stopped, exiting passengers stepped off. Stoker blended in by following the people in front of him onto the train. Once aboard, he remained standing and took out his phone to send a text to update Ahmadi. Halfway through the message, he took a quick glance toward the front of the train car. Nazem was surveying the other passengers. Stoker pretended to pay particular attention to his phone as he finished the text. He knew Nazem couldn't go far while the train was in motion.

As they arrived at the next stop, Stoker glanced toward the front of the train and watched people start to exit. Nazem stepped out of the train, so Stoker moved toward the door and stepped out. He glanced toward the platform to find Nazem, but just in time to see the Iranian jump back on the train. Stoker just continued walking. He relaxed his face muscles to remove any appearance of surprise or disappointment from his expression. But inside Stoker was incensed. This Iranian was able to give him the slip. He quickly called Ahmadi. "I lost him."

"That's okay," replied Ahmadi. "I hid behind a column at the train station where you are. I slipped undetected into the rear train car."

"Excellent," Stoker said. "He's in the front train car. How do you know this guy?"

"I've never met him, but I know all about him. Homeland Security's been watching him for two years. I've seen his file. He's been back and forth between Mexico and Tehran many times. The group you witnessed as it crossed the border is a group of science technicians. But, this guy is not only a scientist, but he's also a well-trained soldier. He *really* knows his stuff when it comes to espionage."

"I'm thrilled our work in Mexico is paying off," Stoker said.

"You caught a pretty big fish there on the banks of the Rio Grande, Stoker. I'm excited we've got this guy in our sights. But if everyday Americans knew he was here, they would be terrified."

Ahmadi did not leave a moment for Stoker to speak. "The train is slowing down; I suspect for another stop. Let's see what happens." Ahmadi and Stoker were silent but stayed connected to the call. Ahmadi's voice came back. "He stayed on."

"Good," Stoker said. "I'll catch the next train, in case he tries any theatrics."

Ahmadi stayed on the call with Stoker for three more stops. At the next stop, Ahmadi saw Nazem exit the train. "There he goes. I'm following him." The man exited the train and walked hastily toward the exit. "He somehow changed his clothes," Ahmadi explained. "It looks like he's in dress pants and a tuxedo shirt. He's also sporting a bowtie like he is going to some fancy event." She followed behind Nazem with at least a dozen pedestrians between them. He jogged down the stairs to the street. He found a garbage can near a newspaper stand and dropped a plastic bag into it. "He just dropped a bag in a garbage can," Ahmadi explained. "I'm going to keep following him. It's the blue garbage can. When you exit the train, veer off from the front of the train, and go down the stairs. It's right by the newspaper stand at the base of the stairs."

"Roger that," Stoker said. "I'm jumping on the next train in about thirty seconds."

Ahmadi followed Nazem. She anticipated he might double back at any moment to detect anyone who followed him, so she crossed the street and kept pace with him from the other side of the road. At one point, he turned around quickly and retraced his steps for forty-five seconds. Satisfied nobody was following him, he turned around again and resumed his intended route. For thirty minutes Ahmadi tailed him loosely as he took a couple of wild turns. She called Stoker again and explained where she was.

"Can you come help me? If anyone is watching him, they will discover I'm tailing him. Can you take a turn?"

"I'll be there ASAP," Stoker said holding up his hand to hail a taxi. "Stay on the phone with me. I just jumped in a taxi. Now, where is this?"

"I'm on Ogden Avenue, going south. It looks like there's a place called Union Park up ahead. Aim for that.

Stoker held out fifty dollars to the taxi driver. "Union Park please, on the Ogden Avenue side. Let's step on it."

The taxi driver took the money and thanked Stoker. Then the

taxi was off. Stoker oriented himself on the map on his phone. "I found Union Park. Where are you from there?"

"North on Ogden Avenue, about three blocks," Ahmadi replied.

"Gotcha. I'm guessing I'll be there in about three minutes."

"Okay. I'm going to take a considerable risk, Stoker. I'm going to turn two blocks before the park. If someone's tailing me, my exit may convince them the route I shared with Nazem—." Her voice went silent. Stoker waited and listened. He could hear the noises of the street coming through the phone. After about ten seconds, Ahmadi's voice returned. He just doubled back and was coming straight toward me."

"Did he see you?"

"Yes. But, I did not make eye contact with him. He was certainly looking at every face he passed. It's the first time he's seen me, so I need to make sure he doesn't see me again."

"Okay, I'm almost to Union Park," Stoker said.

"Uh-oh. Change of plans," Ahmadi said. "He turned west on Fulton Street. So why don't you aim for Fulton and Justine."

Stoker revised the drop-off site with his driver. As they approached the intersection, Stoker gave the cabbie instructions to drop him off a little shy of the location. Stoker got out and walked up to the intersection of Fulton and Justine and turned right. Across the street, he saw his man. Nazem was walking in the opposite direction as Stoker, and Stoker started contemplating how to change course and fall in behind him. But, Nazem passed through the doors of a building.

Stoker intentionally slowed the pace of his aggressive stride. It required some discipline to restrain his usual dynamic vigor. He contemplated his next move as he walked across the street and slipped into an alleyway that led to the back of the building Nazem had entered. As Stoker turned down the alleyway, he saw Nazem jump into a white van. He advanced close enough to the terrorist to hear him speaking in Farsi with a woman, a driver. She also appeared to be of Iranian descent. Stoker quickly turned on the video recorder on his phone and proceeded in their direction. Navigating the van into the alleyway, the woman turned the automobile toward Stoker, who just kept walking. He ignored the van as if he were aloof about it. But, his phone was recording as Nazem and Roya passed. Once they were behind him, Stoker looked at the movie he'd made on his cellphone hoping he captured a reasonable frame of the license plate.

The van turned a corner and was gone. Stoker called Ahmadi. "Nazem got in a van at the back of a building on Fulton Street. He was a passenger, and there was a woman. I bet she was Iranian. I captured a brief video clip."

"Sounds good. Let's see if we can find out who owns that van. I'll have Z set up an on-the-spot phone conference, and we'll invite the whole team to call in."

Two minutes later, Rivera, Jessica, and Z had joined the phone call. They each reported their individual experiences. Rivera yielded the leadership role to Stoker who summarized. "We have terrorists entering the red brick building. Ahmadi will go with the FBI and pursue that lead. I'll send everyone the video I took of Nazem and this woman in the white van. Z will share the movie he made of that woman at the bus stop. Ahmadi will have the FBI crime lab analyze all of this, along with Nazem's clothes from the garbage bag at the train station.

We'll all need some shuteye, while we're also making twenty-four, seven progress on this investigation. So, a sleep schedule will benefit everyone. And, Rivera and I are going to loop the CDC back into what we've got going on here."

"That should be interesting," Rivera said. "I think we may finally have enough information to wake up the CDC."

CHAPTER 20

Chicago, Illinois

Even before Stoker and Rivera could place a call to the Centers for Disease Control, Stoker's cell phone rang. "Now this is interesting. It's a 404 area code," Stoker said with a wry smile. "Atlanta."

"That's got to be the Office of Public Health Preparedness at the CDC, calling from somewhere behind the eight ball. My money's on Dr. Kaitlyn Steele, complete with a new attitude. I'll bet Agent Ahmadi and the FBI have rattled the right cages. I'm looking forward to this call."

Stoker answered the phone on the fourth ring. "You're on speaker phone with Rivera and Stoker."

"Hello, Doctors. I'm so glad I caught you both." As predicted, it was Steele. Her tone was friendly and upbeat. "Your story checks out. The data is overwhelming. We'll take it from here."

"I agree," Stoker said as he gave Rivera a wink and a nod. "We'll *all* take it from here."

Rivera could not help but rub salt in Steele's wounds. "The FBI is way out ahead on this one. They've already activated their Weapons of Mass Destruction Directorate. Is that who called you?"

"Yes, and I'm co-chairing a task force—

"Task force? We don't need a task force growled Stoker as he held his finger over the call disconnect button. Just before he pushed it, he said, "This is a war, and we're here on the battlefield. Try to keep up, Director."

• • •

"Ah, Roya. It is so nice to see you," Nikolas said as she entered his office. "You have brought great honor to our cause. Your attacks are starting to afflict the Great Satan. There will be millions who suffer. Then, one day soon, you shall rise for your morning prayers, and you will hear the terror in some random American news reporter's anxious voice describing how our attacks have killed a million. Or, perhaps it will be a zealous Muslim brother who whispers it to you with elation in his voice. Then you will look to the East and new strength—the Caliphate emerging. You will look to the West and see America in chaos. The sun shall rise that day on Tehran."

"I've never been there," Roya said. She always thirsted for his extravagant accolades. "I am only a peasant, blessed to do the will of Allah."

"You shall see Tehran! You will be revered there as a hero, perhaps a new princess of Persia. You shall be adorned in fine silks and eat of the fat of the lamb. Your gardens will overflow."

"No, I am just a simple girl who lives to serve Allah. I desire no opulence or adornment. All my needs are surpassed. I am still overwhelmed as I walk through this pristine hotel."

"Are you conflicted, Roya? Does it give you pause while you wonder how we can exist here in this beautiful building while our brothers and sister live in poverty and distress in other parts of the world?"

"Forgive me. I do not want to appear doubtful or ungrateful. But, yes. The Koran teaches, 'And the slaves of God are those who walk on the earth in humility and calmness.' I wonder why it is okay for me to partake in the bounty of this corrupt land enjoying conveniences and pleasures not available to so many."

"I applaud your thoughtfulness. These are noble inquiries borne of a quest to do the will of Allah. He has answered your humility." Nikolas could see how his honeyed words mesmerized her. Yet again, he fanned Roya's yearning for attention and praise while also fanning her fanaticism with his pretended belief in Islam. This is how he always manipulated her into doing anything. "The Prophet once said, 'And no one humbles himself before God but God will raise him.' Allah has raised you."

Roya's eyes relaxed. She said nothing, so Nikolas continued. "Let me tell you a story. When I was a little boy in Iran, before I left for Greece, my sisters kept chickens. They started with two hens and one rooster. One spring, we allowed some of their eggs to develop to maturity. Four of those eggs hatched. With seven chickens, our inventory was too large. So, we sold two and kept two.

A few months later, one of our chickens matured; and it turned out he was a rooster. We already had a rooster. And, in the world of chickens, there is never room for two roosters. So, my father instructed me to kill a rooster.

Well, I had not ever had any interest in my sisters' chickens. I had never gained the animals' trust. Coincidentally, catching the rooster was very hard. Impossible as a matter of fact. So, I started endearing this rooster to me. I would feed it special treats. I would never share the treats with the hens. Within two days, I won him over. After all the pampering and special treatment, he trusted me enough to sit on my shoulder.

"Do you know what happened next?"

"Yes. You killed the rooster."

"The same hour he trusted me enough to roost on my shoulder, he went willingly to the chopping block."

"This hotel is the chopping block," Roya said.

"Yes," Nikolas slowly nodded and allowed a slight smile to grace his face. "Within the next few days, yes. But, at this exact moment, all these trusting Americans are the proverbial roosters standing on our shoulders and trusting us. Hotel Esatto is the fishing lure, the bear trap, the Venus flytrap, —"

"The center of the spider's web." Roya had interrupted him for the first time ever. Nikolas did not mind.

"Exactly."

• • •

"Okay, Boss," Rivera said to Stoker. "What's our next move?"

"We're going to invest our time and energy into our ongoing work with the FBI," Stoker said. "So, we need to give this investigation everything we've got. Let's pull the team together, regroup, and execute."

Thirty minutes later Stoker, Rivera, Ahmadi, Jessica, and Z assembled in a conference room at the FBI Chicago Field Office. Two other members of the JTTF joined on a speakerphone.

Stoker led out. "Okay, people let's put pieces together. First, I have this video." Stoker projected the video he had made of the white van as it passed him, just a few hours before, in the alley behind a wedding center.

"That's Nazem, in the passenger's seat," Ahmadi said.

"I know that driver," Z said recognizing Roya. "She's the woman I observed at the bus stop. She was a visual contact for the unknown tangos when they made their on-foot arrivals in Chicago. Her presence directed them to the red brick building."

As the video ended, Ahmadi asked Stoker to pause it. "What's the license plate number?"

Stoker only needed to zoom in a little, and he read it off. Ahmadi used her laptop computer to enter this plate number into the National Crime Information Center database. "That van belongs to Hotel Esatto here in Chicago."

Jessica chimed in. "Which is right behind the gym where that Iranian woman, the driver on your video, gave us the slip."

"There are no coincidences," Stoker said.

"What are you referring to, Troy?" Rivera asked.

"Mexico and Chicago are linked," Stoker said. "We need to check out this Hotel Esatto. Allie's staying at another hotel nearby. She's here working on a project in Chicago. I'll join her tonight and look for an excuse to walk to Hotel Esatto and look around. Rivera, Ahmadi, and Z should check into Hotel Esatto. But, not all at once. You should all book your reservations through different websites, so our arrivals don't appear orchestrated." Turning to Jessica, Stoker gave her different instructions. "You should stay in a different hotel close by. We need another set of eyes, besides mine, that is on the outside looking in. Find one and get checked in."

Ahmadi changed the subject and spoke up. "I'll have some of my agents find out about the red brick building. They can snoop around to find ownership and occupant information for that property."

"I'll find out exactly who owns that building, right now," Z said as he started typing on his laptop.

Stoker pointed toward Rivera and said, "While Z looks up that data, let's have Dr. Rivera bring us up to speed on the CDC."

"Thanks to Agent Ahmadi, the CDC is finally on board. Let's see if they can keep up."

Ahmadi chimed in. "I informed the FBI Weapons of Mass

Destruction Directorate about your findings. They sent three of their agents to investigate in Mexico. And four agents have just arrived here in Chicago."

"We're not waiting for that bureaucracy, the CDC," Rivera said. "We're already using some of our contacts at Military Health System to make phone calls to the most highly qualified reservist physicians. They are also reaching out to retired military doctors with specific expertise in advising the dissemination of disease information to particular tertiary care situations. These are not the usual slow CDC protocols. These are well-connected docs who know the most effective ways to get this information out to other medical professionals on the front lines of care. If the powers that be at the CDC don't like our methods, to hell with them. They can't censor us or stop us from communicating this vital information. Infectious disease specialists and neurologists are the highest priority. We're reading them in on the weaponized Campylobacter jejuni and its ridiculously high rate of Guillain-Barre syndrome.

"We're probably a day away from the CDC activating the Armed Forces Physicians Control Group for emergency duty. With the help of our new friend, Governor Horton of South Dakota, we also secured some money from a few extremely wealthy private donors to ramp up the supply of intravenous immunoglobulin and bag valve masks. We've got military brass getting involved as well. Making plasma exchange more available to millions of Americans is a high priority. This disease is coming with a vengeance. We just want to do everything we can to minimize Americans' symptoms and keep as many people off ventilators as possible."

Z spoke up. "Let me tell you about the red brick building. It contains a large Airbnb unit, where these combatants could sleep. It was rented out under the fake name of some Joe Blow ostensibly from Miami, Florida."

"How did you find that information?" Ahmadi asked Z.

"Why do you ask such questions?" Z responded.

Ahmadi realized Z had hacked the information out of a supposedly secure system. She looked him directly in the eye. "Ok, Z. From this point on, I only want to know the information. I won't ask about the source or how you got it. You get info, I use it. Now let's go balls to the walls and nail these bastards before they turn this country into a living hell. Let me take that information about the

Airbnb and have my people investigate it. Give us a few hours."

Agents from the FBI's Chicago field office used the next hours to do some checking with the owner of the Airbnb property. The Iranians had indeed spent one night at the unit. Their stay was paid for with a prepaid debit card. The FBI agents also spoke to the cleaning crew. Unfortunately, they had already cleaned thoroughly, leaving little evidence to examine. The FBI determined it would not be worth further investigation.

• • •

Rivera just smiled as he brought up a large screen. Only he and Stoker occupied the high-tech conference room within the FBI's Chicago field office. "I'm about to introduce you to a fascinating person in Boston. He's an Air Force guy with extraordinary technological skills in the world of military intelligence and space satellites. But, rather than explaining my friend, Mr. Bojangles, I think it's just best for you to experience him."

Rivera activated a speakerphone and dialed. Almost instantly Mr. Bojangles answered. "Colonel Rivera, sir."

"At ease Colonel Bojangles," Rivera said.

"Yes sir, Colonel Rivera!" Bojangles replied. "I am at ease."

Rivera responded with, "Okay. New rule. Call me Rivera."

"Okay, Rivera. Why are you calling me?" Bojangles asked.

Before Rivera could answer, Stoker covered the phone and whispered, "Answer his questions as succinctly as possible. Let him know you're working on an investigation that needs perfection or near perfection."

Rivera understood. His next statement proved it. "Because of your one hundred percent success rate at helping me find information with satellites."

Stoker gave him a nod of approval and covered the phone again. "Now tell him how vital he is in your quest for perfection in this endeavor."

Rivera continued talking. "I need a bullseye. Why do you think I'm calling you?"

"I'm listening," replied Mr. Bojangles.

"I'm here with Dr. Troy Stoker."

"I know of Doctor Stoker. Hello Dr. Stoker."

"Hi Colonel," Stoker said. "So how do you know me?"

"Please tell Rivera I know many people. And, can we get on with our business here? How can I be of service?"

"It's a pleasure, Colonel." Stoker did not know his real name, so he decided to let some time pass before using his strange nickname.

Rivera steered the conversation back. "We need to analyze any historical images our satellites captured at a hospital in Chihuahua, Mexico over the last couple of weeks."

"I can do that," Bojangles responded.

Rivera gave Mr. Bojangles more precise dates and times. He also explained how the CDC had sent a team down.

A few short minutes later, Stoker and Rivera were staring at giant screens in the Chicago FBI field office. They were reviewing satellite images Bojangles accessed in Massachusetts and shared via a telepresence platform. On the screen, Stoker and Rivera viewed overhead images of the hospital in Chihuahua.

"Here's when you arrive at the hospital." Bojangles showed them an image of Stoker's ambulance bringing him in for snakebite treatment. "Here's when you left." There was an image of Stoker and Rivera, about thirty feet from the main entrance to the hospital, walking away from the building."

Stoker looked over at Rivera and quietly said, "How does he get these images so quickly?"

"It's the Bojangles effect. I don't know how he does it. And, don't ask."

The men continued to watch image sequences. "We're looking for an exodus of patients, probably twelve or thirteen days ago, who would need to leave in ambulances," Stoker said. "They were all very sick, most on ventilators."

After a few minutes of indexing and searching, Bojangles found the images they were looking for. "This was thirteen days ago." They observed six patients leaving in ambulances. Three were in body bags. The other three were severe Guillain-Barre syndrome patients, close to death. Images showed these three patients being wheeled out to the ambulance bay on stretchers. The nurses were bagging them to help them breathe as they transferred the patients' care to EMTs.

"Wait," Stoker said. "Let's take a closer look at this image. Check out that person in the lower-right quadrant. I think it's someone pushing a wheelchair away from the hospital."

Bojangles zoomed in, and it took a moment for the image to render. But, when the picture sharpened, Rivera recognized one of the people immediately. "Good eye, Troy. That's the Iranian lab tech, the one you treated with your fist to correct his TMJ problem. And, he's pushing a female patient in that wheelchair. It looks like he's transporting her somewhere. Can you use the satellite image history to follow those two, Bojangles?"

"Watch this," he responded from Boston.

Stoker and Rivera watched different frames, each about ten seconds apart. The images captured the lab tech pushing the patient to an industrial building three blocks away from the hospital. "That building's a factory," Bojangles said. "According to my data, they manufacture windshields there."

In the next frame, the lab tech wheeled the patient through a roll-up garage door. The next frame showed the lab tech walking away with an empty wheelchair.

"There's your cover-up," Stoker said. "Now we know why the CDC investigators didn't find any Guillain-Barre syndrome patients. That image just showed how the Iranian lab tech simply delivered her to that building."

"He probably had a few patients to unload," Rivera said.

For the next twenty minutes, they watched more satellite-captured views. The days-old images showed a history of the lab technician taking more than a dozen patients to the windshield factory. "I hate to imagine what happened to those innocents in there," Stoker said. "I think that was the end of the road for those patients. We're watching images of a terrorist at work. Instead of the stereotypical madman who runs around with guns and bombs yelling 'Allahu Akbar,' he's quiet, cold, and calculating. He wears scrubs and brandishes silent weapons. Getting rid of those patients—the evidence—was his only aim. There are no survivors."

Bojangles started speaking as if Stoker had not said anything. His logic-driven personality was not sensitive to the empathy Stoker felt for the victims in Mexico. "After this point in time, our satellites rarely saw anybody leave that building on foot. Anyone who left seemed to be a factory worker." He pointed at the map and outlined a few adjoining buildings. "All of these buildings are connected. There were a few automobiles that came and went from this location, mostly delivery vehicles like box trucks and vans. The patients were probably removed from the windshield factory in one of those trucks."

Rivera nodded his head in agreement as he listened. Then he asked, "Do you have any other footage that provides clues?"

"Yes," Mr. Bojangles said. "Watch this. Here's more evidence of the cover-up."

Stoker and Rivera paid attention to the screen in front of them. They watched the lab tech working on the hospital loading dock. He was filling a panel truck with ventilators. Then the satellite images followed the truck to a large shipping distribution warehouse on the outskirts of Chihuahua. "He drops the ventilators off," Bojangles explained. "They enter this big building, and we can't track the ventilators any further. We can be pretty certain they were loaded up into a big eighteen-wheeler, but we don't know which one."

"The large distribution center has dozens of trucks loading or unloading at any given moment," Stoker pointed out.

"It would be hard to find out what happened with the ventilators," Bojangles said.

"Let's leave it to the FBI to decide if they would like to pursue this lead any further," Rivera said.

"Yes. It's time to assess our situation," Stoker said. "We've gotta fast forward to the here and now. What's the big picture? Thanks to Mr. Bojangles, we have a pretty good idea of what happened in Mexico. From now on, we need to concentrate on the Homeland, putting together the pieces of this horrific puzzle, and finding the right people to kneecap." Stoker paused for a moment. "Hey Bojangles, do you have a problem with that?"

"Absolutely not!"

• • •

Z checked into Hotel Esatto first. Ahmadi did the same about an hour later. The two met in the lobby and chose a secluded place to sit down and fire up their laptops. "It sounds like you fancy yourself a hacker?" Sarah Ahmadi asked Z. It was more of a statement than a question.

"I am an aficionado of everything tech. I love it all. Hardware, code, cables, Wi-Fi signals, automation. I love what it can do. And, if I need to occasionally use some code to get information critical to the nation's defense, I guess I'm an occasional hacker."

"Good," Ahmadi said. "Can you hack into their cameras here at Hotel Esatto so we can keep an eye on the place?"

"We could. But why hack, when you can create your own network of cameras?" Z asked. We can place tiny cameras outside the exits of the hotel and monitor who comes and goes."

"Good point. I guess do-it-yourself solutions are often best," Ahmadi said.

"Right. It's just not very fun."

"And it may *not* require a search warrant to sit here and do reconnaissance in the hotel," Ahmadi pointed out. "We've got probable cause with Nazem and that other woman leading us here."

"Let's meet back here in an hour," Z said. "I've got some hardware to install."

Z walked through the hotel's main doors to a busy Chicago street. Scanning down the sidewalk in front of Hotel Esatto, he identified his first target. A curbside United States Postal Service collection box would soon become the home base for a small device. As he walked past it, Z casually swiped the mailbox with his hand, adhering a button-sized camera with adhesive gel on the side. He walked thirty more feet down the sidewalk, fished his phone out of his pocket, and pretended he was getting a call. He stepped toward the post of a No Parking sign, leaned against it, and pretended to engage in the call. When he ostensibly finished, Z put his phone back in his pocket and used his hand to push off the signpost. As he pushed away, he deposited another small camera onto the post—this one at about chest height. Z repeated this process at two additional locations, adhering the small cameras so they could see people on foot entering and exiting the hotel's main doors. He also took notice of a planter out in front of the hotel, where he would place an infrared camera later that night under the canopy of darkness.

As Z was placing cameras, Sarah Ahmadi was walking

around and checking out Hotel Esatto. She was dressed in a smart business suit. In case an employee or guest were to ask, she was ready to pose as an IT security consultant from San Francisco. Ahmadi used glasses and some make-up alterations to transform her appearance. Because Roya had seen Ahmadi once, it was essential for her to remodel her look. The changes were sufficient to make it hard for an acquaintance to recognize her, but not so drastic she could've fooled family.

After Ahmadi had explored most of the hotel's public areas, she took her cell phone and laptop back to the main lobby. She ordered a sandwich, salad, and tangerine juice. She then took her food and sat down on a couch in a high traffic area of the hotel lobby. Ahmadi spread her food, phone, and computer on the coffee table before her. There she pretended to be engrossed in work on her computer screen. But, appearing fascinated was difficult, because the work on her display was not engaging. Her computer was networked into the cameras Z had set up. Sarah was watching people walk by on four different quadrants of her screen, and it was monotonous. Surveillance always was. Nevertheless, she was thrilled to be surveilling from the comfortable couch of a nice hotel. In her line of work, stakeout work often meant spending long hours in a car or van.

She also paid attention to all the people who walked by her on the inside of the hotel. For the next few hours, she pretended to be an overachiever. It came very natural. There Ahmadi camped out in the lobby of Hotel Esatto, ostensibly analyzing data, preparing a report, or doing whatever relentless business executives did to guarantee victory on the vast playing field of the corporate world.

By 10:30 p.m. Z had placed six more cameras outside. At 10:45 he redirected the camera feed to two computer monitors set up in Jessica's room—in a lower caliber hotel than Hotel Esatto. She would take the night shift. Z sent Ahmadi a text encouraging her to get some sleep.

The suggestion of sleep thundered through Ahmadi's mind. She realized she had not slept in a comfortable bed for a few days. She had not had eight hours of continuous sleep in over a week. She was ready for deep, refreshing slumber. At 11:20 p.m., Sarah Ahmadi was slumbering.

• • •

When Stoker told Allie he was staying in Chicago that night, his wife was thrilled. He did not often hear his stoic wife express so much enthusiasm. Later that night he met her in the lobby of her hotel. "Nice place," Stoker said feeling a little out of place in combat boots and black tactical pants.

Allie embraced him and kissed him warmly. "Let's get room service," she said. "I'm thrilled you're here. But, I'm not feeling so great."

"Really, Allie? What's wrong?" Troy took Allie by the hand. "I'm only concerned because, well. Let's just say that anything that makes Allie Stoker sick would land the average person in the hospital. It must be serious."

Allie smiled and issued a three-syllable chuckle. "I feel unusually fatigued. During my workout yesterday, I ran the path along Lakeshore Drive. My legs were just not themselves. They felt weak. Now I am feeling more exhausted than I have in a long time. I wonder if I'm coming down with a cold or one of those other pesky viruses."

"Any other symptoms?"

"No. I don't have a headache. I'm not nauseous. And, I really want to sleep."

"I'm drained, too. Let's hit the rack."

Forty-five minutes later Allie Stoker was asleep in the quiet comfort of a hotel room just four blocks from Hotel Esatto. But, Troy Stoker was awake and uneasy. The love of his life was showing early symptoms—the same symptoms he'd seen in Mexico.

• • •

An all too familiar discomfort awoke Sarah Ahmadi. She let out a huff of dismay, as she leaned up on an elbow and turned on the bedside lamp. Pulling back her covers, she looked down at her panties. She saw an unmistakable drop of menses blood. "Really?"

She complained out loud. "The first night I've had any reasonable chance at sleep, and I get my period." Ahmadi went into the bathroom and cleaned up a little. She didn't have any other pajamas, so she just draped on the robe bearing Hotel Esatto's logo. She picked up her phone, noted it was two fifteen a.m., and exited her room.

An elevator ride and a few more paces took her into the gift shop. There she bought a box of tampons. *Not my brand, but they'll do in a pinch*, she thought. She paid for the tampons and left the gift shop still in a bit of a sleepy fog. As she approached the lobby, the door to the women's bathroom opened. A woman exited the bathroom. The face she saw triggered the FBI veteran's fight or flight response. Adrenaline poured into her bloodstream. Her training helped her sublimate this adrenaline response into controlled thought and action. She made mental notes of the person with all the details she could capture. Her hijab, facial features, and name tag inscribed with "Roya" were all recorded in Ahmadi's memory. The FBI agent issued a subtle smile to this Roya woman, apparently a housekeeper at Hotel Esatto, and made brief eye contact. The woman they had been looking for just walked right past her. Roya issued the automated, polite nod and the rehearsed smile virtually all workers in high-end hotels knew how to render.

Ahmadi kept walking. Despite her desire to follow this mystery woman, she realized doing so, at two thirty in the morning, would raise Roya's suspicions immediately. At least Ahmadi had confirmed where this woman worked, and where she was likely to find her again soon. Ahmadi subdued the effects of her adrenaline by breathing profoundly and walking calmly back to her room. Once inside her hotel room, she let the adrenaline propel her. She picked up her cell phone and called Z.

"Why are you bugging me at two forty-five in the morning?" Z said in a groggy and accusatory tone.

"I found her!"

"The mystery woman?"

"Yes! Her name is Roya," Ahmadi said. "She's an employee of the hotel. She works here."

"How do you know?"

"Because I saw her coming out of a bathroom wearing her hotel uniform and name tag—just less than five minutes ago."

Z yawned as he asked. "What were you doing wandering the hotel at this early hour?"

"I started my period while I was sleeping, and I needed some accessories."

"And you thought you were finally going to get a good night's sleep."

"So much for that."

"But, we have a problem," Z said.

"What's that?"

"Do you think our mystery woman committed your face to memory?"

"If she did," Ahmadi said, "she'll never see that face again. I had on no make-up, and my hair was all over the place. My other face, the public face she saw a few hours ago, was enhanced with base, eye shadow, blush, eyeliner, and mascara."

"No lipstick?" Z asked?

"Oh yes. Add that to the list. A nice subtle mauve shade. That will be a nice enhancement to my new disguise."

"Good. Let's stick with your latest look. Because something tells me trying to find another female Iranian FBI agent to figure this mystery out would be challenging."

"At least one who's as good as me and can arrest people. Not likely."

"Should I get up and see if I can go find this Roya woman?"

"No. I think she'll be back to work a shift in the next day or two. How about we get some sleep. In the morning we'll put a plan together for tailing her the next time she shows up for work."

"Deal," Z said. "How about you go to human resources tomorrow, disguised as a job seeker, and see what you can find out about housekeeping in this hotel. Then I'll spend the morning by walking around the hotel observing what I can from the housekeepers as they work."

Ahmadi yawned before she could reply. "Sounds good. With my body fighting this little monthly battle, I could really use some sleep. See you in the morning."

Ahmadi hung up the phone. Within fifteen minutes she was asleep. Z was wide awake. He was on his computer ordering some essential surveillance equipment that would arrive by the afternoon.

CHAPTER 21

Chicago, Illinois

Troy Stoker awoke at 5:20 a.m. The summertime sun was minutes away from rising over Lake Michigan. Allie was still asleep, so Troy quietly put on some workout clothes and slipped out of the hotel room. Stoker was on his way to Hotel Esatto. He figured he could observe the hotel during a workout and breakfast there. Stoker walked a few blocks, accessed Hotel Esatto through the main lobby, went downstairs, and walked into Hotel Esatto's well-appointed gym. As he looked around the gym, he was amazed at the size of the facility. And, it was jam-packed. He found a stationary bike and rode with persistent vigor for thirty minutes. This workout was very refreshing because most of his fitness routine during his *Espada Rápida* training had consisted of running. Then, for the next forty-five minutes, Stoker attacked the weight room. At the end of his session, his muscles quivered. Troy Stoker felt the deep, satisfying invigoration that comes from a long, fierce workout. His body was screaming for calories and protein. He knew lactic acid was building up due to the anaerobic punishment he doled out upon his muscles.

Back at her hotel, Allie Stoker continued to sleep. She was oblivious to her robust immune system as it was attacking the nerves in her body.

After his workout, Troy went to breakfast at Hotel Esatto's restaurant. When he sat down at the table, an attendant immediately served him a glass of juice. "How did you do that?" Troy joked with the man.

"Do what?"

"Read my mind. How did you know I wanted orange juice?"

"Is this your first time visiting Hotel Esatto, sir?"

"It is."

"The juice is actually tangerine juice. Our fresh-squeezed tangerine juice is complimentary, as well as our Colombian coffee. A lot of people are taking their coffee BulletProof these days."

"Thank you. Do you do that for all first-time guests?"

"No. We do it for all our guests all the time. It's one of our trademarks."

"It's a nice touch. Do you have a trademark breakfast that goes along with the trademark tangerine juice?" Stoker asked. Then he interjected, "I mean trademark as in special, not implying it should be free."

The waiter smiled as he responded. "Our healthy power breakfasts are indeed one of our trademarks. I recommend the whole-wheat turkey sausage sandwich. Our whole wheat is the course, grainy type of wheat your body needs. The turkey sausage is low-fat, delicious and high in protein. The sandwich includes tomatoes, arugula, spinach, and thin slices of zucchini. If you want mayonnaise, we'll put it on there; but you must ask for it."

"Sounds great. No mayo. That stuff will kill you."

"Anything else I can bring you?"

"Come to think of it, I'll have two of those sandwiches. If I'm not too hungry, I'll share the second one with my wife."

"Excellent, sir."

Stoker sipped the tangerine juice. It was delicious. He took three more swallows. Then he started to look at email on his phone. Before he could thoroughly read the first email, his coffee and sandwiches arrived. Faster than he could thank the server, his tangerine juice was topped off, too. He was thoroughly impressed with Hotel Esatto. His breakfast sandwich was very satisfying, and healthy to boot. Because he had worked out so hard, he ate the second sandwich as well. He finished off his coffee and decided to look around a little.

Stoker paid, left the restaurant, and walked into the lobby. Everything in the hotel was perfect. It was not the luxurious, extravagant kind of perfect. It was the sleek, pristine kind of perfect. The attention to small details evident in the building's architecture was remarkable. The design of the hotel embodied motion. This was not a place to stay for a luxurious weekend. Hotel Esatto was a place for the ambitious. The people who were going places. Stoker looked at the people around him. They were the achievers and innovators. He could see it in their demeanor, expressions, and body language. As they walked, they executed each step with purpose, drive, and passion. And every aspect of the hotel's architecture and processes catered to this cross-section of society's psychology.

I must tell Allie about my observations of this Hotel Esatto, he thought. He headed toward the elevator. When he got there, he noticed there were flights of stairs that rose alongside the elevator. "Brilliant," he said to himself as he looked up. Many of these A-type personalities were choosing the rigor of taking the stairs, preferring the action instead of the elevator. "Whoever designed this hotel anticipated that instinctive preference within this group of over-achievers," Stoker said to himself almost in a whisper. He considered taking the stairs to explore Hotel Esatto further. But, Stoker had plenty of exercise already this morning. *After all*, he thought, *I should be getting back to Allie.*

Ten minutes later, he quietly entered her hotel room. His wife was still in bed. He softly stepped into the bathroom intending to take a shower.

"Good morning, Troy," Allie said in a tired voice.

"I was trying not to rouse you."

"I woke up about fifteen minutes ago."

"And, how are your legs and fatigue this morning?" Stoker asked, keeping any tones of concern out of his voice.

"I haven't tried using my legs yet, but my energy level is still shallow. Could it be a nutrition thing?"

"I doubt it. Not if you've been eating breakfast at Hotel Esatto?"

"You discovered the healthy power breakfast they have over there?"

"Yes. And, I even had seconds."

"What did you have? And, how did you like the tangerine juice?"

"I've never been so transfixed by a health-nut breakfast in my life. Hotel Esatto was a fascinating piece of architecture."

"Isn't it amazing? I love that place."

"And I know why," Troy said. "The place was designed to cater to your type A personality."

"Now you're thinking like a designer," Allie said. "We consider psychology in the architecture of workspaces."

"Right. But, I think your discipline, interior design, prioritizes other design demands above psychology. You must consider square footage constraints, efficiency, aesthetics, and budget. I suspect the latest trends in color palettes come into play even before the type of people with this type A mental make-up—

the movers and shakers—who stay here."

"You're right. We rarely start with the personality of the users. It's more about the function or processes that will occur within the space." Allie sat up and dangled her legs over the side of the bed. Her bangs fell over her eyes. "You think I'm a type A personality?"

"You're an achiever. You love to get things done. You work hard. Even your favorite means of recreating is all about achievement and kicking butt. When you cross-country ski around that track, you're pushing yourself with every muscle in your body."

"It's July, and I miss my cross-country skiing. But, running half marathons will suffice." Allie pushed her bangs back up behind his ears and shifted on the bed. "If I'm an achiever, what are you, Troy?"

"I'm an experiencer. If I were an achiever, I would be more concerned about the number of patients I see. But, every patient is an experience for me. I like to figure people out as well as their problems. I provide people with effective medicine. I use therapy to coach them through the process of changing their lives."

"I never wonder why you go to Mexico with *Espada Rápida*," she said. "That adventure matches your personality. You need out-of-the-ordinary experiences."

"That's also why I married you," Troy said.

Allie winked at Troy and smiled. "You sense there's a problem down in Mexico, and you want the whole experience of fixing it."

"You're a pretty good shrink, Allie."

"So why are you on this architectural psychology kick?" she asked.

"Because every square inch of that hotel is designed to cater to—no, to catalyze—the hard-driving, high achieving cross-section of society. That's why you like it over there."

"I love the place. It's a little pricey, so I've only stayed there once. But, enough of this philosophy and psychology. I'm an achiever. Forget this fatigue and weakness. I'm getting up to go take on the world." Allie pushed off from the side of the bed with exaggeration. But her legs failed her, and she stumbled and caught herself on the desk. "Whoa," she said.

Troy tuned into an instinct he often suppressed. He usually avoided lending a minor helping hand to the fiercely independent

Allie. In this instance, he noticed her stumble, and he jumped to her side.

"What was that?" Troy asked.

"I don't know. My legs are not behaving like the legs of an achiever." Allie made her way back to the bed. "This is alarming. Do you think I could've injured my legs and not known about it? Do I have a pinched nerve in my spine, and I'm only now getting the news?"

"I don't know. Let me take a look at you," Stoker said as he held out his hands. "Cross your hands and grab onto my fingers." Allie followed his lead. "Now squeeze hard with both hands." Allie squeezed as Stoker observed. "I'm testing to see if one side of your upper body is stronger than the other. Now shrug your shoulders while I apply some downward pressure." Allie followed his suggestions. Stoker noticed the right side of her body was slightly weaker than her left.

With his brow furrowed, he hid the alarm swirling in his mind as he considered the odds of Allie contracting Guillain-Barre syndrome. "Hmmm. That's weird. It could be me, but maybe there's a little bit of asymmetry—some mild weakness—on one side. Do you have any pain?"

"No. Nothing unusual. Just weakness in my legs."

"How about you lie down on your back and let me try some things." Stoker grabbed Allie's ankle and lifted her foot into the air about eighteen inches. Then, he ran the tip of his thumb up, from heel to toe on Allie's right foot. Her reflexes reacted, and all her toes curled downward. He repeated the test on her left foot, and her toes curled downward again. "That's called the Babinski reflex, Honey. And yours is normal. That's good. I don't think there's anything wrong in your brain."

"Now sit up here and dangle your legs over the side of the bed." Stoker walked into the bathroom, found Allie's hairbrush, returned to his wife, and used the handle to tap just below one kneecap. Her leg shot out briskly. Then he performed the same task on her other leg. The response in this leg was much weaker than the first. Allie noticed the difference. "Wow. Every time the doctor used to tap my knee, I thought it was kind of goofy. But, there is a vast difference between the reflexes in my two legs. What's going on?"

"Well, I'm not sure. The first test I did, on the bottom of your foot, made me pretty sure there is nothing dangerous going on in your brain. But, your reflex test tells me there may be a problem with your muscles or nerves. Out of an abundance of caution, I want to have you see a specialist and get you checked out some more.

"Okay. Do you think it could be something serious?

"There are a lot of things this could be. Allie, do you have any shortness of breath or difficulty breathing?"

"No."

In a short time, Dr. Stoker had narrowed down his possible list of diseases or problems from hundreds to less than twenty. But, Guillain-Barre syndrome was looking more and more likely. He noticed how Allie was uncomfortable with his concern.

"Who knows?" Stoker said. "Maybe you hurt something while you were training. But, do you remember when you had diarrhea about two weeks ago?"

"Yes."

"Me, too. And, I think we should get you to a neurologist in the next few hours. Let me make some phone calls."

At three o'clock Allie, Troy, and Errol Rivera met with a neurologist at Northwestern Memorial Medical Center in Chicago. The neurologist ran many of the same tests Stoker and Rivera had seen administered to patients in the hospital in Chihuahua only weeks ago.

After ninety minutes, the neurologist had a diagnosis. "You have a disease that's not permanent or fatal. But, you probably have a few very tough months ahead of you."

"Okay, I'm glad to know I'm not going to die or end up in a wheelchair. I'm pretty good at toughing things out and enduring pain. What's this disease called?"

"Guillain-Barre syndrome," the neurologist said.

"Well at least it's French," Allie joked. "Is it also fashionable?"

Stoker and the neurologist flinched a little. Rivera let out one quiet syllable of an uncomfortable laugh. Overriding the awkward pause, the neurologist continued. "The infection you had two weeks ago triggered your body's immune system, just like it was supposed to. But, your immune system not only attacked the infecting bacteria, but it also attacked your nerves. Your own immune system is attacking the protective sheath around your nerves. Over the next few weeks, you will lose even more strength. Odds are about fifty percent this disease will paralyze you for a few days or weeks."

The mention of paralysis stunned Allie Stoker to her core. She had always been so good at enduring pain. But, the impending loss of control, the loss of motion and freedom, shocked her in a way she never imagined. This new angle on suffering terrified her.

"And you can manage this paralysis?" she stammered. "I mean, how do we handle this?" Troy had never seen his usually stoic wife react with so much trepidation. He put his arm around her. She melted into his embrace, which was also unusual for the fiercely independent Allie. But now, her tears flowed freely. "How do you treat paralyzed people for those days or even weeks? Is there some kind of daycare for paralyzed people?"

Stoker spoke up with a calm, confident tone. "We admit you to the hospital. If you reach the point of paralysis, we put you on a ventilator to help you breathe."

"And what do I do while I'm on the ventilator?" Now Allie was angry. Her voice trembled. "Listen to talk radio, to books on the Audible app? Do I just lay there and count my many blessings? How the hell did this happen? Is somebody going to have to feed me, and bathe me? No way is that going to happen." She broke free from Troy, pushed her hair back, and wiped away tears. But, more tears deluged her eyes and moistened her cheeks. "We're going to beat this." The look on her face was determination. Her voice was too fierce to tremble "There has got to be a treatment for this. I want a second opinion from the Mayo Clinic." Then Allie went silent.

Stoker waited for a few seconds before he interrupted the hush. "Sure, Honey. We'll call Mayo as soon as we finish here." He knew a phone call to the Mayo Clinic, or any other medical facility in the world, would be futile. There were no new or better treatments for Guillain-Barre syndrome. However, he was willing to make the call to support her through the coping process. "But, before we go the Mayo Clinic route, can we please start treating you today with some medications that will strengthen you for the battle to come?"

"No. I'm not ready for that." Her denial was palpable.

Stoker paused for a moment before he renewed his plea. "A treatment today may help lessen symptoms down the road. It's crucial."

"No, Troy! I said no, and I mean no!"

Stoker wouldn't back down. "Your body is fighting a war right now. It needs help. A treatment called immunoglobulin therapy may help you avoid paralysis or shorten the number of days on a ventilator."

"I'm not ready. Maybe further down the road."

Stoker made it a rule to avoid manipulating Allie with "tricks" he had learned as a psychotherapist. But today he knew how important it was to coax Allie into accepting the treatment. "For me, Allie? Will you please do it for me? So, I don't have to spend extra days watching you on a ventilator, agonizing. For your family? You know your sister's going to fly in. There will be people here supporting you. Please don't extend their suffering."

Allie's tone was low and angry. Her words came out slowly. "Don't you use your mental, intellectual malarkey on me, Troy Stoker."

"Yes, I'm trying to persuade you. This treatment is that important. But, I'm mostly thinking of you—"

Allie cut him off and attempted to finish his thought with a sassy expression. "And you'll support me, like you always say you will, if I reject this immunoglobulin treatment?"

"No," Stoker said. "While my love is unconditional, I do not want you to make this foolish decision to avoid the immunoglobulin therapy. Hours count right now. I want you to ski this winter."

It struck Allie to realize her cross country ski season was in jeopardy. "Troy, you're such an oaf sometimes. I'm sure I would've responded to empathy eventually. But, if you want instant results, tell me my ski season's in jeopardy. What's the treatment you're talking about?"

Rivera interjected. "A shot in the butt, for a real pain in the—"

The neurologist interrupted Rivera. "We inject immunoglobulin into the top of your buttocks." She smiled wryly at Dr. Rivera. "And most of the time without insulting our patients. Isn't that right Dr. Rivera?"

Rivera ignored the neurologist's question and used the opportunity to explain the treatment further. "The antibodies from this shot will counteract the antibodies eroding away your nerve sheaths. Less nerve damage now means more cross-country skiing next winter." Rivera smiled and nodded slightly toward Stoker. "And this is an excellent moment to manipulate your husband into committing to a ski vacation."

"Colorado, Troy. You're taking me to Colorado this winter. We'll hire a guide. And, we'll strap on backcountry skis with skins. We will climb the peaks in the wee hours of the morning. Then we will reward ourselves with spectacular descents through virgin powder snow."

"It's a deal," Stoker said. "Now pull down your pants a bit and let the doctor give you this shot. I warn most people this injection hurts. But I know better than to concern you with pain."

That evening Allie and Troy Stoker walked along Chicago's North Avenue Beach. Allie had suggested the stroll by emphasizing how much she wanted to walk, while she still could. They stopped at a diner and ordered hearty spinach salads. Allie ordered Mahi Mahi fish tacos and a glass of Riesling. Stoker chose a jerk chicken sandwich and a dark tap beer. After dinner, they walked further up the beach. "What do we do next, Troy?" Allie asked. "Do I rest and wait, or do I go about my daily business as long as I can?"

"What do you think?" Stoker asked.

"Every once in a while, I hear you talk about how so many of your patients just have to take their lives one day at a time. Now we're the patients. I'm terrified of being helpless and dependent." Troy did not reply. He wanted Allie to continue to process her thoughts out loud. "I guess I just take it day by day."

"We can do that," Stoker said, making sure Allie knew he was listening.

• • •

That morning, Z slept in until nine-thirty at Hotel Esatto. After breakfast, he walked around the hotel. He noted two interesting patterns. First, there were many housekeepers with Iranian first names. Second, there were few Arabic first names among the housekeepers. He wondered, did this hotel favor Shiite Muslims? Was this part of the Iranian connection?

At one point Z also walked down a service corridor into the bowels of Hotel Esatto, an area most guests would never see. It connected the kitchen, laundry, and housekeeping functions of the hotel. He placed additional tiny cameras in hidden places where people were not likely to notice. He also found the employee entrance and hid a small camera in a position to monitor the entrance. Because Roya was more likely to arrive at night, the camera had infrared capabilities. Later that day, he would take delivery of additional cameras and pieces of impressive technology. He would use them to learn more about Roya. With a little luck, she would lead *Espada Rápida* and the FBI to the Iranian cell.

Later that afternoon Z met with Ahmadi. "Tell me what you learned in your job interview?" Z asked.

"It was not an interview. It was just me pretending to be a woman, recently arrived from the Middle East, trying to find a housekeeping job. I just dropped in at the HR department and filled out an application." Ahmadi had dressed in plain clothes, dawned a headscarf, and visited the human resources office to apply for a job at Hotel Esatto.

"Did you apply using a Persian name or an Arab one?"

"Yasmin Mir-Khatibi."

"Very Persian," Z said. "I noticed a lot of housekeepers had Persian first names as I walked around this morning. What did you find out about the housekeeping world?"

"They work in eight-hour shifts. I told them I would prefer to work nights. But they don't need people on nights. They need new employees on the day shift from seven am to three pm. Still, I found out the overnight shift starts at eleven o'clock."

"Good to know. That's when Roya will arrive. That's when we'll start snooping and pooping."

"What? Snooping and pooping?"

"It's military lingo for reconnaissance."

"Good. I've got a few cameras set up. And, I'll put up some special little ultrasonic strips—"

What?

"It's just some new technology I'll receive today. Did you know the newest smartphones can hear ultrasonic sounds out of our human hearing range?"

"That's bizarre," Ahmadi said.

"Well, whatever it's for, I'm using this. I'm going to adapt this ultrasonic technology so I can put it along the ceiling corners. All I have to do is use it to detect these ultrasonic sound waves as they travel through the microphone on Roya's phone. We'll get close enough and hack into her phone through Wi-Fi or Bluetooth. It's a lot like the scammers do at airports. I start by capturing her phone's unique identifier information. After that, we're using high-frequency sound waves to track her whereabouts. I place one of these ultrasonic strips every 150 feet or so. We'll always know where she is."

"Excellent. Let's do it."

An hour later, Z received his shipment of customized ultrasonic sound wave generators. He found a few places to hide the generators. At 10:45 that evening Z was the only person sitting in the lobby of Hotel Esatto. He was monitoring the many cameras on his laptop computer. He also had an attaché case, just to make him appear as if he was one of the aspiring businesspeople. Ahmadi stayed glued to monitors in her hotel room. They also projected images from the cameras Z had placed around Hotel Esatto.

At 10:50 p.m. Roya passed through the employee entrance.

"We're on," Z whispered under his breath.

• • •

Tonight was a trial run. Roya was testing the ability to change the mist canisters with surgical gloves on while wearing a respirator. But, when it was time for the amoeba to go live, she would need to don a full HAZMAT suit. The ingredients in tonight's containers were only harmless scents. But, she needed to practice swapping out canisters quickly and safely. At least safely for her.

She loaded the scent containers into her housekeeping cart, put on the thick surgical gloves, and donned the respirator. Then she started with one of the men's bathrooms on Hotel Esatto's main floor. Wearing gloves and a respirator was not new to Roya. She had worn the protective gear hundreds of times when she worked in the lab hidden in the hotel's basement. But, that was a highly controlled environment. The risks to her health would be more considerable out here in the hotel. Within the next 24 hours, she would be deploying the canisters containing the deadly pathogen. If the pathogen got into her system, she would find herself amongst the miserable throngs of people pounding on hospital doors, clamoring and begging for scarce treatment.

But tonight, there was no danger. *How anticlimactic*, she thought. Rehearsing terror was not invigorating like executing the real thing.

• • •

For three hours Z had waited. Finally, at almost two o'clock in the morning, Roya walked through the lobby. She was pushing a cart while wearing thick surgical gloves and a respirator. Then she knocked on the men's bathroom door. She opened the door a crack. "Housekeeping." There was no answer, so she entered.

Z left his computer and walked over near the door to the restroom. Utilizing his homemade scanner, he stood next to the wall separating him from Roya. He pressed a couple of buttons and let the scanner work. A few minutes later, Z returned to the same spot where he'd been sitting. Looking at some readings on his device made him smile. He had captured the unique identifying number for Roya's phone.

When Roya emerged from the bathroom, Z started using high-frequency signals to get a fix on her phone. Z was ready to track her, virtually, throughout Hotel Esatto.

For the next fifteen minutes, Z observed his computer screen as he followed Roya's icon. She traveled to many bathrooms on the first floor.

Z called Ahmadi. "I just noticed something troubling."

"What's that?" Ahmadi asked.

"This Roya woman is wearing biohazard clothing that resembles the protective gear I saw in the hospital in Mexico."

"Like a mask? The gloves I can understand. Housekeepers wear gloves."

"A mask, yes," Z said thinking for a moment. "It's even more than that. When she exits a restroom, she observes a protocol, perhaps like we might expect to see in a lab? I'm not a medical lab expert, but her behavior seems out of place in a hotel."

"So, who could we ask?" Ahmadi said. "Do we know anyone

familiar with hospital and lab stuff?" she said sarcastically.

"Don't bug Stoker. Allie never complains about his extended absences when he works with us. And, she needs him right now."

"Let's wake Rivera," Ahmadi said. "You know he would never hesitate to wake us."

Z agreed. "Get him down here. Let's see what he observes."

Ten minutes later, Rivera was fully dressed. Ahmadi and Z briefed him on the situation with Roya and her protective gear. Rivera started walking around on the main floor looking for Roya. When Rivera saw the woman from Iran, he pulled out his cell phone and pretended to be having a phone call with someone in Spain, where the sun had already risen for the day. He strolled casually in her general direction. Roya stopped her cart at a men's bathroom near the banquet halls. He watched her put on gloves and respirator. Then, with a stepladder and aerosolized container in hand, she knocked on the door. "Housekeeping."

Rivera waited for less than a minute before Roya emerged from the bathroom; and she placed a different canister in a plastic bag. Then she put her gloves in the bag. Using tape, she double sealed the bag. The hair on the back of Rivera's neck stood up. He walked a few paces away from Roya, still pretending to participate in a phone conversation. Out of the corner of his eye, he saw Roya re-glove, and grab a new canister. He rounded a corner as she was about to enter the women's bathroom. He picked up his phone and called Z. "This is serious. She is showing a lot of caution toward those canisters. Something's not right."

"Look, Rivera. You're watching a woman, who is most likely from Iran, doing dangerous stuff within a stone's throw of millions of people. Let's act on this."

"Can you hack into the fire alarm system in this building?" Rivera asked.

"Sure, anybody can," Z responded. But, can't you just go pull a fire alarm?"

"No, Z. If I pull the fire alarm, it's not a big deal. We need a bigger distraction. I want to use you for your expertise. We need you to figure out a way to make Hotel Esatto, the police department, and fire department think they have a five-alarm fire on their hands here."

"Okay, give me a few minutes."

"I'll be waiting," Rivera said. I'm going to try to distract this Roya woman."

Rivera meandered slowly toward Roya's cart. When she came out of the bathroom, he smiled. "Hello." Then he pretended to do a double take on Roya's face. "I just can't help but notice. I'm a doctor, in town for a medical convention. You have a big red area just below your eye. You might want to get that looked at, and soon."

Roya put a false smile on her face. But, her smile could not hide the alarm present in her eyes from the unsolicited medical news she was receiving. She stammered for a moment. "Thank you, sir," she said with a quiver in her voice. "I'll make an appointment tomorrow morning."

"That would be wise. We're so good at curing that particular skin disease, at least when we catch it early. At that point, it's still easy to beat. If you get in quick, your treatment will be straightforward for that condition."

"Have a nice evening sir," Roya said as she hastily made her way back into the lady's restroom to examine her face.

Rivera immediately turned toward her cart and grabbed three of the canisters. He placed the containers on the ground in a disarrayed fashion, making it look like they had spilled out of the cart. Then, he saw a text from Z telling him he was ready to sound the alarms. Rivera spun the cart around and threw some of the cleaning supplies on the ground. Then he called Z. When Z answered, Rivera's voice sounded urgent. "Okay Z. Now! I need that alarm."

The fire alarm blared. Grabbing a towel from Roya's cart, Rivera and wrapped it around one of the full canisters. Then he took off running toward the front door.

At first, it was mostly hotel staff members who entered the hallway. When Roya opened the door and looked out, she saw her cart in disarray. She also noticed three canisters on the floor—one of them had rolled almost twenty feet from the cart. She sprinted to grab the furthest canister, picked it up, and returned it to her cart. As she turned to pick up the other two containers, the first wave of hotel guests came walking down the hall in an orderly but determined fashion. Just as they reached her and her cart, she put the two remaining canisters back on the cart. Then she grabbed the cart and shoved it over toward the wall, making more space for the bleary-eyed crowd to proceed down the hall toward the exit. There Roya waited until the crowd began to thin. Then she started to push her cart in the opposite direction of the flow of people. Eventually, she made her way to the main corridor that forked away from the kitchen and into the housekeeping bowels of the hotel.

Z was following her virtually on his computer. With all the uproar, Z felt like he had enough cover to follow Roya on foot. He wanted to delve deeper into the hotel. There was more to this place, and he wanted to know what it was.

Z scanned the faces that walked by. None of the people looked familiar. Most looked perturbed by the inconvenience of an alarm. Some faces appeared anxious. Other faces wore resolute and duty-bound expressions to exit the hotel quickly.

Z remained far behind Roya. Thanks to his ability to follow her digitally, he was always behind her by at least one corner, staying out of her sight. After some twists and turns through corridors, her icon stopped. After a brief pause, the icon continued forward for a foot or two, and then faded away.

"So where have you gone Roya?" Z wondered aloud. Cautiously, he peeked around the corner. He saw no Roya. But, he also saw an opportunity. Right here, in this corridor, Z placed a small camera as well as one of the locator devices. If Roya came this way again, he would pick up her signal.

● ● ●

Nikolas often worked during the earliest hours of the morning in his office on the third level of Hotel Esatto—a floor where Roya would install no mist canisters containing the Balamuthia amoeba. If he wanted to do business with Tehran, Nikolas needed to be awake while his bonyad director was working. "My Sayid. Initial reports from local hospitals are very encouraging," Nikolas said to his director. "The intensive care units are filling up."

"I did not ask for full hospitals!" the director said sternly. "I need to hear news reports of overflowing hospitals, of people lining up at the hospitals with tear-stained faces. When will I hear those stories?

"Within two weeks," Nikolas said with confidence.

"That is the first time you've ever given me a concrete answer," the director said. "I'm so accustomed to hearing the vague word 'soon' that I'm somewhat thunderstruck by this experience."

"It will happen, my Sayid. We've blanketed America with our pathogens."

"It better happen! I better see the weeping and gnashing of teeth their Christian Bible anticipates, or I will be sending some special friends to visit your loved ones in Jubail." Director Alireza Pour-Mohammadi was referring to a city on the eastern coast of Saudi Arabia that overlooked the Persian Gulf. He was holding Nikolas's family there.

"Director, sir. Here's another first." There were resolve and bravado in Nikolas's voice. "This is the first time I've had a positive bargaining position with you, ever. Now I've got the upper hand, and I will not stand for your threats. Let me be clear. If any harm comes to my family, purposeful or accidental, I will—"

Hotel Esatto fire alarms rang out and interrupted Nikolas. From Tehran, the director stammered before he shouted back at Nikolas. "How dare you!"

But Nikolas couldn't hear his rage-filled words. All the director in Iran could hear was the fire alarm coming through his computer's speakers. He could also see some confusion. "What is going on there?" the director demanded. In the background, he saw Nikolas having an animated conversation with a bodyguard. It surprised the director when the bodyguard seemed to win the argument, and Nikolas exited the picture. Then the face of another bodyguard came onto the camera. He started to type on the keyboard.

A moment later a message came across the computer in the online chat feature.

> *The fire alarm has sounded in the hotel. We are escorting Mr. Antoniou from the building. Many of us are very loyal to him. If anything happens to his family, our little army will sneak into Tehran, find you, and behead you very slowly.*

Then the bodyguard flipped the director the bird and slammed down the computer's screen.

By now Nikolas had made his way down a little-known stairway to the basement parking. He and his bodyguards exited the elevator and walked briskly into the garage. As they had rehearsed many times, a man was waiting by a bulletproof Lincoln Town Car. Ahead of it sat a black Suburban, with Texas plates, filled with more bodyguards ready to defend Nikolas. Still flanked by the two bodyguards, Nikolas dipped into the Town Car. The door slammed, and the car took off.

"Where would you like to go, sir?"

"Take me to the marina for an hour. I will work from my boat."

• • •

Rivera watched as the guests continued to exit Hotel Esatto. He sent a text to Stoker:

> There is a false fire alarm at Hotel Esatto. But I need an enhanced Stoker sit rep evaluation pronto. The perspective of a psychiatrist would be valuable. Can you walk around and see if you observe anything out of the ordinary?

Stoker's phone chime woke him. He texted back to Rivera telling him he would be right over. Then he pulled on his tactical pants and quickly laced up his boots. Jostling Allie's shoulder, he whispered, "There is a false fire alarm at Hotel Esatto. Something tells me Rivera triggered it. Stay in bed and sleep." He kissed her on the cheek and headed out the door.

Stoker walked to the hotel and arrived to witness a sea of pajama- and robe-wearing hotel guests waiting on the sidewalk. Fire trucks and police vehicles filled the street. The firemen were relaxed. In the last minute, they had concluded the event was a false alarm. Stoker started to walk around, to observe. As he walked down the sidewalk, watching the people and studying the situation, he didn't see anything he would not expect to see in the middle of the night amongst a group of alarm-rattled hotel patrons. Glancing ahead, he suddenly caught a glimpse of the Iranian woman, Roya, coming down the sidewalk toward him.

Stoker stepped aside, to the edge of the sidewalk and turned his back, so she would not see him. After she passed, Stoker turned and followed her. As he observed, Roya's determined stride and body language conveyed to the psychiatrist that she was looking for someone or something, with hunter-like intensity.

• • •

Roya stopped. She removed a small radio from her pocket and spoke into it. "I'm looking at this man who spoke to me a few minutes ago. The one who said he was a doctor."

"Yes," replied Nazem. "We too were watching him on the hotel's security cameras, before the fire alarm went off. That man definitely has us curious. He's not acting like a hotel guest. His behaviors are those of an investigator. He holds himself like a soldier."

"Do you think he's some type of law enforcement?"

"Yes. But, let's find out exactly who he is. I'm coming outside to take care of this man—to take him to Nikolas's boat."

• • •

In the distance a siren from an arriving fire truck, perhaps still sixty seconds away, was audible. Stoker eased to within twenty feet of Roya. He looked out into the sea of people, in the same direction where Roya's gaze appeared to concentrate. Then he saw who Roya was watching. She fixated on Errol Rivera. He was talking on his phone.

As the fire truck approached, Rivera covered his other ear to help him hear the phone conversation despite the loud siren. The fire truck eventually made it impossible for Rivera to listen to his discussion, and Stoker saw him end the call with a look of frustration on his face.

As Rivera slid his phone into his pocket, Stoker saw five men emerge from the crowd and come up behind Rivera. Two of them were carrying a large device that looked like a black windsock. Stoker cried out to warn Rivera, but the siren canceled out his yell. Stoker fought through the crowd to get to Rivera. But, even after nearly throwing a few people to the ground, he could not reach Rivera in time. In less than a second, the men lifted the sizable wind-sock-looking bag up over Rivera's head and brought it down around him disabling his arms and legs—even making it impossible for him to bite or head butt. The men hoisted Rivera, threw him into the back of a black Suburban, and slammed the tailgate shut. As the Suburban started to pull slowly away from the curb, Stoker broke through the crowd thinking he could catch up with the automobile on foot.

When a wallop struck him hard in the shins, Stoker found himself sprawling out into the street. Instinctively he tried to jump up and continue his run. But, one of his calves cramped. He hobbled a couple of times, and the other calf seized up. Stoker fought through the pain, but his muscles refused to cooperate. He stumbled back to the ground but had the presence of mind to capture the Suburban's license plate number. The Texas plates read LS3-C4891.

Stoker spun around to see who had hit him. His eyes met a satisfied smirk on Roya's face as she held a black baseball bat. His iron will commanded him to rise to his feet. When he stood, Roya's smirk turned to fear. She disappeared into the crowd while Stoker took some initial tentative steps. His next steps were slow, but at least he was walking, and in the right direction. Stoker hobbled through the crowd, and he searched to see if he could reacquire Roya. To his right, he saw her shoving her way past people. Then he was thrilled to see Agent Ahmadi just a few feet behind her. She was also trying to reach Roya, but the crowd was impeding her progress. Eventually, Roya made it to the edge of the throng, and she made a clean breakaway. She started running down the sidewalk, and then she turned around a corner into an alley. Ahmadi was not far behind her. Stoker continued to struggle, trying to free himself from the mass of hotel guests.

When Stoker finally made it to the edge of the crowd, he also ran toward the alley. He rounded the turn into the darkness just in time to see Ahmadi. She was circling a corner toward the back of the hotel. Stoker continued to follow, increasing his velocity with every stride. When Stoker arrived at the rear of the hotel, he saw Ahmadi had almost caught up with Roya. Roya swiped her badge, which allowed her through the entrance. Then she pulled the door closed behind her. Ahmadi was locked out. It looked as though the chase had reached an end. But, then the door opened, and another employee exited, a woman wearing a hijab.

Ahmadi pretended like she worked there. "See you tomorrow," she said in Farsi as she passed through the door flashing a smile. Then the door slammed shut again.

Seconds later, Stoker, with shins burning in pain, limped up to the door but remained outside, hoping another employee would exit soon. He took out his phone and made an encrypted call to Z. "Rivera was just kidnapped by a black Suburban, Texas plates, LS3-C4891. But, something tells me calling in the FBI to find Rivera would be the wrong call."

"I'll scour cameras around the city," Z said.

"That's great. Ahmadi's chasing down that Roya woman." Stoker knelt, rolled up his pants, and started inspecting his shin injuries. "And I'm a couple of minutes behind her." His shins were throbbing. "You and I need to rendezvous with Ahmadi as soon as we can. We'll come up with a game plan that will help us get Rivera back and figure out what's going on around here." Stoker ended the call and stood up waiting for another employee to exit.

When someone finally opened the door, Stoker pretended to be an employee who was arriving. "What's up with this fire alarm?" he asked. "I've got tangerine juice to squeeze."

"They just made an announcement. It's a false alarm." The woman said.

"That figures," Stoker responded as he passed through the door.

When Stoker got through the door, he had no idea where to go. So, he started to run. This time his pace was brisk, and every stride sent lightning bolts of pain up his shins. Yet, he snubbed the pain and ran. He sprinted until he arrived at the laundry. Four employees were working there. "Did you see two women run through here?" he asked.

"No. Of course not. We're not that kind of hotel," one of the employees joked. The other three laughed.

Stoker smiled and said. "Good. That's why I need to catch them. We must keep it that way." The four laughed again, and Stoker turned around and ran back the way he came.

He hit similar dead ends at a kitchen entrance and then at the loading dock. As he ran down a new corridor, he heard yelling—in Farsi. He turned again to follow the sound. Turning one more corner, he saw Roya and Ahmadi engaged in hand-to-hand combat. Roya was verbally insulting Ahmadi. "You're a Western-brainwashed whore!"

But now Ahmadi was holding the baseball bat. She faked a swing to her left, adjusted to her right and commenced another swing. As Roya started to sidestep the blow, Ahmadi tossed the bat right to her. Roya could not ignore the instinct to catch the bat, and she reached both hands out involuntarily. Just before the baseball bat reached her palms, her throat caught a crushing blow from Ahmadi's knife-hand strike. Her vision went black for a fraction of a second, wherein an elbow strike shattered her cheekbone. Ahmadi jumped forward and threw her leg out into a front sidekick impacting just above her knee and snapping it backward. The sound of tearing ligaments was brief, loud, and horrific. Roya's sickening scream echoed from the concrete walls as she tumbled to the ground. Ahmadi dropped to her knees simultaneously throwing a reverse front strike to Roya's eye socket. Roya felt no pain from her shattered eye socket because the blow knocked her unconscious.

"Ahmadi!" Stoker yelled. She turned around instantly with fists clenched, fire in her eyes, and blood on her teeth. "Whoa, whoa. It's me, Stoker." She relaxed. "Are you alright? I saw the end of your fight, but I don't know how the battle went before that."

"My dentist will be glad to see me," Ahmadi said as she spat two teeth onto the ground. "My neck will be sore tomorrow. I caught a kick to the head."

"She knew how to fight?"

"Yeah, like a dragon," Ahmadi answered. Then her tone became a little annoyed. "Where were you, Stoker?"

"Locked out at the employee entrance."

"If you would've seen the fight from the start, you would've been worried. Our little Roya here has obviously trained for years.

She has better skills than me."

"So why is she the heap on the floor and you the standing conqueror? Didn't she also have the bat?"

"Because I'm more fit. Roya burned through all her adrenaline, and she trusted her weapon too much. I usually try to end a fight within seconds, but that doesn't work when your Kung Fu master opponent's holding a bat."

"So, you disarmed her?"

"I took a shot to my abs, which are well-prepared for such a blow, and ripped the bat right out of her hands."

"Giving you the upper hand," Stoker interjected.

"I'm not much of a weapons girl. But it sure made for a nice distraction. But, enough about the fight. Look at this door right here."

"Well-reinforced. Why do you mention it?"

"Because she was trying to get through it when I came around the corner. But, when she saw me, she made a stand as if she was protecting this area. She seemed to feel real territorial about this space."

"I bet you're right. This may be Roya's lair."

"I bet we find a stockpile of baseball bats," Ahmadi joked. Let's see what's inside.

"Where's the key?" Stoker asked.

"I'll search her," Ahmadi said. "A Muslim woman would not want a man searching her." She frisked the unconscious Roya, and quickly found the key in Roya's sock. She held up the key. "Let's find out what's waiting for us

Stoker slipped his hand behind his back and under his shirt, removing a .45 caliber Glock 21 pistol. "You open the door, Ahmadi. I'll be the first one through."

Ahmadi slid the key into the lock slowly and quietly. "Five, four, three, two," Ahmadi twisted the handle and threw the door open. Stoker slid through the door, pistol extended. The room was empty. "Clear in here."

Ahmadi dragged Roya through the door and closed it. "Look, Stoker. There's another door. This one has a fingerprint reader and retinal scanner."

"Well, let's see here," Stoker said as he stowed his pistol in the small of his back. He picked up Roya by placing his hands under her armpits. Ahmadi grabbed Roya's hand and pressed her index finger against the reader. A green light came on. Stoker shifted Roya to the right, lined up her face with the retina scanner, and boosted her limp body up to sit on his knee. "I'll hold her still; you pry her eye open and see if you can get her eyeball lined up for long enough to let the scan occur." His left hand grabbed her hair and held it upright and steady.

Ahmadi reached over, and with the thumb and index finger of her left hand, pried Roya's unswollen eye open. After some attempts to manipulate her eye, the laser scanned it successfully. There was a click in the door. As Stoker gently returned Roya's body to the ground, Ahmadi turned the handle and cracked the door open.

Stoker again brandished his weapon and held up his hand with all five fingers extended. Silently he used his hand to signal a countdown back from five, four, three, and two. Ahmadi swung the door open, and Stoker stepped through it with stealth. After surveying the room for less than two seconds, he yelled to Ahmadi. "Get out of here! Now!"

Ahmadi leaped backward but didn't close the door. Stoker reached quickly into a pocket of his tactical pants and retrieved a lock picking kit. He deftly removed one of the metal picks and wedged it between the door bolt and strike plate, keeping the door unlocked. "Let's back out of here, and fast."

Ahmadi followed his instructions and walked in reverse toward the first door. "Is that a lab?"

"Yes. No doubt about it."

"What kind of lab?"

"That's a question laden with doubts and mysteries. It's biological. They're growing cultures. And, nobody should go in there without a complete biohazard suit."

They backed through the first door. Stoker closed it until it was only open a crack. There was a light whistling sound as air passed through the gap. "Feel that," he said as he held his hand up to the separation.

"That's some pretty aggressive ventilation," Ahmadi said.

"It's negative pressure to protect lab personnel. The air is being constantly sucked into the room and filtered. So, if a germ gets into the air, it will be sucked into the filtration system within the room."

"So that space is a biohazard?"

"I'd bet my restored Ford Bronco on it," Stoker said.

"While you're wagering your antique SUV, I'm going to call in the FBI Weapons of Mass Destruction Operations Unit."

"No!" Stoker replied. "Only you, Z, and I know what's going on here. If we must bring in large teams and bring them up to speed, they'll fajangle everything while they try to figure things out. More importantly, they'll scare off the people who run that lab in there."

Ahmadi turned around to the unconscious Roya, knelt beside her, and put flex cuffs on her. "We'll interrogate Roya when she wakes up. She's our only lifeline back to Rivera."

"I'd love to help," Stoker said. "With that mangled knee, she'll tell you all her secrets in return for a merciful dose of a typical opioid."

"This is one time when I may look the other way while you coerce a criminal," Ahmadi said.

"Well, the pain medications—our bargaining chips— are at my hotel," Stoker said. "Let's get her upstairs before she wakes up."

"Let's get her up to my room," Ahmadi said. Then you can retrieve the pain meds. I'll grab one of those big laundry carts. We'll put Roya in it and cover her with some sheets."

"Great. While you're looking for your laundry cart, I'll get Z down here to set up some cameras. Let's see who else comes calling at this little lab."

Stoker called Z and directed him down to the bowels of the building where he was waiting with the unconscious Roya. "Get cameras on these doors right away. And let's watch this door twenty-four seven. Roya is our first lifeline to Rivera. But, the person who comes down to this lab is going to be our second critical link."

A few minutes later, Z finished installing two additional hidden cameras positioned to watch the doors.

"Okay Z," Stoker said. "I don't want you to take your eyes off of the camera feed."

Stoker and Ahmadi loaded the unconscious Roya into the laundry cart and covered her with sheets and towels.

Five minutes later Ahmadi and Z pushed the cart into Ahmadi's hotel room. Stoker made a quick trip to retrieve his medical bag and pain medications. Once he returned to Hotel Esatto and Ahmadi's room, Stoker took charge. "Okay guys, Errol Rivera may be missing, but he's not our mission. We've got another objective. To find out who is infecting a few hundred thousand people with Campylobacter jejuni. Let's focus on saving the world. However, I'm thinking we may fill two needs with one deed."

"I agree. The two are connected," Ahmadi interjected.

"That assumption will keep us focused," Stoker said. "And, when Roya wakes up, you've got to do what you've got to do, Ahmadi. But, I just need to know one thing. Would you believe, Roya as a woman, could be running this whole operation here?"

"In the Muslim world of the Ayatollahs? Never. She's a pawn. Someone else is the mastermind."

"Good to know. As we interrogate, we can assume there is one or more males higher up the chain of command."

A soft moan emanated from the laundry cart. "Our princess awakes," Z said. Ahmadi reached into the bin and removed the laundry. Roya was sitting sideways with her lower leg askew. Roya moaned again. Then her face winced. She involuntarily began to stretch out her injured leg, when a bolt of pain made her eyes shoot open. Her scream was ear-splitting. But it was over as fast as it started because Ahmadi stuffed a washcloth into her mouth. The screams turned to muffled yells.

"Fine. We'll give you something for your pain," Stoker said. But he saw an opportunity to extract some information from Roya. So, he took a gamble and asked a question that contained some assumptions. "Listen Roya, who is that guy we've seen you with?"

"Never. I tell no one about him," she hissed.

We know she's working with at least one other person, Stoker thought. *A man.* He pulled a pre-filled syringe of morphine and midazolam out of the medical bag and considerately injected the needle into her shoulder. Her pain-twisted face shifted to a look of serenity. Then her eyes closed as the sedative kicked in.

"It will do us no good to see people entering this basement laboratory from up here. We won't have time to run down and capture them. Someone needs to be there waiting to nab whoever comes to the door. One of us needs to be right there. And, Roya is not the only person who can fit in this laundry cart. Stoker tipped the cart forward while Ahmadi and Z each grabbed Roya under her armpits and dragged her onto a spot on the hotel room floor.

Stoker volunteered. "Okay Z, you know your marching

orders," he said as he climbed into the laundry cart. "Don't take your eyes off that screen. We're going to leave you here with Sleeping Beauty." Stoker looked at Ahmadi. "Wheel me down to the corridor where the lab is. And, where is that baseball bat?"

"Why the bat?" Ahmadi asked as she handed it over to him.

"It's not what you think it's for," Stoker replied as he sat down inside the cart. "Let's stay in radio contact," he said as he put a radio earpiece in his ear. Ahmadi threw the laundry on top of him.

For the next few hours, Stoker remained concealed underneath sheets and towels in the laundry cart while listening intently for somebody to arrive at the door to the lab. While he hid under the laundry, he reflected on the events of the last few days. When he thought of the wave of disease about to hit the United States, his indignation broiled, sharpening his focus and forging his resolve. Occasionally Z would check in with Stoker through his earpiece. Their brief conversations consisted of Z asking questions. Instead of answering verbally, Stoker would respond by keying his radio switch once to generate a single click for negative. He keyed two clicks for affirmative. After a few hours, Stoker heard footsteps coming toward him. Z's voice came through his radio earpiece. "We've got a tango in the hallway," Z said. "The man's turning toward the door. He's removing keys from his pocket. Get ready Stoker. I think this is our guy."

Stoker heard the key enter the lock. Then he heard the door open. In one strong fluid motion, he lunged sideways slamming his shoulder into the side of the utility cart and tipping it over. Rolling out with the bat in hand, Stoker lunged for the door, swinging the weapon in a swift downward arc. Nikolas heard the commotion at his back. He stepped quickly through the door, attempting to slam it shut. Just before it swung closed, Stoker's bat wedged its tip between the door and the door frame. To gain a more significant advantage, Stoker forcefully shoved the bat toward Nikolas. It struck him square in the forehead, almost knocking him unconscious. Nikolas stumbled away from the door and deeper into the lab's anteroom. Stoker swung the door open and advanced on Nikolas in two quick steps. "Listen, I need to talk to you. But for now, you need to go to sleep." With a mighty swing of his arm, Stoker slammed his elbow into the side of Nikolas's head and knocked him out cold. Nikolas slumped to the ground.

Stoker picked up Nikolas and lifted him up, over his shoulder like a rag doll. "We're going on a little excursion, you and I." Then Stoker carried Nikolas over to the tipped laundry cart. He used the top of his foot to flip the cart into its normal standing position. Then Stoker tossed Nikolas on top of the dirty laundry. After he secured the lab by shutting the door, he pushed the laundry bin down the empty corridor while he whistled the song Don't Worry Be Happy.

• • •

Back in Ahmadi's hotel room, Stoker was slapping Nikolas's face. "Wake up, come on. Wake up."

Nikolas was zip-tied to a chair, and he started to awaken.

"Hey Z, is the camera recording right now?" Stoker asked with a menacing intensity.

"Roger that," Z said. "The camera's ready."

When Stoker saw Nikolas was alert, he said, "Okay, where's the man your goons kidnapped? You better know where the hell he is. You're going to tell me everything, and you're going to tell me now," Stoker snarled.

"I can explain. I *will* tell you everything. I'm a hostage, in the most ironic of cruel circumstances." Nikolas had prepared for this moment for years.

"I don't give a damn about your circumstances. I don't have time to play your games. I have a forty-five-caliber pistol trained on your left kneecap. Where's the man you kidnapped?"

"I will take you to your friend, and you'll get him back. I promise you. No negotiation necessary."

Stoker looked at Nikolas and wondered. *Why is he so quick to be agreeable, to conform?* He decided to explore the issue. "And, why would you do that?" Stoker asked incredulously. "Why should I believe a man who is days away from being a mass murderer?"

"Okay, listen. Let me get your friend back and prove I'm telling the truth. I'll show you. I'll walk the walk."

"Let's see where this goes," Stoker said. He knew Nikolas was starting a war of wits, and the psychiatrist knew it would take some time to figure out his true end game. "Show us this instant gesture of goodwill."

"My family is in Saudi Arabia. They're hostages in that country. I need your help to get them out, to rescue them. That's the truth. To prove my good intentions—indeed to curry your favor—I will take you to your man, Rivera. But we'll need a car to get to him."

"Agent Ahmadi's got an FBI cruiser," Stoker said. "Now come on. You're coming with us. And if you try to get away, I remind you about this forty-five handgun with hollow point rounds that'll splatter your mind before you can change it."

Then Stoker turned to Ahmadi and asked, "Would you lend me your nine-millimeter and its silencer?" Agent Ahmadi spun the silencer onto her gun and handed it to Stoker. Stoker took the gun, aimed it at Nikolas's right leg and took a shot. The bullet grazed the inside of his thigh. Blood gushed out of the wound. Nikolas screamed. Stoker stuffed a rag into his mouth. "If you screw around with us, the next bullet will not *graze* you. With everything you're doing to suck up to us, my bullshit meter is pegged at infinity."

Stoker wound a piece of duct tape around Nikolas's leg. The crude bandage over the bullet wound stopped the superficial blood flow. When Nikolas stopped screaming, Stoker pulled the rag out of his mouth.

"You will meet no resistance from me," Nikolas said almost hyperventilating. "You are my rescuers. You see me as a hostage. I see you as liberators."

"Well, here's your train to any sliver of liberty you may someday regain," Stoker said as he restrained Nikolas's ankles and wrists with zip ties. Then Stoker picked him up and laid him in the laundry cart. "Now shut up until we're in the car."

Stoker threw a sheet on top of Nikolas. He and Ahmadi pushed the cart to an elevator. After descending into the parking garage, they approached Ahmadi's FBI cruiser. Stoker lifted Nikolas out of the bin and put him in the back seat of the car.

"Okay, where are we going?" Stoker asked. "Take us to Rivera."

Nikolas gave Ahmadi directions to a yacht club on Lake Michigan. "Your friend's there, in the marina, on my sailboat."

Stoker paid very close attention to Nikolas, just in case he tried to attack or escape. But the captive never showed any hints he was scheming to escape.

When they arrived at the yacht club, Stoker cut the zip ties binding Nikolas's ankles, but he left his wrists secure. "Remember, Agent Ahmadi and I each have a pistol trained on you."

Nikolas started to lead the way. But, then he stopped and winced with pain. "It's hard for me to walk without my arms to balance."

"Exactly!" Stoker said. "You're not getting those flex cuffs off right now."

The threesome made its way along a network of docks to Nikolas's sailboat. "Let's be very quiet when stepping aboard the boat," Nikolas said. He pointed at Stoker and Ahmadi. "You'll board the boat first. My men—two of them—are prepared to kill you." Nikolas pointed to one of the fold-down seats on the port side of the helm. "That's where one of my men's hiding. Under the cushion, you'll find a storage space. It's kill or be killed. If you want your Rivera friend to live, you must eliminate this man. While he is my bodyguard, he's also here in Chicago to make sure I do my bonyad director's bidding. I'm finished doing my bonyad's bidding, so I'm willing to sacrifice him."

"You're not in charge here," Stoker said as he removed his .45 caliber pistol from a holster in the small of his back and screwed on a suppressor. "The day will never come when I believe you." Then he gave Ahmadi the hand signal for her to cover him. She raised her nine-millimeter Glock as he advanced on the storage area. Secretly, Stoker hoped for the opportunity to take more of Nikolas's men alive.

In his mind, Nikolas had rehearsed this moment. By design, he had placed the man inside the stowage. A soldier who had lived most of his life in a small Iranian village was lying facedown. He whispered some verses from the Koran. Nikolas had taught him the passages, many years before, specifically for this occasion.

"And do not say about those who are killed in the way of Allah, 'They are dead.' Rather, they are alive, but you perceive it not. And we will surely test you with something of fear and hunger and a loss of wealth and lives and fruits, but give good tidings to the patient, who, when disaster strikes them, say, 'Indeed we belong to Allah.'" His pistol sat on the ground next to him.

Stoker quickly threw the stowage door open and aimed his

gun downward. The man inside grabbed his weapon and raised it. But, his draw was slow. Stoker squeezed the trigger and sent a subsonic round into the man's head. Then he put a second round into the man's heart.

Ahmadi swept in behind Stoker. "There's a good chance there are more people on the boat. You cover me—"

Stoker cut her off. "Not yet. Hang on, Ahmadi," he said. "Something's not right here. That man drew on me, but his reaction was dull. It was almost as if he was impaired."

"Now do you trust me?" Nikolas stood on the dock. "I gave away the position of one of my finest men. I sacrificed him to win your trust."

"This still doesn't feel right," Stoker said. "Where's this second guy? And, I just want to remind you, we've got a fiery lady, Agent Ahmadi, with a real gun trained on you, bud."

"I get it," Nikolas said. Then he pointed down into the boat. "My man's below. I told him to hide in a storage compartment, aft berth."

"I don't speak boat very well," Stoker said. "Where's the aft berth?"

"The bedroom in the back," Nikolas clarified.

"Now fall in line between Agent Ahmadi and me," Stoker ordered.

Stoker held the gun in front of him and then he passed through the companionway. He quickly descended the ladders into the saloon, moving his firearm from one side to another. Nikolas and Ahmadi followed. Then Stoker stepped into the berth. Turning to his left, he saw the storage compartment. Stoker threw open the door. Through the dim light, he saw the whites of another man's eyes. Grabbing the stranger, Stoker yanked him out of the compartment. Intending to capture the man alive, Stoker threw him on the bed and landed on top of him. He reached down to try and subdue the man's hands. He grabbed the man's forearm and twisted it inward. The man shrieked, and bones snapped in his arm. Stoker pushed the bed sheets away, and he looked down at the pain-contorted face.

"It's Nazem," Stoker yelled.

Ahmadi noticed Nazem's free left hand pulling a nickel plated snub-nosed .38 Special from an ankle holster. "Gun!" she yelled. Ahmadi switched her gun to her left hand as she jumped to grab his arm. A shot rang out, and a bullet flew toward the boat's stern. Ahmadi slammed his forearm on the side of the wall, and the gun popped out of his hand.

"Nobody moves!" Stoker yelled. "I'm good!"

"Me too!" Ahmadi responded. "Nikolas, are you hit?"

"No."

Nazem was screaming. Stoker checked him over. The bullet had not struck him.

"Where did the round go?" Ahmadi asked.

"Right there," Nikolas pointed at a wooden panel. Then his face went ashen and dread filled his voice as he exclaimed, "Oh no. Rivera."

"What?" Stoker asked. "Is Rivera back there?"

"Yes, he's in the dinghy garage."

"Ahmadi, you handcuff this guy," Stoker ordered.

She grabbed Nazem, pulled his arms together. "Done. Let's get out of here."

Stoker turned to Nikolas. "I don't know what a dinghy garage is. But, you'll take me there, right now."

"Follow me," Nikolas said.

"I've got this gun trained on your other leg, Nikolas. If anything funny happens, you won't be so lucky."

Nikolas climbed up the ladders. "Have I resisted you at all?"

Stoker didn't answer as he followed Nikolas onto the main deck of the boat. Instead, he ordered, "The dinghy garage. Double time it."

"It's at the very back of the boat. The little garage holds a much smaller boat, a dinghy, which we use to get to shore. It was sufficiently spacious for your Rivera friend. But, I'm afraid it's not very comfortable."

"I'm not worried about his comfort. I'm worried about the bullet. If Rivera's hurt, you'll never feel comfort again."

Nikolas opened an access panel that contained some controls. When he pressed a button, the back panel of the boat seemed to open downward toward the water. Stoker kept his gun trained on Nikolas.

When the door was about one-third open, Rivera suddenly flopped over the edge of the door, fell into the water and disappeared into the water's darkness.

"Quiet!" Stoker ordered. They all scanned the water, waiting for Rivera to surface. After twenty seconds Stoker yelled out. "Rivera!" There was no response. He waited for another twenty seconds and yelled his name again. After a full minute had passed, there was no sign of Rivera.

"I fear for this man, Rivera," Nikolas said. "Nobody can hold their breath that long."

"Quiet!" Stoker ordered again.

Nikolas stepped toward the dinghy garage. "Hold it right there," Stoker said. "Where are you going?"

"To look for traces of blood in the dinghy garage."

"You stay there. I'll look." Stoker peered down into the chamber where Rivera had been held captive. "No blood here. But it looks like he made short work of the ropes you bound him with."

"Only half the ropes, *loco*," came the voice of Errol Rivera. "And, who shot the bullet that buzzed past me?"

"Rivera!" Stoker called out. "Where are you?"

"Other side of the dock. Come help me get out of the water. My hands are bound, and I didn't have a chance to change out of my clothes and into my swimming suit before I went for a dip." Stoker leaped to the side of the boat and looked at the dock. Rivera was using both hands, joined by ropes, to hold onto the dock.

Stoker turned to Nikolas. "Stay right there."

"Have I not obeyed your every order?" Nikolas replied.

"Silence!" Stoker said. Stoker disembarked from the sailboat and jogged down the dock where Rivera was waiting. Tucking his gun into the small of his back, he reached down, grabbed Rivera by his belt, and lifted him out of the water. "Why are you screwing around and playing games at a time like this? After two minutes under the water, I thought you were in real trouble."

"I wasn't screwing around. I dove down and stayed under for about ninety seconds. I surfaced very quietly on the other side of the dock. When I heard your voice, I listened a little more to see what was going on. I didn't know if you were in charge, or if someone was in charge of you? For all I knew, they had captured you, too."

"No, I was here to rescue you."

"Damn! After freeing myself with that beautiful flop into the water, now I have to pretend you rescued me?"

"Well, who do you think arranged to have the terrorist open the dinghy garage?"

"Okay," Rivera said. "You make an excellent point. Thank you for rescuing me."

"You're welcome. I am very impressed with your armless swimming."

"Not bad for an old guy," Rivera said as he dripped water all over the dock. "Can you cut my arms loose?"

Stoker retrieved a knife from his pocket and slashed the ropes that bound Rivera. "So, you're okay?" Stoker asked. "We thought the stray bullet might have hit you."

"I heard the round buzz by," Rivera said. He walked back to the boat with Stoker. He seemed oblivious to his wet shirt, pants, shoes, and socks. "Who shot at me?" Rivera asked.

"The guy with the broken arm inside the boat. It's Nazem. Ahmadi has him in flex cuffs."

"And who's that guy?" Rivera asked pointing at Nikolas. "And why do you have him at gunpoint?"

"That is Nikolas Antoniou. He's a terrorist—the man behind the manufacture and disbursement of the Campylobacter jejuni bacteria we've been chasing down for the last few weeks."

Rivera's jaw clenched, and his eyes flashed anger. His short military haircut exposed the bulging blood vessels on the side of his head. He bounded up onto the sailboat, balled up his fist and swung for Nikolas's face. Carefully sidestepping the punch, Nikolas offered no additional resistance or defense. Rivera's left jab caught him squarely in the nose and sent him flying onto the deck. "I've seen the people in Mexico, on ventilators, suffering from your creation. I'm watching my best friend's wife depleting to a fraction of her former self because of your bug." Rivera reached down and picked him up by his shirt. "You're about to meet the depths of Lake Michigan. Let's cast off, Stoker."

"Not just yet," Stoker said. "If we want to quell the epidemic, we may need some of Nikolas's knowledge."

"Good point. Let's start extracting some intel."

"Yes," Nikolas said. "I want to tell my story. I will give you all the intel you need."

"Just like that? You'll just give us all this intel?" Stoker asked in palpable sarcasm. "Yesterday you were an evil terrorist, but today you're a helpful ally?" Stoker sneered at Nikolas. "I don't know your scheme yet. Now, get into the boat." Nikolas quickly complied and stepped down the ladders into the boat's saloon. Stoker and Rivera followed.

Down in the cabin, Nazem was chanting and saying some kind of prayer. "What's going on here?" Stoker asked.

"He has been supplicating Allah for the last few minutes," Ahmadi said.

"Can you translate his Farsi for us?"

"We Muslims pray in Arabic. I would describe this as a sort of martyrdom prayer. He believes suicide's in his future. He's asking Allah for mercy for his sins. He is mixing a lot of verses into his prayer from the Koran about martyrdom."

Stoker frowned. "I don't understand this at all. I don't see this motivation." Stoker glanced over at Nikolas. "Care to enlighten us Mister Altruistic?"

Rivera didn't allow Nikolas to respond. Interjecting his own question, he asked, "Have you checked Nazem for explosives?"

"Yes," Ahmadi said. "Right after he discharged the gun, we got flex cuffs on him. Then we frisked him and looked for weapons."

"Usually I would be very concerned about a suicidal person," Stoker said. "But with a terrorist, I only care about what they can tell me. How and when he leaves this world is of no concern to me."

Just then, the man smiled. "I will not be telling you anything, Stoker," the man said. His smiled disappeared for a moment and then returned. "Indeed we belong to Allah, and indeed to Him we will return. Those are the ones upon whom are blessings from their Lord and mercy. And it is those who are the rightly guided." Nazem paused for a moment of discomfort, then looked up at Stoker with a menacing glare. "I belong to Allah. I am rightly guided. And, may your lost American soul rot in hell." Then he fell sideways onto the bed. When his head hit the mattress, his mouth expelled a stream of foam. All signs of life left his face.

"Cyanide?" Ahmadi asked.

"Most likely," Stoker said. "But, let's not worry about the dead guy right now."

Suddenly Stoker grabbed Nikolas, wrestled him to the ground, and pinned him on his back. Then he pounded on his sternum. "What the hell is going on?"

Nikolas winced at the pain. Then he looked away from Stoker and toward the ground at his side. "I find it very interesting he ended his life with cyanide. I have suspicions about Nazem's motives, but I do not know why he chose to die."

"What do you mean?" Rivera barked.

Nikolas spoke calmly. "I need to think about the facts. That's all. There is much more I can tell you, that I want to tell you."

"I don't like what's going on here," Stoker said. "It doesn't make sense when terrorists, like your two men here, allow themselves to die—without killing any other enemies at the same time? It seems like a pretty empty jihad for those guys."

"Those guys were such brainwashed religious lemmings," Ahmadi interjected. "They'll do anything the bonyad or Nikolas asks."

"The experiences I just had with your two men seemed bizarre to me. The way they behaved just didn't seem right. They went down a little too easy."

"Oh, Stoker. You're just paranoid," Rivera said.

"Yeah right," Stoker responded. Then he asked Nikolas, "Do you always give your agents cyanide capsules?"

"They have been trained to die," Nikolas responded, "rather than suffer a degrading interrogation by your people."

Stoker just looked at Nikolas and thought, *I'm starting to understand a method to this madness. He's bartering for our trust, and these men are his currency. But, his submission must be shrouding something bigger. I can play this game.*

Rivera pointed to Nikolas's mouth. "And, do you have a cyanide capsule ready to swallow at a moment's notice?"

"These are my men. Why would I need to die?" Nikolas said. "I have no cyanide capsules—because I am willing to tell you everything without any compulsion. I don't want to die. I only want to tell you the truth."

"Of course," Stoker replied. This time he was ready to pretend some trust in Nikolas. "Tell us more of your truths. Give us the whole story."

· · ·

"I know you don't trust me," Nikolas said. "But, I have

shown you good faith. Two of my men are dead. What else needs to happen for you to believe me? You should trust me at least a little by now."

"Okay," Stoker said. "Let's hear everything you want to tell us. Let's keep exercising this trust thing right here and right now. I'm recording this." Stoker removed his phone from his pocket and started recording.

Nikolas looked into the camera and began. "For the past thirty years, my name has been Nikolas Antoniou. I have committed many crimes and acts of terror against the United States of America. My greatest crime is unleashing a weapon of lethal silence."

"You've poisoned America with a highly virulent strain of Campylobacter jejuni," Stoker interjected. "One you brought in from Mexico."

Nikolas looked surprised. "Yes. How did you know so much about the Campylobacter jejuni?"

"Not only am I a warrior. I'm also a physician. My team and I have been working in Mexico. We've seen your victims there."

"I shall not share words of apology with you. I hope to show contrition through my actions. I came to America on a Greek passport, a passport fabricated by the Iranian Ministry of Intelligence. My government singled me out at the age of thirteen as a person with the attributes necessary to lead a business empire. I also showed some promise as a scientist. The Iranian government invested much time and money training me ruthlessly for my grand mission. They started by helping me master the Greek language, while also providing me with a legend that injected me into Greek society's privileged class. I attended the best schools in Athens. I was a good student. But, my Iranian handlers tutored me, and I earned superb marks. I then attended Cambridge University in the UK, where I excelled, double majoring in biology and economics. The next step in the Iranian plan was for me to complete an MBA at an American university. My bonyad director selected the University of Chicago's MBA program. After completing that degree, the Iranian government had what they wanted. A person ready to take their venture capital, build a vast business empire, and use that empire as a shroud to camouflage a bioterrorism attack on your country.

"And, I must correct one point from your story, Dr. Stoker. Mexico was where we tested our Campylobacter jejuni strain. We engineered that germ in the Middle East, and I multiplied the bacteria there. We stored it here in the underground levels of Hotel Esatto in a specially built laboratory, as your FBI experts will soon confirm." Nikolas looked at Ahmadi. "Do you know what a bonyad is, Agent Ahmadi?"

"They are a type of Iranian charitable organization. Most of them noble."

"Yes," Nikolas took over the description from Ahmadi. "Bonyads are somewhat similar to American charitable trusts, foundations, and not-for-profit organizations. Bonyads, on the surface, are an Iranian equivalent. Many are good. But, a few of them are rife with corruption. The evil ones may put some money and publicity into building a hospital, funding scholarships, and feeding and clothing the poor. However, beneath their front, they operate like a private equity firm to fund activities to undermine Israel, America, and the West. For many years I have been virtually an indentured servant to a bonyad director. He's the equivalent of the chairman and CEO. His board of directors is a group of mullahs and ayatollahs who run Iran. My orders? Use hundreds of millions of the bonyad's dollars to build and operate my hotel. They are the investors, and I am the entrepreneur.

"People who report to me are also running the Little Italy sandwich shops. Anyone who has purchased a sandwich, with mayonnaise, at one of those shops in the last few days, has been exposed to our genetically weaponized strain of Campylobacter jejuni. I suspect about fifty percent of those people will contract Guillain-Barre syndrome."

Rivera spoke up. "Let me guess. You're about to tell us you have numerous companies fronting and producing terror?"

"Yes," Nikolas replied. "I want to come clean about all of them. We planned and implemented a new venture called CoolSolar. We take our solar-powered mist machines to events such as concerts, state fairs, triathlons, and marathons. We also have contracts to provide misting systems all over the United States. People find the cooling mist very appealing, and they gravitate—"

"But the mist also contains Campylobacter jejuni bacteria," Stoker said while cloaking his indignation.

Then Ahmadi spoke up. "But, you still have not explained your *supposed* captivity. You run a beautiful hotel. I see this stunning boat. I think you're living a charmed life. I don't see evidence you're the hostage you claim to be.

"I have a beautiful American wife," Nikolas paused for effect while pretending to be very sad. Stoker sensed his fabricated sorrow. "Together we have three children, the oldest being sixteen. They've been in captivity for four years, hostages in Saudi Arabia by Iranian agents, unknown to the Saudi government. And, if I fail in my attack on America, I will witness their execution, one by one. I will be allowed one week to mourn them, to live in misery. Then they will hang me."

"But, you've now kept your end of the agreement," Ahmadi said. "Why are you not reuniting with your family? That doesn't make sense."

"It does make sense," Stoker said. "Mullahs don't keep all their promises."

"This attack is in its early stages. My bonyad director is screaming at me for results. He will not be satisfied until this attack brings America to its knees."

"Until your weaponized pathogen overwhelms every hospital," Stoker said. "Until victims of Guillain-Barre syndrome overcome the ICUs and outstrip the capacity of all the ventilators in America."

Yes, Mr. Smarty pants Doctor, Nikolas thought. *You don't know about the amoeba and a few other plans.* Then he continued with this incomplete story. "Until the hostile families are showing up at hospitals and demanding services at gunpoint. Until the docile families are using Ambu bags to keep their loved ones breathing and alive," Nikolas said, "exhausting themselves by taking shifts squeezing that bag repeatedly for hours that turn into days and compound into weeks. With this potent strain of the bacteria, it may be months. Nevertheless, even this death toll and level of misery may not satisfy my bonyad director and the ayatollahs. They still may not free my family."

Rivera chimed in. "In three weeks, your director and the Ayatollahs will see the newspaper headlines, read the tweets, and watch the live news feeds. They'll have their short celebration. But, I think they'll be disappointed. This trial will be hard for America, but we'll figure it out."

"You're never going to see that family of yours again,"

Stoker said. "You'll be locked away in a maximum-security prison awaiting execution."

"You're right about my fate. But, if Allah hears my prayers, my family will return safely to America."

Stoker interrupted him by clamping his powerful hand on his shoulder. Then he leaned in and whispered in Nikolas's ear, so only Nikolas could hear. "Drop the charade, Nikolas. You're not a religious man, a believer. It's not in your nature. You're a master manipulator."

Nikolas frowned and he took a moment to rethink his approach. "My wife and children are Americans. They have done nothing wrong. Will you please extract them, before the bonyad director orders their execution?"

"I've heard enough," Ahmadi said. "Let's get this Bozo into an interrogation room and find out how to stop this epidemic." She stood Nikolas up.

"I'll tell you everything," Nikolas said.

"Yes, you will. I guarantee it." Stoker said. Then Stoker made a snap decision to leverage Nikolas's family. "Your story sounds off the wall to me. But, if you tell our experts everything. And, if our experts tell us your story holds water, we'll go find your wife and kids. But before we go, we need all the information about this disease you can provide ASAP, or we don't go—period."

"Tell it all," Rivera said. "What about the Campylobacter bacteria? How did you get the bacteria so potent?"

"We genetically engineered a new strain. We increased the number of antigens likely to trigger Guillain-Barre syndrome. Our bacterium increases the incidence of Guillain-Barre more than 100-fold.

Then Ahmadi took a turn to ask a question. "With this strain, what percentage of people infected develop Guillain-Barre?"

"Close to half."

"We know those trials were in Mexico," Stoker said.

"Yes. From what you said earlier, it sounds like you were there?"

"We were there, in Chihuahua."

"Fifteen of our trainees," Nikolas said, "and their leader died during a training exercise outside of Chihuahua."

"Yes. That was me." Stoker said. "They fired on me."

Nikolas was speechless. The realization that he was being interrogated by a soldier with such a violent history froze him with fear.

Stoker continued. "Yes, we found your test subjects in Chihuahua. Do you know the lab technician? He was Iranian."

Nikolas made a quick nod of his head.

"I'm the one who knocked him out. Did you hear about your guys in the *Soltolería*? What about your guys in trucks who met the grenades on a dirt road northeast of Chihuahua?"

Nikolas's eyes opened wider. He made no effort to hide his surprise or alarm.

"Yes! That was us! And now, here you are, attacking the United States of America." Stoker looked at Ahmadi as if to suggest she ask the next question.

"The Campylobacter," she said. "Who were your targets in the U.S.?"

"Customers of Little Italy sandwich shops. Participants in athletic events like marathons and triathlons. Hotel banquet attendees. I had more than 100 people working as banquet chefs and large hotels around the country. We've infected the food at NASCAR races and at some NCAA football games."

"You must've infected millions of people."

"I'm ashamed to say, our estimates project infecting tens of millions of Americans."

"What else is there?" Stoker asked.

"I've told you everything," Nikolas lied.

While this was not a boldfaced lie, it was an omission—an enormous one. Nikolas said nothing about the Balamuthia mandrillaris amoeba he was also circulating using mist machines and other methods. And there was more, so much more.

"Our experts will interrogate you further. But, we need to start to make good on our promise," Rivera said, giving Nikolas a degree of hope he might get what he wanted. "Where is your family being held?"

"You should fly to Jubail, a city on the Persian Gulf side of Saudi Arabia. There's an industrial building north of the airport. Take Tapline Road for 36 miles to the north. You can't miss it. When you arrive, tell the guards you wish to visit with Elizabeth. She's my wife."

"That's a nice suggestion," Stoker said with sarcasm in his voice. "We will not be entering in the traditional, cordial manner you suggest. We'll be arriving in darkness with a group of very well-trained operatives."

CHAPTER 22

Chicago, Illinois

The FBI detained Nikolas Antoniou at the Chicago FBI field office. They also arrested Roya. Ahmadi sent the recordings of Nikolas's confessions to the FBI director.

Interrogators went to work on Nikolas, asking him for meticulous details about the Campylobacter jejuni bacteria, his business holdings, and his history with the Iranian bonyad. They ran background checks and froze bank accounts. But most of the funds had been conveniently swept into accounts in Asia and the Middle East over the last few hours. So, the FBI could not freeze that money immediately.

Roya was only somewhat cooperative. Nikolas provided lengthy answers to all their questions. Yet, he still held back. He revealed nothing about the cruise ship Tropical Solace, the Balamuthia amoeba, or any other plans the FBI did not already know something about.

It took less than three hours for the FBI, the Centers for Disease Control, and local police departments to shut down all the Little Italy sandwich shops owned by Nikolas throughout the whole country. They closed and evacuated Hotel Esatto, much to the chagrin of thousands of loyal guests. They also found paper trails to the Benevolent Iranian Student League—just like Nikolas had set them up to be found. Hundreds of hotel-based banquets, across the country, were immediately canceled; and the cooks and chefs were interrogated. CoolSolar documents were uncovered, again like Nikolas wanted them to be. The mist machines were turned off.

The FBI closed down the lab in the basement of Hotel Esatto. But, the lab had completed its work. It was virtually empty.

The FBI continued to dig into Nikolas's office as well as the offices and computers of his accountants and managers. But, there was almost no additional paperwork to be found. Nikolas's enterprises ran on a near paperless system—all cloud-based with server farms co-located in Iran, Lebanon, and Yemen. The moment the FBI had set foot in the hotel, Nikolas's head of security notified the bonyad in Tehran. In turn, the bonyad's IT gurus disabled everyone's usernames and passwords, even Nikolas's. The FBI had little access to corporate records for Hotel Esatto, CoolSolar, the Benevolent Iranian Student League, or any of Nikolas's other businesses. They were sealed out by technology and the borders that lie between them and an enemy state.

"Bravo, Stoker and Rivera," Ahmadi said after a sleepless night of investigating and interrogating. "It turns out that Roya's mist containers contained no pathogens. Nikolas tells us Roya was just rehearsing—making sure that she had her safety procedures down before they started to use live canisters in the next 24 hours. The plan was for Nikolas to leave the hotel today, and never return. Roya would plant all the infectious canisters during one shift. Then she would leave, never to return. I know you doctors have saved a few lives during your career. But tonight, you can add a few thousand more. First, you prevented thousands of Hotel Esatto guests from lethal infections. But, there's more."

"What do you mean, more?" Stoker asked.

"We found a few hundred canisters, still in their shipping boxes. One of the boxes had a shipping manifest from a factory here in Chicago. There we found an active operation that was shipping out tens of thousands of canisters every week, all over the country. That's been shut down. And, with the help of the shipping company, we've been able to trace all the shipments and alert the purchasers."

"Wow," Rivera said. Rarely did he have one-word answers.

"We estimate that you've saved at least ten thousand lives by interrupting Nikolas's mist canister plan. Add to that tens of thousands more because we shut down his silent strikes at Little Italy sandwich shops and all of the other places he was infecting food."

• • •

The next morning Allie went to work with her client in Chicago. But, when she got back to her hotel, she was exhausted. She went directly to her room and climbed into bed. Troy picked up takeout from a quaint restaurant. In their room, they ate small portions of grilled salmon, fresh peach slices, baked potatoes, and steamed carrots.

"Thank you, Troy," Allie said as she sat up for a moment to eat. "There's nothing like salmon to warm my cold Nordic heart." She took a bite and chewed slowly. "I guess I better enjoy it while I can. In a few days, my nourishment will probably be through a feeding tube."

"A Nordic feeding tube. They have those you know. They're inflexible and kind of stubborn."

Allie laughed. "With everyone treating me so delicate lately, I actually welcome your snarky insult."

The second day after her diagnosis, Allie went to the hospital infusion center for plasma exchange. The procedure removed some of the antibodies that were attacking her nerves from her bloodstream.

Again, on days three and four Allie went to work. She barely had the energy to work eight hours. Like she had done the previous two nights, she came back to the hotel and collapsed into bed. Each night Troy brought her a meal. During the days that Allie was growing weaker, Stoker spent his precious downtime with her. When she was at work, Stoker was participating in the hunt for the Iranians who had crossed the border.

Allie's workdays grew shorter and shorter. "Why did I have to get sick for us to make time like this, Troy?" she asked before fading off to sleep at the end of day six. Seven days after Allie Stoker's diagnosis, she was so tired, she could only work from her bed, on her laptop computer, for three hours. That prompted her sister, mother, and father to come into town.

Over the next few days, Rivera led the ongoing surveillance in Chicago. Z became his right-hand man in Stoker's absence. The tech genius proved himself very valuable by orchestrating all the technical work. With the blessing of a federal judge and a FISA warrant, Z's facial recognition software was scanning images captured from cameras all over the city. But, the men they had been searching for must have been avoiding the streets. They never succeeded in identifying any of the Iranian border crossers.

For Allie Stoker, the disease was progressing more rapidly than Stoker, Rivera, and her neurologist had expected. On day ten Stoker drove her to the hospital, and the neurologist admitted her. On day eleven, it was time for Allie to be transferred into the ICU.

There a ventilator would take over her breathing as the disease progressed through its most cruel phase, paralysis.

"We're having some trouble opening up a bed for you, Mrs. Stoker," her neurologist reported. Allie looked alarmed.

"Don't worry, honey." Stoker's tone was calm a reassuring. "This happens all the time." In a few hours, they'll be able to transfer a patient out, and a spot will open up for you."

"This situation is different." The neurologist had almost interrupted Stoker. She was very serious. "There are nine other cases of Guillain-Barre syndrome in the ICU, and they progressed unusually fast, much like Mrs. Stoker. It may be a day or two before a bed opens up here."

"Then let's transfer her to another hospital," Stoker said.

"I was about to explore that possibility with you," the neurologist replied. "But, here's the problem. All of the ICUs in Chicago are maxed out for some reason."

Stoker's heart started to pound. People can go weeks without food and two or three days without water. But, humans can only go for a few seconds or minutes without breathing. For her very survival, Allie needed to be in an ICU and on a ventilator. "Let me call Rivera. We'll figure this out."

Twenty seconds later Stoker was on the phone with Dr. Errol Rivera. "Allie needs to be on a ventilator, perhaps in the next six to twelve hours. But, all the ICUs in Chicago are full. They have nine other Guillain-Barre cases in the ICU here. Can you help me out?"

"I've got a bad feeling about this, Stoker. The disease is progressing throughout the nation this quickly, and America's not ready. I'll make some phone calls. If there are any veterans in the ICUs, I'll get them transferred to the VA hospital and open up a spot for Allie." Then Rivera made another suggestion. "Why don't you suggest transferring one or more ICU patients to a long-term acute care facility?"

"The LTAC is a brilliant idea," Stoker responded. "Let's not transfer patients to make room for Allie. Let's send Allie to the LTAC. It may be the perfect place."

"I like it," Rivera said. "These long-term hospitals may be a good match for people with Guillain-Barre syndrome. They can keep them breathing and keep their pain managed. Can I call around and find out which ones have the best reputation?"

"I would appreciate that," Stoker said. "And the long-term hospital will probably allow more family visits and support," Stoker said.

Twenty minutes later, Rivera called back and recommended the Sunrise Long-term Acute Care Hospital. Stoker kissed Allie on the forehead. "I'll be back, honey. I've got a visit to make."

Stoker walked quickly out to the street. Then he took a cab to the Sunrise Long-term Acute Care Hospital in the Suburbs of Chicago. After walking in through the front door, he followed a sign to the admitting office. When Stoker walked into the simple office, a woman was on the phone. She acknowledged him with a smile, then she held up her index finger as if to say, just a minute.

Stoker picked up a brochure. Its pictures showed patients and families smiling as if staying in this hospital was akin to a night on the town. Long-term acute care hospitals, or LTACs, were a little-publicized phenomenon in the American health care system. Patients who needed a month or more of acute care qualified to stay in LTACs instead of a traditional hospital. Paralyzed patients and people in long-term comas made up a large proportion of the hospital's clientele. The brochure also included a picture of a pulmonologist who was the medical director.

The woman finished her phone call. "May I help you?"

"Yes, my name is Troy Stoker. I'm a doctor, and I would like to admit a patient here."

"Very good. Let's get that process started."

"This patient is not my patient, per se. She's my wife. Her diagnosis is Guillain-Barre syndrome. I think she's going to need to be on a ventilator in the next few hours. Can you accommodate her that quickly?"

"Assuming we can get your insurance to authorize her visit, yes," she said. "My name is Grace Dean. I'm the admitting nurse. Let's get going on some paperwork."

"I don't want preauthorization or insurance hurdles to slow the process. I'll just pay for it. If you need anything else, just let me know."

Grace smiled. "Thank you, Dr. Stoker."

"Yes. There's some definite urgency here. Let's do it now."

"In my opinion, we should get most of the Guillain-Barre syndrome cases," Grace said. "We have more liberal visitation policies, and our floors are much quieter than hospital ICUs."

"Great. I want my wife to walk in here under her own power while she still can. She's a strong and independent soul. She will accept her treatment better if she chooses to walk through the doors on her own."

"Can you have her attending physician at the hospital call me?" Grace asked.

"I've got her on speed dial." Stoker dialed the neurologist, and she answered. Stoker introduced the neurologist to Grace.

After a five-minute conversation, Grace ended the call and handed Stoker his phone. "You go get your wife. I'll assign her a bed right now."

An hour later Stoker and Allie were both in a rental car, on their way to the LTAC. They pulled the car into the parking lot and parked. Allie got out of the car and began her trek into the hospital. "It's afternoon, and the temperature's about eighty-eight degrees," she said. "I guess these are my last breaths of fresh air for a few weeks." Her pace slowed. "They'll keep me cooped up in my room with a temperature of a constant seventy-two degrees or something like that." She stopped and wrapped her arm around Troy's bicep. "I don't like constant, with one exception." She transferred a fair amount of weight to her husband. The short walk had depleted most of the strength in her legs. "That exception is you, Troy. Thank you for being so constant."

"You're welcome, Allie. I like constant you, too."

"That's why the next few weeks are going to be tough for us."

"What do you mean? I'll be right here by your side."

"No, Troy." Allie stopped. "There's something bigger out there than you and me—than our desire to be constant." Allie was catching her breath. "There's a puzzle out there. There are only a few people in the world who see this act of bioterrorism in its entirety. There are only two doctors in the whole United States who are ahead of this situation. And, you are one of them. There are millions out there who need you right now. It's easy math."

"Well, they may have to wait for a few days. I can do quite a bit right here from the hospital."

Just then, Allie's parents and sister pulled into the parking lot. "I told my parents and sister your story of the past few weeks—everything you've experienced. The Shiite extremists in Chicago,

Guillain-Barre syndrome in Mexico."

"They must think I'm crazy."

"No, Troy. They think you're the man for this season, and so do I. It's not by chance you were in Mexico. It's not by chance you had a detour to the hospital in Chihuahua. I'm coming to accept that I needed to be one of the first cases so you would have the conviction—the indignation—you need to go out there and save millions of other people like me."

"But, the millions of people have Errol Rivera and Z," Stoker rebutted. "Those two have the tools and information everyone needs."

"No, Troy," Allie said as they reached the front door to the hospital. Troy opened it, and she stepped through. They walked into the lobby a few steps and Allie sat down on a couch. "Look at how well you've taken care of me. You thought outside the box. I'm here in this specialized hospital, a kind of hospital I never even knew existed. I'm far away from the craziness of a big general hospital. It's peaceful here, and my family can be by my side the whole time. My parents and sister have already set up a schedule to make sure someone is always with me. They worked out their shifts. And, I asked them to exclude you, because the world needs you more than I do. You need to be out there fighting this war."

An automatic door opened. Grace, the admitting nurse, and another person dressed in scrubs emerged from a treatment area. "Welcome Mrs. Stoker," Grace said.

Allie smiled at her. "Thank you, I guess." Allie's parents and sister entered the lobby. Allie stood up, and her legs trembled. She squeezed Troy's hand. "As you can see, I have a lot of support on my admission day. I need you to go out there, solve this problem, and be here for my discharge."

Allie's dad spoke up. "You're an incredibly supportive husband, Troy."

"You can prevent moments just like this one for millions of people, Troy," Allie whispered as her eyes moistened. "It's a small sacrifice, this bookmark. Leave me here. Then come back and burst through that door when you've saved the world."

Allie was right—and he hated it. Troy Stoker, MD, then did the hardest thing he'd ever done in his life. The husband, doctor, and warrior spun around and started for the door. Each pace was resolute, and he did not look back.

CHAPTER 23

Chicago, Illinois

Dark gray clouds floated above Stoker. Looking toward downtown, he could see fog floating amongst the skyscrapers, dropping a welcome summer rainstorm on the streets of Chicago. Z navigated the rental car into the parking lot and pulled up to Stoker, who was standing curbside outside of the Sunrise Long-term Acute Care Hospital.

As Stoker crawled into the car, Z asked, "How's Allie?"

"There's not much to say. She's in a tough spot. But, she recognizes that a few million people are going to be in her same boat. So, she kicked me out with orders to go fight this battle. She wants us to save as many people as we can from this miserable disease. Now, bring me up to speed on the last few hours."

Z pulled the car away from the curb. "Not until you give me a little more detail on Allie." The windshield wipers fanned back and forth, not on the highest setting, but close. "Her parents and sister are with her," Stoker said. "We found this hospital for long-term situations like this one. She should be safe here, even when things get crazy."

"Will she be awake when she's in those worst few days, the days when the ventilator is breathing for her?"

"She'll be heavily sedated, and probably will spend some time in a drug-induced coma."

"I'm so sorry for Allie," Z said. "There's not much any of us can say, other than that sucks."

"There's my update about Allie. What can you tell me to help us win this fight?"

"First, we got results back from the CDC in Atlanta. The samples from the lab in Hotel Esatto's special basement lab contained the same strain of Campylobacter jejuni we uncovered in Mexico."

"That's no surprise," Stoker said.

"Second, we've been searching high and low for these would-be Iranian terrorists, the ones we followed in from Mexico. But, they've all disappeared. We have, however, shut down Hotel Esatto. We made the media think it was because of a significant natural gas leak. We've also arrested a bunch of Nikolas's key employees. The accounting and IT personnel have been particularly helpful. We've collected a lot of valuable intel from them."

"How did you like Hotel Esatto?" Stoker asked. "I'm referring to the experience you had before we learned it was a node of international terrorism."

"That fresh-squeezed tangerine juice tastes amazing," Z replied. "But, I think I may be allergic to it. I got a headache shortly after drinking it two days ago."

"Have your headaches gone away?"

"They did. So yesterday I took a risk and drank more tangerine juice."

"And, it gave you a headache again?"

"Yes. But, I also felt some stiffness in my neck."

"If it was just headaches, I may be willing to entertain your allergy diagnosis. But, the stiffness in your neck would steer me more toward an infection of some kind. Perhaps a virus. Have you had any other symptoms? Skin rashes, nausea, or swelling?"

"No, just the headaches and stiffness in my neck."

"No fever?"

"None I can think of."

"Okay. Just let me know if you get any other symptoms." Stoker thought for another minute. "Have you been working out?"

"Almost every day," Z replied as he maneuvered the car around a right turn at a busy intersection.

"Is there any part of your workout feeling out of kilter? Like, have you noticed any part of your strength or stamina decreasing?"

"Strength and stamina when I lift weights are good. My legs have felt a little rubbery lately. I've been favoring my left leg a bit."

"How about running?" Stoker asked. "Have you noticed any difference there?"

"Yes. During my workout at Hotel Esatto's gym a couple of days ago, I just didn't feel as good when I was running. I'm slower."

"Okay then, let's have Rivera and me take a better look at you this afternoon," Stoker said.

The weakness in Z's legs, a common Guillain-Barre syndrome symptom, concerned Stoker, but he did not want to cause his friend any alarm. "I suspect you've got some kind of virus," Stoker said to placate Z. "You're just such a tough guy. A little virus isn't going to keep you down. What else can you tell me about the latest investigation here in Chicago?"

"There's not much more to tell you. Ahmadi's FBI agents have been scouring the streets.

Stoker pointed up at the clouds in the sky. "At least her agents won't have to be working the streets in the rain. It looks like this storm is letting up."

Z turned the car onto Interstate 55 and drove toward downtown Chicago. "Yes, it is. The clouds are lifting. But, I welcome rain in the summer."

Z and Stoker continued down the freeway. Most of the conversation was Z updating Stoker on minor details. Suddenly brilliant rays of sunshine broke through the clouds. Z squinted. Then he let loose a pain-laden yell while holding up a hand to shield the sun from his eyes. It was all he could do to keep the car under control.

Stoker looked over at him. "Are you okay? You're acting like a vampire sunbathing on a beach."

"No, I'm not okay." Z veered the car over into the right emergency lane and decelerated to a rapid stop. "The sunlight just triggered a beast of a headache," Z said as he rubbed his temples and kept his eyes closed. Stoker chose to remain silent. Z gritted his teeth and exhaled between audible murmurs. Then suddenly he bolted up in his seat, opened the door, jumped out of the car and ran to the right edge of the freeway shoulder. Stoker followed him. By the time he caught up to Z, the young tech enthusiast was bent over with his hands on his knees, puking up the contents of his stomach onto the rain-washed asphalt at the edge of Interstate 55.

Stoker came up behind him and placed his strong hand on Z's shoulder. "Don't worry, man. We're going to get this taken care of." When Z finished vomiting he slowly straightened from his hunched over stance. Then Stoker helped him over to the car, and Z leaned against the passenger-side door.

"Whoa. I don't know what just hit me. It came from nowhere, just out of the blue."

"Let me check you out a bit," Stoker said as he reached out and put his left hand behind Z's neck. "Just go with me here. I'm just going to move your head. Move with me." Stoker pushed Z's head to one side.

"Ouch. That kind of hurt," Z replied.

Stoker pursed his lips, furrowed his forehead, and reached his hand up to feel Z's forehead. "Your temperature feels a little high. We call your response to the sunlight photophobia. It's a symptom of a few things, including certain infections. Where's Rivera?"

"He's working out of the FBI field office."

"With the weakness in your legs, photophobia, the stiffness in your neck, and the headaches, you've got something going on. Let's get you treated ASAP—get you better. We need you on the team during this critical time."

"You're driving," Z said as he opened the passenger door and slumped into the car.

Less than thirty minutes later, Z had Stoker and Rivera poking and prodding him. After a few questions, Rivera spoke calmly. "We need more information than we can capture here in the field office. Let's take you to the hospital and run a few more tests. This should all be pretty routine stuff we can do right from the emergency room."

● ● ●

"How come I'm just learning about this Guillain-Barre syndrome epidemic now?" yelled president James Riddell in the face of his Secretary of Health and Human Services. "Come on Albert. I have confidence in you. Help me cut to the chase and get to the bottom line. What's your hunch?"

"Mr. President, my instincts tell me this is big. My hunch is this infection's not natural. Someone with sinister motives is the catalyst here."

"I'm issuing an executive order," the president said. "I want every new case of Guillain-Barre syndrome reported to state health departments within twenty-four hours of diagnosis. States will have twenty-four hours to forward those results to the Centers for Disease Control. I want daily updates." The President paused for a moment before he asked, "What else should we do?"

"Two things, sir. First, we need to get lab experts looking into what is causing this spike in cases. Second, we should have you meet with two doctors who have been raising a stink about this issue for a few days now. One is a military physician, Colonel Rivera. The second doctor is a psychiatrist from South Dakota, a Dr. Stoker. The FBI is crediting them with preventing tens of thousands of infections."

"I want a meeting with these doctors, ASAP," the President ordered. "What have they been saying?"

"They stumbled onto an epidemic in Chicago," explained the Health and Human Services Secretary. "And they have preliminary data about an inordinate number of cases in other metropolitan areas. Dr. Stoker's wife developed Guillain-Barre syndrome. They also mention some tie to Mexico. But my people need more time to verify the Mexican link."

"Have Stoker and Rivera bring any and all information they have. These guys don't sound like they're just playing doctor. They sound pretty serious. If what they're saying is true, we could have a national horror to deal with."

• • •

The emergency room doctor started to examine Z. "Your symptoms are interesting. A couple of them match up with an illness called Guillain-Barre syndrome, such as the weakness in your legs. We've seen a sudden spike in the number of Guillain-Barre cases here in Chicago, and the CDC has put out an alert."

"Guillain-Barre syndrome crossed our minds very early on," Stoker said. "But, Z's photophobia and neck pain are bothering me—"

The emergency room doctor interrupted Stoker. "I agree. Those two significant symptoms make me think it is much less likely to be Guillain-Barre. Let's check this out again," the doctor said. He grabbed the overhead exam light and tilted it down into Z's face.

"Ouch!" Z winced, closed his eyes and covered them with his forearm.

Then the emergency room doctor took hold of the back of Z's

neck and pushed his head backward and then forward. Again, Z complained. "That really hurts, Doc."

The emergency room doctor looked over at Stoker and Rivera and raised one eyebrow in an expression of concern.

"I hope you're good at spinal taps, Doc," Rivera said. Z flinched at the mention of a spinal tap.

"I think I'm pretty good at them," the ER doctor said.

"No way!" Z said. "No spinal taps." Z stood up and reached for his clothes. "I'm getting dressed and going back to my hotel."

"Relax loco," Rivera said.

"I've done hundreds of these," the ER doctor said. "I believe it will hurt a lot less than you think. I'll do my best to keep the pain down. Besides, we need to do this little procedure. But, let's get a CT scan first."

They gave Z an injection of lorazepam to diminish his anxiety. Then he had his CT scan. The spinal tap went well, and Z was pleased it hurt less than he had heard. During the next three hours, Z also had some other tests and exams, including an MRI. The results from his spinal tap showed elevated lymphocytes and an increased protein concentration—both evidence of infection in his brain or spine.

Finally, Z waited in the exam room while the three doctors reviewed his MRI. "Look at that lesion," Rivera said.

"It's sitting barely behind the prefrontal cortex," the ER doctor added. "He's also got some edema."

"Let's show Z what we're looking at," Stoker said.

The ER doctor swung a large monitor toward Z. It displayed many images of Z's brain. The doctor pointed to an area just to the side of the center of his head. This is the part of your brain that controls motor function. We suspect your leg weakness is due to a lesion you have at this location." The doctor circled his finger around an area on the MRI colored much lighter.

"Do I have a tumor? What do you mean a lesion?" Z asked.

"While I doubt it's a tumor, we're not sure what your lesion is. But we need to find out."

"Hey, Z. You're lucky it's not in your frontal lobe," Rivera said.

"Yes, really lucky," Z replied with lots of sarcasm.

Rivera explained. "You're unlucky to have a lesion like this.

But, if this lesion were situated a couple inches closer to the front of your skull, it would really affect your behavior. You would have severe impulse control problems.

"I am having impulse control problems," Z said. "I want to tell you to shut up. I want to just grab my clothes and run out of here. I just found out a lesion is occupying some valuable real estate inside my head."

The ER doctor started to speak. "There's a minimal procedure we need to do, Z. It's called a biopsy. We have to find out precisely what this lesion is. It's about the most straightforward procedure a neurosurgeon performs. We take you to the O.R. and put you under general anesthesia.

"It's also very techie," Stoker said realizing how the presence of technology would reassure Z thanks to his faith in technology. "A robot does a lot of the work."

"I'm having brain surgery?" Z asked in shock and disbelief. "Within the last few hours, I've gone from wondering if I'm allergic to tangerine juice to having brain surgery?"

"Yes," Stoker said firmly. "It's the best course. And it really is a very small brain surgery. Your pain will be minimal."

Z stood up and started to pull on his pants. When the hospital gown he was wearing got in the way of zipping up his fly, he ripped off the shroud. "This is bogus!" Z tossed the gown to the foot of the exam table. "I don't want anyone cutting into my brain. It's a brain filled with music, computer programming code, foreign languages, a knowledge of the world, and a love for the simplicity of warm pita bread." Z thought back to his time in the Nevada desert a few weeks ago. He longed to be in that place. He ached to feel free of burdens as he had, for just a few hours in the middle of the chaos of the Burning Man Festival. "Stoker, you've been teaching me to analyze people and read body language. I don't want to lose what I've been learning. How can I be sure Farsi will continue to roll off my tongue?"

"Did you say Farsi?" the ER doctor asked.

Two hours later, Z sat in front of Dr. Hosseini. Stoker and Rivera were there. And his girlfriend Jessica had found her way there, too. It was the first time Z had ever seen her worried.

The Iranian neurosurgeon was explaining the procedure, first in Farsi and then in English. Z asked a question in the doctor's native tongue. The doctor answered in Farsi and Z translated it into English. "The procedure takes about twenty minutes, and you use the x, y, z matrices to tell the robot where to remove a small piece of my brain tissue."

"I don't think you need to worry about your intellect, Mr. Z," the neurosurgeon said in perfect English. "The location of your lesion is not involved in your memory, cognition, or thought processing. It is more likely to affect your motor control, probably your left leg."

"Let's do this," Z responded. "Before the charm of language and robots using x,y,z matrices to operate on me wears off."

"In that case, we'll wheel you into the OR," the doctor said.

"No way is anyone pushing me around like a sick guy," Z said. Then he got up from his chair, kissed a teary-eyed Jessica, and walked toward the double doors that led to the operating room. He stopped right next to a sign that read "Operating Room." Z removed his phone which he had hidden held in place by his underwear's elastic band next to his hip. He put his head next to the operating room sign, pointed to the spot on his head where he would have the procedure and shot a Snapchat. "Hi, all. It looks like I'm having a little spontaneous neurosurgery. Pray for me."

After he sent the Snapchat, he hid the phone on his hip, held in place by his underwear's elastic band. Then he pushed the door open and entered the operating room under his own power.

• • •

While Z was in surgery, Stoker and Rivera made some quick phone calls. They each identified ten high-volume emergency rooms, in different cities across the country. Rivera connected first with an emergency room physician on duty at Montefiore Hospital in the Bronx, in New York City. "Hello. My name is Dr. Errol Rivera. I'm calling from Chicago. As you know, there have been more Guillain-Barre cases in the United States. How have your Guillain-Barre volumes been?"

"We've admitted nine cases in the last two weeks, which is abnormally high" the doctor responded. "We usually see about two cases per year. Most of those patients are in our ICU right now."

"That matches what we're seeing," Rivera said. He captured the doctor's email and promised to share the results of their informal study. After phone calls to hospitals in Orlando, Houston, Denver, San Francisco, Seattle, and fourteen other hospitals, Stoker and Rivera had some preliminary data suggesting cases of Guillain-Barre syndrome were skyrocketing all over the country. There were seventeen cases at a hospital in Atlanta, right in the CDC's backyard.

"This is just the very beginning," Stoker said. "In two weeks, each of these hospitals will have a hundred cases. In a month, they'll have thousands."

Then Stoker's phone rang, and he looked at the display. "If Z weren't in surgery, I would think he was spoofing me."

"What do you mean?" Rivera asked.

"My caller ID says this call's from the White House. It's a 202 area code and everything." Stoker answered the call.

"Is this Dr. Stoker?" a voice said.

"Yes. This is Dr. Stoker."

"This is Secretary Karin Danielsen from the Department of Homeland Security."

"Hello Madame Secretary," Stoker said. "Are you calling to talk about the Campylobacter jejuni bacteria and Guillain-Barre syndrome?

"Yes. More specifically I'm calling to arrange a meeting with you and Dr. Rivera to brief the President and select members of his cabinet."

"With respect, Madame Secretary. We're fighting a battle, and we cannot leave the front lines. Could we arrange a teleconference? We are prepared to brief you immediately."

"Dr. Stoker, you're being summoned by the President of the United States. It's rare that someone attempts to decline this invitation."

"I understand," Stoker replied. "But the issue is where can we be best utilized?"

"You need to tell us all you know. We need to talk about how to best deal with this crisis. We need to put together a battle plan, and nobody sees the battlefield as well as you and Dr. Rivera."

"And, Rivera and I can describe our battlefield very concisely from right here in Chicago via secure teleconference from the FBI field office. Delaying this meeting because of travel time will cost lives."

"I agree," the secretary said. "I'm not asking you to fly to Washington D.C. I'm aboard Air Force One with the president. I'm asking you and Dr. Rivera to meet us on the tarmac at O'Hare International Airport in 30 minutes. The Marines will send a helicopter to pick you up. Where in Chicago are you?"

"Northwestern Memorial Medical Center," Stoker said. "I'm sure they have a helipad."

Secretary Danielsen's voice was stern. "Doctors, find the helipad and be there in fifteen minutes."

Thirty minutes later, Stoker and Rivera climbed the mobile stairway up to Air Force One.

CHAPTER 24

Chicago, Illinois

In her room at the LTAC hospital, Allie Stoker was alarmed by her weakness. She had always been so strong. And, her strength had helped her push through virtually any pain and discomfort in her life. Just months ago, she had amplified her patience, endurance, wits, and pain tolerance to survive a kidnapping ordeal. But now, her own immune system was attacking her nerves. And those nerves were losing control of her well-toned muscles. Her strength was zapped, and she was weak. And being weak made her scared. And, her fear produced anxiety.

She knew a fair amount about anxiety. Being married to a psychiatrist gave her insight into anxiety and dozens of other conditions that profoundly affected the human psyche. And now, her psychological fortitude crumbled as her immune system had kicked out the crutch of physical strength from under her. *Was it all a facade? Was my physical strength the only quality making me feel emotionally strong for all these years?*

Breathing. It was so hard. *Am I struggling to breathe because of the Guillain-Barre, or is this anxiety talking? Is this what a panic attack feels like? And which came first, the chicken or the egg?*

A white-haired doctor walked into her room. He introduced himself to Allie, her parents, and her sister. "I'm Doctor Paulson." He paused for a minute. He noticed profound worry in Allie's eyes. "I'm an expert at keeping people breathing, a pulmonologist. And, I'm sorry you have a disease, Mrs. Stoker—"

"Allie. Please call me Allie."

Dr. Paulson observed how Allie was biting her lip, playing with her necklace, and blinking more frequent than usual. "Allie. I'm sorry you feel alarm bells going off in your head as your ability to breathe slips away." The doctor paused for a moment and looked at Allie's family. "Between your parents, your sister, and our staff here, we'll keep you breathing strong. We'll also have the help of this machine right here." He pointed at the ventilator. "Over the next few minutes, our team will start to prepare you."

• • •

"Okay. You're all done," came a nurse's sing-song voice. Indeed, this nurse had been trained to use happy and optimistic tones to welcome patients out of anesthesia.

To Z, she sounded like an amusement park ride attendant at Disneyland saying something like, "We hope you enjoyed the ride."

"Everything went very well," the nurse said. "Z struggled to open his eyes for a moment. He felt different. He felt great. He felt much too cheerful and energetic to be coming out of surgery.

"Is waking up from anesthesia supposed to be such a rush?"

"Um, no," the nurse replied.

"I know. I was just making sure the neurosurgeon didn't jack up my ability to speak or be funny!"

"Well, your speech is fine. But we'll have to see if your sense of humor returns."

"Hah. But, I bet you don't know who killed Jack Kennedy!"

"I don't know. But, I bet you do."

"I know all their names. It was a well-orchestrated hit."

"Okay, I think the anesthesiologist may have been a little generous with his potions. But, besides high and appearing a bit manic, how are you feeling?"

"Remarkably well for someone who just had a section of brain bored out of his head."

"It was a tiny sliver," the nurse said. "Here, let me check your vitals and this minimal incision. Your doctor will be here shortly." She started to probe the spot on his head where the neurosurgeon had worked.

"And Rivera and Stoker?" Z asked "They're doctors. Are they allowed into the recovery room?"

"No, and neither is your girlfriend, for now. But the doctors did leave you a note," the nurse said as she handed a folded over piece of paper to Z.

Sorry to not be there when you woke up. We were asked to talk to the president of the company.

Z smiled. He knew immediately. Stoker and Rivera finally had the ear of the president of the United States.

Now he was tethered to an IV bag supplying miltefosine, fluconazole, albendazole, and clarithromycin into his bloodstream. And, he was confined to a recovery room in Chicago. Z remembered his smartphone he snuck in, and he removed it from his underwear's elastic band next to his hip. A Snapchat had arrived from his newlywed friends who had been married at the Burning Man Festival a few weeks ago. On the short video, they wished Z well. Then the couple shared a selfie while the bride complained, "Too bad we're sharing our two-month anniversary as sickos."

About ten minutes later, Z saw another Snapchat arrive. One of the people he remembered from the wedding chimed in. "Something must be going around. I've been really sick for three days, and it's not getting any better. Time to call the doctor."

Within thirty seconds, another person responded. "It is going around. I'm vomiting, any amount of light gives me a horrible headache. What is this stuff? Ugh!"

On the heels of that message another Snapchat arrived. This person had been to the emergency room a few days back. The doctor told her to drink more liquids, take ibuprofen, and rest. But now, she felt even worse.

Z instant messaged all of them.

> *What are your symptoms? I had similar symptoms, and now I'm in the hospital with four different drugs being pumped into me. Not to mention the brain biopsy.*

Twenty minutes later, Z was in communication with twenty people who had been at Burning Man and who were experiencing the same symptoms. "Get your butts to the emergency room," he told them. "But, let us know what you learn."

Dr. Hosseini walked into the recovery room. "*Salâm!*"

"*Salâm, chetori*, Z. It looks like you've emerged from anesthesia feeling perhaps a little too good."

"I feel great. A little thirsty. But other than that, I feel great."

"I'm sorry I was not here when you woke up. I personally

delivered your sample to the pathology lab. The pathologist and I took turns looking at a small piece of your brain tissue under the microscope. We can see some damage from a parasite of some type, but we don't have the tools at this hospital to distinguish which parasite it is. So, we're sending your sample to the Centers for Disease Control. It should be there within hours. I hope to have specific results very soon."

"So, what's going on with me? Is this something rare? Am I going to be okay?"

"We're not sure if your situation is unique, but my hunch tells me it is. You may have a rare germ. It could be one of many pathogens. We'll just have to wait and see."

"What do I do while we're waiting?" Z asked. "Can I go back to my hotel room?"

"I don't think so," Dr. Hosseini said. "Until we hear from the CDC, I need you to stay here. We're already administering drugs through your IV that kill bacteria, amoebas, and fungi. That will give us a head start regardless of what this turns out to be. One of them, called miltefosine, is actually an orphan drug. It was recently approved by the FDA. We're using it as a precaution."

"Okay. Hopefully, I can go home in a day or two?"

"I think you're going to be in the hospital for longer than that. You may feel good now, but you arrived here after an alarmingly quick onset of some serious symptoms. Let's see how you're feeling in a few days."

"Okay. I guess I'll be checking into a room here."

The doctor smiled. "Let me go talk with your doctor friends."

"They had to leave. It was an emergency."

"With doctors it always is," Dr. Hosseini said.

Z smiled and blinked three times, in quick succession. "I've got some other information I want to share with you. It's a bit of a wild theory."

"What's that?" asked the doctor.

"A couple of months ago, my friend got married at the Burning Man Festival in Nevada. Have you heard of it?"

"Yes. I've heard about it, read about it."

"I went to support my friend. I was there for less than twenty-four hours. But, on social media, I'm seeing a lot of people who attended have my symptoms. I'm counting twenty so far."

"Please, keep talking with these people," Dr. Hosseini said. "You may be onto something. Usually, when we see emerging clusters of symptoms like you're seeing in a specific population, our theories end up evaporating. But occasionally, vigilance and early detection pay off, and we find an epidemic. Please let me know if anyone else is diagnosed with a growth or infection in their brain. It's worth watching."

• • •

As Stoker and Rivera entered Air Force One, they were greeted by Ethan Musgrove the surgeon general as well as the head of president James Riddell's Secret Service detail. After a brief security check, Surgeon General Musgrove asked them, "Doctors, have either of you been exposed to the Campylobacter jejuni bacteria?"

"We cannot be sure," Stoker said. "But, we're both asymptomatic and have been for weeks."

"Have you walked under any mist machines? Have you eaten at any Little Italy sandwich shops?"

"We haven't," Rivera said.

"I'm going to ask both of you to wash your hands and wear gloves while you meet with President Riddell. Also, please do not shake anyone's hand during our meetings here today, because of the infections, especially the president."

Rivera rolled his eyes. And then they walked to a bathroom, where they washed their hands and donned disposable exam gloves. Then they were accompanied into the Air Force One conference room. The president and Secretary Danielson stood up immediately. Surgeon General Musgrove introduced Stoker and Rivera to Danielson and the president.

"It feels strange not to shake your hands, Doctors," President Riddell said. "I'm sorry for the abundance of caution." The president gestured toward the chairs in the conference room and instructed everyone to take a seat. "First, Dr. Stoker let me say how sorry I am that your wife is a victim of this horrible attack."

"Thank you, Mr. President. She's in good hands."

"I want to thank you both for all you have done to get ahead of this terrorist epidemic. Frankly, you two were ahead of two major government agencies in uncovering this plot. We owe you a debt of gratitude for the tens of thousands of infections you've prevented and numerous lives you've saved." The president pointed to a large color monitor hanging against a wall. "I'm conferencing with Glenn Brookfield, the Secretary of Defense, and Albert Bostock the Secretary of Health and Human Services. We're familiar with the basics of your story."

The Homeland Security secretary spoke. "We know you found a cluster of this infection in Mexico. You also followed some Iranian agents to Chicago, uncovered this Nikolas person at his hotel in Chicago, and then found the lab instrumental in distributing Campylobacter jejuni. We want your input on our strategy going forward."

It was the president's turn to speak again. "How should we be preparing to treat all of the people who develop Guillain-Barre syndrome?"

Stoker responded. "First and foremost, we need to figure out how to keep millions of people breathing. We must get our hands on more ventilators. We could go over the approximate numbers with your cabinet members, Mister President, ASAP."

"Is there anything we could do to reduce the severity of the illness so more people can avoid going on ventilators?" the president asked.

"Perhaps a little. If people get an injection of immune globulin early in the treatment, their disease course may be less severe. Patients can also have a plasma exchange. An infusion center removes a patient's blood and separates out some of the offending antibodies."

"The antibodies that attack the neurons," the president said.

"That's correct," Stoker said. "But, those treatments typically only help a little bit. Besides, if there are hundreds of thousands of people battling this disease, we will run out of immune globulin very early. I also doubt our medical system has the capacity to provide plasma exchange to so many people."

The president turned toward the other two physicians in the room. "So, more ventilators. Do you concur Dr. Musgrove And Dr. Rivera?"

Both doctors agreed without adding any additional commentary.

"Dr. Stoker, what are your impressions, as a psychiatrist, of Nikolas Antoniou?"

"They are the same impressions the Iranian intelligence community realized when they identified him in his youth. He's a callous, manipulative psychopath who's extremely intelligent and knows when to take the right risks. He's a ruthlessly brilliant sleeper terrorist. There are still some things bothering me about him, and I can't put my finger on it. He invested Iranian money, through an organization called a bonyad—"

Stoker's and Rivera's phones simultaneously vibrated.

The president held up a hand. "Please answer it. I know you're also concerned about your friend, Z." Even though they were sitting with the president of the United States, cabinet members, and the surgeon general, they both took a moment to glance at their phones. Z was very much on their minds, and they were anxious for an update. The message was from Dr. Hossein, Z's neurosurgeon.

CDC reports infection is apparently caused by very rare amoeba, Balamuthia mandrillaris. Usually 1 or 2 annual cases in the US. Now 60 new cases in last two weeks. Z appears to be #61.

"Mr. President, this changes everything," Stoker said. Suddenly, everything came together in Stoker's mind. "This bio attack just got more complicated, and more lethal."

"What do you mean?" the president asked.

"What I'm about to state is a theory," Stoker said. "But, it all makes sense. Our friend, Z, has just been diagnosed with a rare amoeba infection in his brain, Balamuthia mandrillaris. In the last two weeks, infections from this amoeba have skyrocketed to 61 cases. We usually see one or two cases per year. Two biological attacks are occurring at the same time. This is no coincidence."

The president turned to the secretary of Health and Human Services. "Can you verify those numbers, Secretary Bostock? The CDC is under your purview."

"I'm checking now," he replied.

The president motioned for Stoker to continue.

"Let me tell you the more salient details about Balamuthia mandrillaris. The initial symptoms of Guillain-Barre syndrome and Balamuthia mandrillaris can be very similar. What I'm saying here is the neurologic signs may overlap, in the initial stages, of both diseases. And this is very concerning to me. Wouldn't it be possible, if someone were to manufacture a very nasty Campylobacter jejuni, one who's virulence could be increased greatly, let's say a thousand-fold, we would see resultant Guillain-Barre syndrome with very heightened numbers, as we did in Mexico? Now, if one could take time, and know how to grow this amoeba, which we know as Balamuthia mandrillaris, which is very rare, and infect people in a very similar way, it could potentially cause chaos among physicians and medical professionals in figuring out the diagnosis between the two. How clever would it be to try to confuse us by these initial symptoms in which one organism could kill quickly, while the other is very survivable if a person is treated properly?"

The Health and Human Services secretary chimed in. "First of all, I've verified the amoeba figures. There are now sixty-two confirmed cases in the last two weeks—another was just reported. And, just like Dr. Stoker said, this organism commonly only infects one or two Americans per year. Until now, it's been extremely rare. And, let's not fail to overlook one crucial fact. It's lethal in more than ninety-five percent of cases. My people also assert it is much too early to report this or act on this Balamuthia data. But, I've just told my people to go jump. I recommend we *not* wait around for the statisticians to sharpen their pencils. Common sense must prevail here."

President Riddell held up his hand, and everyone went silent for a moment. "Doctors Stoker and Rivera. Nobody sees this more clearly than you two. What do you recommend?"

"Stoker gets it better than anybody," Rivera said. "What should the nation do, Troy?"

"We're under attack from two different pathogens," Stoker said. "The key is helping doctors and healthcare professionals make the right diagnosis as early as possible. We need to release a guideline informing the medical community about their similar symptoms. For example, if a patient exhibits photophobia, or has soreness in their neck, the next step, most likely, would be a CT scan of their brain. Soreness of the neck along with photophobia is much more likely to be the Balamuthia amoeba. And therefore, Guillain-Barre could be ruled out. However, if we had a patient, for example, with a history of diarrhea and slowly progressive weakness—with no neck pain and no photophobia—most likely they would have the beginnings of Guillain-Barre syndrome. That's what American doctors need to know right now."

"Surgeon General Musgrove," the president said, "let's make a chart to share with doctors and the rest of the medical community. Let's help them get the diagnoses ASAP for proper treatment. This is imperative." Then he nodded toward Stoker prompting him to continue outlining his strategy.

"When it comes to treatment, as most doctors know, this is the easier part. We have protocols in place for each specific diagnosis. For the amoeba, the most important drug is IV miltefosine. It's a drug with FDA orphan drug status, just approved in 2017, that has saved some amoeba victims' lives. Patients should also get I.V. fluconazole, albendazole, and clarithromycin. But, there is a bigger issue here. Most of these Balamuthia mandrillaris patients will also need ventilators. We're in serious trouble."

The surgeon general spoke up. "You know, if that's the case, this two-pathogen attack would be incredibly sinister. And, Dr. Stoker, that would make sense. That's an incredible deductive leap. But, it makes complete sense."

"However, if we need ventilators for Guillain-Barre syndrome patients and Balamuthia patients," Stoker said, "this is going to get ugly. We need to stock up on Ambu bags, devices we use to hand ventilate patients. Friends and family will have to learn how to ventilate victims by hand."

"Dr. Stoker," the president said. "You've given us incredible insight."

"Actually, many doctors I know would arrive at the same conclusion. Rivera and I have merely been in the right place at the right time. It just makes sense."

"The important thing is to get the IV drugs flowing into the amoeba-infected patients," the president said. "We also need to get our hands on more ventilators."

Secretary Bostock from the Department of Health and Human Services chimed in. "Mr. President, miltefosine is an orphan drug. We have a minimal supply of it. We need to *manufacture* more."

"The military has a small supply," the Secretary of Defense said. He had been quiet up to this point. "We also have the ability to spin up some medical services."

Secretary Danielson from Homeland Security spoke up. "We do *not* have stockpiles of miltefosine in our Homeland Security warehouses. After this blows over, we'll add them."

The president spoke up. "Okay, Dr. Stoker has outlined the plan. Now I'm issuing executive orders. We'll distribute the protocol about distinguishing between Guillain-Barre syndrome and the Balamuthia mandrillaris amoeba to health care professionals in the next twenty-four hours. We'll label the protocol version one point zero. And, let people know we'll revise it as we get smarter. Getting out a proper protocol fast is much better than a perfect protocol slow.

"We will direct billions of dollars into increasing our nation's supply of ventilators, Ambu bags, miltefosine, immune globulin, and any other critical drugs. I'll call in favors from other countries to lend us ventilators and other critical pharmaceuticals and supplies. We'll also amp up the capacity of infusion centers so they can do more plasma exchanges. I know you said the immune globulin and plasma exchanges only help a little. But, if they keep a few thousand people off ventilators, the spend will be worth it.

"Finally, I'll address the nation this evening. We're going to mobilize America, do everything we can, and overcome." The president turned to Stoker. "What else do you need from me?"

"Permission to interrogate Nikolas Antoniou even further," Stoker said. "If we're right, and these two pathogens are being used together, Nikolas has committed a huge sin of omission by not telling us."

"Let's think about it," Rivera said. "If he left us in the dark about the Balamuthia mandrillaris, there may be even more assaults we don't know about."

"Use your best judgment as physicians," the president said. "This is war, and we're under serious attack."

"We should also get Nikolas's family out of Saudi Arabia," Stoker said. "They are Americans, being held hostage there. That's just one more piece of leverage we can use to help Nikolas remember things he's been omitting."

"Get with the CIA, Dr. Stoker. Make it happen yesterday.

The family may have critical intel," the president said. "And Dr. Stoker, I insist the spooks take you along on the mission. Having a psychiatrist on a hostage rescue will indeed help the victims. I also want to keep you in the center of things, like you have been. But, my motives for sending you go even deeper. We need more men like you, Stoker. While you'll never be in the CIA, building your relationship with the CIA will be very important in the future. I know because of Dr. Rivera's history."

"Yes sir, Mr. President," Stoker said.

"Are you really up to snuff on your training?" the president asked.

"Yes, sir. Thanks to my mentor, Rivera."

"If it weren't for you, Dr. Stoker, we would still be a month away from figuring all of this out."

Stoker's phone vibrated again. The message was from Z.

> *Using social media, identified three other Burning Man attendees who had brain biopsies and diagnosed with Balamuthia. I think Burning Man was a target.*

"Z's been using social media. He's found three more cases from people who attended Burning Man. These are people who've also been positively diagnosed by a brain biopsy."

"Those people are three more reasons to execute our plan within the next few hours," the president said.

The president arose, and everyone else stood out of respect for him. "There's one more thing, Dr. Stoker. You're at the tip of the spear in this war. We want your wife to be secure and well cared for. I also don't want you worrying about her. I insist we transfer her to Bethesda Naval."

"I understand, Sir," Stoker said. "Thank you."

"Let's get Z there, too," the president ordered. "Get Allie and Z on the same transport."

"Yes, Sir!" came the enthusiastic reply from Glenn Brookfield, the Secretary of Defense.

"Thank you, Secretary Brookfield and Secretary Bostock. That will be all." The two men's images disappeared from the screen. The president spoke to Rivera, the Surgeon General, and the secretary of Homeland Security. "Can you please give Stoker and me the room?"

The three quickly complied and left Stoker speaking with the president. The president held out his hand, "May I please enter my contact information into your phone?"

"Of course, Mr. President," Stoker said, as he opened a new contact and handed his phone to the president.

"I'm putting my contact information under the name Ron Reagan. Call or text that number anytime. If I don't answer it, my special assistant or chief of staff will. I've also included my encrypted email address. But, it's almost always best to call me."

"Thank you, sir," Stoker said. "I will reach out if I need your help."

"Perfect," the president said. "Now, I'm going to share something with you. And, I'm going to ask you to read between the lines." The expression on his face turned grave, and he looked Stoker right in the eye. "We should never take the power of the presidential pardon lightly. That being said, if you ever find yourself in the situation where you need to make some tough decisions, always do what you need to do to save lives and defend our country. If you must break the law here and there, remember I'm here. Does that help you with your question about interrogating this Nikolas terrorist?"

"Yes, sir. Thank you, sir," Stoker said.

"I hate people who claim to be a good judge of character," the president said. "I love getting to know people who accomplish amazing things. Last winter, in South Dakota, you did an amazing job of uncovering some deep-seated corruption. In Mexico, you figured out what hostile Shiites were doing there. You followed enemy combatants to Chicago and blew their operations wide open. The game plan you just outlined will save millions of lives and curtail untold hours of misery. Nobody needs to judge your character. Your actions speak louder than words. Thank you, Dr. Stoker. Now go out there and win this war."

• • •

Sixty minutes later, Rivera and Stoker were in grim moods. They did not try to disguise the somber moment, as they sat with Z and Jessica in a hospital room. "Z, the test results from your brain biopsy are back from the CDC," Rivera said.

"And, we're not going to sugar coat this," Stoker chimed in. "You have a dangerous amoeba living in your brain called Balamuthia mandrillaris."

"But the good news," Rivera said, "is the I.V. medications we've been giving you are almost a perfect match for killing off this organism."

"I'm going to be okay?" Z asked.

Rivera hesitated for a moment, so Stoker jumped in. "You're in a fight for your life. We caught this sooner than average, and you've been getting the right drugs. But, this rare amoeba kills more often than not."

"It's a little worse than fifty-fifty?"

Stoker looked Z in the eye. "No, the death rate is quite a bit higher than fifty percent. It's closer to ninety percent."

Z said nothing. He was so stunned he could not speak. He closed his eyes, and his whole body visibly started to shake. Jessica also trembled, but she refused to cry. Z bowed his head for a moment and inhaled a few times deeply, helping the trembling to subside. When Z opened his eyes, they were determined. "I just transformed my fear into a fight. How do we defeat this bug?"

• • •

"Forget something?" Stoker asked. He was sitting across the interrogation table from Nikolas. Agent Ahmadi stood beside Stoker. Rivera looked on from behind the one-way glass from the control room.

"Can you please be a little more specific?" Nikolas asked.

"Sure," Stoker said as he stood and walked out of the

interrogation room.

He returned a few seconds later with a test tube full of liquid. The test tube was from Nikolas's lab in the basement of Hotel Esatto. It contained ordinary tap water and nothing else. But Nikolas didn't know what it held. "Nikolas Antoniou," Stoker said in an exaggerated game show host voice. "It's time to play Name That Pathogen." Stoker walked up to Nikolas, grabbed his shoulders, lifted him up, and pinned his back against the metal desk. Then Stoker climbed on top of him and pinned his knee to Nikolas's chest. He spoke in a low, menacing voice. "Here's your first clue. I have this test tube we found in your lab." Stoker held the test tube above Nikolas and used his thumb to pop the lid off. "Let's pour this in your nose." Stoker put his thumb on Nikolas's nose and shoved his nose upward, and his head followed easily. Terror blazed in Nikolas's eyes as he flailed and protested.

"These little guys inside this liquid will start eating their way along your olfactory nerve pathway until they reach your brain. Then they'll set up shop in there." Stoker held the test tube above Nikolas's nose. "Now, name that pathogen."

"Balamuthia mandrillaris," Nikolas said.

"Winner!" Stoker said. "That's correct!"

Ahmadi took the vial out of Stoker's hand. She held it above Nikolas's nose and started tipping it as if she was going to pour it in a nostril. "I remember what you told us, on the sailboat in the harbor on Lake Michigan. You said you were willing to tell us everything. You *purportedly* didn't need any encouraging or persuading. You just wanted to tell the truth. At least that's what you claimed. But, omitting facts is just as bad as lying. There were more layers of the onion, but you wanted us to think we had an apple."

"Yes," Nikolas said. The truth was he was holding back. He knew so much more of the bonyad director's plan. "I was telling you the most important information, first."

"You must think we're senseless." Stoker scoffed. "And, we would be idiots if we bought this crap—your claim you were merely prioritizing. But, because I'm such a Neanderthal, let me put this to you plainly. Tell us everything, all the information, right now! No omissions. If there are any other assaults beyond these two pathogens, tell us. If there are attacks outside of biological warfare, tell us. If there are any other actors—our counterparts—tell us. If there are any other terrorist groups or countries involved, you need to spill it all. We want the *whole* big picture. Now talk! Because the deal with your family is off until we have the whole story."

"Your greatest threat is the Campylobacter jejuni bacteria. It is the easiest to propagate and spread. We could not make as much of the Balamuthia amoeba, and the amoeba has a lower infection rate. Yes, I did omit that pathogen, but there are no other pathogens I have not already told you about."

"What about non-biological attacks?" Stoker asked. "Do you know of any other attacks or acts of terror or war?"

"No," Nikolas said. He did not hesitate for a moment to lie. He felt safe taking a calculated risk to conceal the Ayatollahs' ultimate plan. Besides, Nikolas didn't care about his family. He wanted Stoker, Rivera, Ahmadi, and other American resources to be distracted by the family rescue. But, Nikolas had a secondary concern. His oldest son had learned parts of the plan. The young man was inquisitive, and he put some pieces together one night after overhearing his father talking on the phone to Tehran. He trusted his father enough to ask a few questions. Nikolas evaded the answers. Yet, he was still concerned his son could be a liability, a source of intelligence for the Americans. So, Nikolas further embellished his lie. "There is one caveat. I don't know what my bonyad director has in his plans. I know they are always thinking of something. By design, I've been left in the dark about anything else. But, if your CIA can capture my bonyad director, Alireza Pour-Mohammadi, he would be a wealth of knowledge."

"There's nothing else to tell us?" Ahmadi asked.

"No, nothing."

"Let's see how honest you're being," Stoker said. "Let's see what's behind door number one!" The door to the interrogation room opened. "Look what we have here!" Stoker continued in an embellished voice. "You've won an all-expense paid trip to an FBI polygraph exam!" A technician wheeled in a polygraph machine. "Agent Ahmadi and I are going to take a little coffee break, while this fine technician tests your truthfulness."

Nikolas smiled a little bit. He was trained to beat the polygraph. "Very good," he exclaimed as he thought; *finally, I get to use these skills I've worked on for years—outsmarting polygraphs.* During his spy training, years ago in Iran and Greece, he had learned to beat a polygraph. Besides, as a psychopath, it was easy for him to shroud his lies. Furthermore, he recently had a surgical procedure on the nerves in his arm that controlled sweating. This subsequently affected galvanic skin response, on his wrist and hands, which the polygraph measured. Once Nikolas completed the polygraph exam, they wouldn't know any more about the activities in Asia or the cruise ship Tropical Solace.

After he was hooked up to the lie detector machine, the technician asked him some questions to establish baselines of truthfulness and lies. Even during these baseline questions, Nikolas was already laying down inaccuracies to help him tell lies that would test as truths.

After a few minutes, the technician got to the core questions. "Has your bonyad director shared anything you've omitted to Doctors Stoker and Rivera, Agent Ahmadi, or any other person who has interrogated you since your arrest?"

"No," Nikolas responded.

"Besides the Balamuthia and Campylobacter attacks, do you know of any other acts of war, violence, or terrorism to be perpetrated on America?"

"No."

"Do you know of any other countries complicit with your plan?"

"No."

"Okay we're done here," the technician said.

"Now do you believe me?" Nikolas asked the technician.

"That's not for me to report," he replied.

Stoker and Ahmadi opened the door and walked in. "That's for us to decide," Ahmadi said. "But, it's time for you to go back to your cell."

"Well, do you believe me?" Nikolas asked her.

"I've not seen the results yet," Ahmadi replied. "But, this isn't prep school. Terrorists don't get to know their test scores."

Two guards came in and took Nikolas away. Stoker and Ahmadi sat down with the polygraph technician. Rivera came in from the control room. "What did you find out?" Stoker asked.

"He's either telling the truth, or he's had some training on beating lie detector tests."

"Since he's a psychopath, it would be easier for him to beat the exam," Stoker said

"Perhaps a little," the technician said. "But, many criminals who fail lie detector tests are psychopaths or sociopaths. It takes a well-trained, disciplined person to beat the polygraph."

"But, the psychopaths have a definite advantage," Stoker said. "I don't believe him. I think it's time we throw Nikolas a curveball."

"What are you thinking?" Ahmadi asked.

Stoker smiled at Rivera. "Let's see if we can get our friend, Dr. Bocelli, to visit us here in Chicago."

Rivera also smiled, this time his grin had a hint of sly to it. "Yes! Dr. Bocelli. Let's get him to do some fMRI testing on Nikolas at the University of Chicago. Nobody fools Bocelli and the fMRI."

"He's pretty busy heading up a bunch of new research," Stoker said. "But, we'll get the president to help Bocelli prioritize a quick trip to Chicago."

• • •

Z had been asleep for two hours. His life consisted of napping for a while and then waking up to interact with the online community of Balamuthia-infected patients he had formed. He opened his laptop to find he had hundreds of Snapchats and Instagrams waiting for him. The first one he opened was a woman who appeared to be about thirty years old.

> *Eight weeks ago, I was at Burning Man. Two days ago, I got so sick I could barely function. Twenty-four hours ago, the emergency room doctor laughed in my face when I suggested I might have Balamuthia. Twenty-three hours ago, I had a spinal tap. Twenty hours ago, I had a piece of my brain removed for biopsy. Twelve hours ago, my brain tissue arrived at the CDC in Atlanta to figure out what's going on with me. And now, I'm in the hospital with an IV pumping me full of drugs, just in case I have an amoeba eating my*

brain.

The next message was a man, probably in his early fifties.

> *I was at Burning Man, and now I'm scared. My hospital started treating me for the Guillain-Barre syndrome epidemic. But, an hour ago I failed some crazy test where they stuck a probe in my arm and shocked me. I think they're starting to believe me when I tell them the Burning Man theory. I can't believe I'm about to request neurosurgery for the second time. Hope they listen.*

In the next post, a boyfriend-girlfriend couple was still in the emergency room.

> *We're being sent home. The doctor thinks we just have the same virus. Rest, ibuprofen and plenty of liquids. We're calling an uncle, who's a doctor, for a second opinion.*

While most messages were from people who had attended Burning Man, Z and Jessica shared the dread every time they saw a message from someone sitting in a hospital. They'd lost count after the first dozen who were recovering from a brain biopsy, diagnosed with Balamuthia, and lying in a hospital bed being treated with I.V. medications.

Z realized he was spending his time as an observer. It was time to be more proactive. So, he went to Snapchat and opened a new account with the name AmoebaEpidemic. Then he went to Instagram and opened an account with the username Amoeba Epidemic. He created similar accounts on Twitter and Facebook. Then, he went back to his personal Snapchat account and encouraged people to start cataloging their experience on the social media channels of their choice. He then went onto Twitter and wrote.

> *Attended Burning Man eight weeks ago. Finding*

many people sick with probable amoeba.
#AmoebaEpidemic.

He repeated the process on Facebook and all his other social media accounts. He watched as even more people started to respond. He took a few minutes to start linking out to resources about Balamuthia mandrillaris. For the next few hours, he interacted with hundreds of people who had been diagnosed, perhaps misdiagnosed, or were showing initial symptoms. Much of the dread he felt faded away, displaced by the empowerment of doing something about this disease—about reaching out to other humans and helping people get an early diagnosis. Perhaps, he could help a few people improve their odds of surviving.

Later, Z realized he had been awake for five hours, running on pure adrenaline. He was identifying an early outbreak of a vicious illness. But, the need for sleep overwhelmed him. He sent a summary email to Stoker and asked him to share the data with his new friends in Washington D.C.

• • •

"My fellow Americans." The nation was watching. This presidential address, scheduled with only a few hours' notice, surprised all Americans. Rivera and Ahmadi were watching from a conference room in the Chicago FBI field office. Stoker had flown out from Chicago to rendezvous with some CIA operatives in Bahrain to stage the rescue in Saudi Arabia. "I come before you this evening to ask us to join together as a nation. There's a crisis starting to ripple across America. If we stand resolute and united, we will emerge victorious."

The president looked directly into the camera. His expression was serious, but he made a conscious effort not to appear grave. "Recently, the Centers for Disease Control detected some unusual cases of two different infections. The first comes from a common bacterium, Campylobacter jejuni. On its own, Campylobacter bacteria is almost never fatal. However, in about one of every three thousand cases, patients infected with the Campylobacter bacteria develop a subsequent disease called Guillain-Barre syndrome. Few people die from Guillain-Barre syndrome, but about half of its victims end up hospitalized, needing a ventilator to help them breathe for a few weeks."

"So far, so good on keeping the medical facts straight," Rivera commented.

"It's a tough speech," Ahmadi said. "The president has to explain a war being fought with weapons we can't see. It's easy to explain bombs, guns, tanks, missiles, or grenades."

"The rockets' red glare, the bombs bursting in air," Rivera replied to Ahmadi. "There are no mentions of pathogens in the Star-Spangled Banner. It's a new battlefield."

The president continued. "Within the last few hours, we have learned a rogue nation, wishing harm to America and democracy, genetically altered a new strain of the Campylobacter jejuni bacteria. Actors, backed by Iran, weaponized this germ by increasing its virulence, or harmfulness. According to data we've collected so far, roughly fifty percent of people infected by this strain of Campylobacter go on to develop Guillain-Barre syndrome. Furthermore, many more of these patients require hospitalization and ventilator support."

The president continued to give a brief and practical explanation. "How does a person contract the bacteria?" he asked. "In this case, our enemies went to great lengths to administer it to Americans via a few different means. Some of the most common include inserting the bacteria into condiments at Little Italy sandwich shops and in several hotels that host large banquets. The Iranian backed agents also sprayed the pathogens into the air from misting machines during summer events. They did this under a company name, CoolSolar."

A web address popped up on the screen: cdc.gov/resolute. The president continued. "You can learn more about the Campylobacter jejuni bacteria by visiting the web address on your screen. The content there also clearly explains how Campylobacter jejuni may lead to Guillain-Barre syndrome. If you have symptoms of Campylobacter jejuni or Guillain-Barre syndrome, please see a primary care doctor. The Red Cross and National Guard are mobilizing to set up clinics in places where infection rates are higher, such as cities. If hospitals become overwhelmed, they will also set up overflow clinics adjacent to those hospitals."

The camera angle changed, and the president paused for just a moment before he changed the subject. "There's a second infection emerging. Balamuthia mandrillaris is an amoeba. It is so rare that only one or two people contract this infection every year in America. However, during the last two weeks, we've seen more than sixty instances reported to the Centers for Disease Control in Atlanta. Sixty cases is a small number, but it is a huge leap. This increase in cases would not occur without human intervention.

"Within the last hour, intelligence operatives were able to verify the same people responsible for the bacterial infection, have also engineered the means to infect numerous Americans with the Balamuthia mandrillaris amoeba. "The president was referring to the information Stoker passed onto him after his interrogation with Nikolas.

"Again," continued the president, "you can learn all about this amoeba at the CDC website on your screen. This is a potent pathogen, and it is often fatal. If you experience any of the symptoms listed on the CDC website, see a doctor.

"Neither the bacteria nor the amoeba is easily transmitted between humans. One person does not pass these to another by touching, sneezing, or kissing. As a result, there is no need to wear a mask to work or school or barricade yourself in your home. Like always, you should wash your hands after you go to the bathroom. That will minimize the spread of the Campylobacter bacteria."

The president changed camera angles once again. He had delivered the bad news. He now projected an air of confidence. "I want to share a word with medical professionals. But, it would be good for all Americans to be aware of the following information. Tomorrow morning, the Centers for Disease Control will publish and disseminate a diagnostic and treatment guideline for this bacterium and this amoeba. It's a version one point zero. It will be revised and improved as we learn more. Please note, it is important to recognize many of the presenting symptoms are similar for these two pathogens." The president paused for emphasis, then continued. "Let me repeat this. Many of the symptoms are similar for these two pathogens, in the initial stages. Patients presenting with weakness in their extremities, pins and needles sensations, or unsteady balance, may have one of these two conditions. Patients should be screened for these conditions. More information will be available on the website for patients and medical professionals.

"Thanks to the diligence of a few forward-thinking doctors," the president said, referring again to Stoker and Rivera, "we're already increasing the production of new ventilators and the drugs used to treat these illnesses. We will also be expanding access to these drugs and specific treatments to reduce the length and intensity of the diseases. The full resources of the Federal Government are working to save lives.

"Finally, let's turn our attention to Iran. First, I want to say to the millions of Iranians living in America, the millions of Iranians living in Iran, and the millions of Iranians living throughout the world, you are some of the most amazing people God has placed on this earth. You are intelligent, warm, diligent, and caring. America is not at war with you. Indeed, we've enjoyed decades of increased peace and understanding with most Iranian people. Our greatest wish is a future wherein America continues to celebrate Iranians.

"Our fight is with a few deranged and blood-thirsty men who have financed and orchestrated this silent strike over many years. We've made some arrests, including the kingpin of this operation. These terrorists will be punished. We're locking up other evildoers as I speak. That's just the beginning. Millions of lives stand threatened by these evil acts of terror. The United States of America has a tenacious history of hunting down her enemies. We warn those of you, be you individuals or corrupt governments, who have financed, harbored, or facilitated this terror. We will hunt you down. We will go to all ends of the earth. We will find you, and we will punish you.

"God bless America."

CHAPTER 25

The Persian Gulf, Due West of Jubail, Saudi Arabia

It was just past four o'clock in the morning speeding through the waters of the Persian Gulf skirting Saudi Arabia. The team's most recent intelligence report showed security was light at a small property forty-three miles northwest of the Saudi Arabian coastal city of Al Jubail. The diesel engines of two experimental Navy M80 Stiletto surface vessels cut through choppy waters thirteen miles offshore. The navigator updated the skippers and team leader on their location, and he reported no other boats in the area. The warm, dry desert air clashed with the fog loitering along the coast of eastern Saudi Arabia. "Did anyone call ahead and secure our reservation for a table of six in Saudi Arabia?" joked one of the two CIA operatives, referring to the six people who would be rescuing the Antoniou family in Saudi Arabia.

A Navy SEAL and the team leader responded. "The head waiter informed me we are not welcome at this particular restaurant. The only food and beverage available are the snack in your pack and the thirty-two ounces of water you're carrying."

A second CIA man chimed in. "Welcome back to the Kingdom."

The skippers turned their vessels with a steep bank toward Saudi Arabia, and the team leader's voice came over their headsets. "Let's get ready guys. We're about twelve minutes from your drop." Then the pilot addressed Stoker through the communication system. "How's it going there, Doc?"

Troy Stoker, M.D, made his preparations including final checks on his medical supply pack, helmet, and night-vision goggles. The last few hours had been a series of firsts. He had never knowingly worked with CIA operatives. And, he had never been to Saudi Arabia. If all went according to plan, he would only spend about an hour in the country. He spoke up and reminded the operators, "Let's be careful here. The family we're rescuing could be confused and hostile."

The Navy SEAL team leader responded. "When we break

down doors, we rarely trust the people on the other side, Doc. I'll keep my third eye open on this one. You know Stoker, when your Spidey senses are tingling, you go with it. I get it. We're good to go."

"Let's rock, Stoker said."

"Sounds good, Doc. Follow my lead, and everything will be just fine."

As the boats crossed the twelve-mile territorial waters limit from Saudi Arabia, the team members went through a series of checks on their weapons and equipment. Once they entered the Jubail Marine Wildlife Sanctuary, the skippers coasted the boats to a stop and extended their rear launch ramps into the sea. The water created a welcome spray as each of the six men boarded a Malloy Hoverbike T3. This was one of the latest technologies *Espada Rápida* had been testing, a hovering motorcycle that flies in the air. Each one could lift two men and some gear. It had a range of about 90 miles. This was a perfect opportunity to use it for its extreme stealth and maneuverability.

"Enjoy the cool while you can," one of the special operators said. "About five seconds after you make landfall, you'll be back in the blazing desert."

Since the moment Stoker and Rivera suggested the mission to extricate Nikolas's family from their house arrest in Saudi Arabia, Stoker felt a conviction he needed to be present during the rescue. So much about Nikolas's circumstances and alleged story bothered him. There were just too many holes. Stoker hoped forming a quick alliance with Nikolas's family would shed more light on their situation. He had always possessed an intuitive gift—the ability to understand people and their circumstances.

On the team leader's command, the group deployed their Hoverbikes in an asynchronous launch sequence. Stoker hovered into the darkness of the night sky. As he zipped across the water, his spirits soared. For the next few minutes, he skimmed over the slightly choppy waters of the Persian Gulf toward the Saudi Arabian desert. Thanks to his night-vision goggles with FLIR thermal imaging technology, Stoker could visualize the beach. He made landfall and scanned the desert before him. He saw the infrared beacons attached to his other teammates, and he steered his Hoverbike toward them. Through his radio earpiece, Stoker heard the Navy SEAL team leader take command. "Count off men." After

Stoker and the other operators had responded, they rode on.

After a few more minutes, the team leader gave the signal for everyone to stop and hover. "We're a little more than a mile away from our destination," came his voice through everyone's earpieces. "Let's leave our Hoverbikes here and fast march it to the perimeter. We'll use a beacon and remote control to summon our Hoverbikes just in time for exfil. Let's move out."

After the men were underway, the team leader radioed Rivera in Chicago. "We hear you've got an eye in the sky."

"Copy that," Rivera said. "We have another Hoverbike hovering a few thousand feet above your destination and using cameras to beam up real-time footage."

"What can you tell us about what's going on inside that building?"

Rivera radioed back. "All's quiet on the Middle Eastern front. Nobody's coming in and nobody's going out."

Then the team leader spoke into his radio. The signal relayed to Chicago. "What about you Colonel Rivera? What can you tell us about your satellite reconnaissance?"

As much as he wanted to participate in this operation, Rivera had elected to stay in Chicago to keep his finger on the pulse of the bioterrorism war unfolding there. "Satellite images have detected no comings or goings for the last few hours. There was a changing of the guard at three o'clock Zulu Time—which was a perfect time for the *Espada Rápida's* NanoBUGS swarm to slip through the open door. We've had the cameras from the NanoBUGS relaying information to us for the last few hours."

NanoBUGS were new to the CIA, but not to Stoker and Rivera. These insect-sized robotic drones were programmed to find an entry point into a building, locate a spot to hide, and then use their cameras and microphones to transmit audio-video feeds to their operators. While a single NanoBUGS unit could operate alone, their power magnified when they swarmed. By combining their collective images and data points, this minute army could infiltrate an enemy undetected and make 3D renderings of their targets for analysis. The acronym BUGS stood for Better than Uncle Sam's Government Surveillance. And thanks to this technology, *Espada Rápida* was a step ahead of the CIA and NSA.

"Right now, I can see the four family members together in a

bedroom, in the southwest corner of the home via the NanoBUGS transmission," Rivera reported. "They're sleeping. We've got two more tangos. One's guarding the front door. He's pretty active—getting up every few minutes to look around. The second one is sitting a little deeper into the house, near the southeast corner. He's asleep."

"Copy that. Two tangos northwest corner, one in a recumbent position. What about any surveillance devices such as microphones and infrared cameras that might detect us as we approach?"

"That's a negative," replied Rivera. "We're not picking up any sensors or cameras."

"This whole situation feels a little too easy and welcoming," Stoker said. "Why don't the people guarding this family have any early warning systems in place?"

"I know what you mean. All we're missing is someone to roll out a red carpet," the team leader said. "Something's hinky, but we've got a rescue to perform." Then the team leader radioed out. "Were getting within 400 yards. We should maintain strict radio silence now. Copy?"

Each special operator replied with their code names.

The team made it to the periphery of the property. The two CIA agents used a FLIR thermal imaging system to confirm what Rivera saw with the NanoBUGSs. There were two tangos in the main living space and four family members in the bedroom.

On the hand signals of their leader, two Navy SEALs snuck to the front door and placed Semtex explosives around the door frame. After a thumbs up, they retreated a few yards and knelt with their backs to their handiwork. The CIA men drew silenced MP-10s and started to advance on the front door. The Semtex explosion rang out. The men with submachine guns sprinted for the door. One entered low and the other high. They visualized the first tango—or what was left of him. Then they advanced on the man who had been sleeping. The startled man reached for his gun, but before he could even think about aiming it, one of the operators double-tapped him in the forehead. Stoker entered the room just as one of the SEALs broke radio silence. "Tangos neutralized. The main room is clear."

There was only a quiet moment before Stoker broke the silence as he yelled toward the bedroom door. "Hello, Antoniou family. I'm here with the United States Special Forces, and we are here to take you home. Please move away from the door. We're coming in."

With a kick, the door flew open. The CIA men entered the bedroom. After seeing the anxious faces of the Antoniou family and conducting a quick search of the room, they declared the bedroom clear. "Let's go," they ordered.

The family jumped to their feet. The oldest son stepped aside and allowed his mom and siblings to exit ahead of him. Stoker observed the concern on his face. During their captive experience, this young man had apparently chosen to be a responsible adult instead of a needy child.

The hum of rotor blades became audible. As the family and special operators exited the building, they looked toward the horizon to see six unmanned Hoverbikes approaching. The transporters stopped to hover fifty yards away from the group, and the special operators accompanied the family toward the machines. Stoker had just started to pick up his pace when he felt something splatter against his back. The shot's report arrived a moment later. He turned around to see the limp body of the seventeen-year-old son lying on the ground.

Stoker's Army medic training kicked in. He fell to his knees and started to search the boy for wounds. Mrs. Antoniou screamed, and she instinctively fell over her son in a protective gesture. Just as Stoker found the bullet's entrance wound in the boy's back, another shot rang out missing Mrs. Antoniou's head by more than three feet. Three men grabbed Mrs. Antoniou and her other children and forced them toward the Hoverbikes. A Navy SEAL located the gunman—a sniper out in a well-camouflaged bunker. He'd been hiding there all along, waiting. Just as he'd been instructed, he had pushed sand away from his small bunker window and pointed the barrel out toward his target and fired.

"I'll cover you!" A Navy SEAL yelled. Then he shot short bursts of rifle fire at the bunker. Pinning down the sniper gave the rescuers and the Antoniou family the precious moments of cover they needed to get to their exfiltration Hoverbikes.

Stoker remained behind for a few moments to examine the boy. On the teenager's back, he found what appeared to be an entrance wound. When he turned him over, Stoker could immediately see how a large-caliber hollow-point bullet had inflicted maximum damage on the boy's thoracic cavity, leaving only carnage and an empty space where his heart and lungs used to be. There was no life to save. Only a body to reclaim and bring home for a proper burial.

Stoker cradled the youthful, lifeless corpse in his arms and stood. Then he double-timed it toward the Hoverbikes, where the special operators were already departing with Mrs. Antoniou and the two surviving children. He heard Rivera's voice in his radio earpiece, "I've got you covered guys," as he took remote control of one of the Hoverbikes. From Chicago, Rivera steered the drone toward the sniper's bunker, hovered the vehicle above the small window, and dropped a grenade. "Fire in the hole," Rivera said. The SEAL who had been laying down suppressive fire, turned and sprinted for the Hoverbikes.

Stoker laid the boy's body on his Hoverbike. He was securing him with Velcro straps when the grenade exploded. Stoker willed himself to disregard the blast and subsequent shower of sand that fell. Stoker and the remaining SEAL climbed aboard their Hoverbikes and took off toward the Persian Gulf.

"Is everybody okay?" barked the team leader over the radio. "Is anybody else hit?" One by one every special operator signaled they were fine. Mrs. Antoniou and her two children realized the big brother's fate. The family sobbed as they flew over sand, then over water, finally hovering to a landing in one of the M80 Stiletto boats. There, the special operators quickly examined the family for any other injuries. They found none.

Stoker flew his Hoverbike back to the Stiletto. There, he floated the machine into the rear docking area, secured it, and removed the body from the Velcro straps. "Can somebody bring me a plastic rain poncho?" One of the SEALs comprehended that Stoker needed a body bag, but he was sensitive of the fact the other Antoniou family members would hear him. A moment later, the SEAL handed him a body bag. Stoker gently placed the young man's body in the bag and zipped it up. Then he carried the boy's body into a storage cabin where it would be secure. When he stepped into the main cabin, everyone was strapping into jump seats. Mrs. Antoniou insisted she sit by Stoker. Once everyone had been properly harnessed into the boat, it accelerated and made a rapid retreat from the boundary waters of Saudi Arabia. One of the special operators put headsets on Mrs. Antoniou and then Stoker.

"I want to hold my boy," insisted the tearful Mrs. Antoniou over the radio channel.

"I'm sorry," Stoker said. "You can't hold him right now. His injuries are devastating. I promise you can see him later."

"I want to hold my boy," she said again.

Stoker apologized again. She shook as she wept. After a few minutes, Mrs. Antonio's strength failed. "Will you please let me see my precious angel?" she asked Stoker.

"There will be a time and place for that. Don't worry," Stoker said.

"Why did this happen?" she asked.

Stoker's thoughts haunted him. *I can take a good guess. The sniper had a chance to score hits on six military men, the enemy. He executed the perfect kill shot—on this innocent young man.* Stoker knew every other aspect of the rescue had been too easy.

● ● ●

He was a low-level spy for the Iranian government. His assignment, for the last year, had been to check on the Antoniou family. But, just one time per day. He was only to report back to Tehran if there was a change in the family's situation. As he approached the home in a white pickup truck, he saw a helicopter lifting off. He pulled over and removed infrared binoculars from the glovebox. Scanning the scene, he could see the front door had been blown off.

Sensing no movement, he threw the truck back into gear and drove toward the front door. Removing a pistol, he advanced on the doorway and breached. He moved through the living space and saw the two dead men and the absence of the Antoniou family. *It's time to call the director*, he thought. He exited the building as he holstered his sidearm. Standing next to the truck was the sniper. "What happened here?" he demanded of the sniper.

"They're gone. All gone."

"And the oldest son? Did you take care of him?"

"Affirmative. Tell the director."

The low-level spy frowned and pulled out his satellite phone. He dialed the most powerful man he'd ever met in the country of Iran. He had strict instruction to speak to the director in cryptic terms. "Director Pour-Mohammadi. As per your orders, they have been carried out.

"And the eldest?" the director asked.

"It is done."

The director ended the phone call, turned to his computer, and sent a brief, encrypted email. "Praise be to Allah. He has spoken. Our true destiny begins."

CHAPTER 26

Washington, DC

After the president's speech to the nation, news outlets all over America scrambled to understand the magnitude of the bioterrorism attack. Because the CDC continued to label all their data as preliminary, reporters in newsrooms across America were stumped. They did not quite know what data to report or how to quantify the magnitude of the silent attacks rolling out in slow motion right before their very eyes. One of the nightly news anchors reported, "Tonight, hospitals across America are filling up with the sudden influx of patients with Guillain-Barre syndrome as well as infections from an amoeba called Balamuthia mandrillaris. On the heels of President Riddell's news conference, we're learning more about these germs and how they attacked so many Americans." The anchor provided no figures or statistics to give his viewers an accurate idea of the enormity. The ominous camera shots that accompanied his dire baritone narrative showed overflowing waiting rooms in hospitals in New York, Washington D.C., Philadelphia, Miami, and Atlanta. And, that's how the panic began. That audience sent a firestorm of texts, tweets, emails, and instant messages to family and friends.

Another popular commentator ascribed a mild label to the crisis calling it a "significant public health outbreak, likely linked to terrorism."

During the next twenty-four hours, news outlets started to calculate. They considered the millions of people served at the Little Italy sandwich shops. They estimated how many people were cooled by CoolSolar, catered for by the Iranian cooks and chefs working in hotel and banquet hall kitchens, and entertained at the water parks. The press's calculations included people who vaped at Nikolas's hookah lounges and ate at the food trucks. They tallied up the attendance figures for Burning Man, KABOO Del Mar, Electric Zoo Festival, Baltimore Orioles baseball, NASCAR, and other events.

The CDC was still tight-lipped with their estimates of the number of people infected. And the White House press secretary also refused to provide any numbers, because it was too early to specify any responsible figures. Behind the scenes, the President's staff was working hard to quash any incendiary rumors.

But, there were dozens of epidemiologists and leading physicians who were willing to go on camera and share their projections. A Johns Hopkins University public health professor emerged as the media darling. She was beautiful, had a Ph.D., and projected a lively personality. She was making the rounds on television and radio programs, and Americans were listening. "I estimate five to ten million people will contract Guillain-Barre syndrome," she would report as she looked directly into the camera. "upwards of a million will be infected by the Balamuthia amoeba. And, keep in mind, my estimates are conservative." The professor was also quick to interject, "Nobody knows for sure how many ventilators there are in service in America's hospitals. But, I've seen rough estimates of about 160,000 in some of the medical literature. We need forty times that many to keep all of these people alive."

Her fifteen minutes of fame led to millions of Americans panicking. By the next evening, emergency rooms were further overrun with people manifesting the initial symptoms of Guillain-Barre syndrome and Balamuthia infections. Some people came requesting to be tested because they had eaten at a Little Italy sandwich shop, run through the mist machine at Burning Man, or had contact with one of Nikolas's many other infectious ventures. Doctors, nurses, and other hospital personnel worked feverishly to rule out the illnesses in most of their spontaneous patients, sending them home with the assurance they were fine. But, the minority of people diagnosed with Guillain-Barre syndrome or the Campylobacter amoeba tallied to tens of thousands of Americans diagnosed that night during the rush. By morning, the hospitals were beyond capacity, besieged with patients who were exhibiting significant symptoms of one of the diseases.

Neurosurgeons and operating rooms were overwhelmed with patients with suspected Balamuthia, awaiting the confirmation of brain biopsies. There were also thousands of people diagnosed with early-stage Guillain-Barre syndrome but were sent home with instructions to return when they started having difficulties getting out of bed and walking.

"Will you have a ventilator for me if I need one?" the patients often asked the ER physicians.

All too often the honest reply was, "We don't know. Start recruiting your family and friends so they can bag you."

Hospitals started converting cafeterias, classrooms, and other spaces into overflow patient care areas. They canceled numerous elective surgeries like joint replacements, hysterectomies, and spine surgeries. But, the real limitation was the number of ventilators. Hospitals were already using every single one of their units, and they were just at the beginning of two waves of disease that would require continuous ventilation.

The CDC sent another team to Chicago. This one was much larger. They finally acknowledged Chicago as the epicenter of the infections. By that time, they were playing catch-up. Troy Stoker, Errol Rivera, the president, the FBI, and the Department of Homeland Security were way ahead.

Supplies of the anti-amoeba drug miltefosine dwindled. The American manufacturer of the drug worked with other pharmaceutical companies and compounding pharmacists to make more of the drug immediately available. Other countries offered to send shipments of miltefosine. Overnight, the orphan drug became one of America's most demanded pharmaceuticals.

● ● ●

Nobody was surprised when Wall Street plunged, and the stock market took a big hit. But stocks in ventilator manufacturers skyrocketed. Plasma exchange companies and the manufacturers of anti-amoeba drugs such as miltefosine also performed very well among investments that day. Hospital stocks also rose slightly, but some investors wondered if the hospitals would ever recuperate the costs of their care from insurance companies.

Many businesses instituted hiring freezes. A new temp industry emerged called respiratory assist baggers. These were people who would take shifts providing manual resuscitation to people who were denied ventilators. The going rate was about fifty dollars per hour. The primary qualification was forearm endurance.

All the medical claims swamped health insurance companies.

Some health plans were refusing to pay hospitals for the respiratory assist baggers' work. But every patient or family was willing to pay out of pocket for their life sustaining services. Rare were the cases when thousands of dollars prevented a patient from choosing death instead of life. Almost everyone used savings or loans to help pay for this non-traditional medical service.

Even though hospitals were overflowing, the Guillain-Barré and Balamuthia amoeba-infected patients were dragging them down financially. Hospitals suffered from having virtually all their beds full of break-even infectious disease cases instead of lucrative surgical cases.

Back in Tehran, the bonyad was cashing out on some financial moves they had made sixty days ago. Based on advice and analysis from Nikolas, the Bonyad had purchased stock in ventilator manufacturers and select drug companies. They also bought short-sell options on many of the Dow Jones Industrial stocks. Within a few days, their investments quadrupled in value.

• • •

Allie Stoker slept in a drug-induced coma. She was unaware of her airlift transfer from Chicago to Bethesda, Maryland. She thought nothing. She sensed nothing. With her father, mother, and sister at her side, a ventilator breathed for her and a nasal-gastric tube delivered food to her stomach. An I.V. supplied her with medication, hydration, and some critical nutrients.

Troy called at least twice each day. "Here's the irony," Stoker explained to her parents and sister. "Allie's excellent health worked against her in this case. She has a very robust immune system—robust enough to execute a vigorous attack on the nerves in her body. This is a disease that can affect healthy people, even more, thanks to their strong immune systems."

Troy was also considering that this engineered version of Campylobacter jejuni was weaponized, and even more potent than other Campylobacter jejuni strains. It created a hyper-immune response. But, he elected not to share this information with Allie's family. It was knowledge that would not help them. It would just introduce unneeded anger. Perhaps he could share the factoid once Allie had recovered.

"What's her long-term prognosis?" her mom asked the rounding pulmonologist at Bethesda Naval Hospital one evening.

"When we bring her out of the coma, she'll be weak. Her legs may be feeble, almost paralyzed. But, after a few months, most of her strength should rebound. Her nerves will heal themselves. For a little extra help, we'll have Allie go to physical therapy. Most people recover completely. Let's be faithful and optimistic that she'll have a similar recovery." Then he backed toward the door awkwardly. "I'm sorry to cut our visit short. Our hospital is more than full. And seventy percent of our patients are Guillain-Barre syndrome victims. So, I must go."

• • •

"I'm cold," Z said to his nurse. "Am I dying?"

"No, Z," she responded. "We think the miltefosine is starting to work on the amoeba infection in your brain. You're fighting a good fight. To help all your organs rally, we're taking you to the intensive care unit. Your lungs need some help, so we'll put you in a medically induced coma and put you on a ventilator."

"Why are you doing this?" he asked. He was only half with it.

"You know, we're just going to put you to sleep so we can keep you breathing well. Drs. Stoker and Rivera have the latest updates on your condition, and your medicine seems to be working. But, we must let your brain rest a bit," She gently placed her hand on his forearm. "Do you understand this?"

Z nodded his head. He closed his eyes and appeared more content.

• • •

It was Stoker's idea. He wanted to watch Nikolas reunite with his family to see if he could observe negative tell signs—abnormalities in their interactions—within his family. And, Stoker insisted Nikolas's family be kept in the dark about all the treacheries he had carried out. So, the FBI removed his prison garb, and they put on some clothing retrieved from Nikolas's closet at home. Then they arranged for the reuniting in a conference room at the FBI field office in Chicago.

Stoker, Rivera, and Ahmadi brought the family into the conference room first and invited them to sit down. The plan was for Stoker to act as an observer. Ahmadi led the conversation. "Your dad's on his way up in the elevator," she told the family.

As Nikolas exited the elevator in handcuffs and leg irons, six guards and two FBI agents accompanied him. Two other guards were brandishing twelve-gauge shotguns. They proceeded for a few feet before they stopped. "Okay Nikolas," said one of the agents. "We're going to remove your handcuffs and leg irons. But, we want you to know these guards are ready to maim or kill you if you do anything stupid. You got that?"

"Yes. I understand," Nikolas replied. Then they walked down the hallway to the conference room.

As Nikolas entered, he smiled and held out his arms. "My *dear* family. It is so good to see you." He walked toward them gesturing for them to stand and embrace him.

The kids hesitated, glancing at their mom briefly. When Mrs. Antoniou gave a barely perceptible head nod, they stood up. They did not move toward their father. Instead, they waited for his steps to close the gap between them. As he embraced them heartily, they returned reluctant hugs. As Nikolas tried to hold them a little longer, the kids pulled away from his embrace. Stoker noticed every move, every reaction, and every nuance in their behavior.

Then Nikolas turned to face his wife. "Hello, my love," he said as he leaned into her and embraced her. "It's so good to see you back here, safe and sound, in America." Then he kissed her right on the mouth—a brief but accentuated kiss.

"Hello Nikolas," she said. "It's good to be back."

Stoker was not surprised to see how Nikolas could successfully feign affection for his children. After all, it was expedient for the moment. But Stoker suspected this psychopathic father felt very little genuine emotion for his wife and children.

Stoker actually felt bad for Nikolas. A genetic shortfall had combined with adverse childhood experiences to deprive him of the ability to form relationships or feel true joy and satisfaction in life. Instead, he could only experience lust, hatred, and the compulsion to dominate and win. His only functioning emotional capabilities were almost like a lizard brain. The quest to yield power over people was Nikolas's core motivation in life. And it was no fault of his own. Yet, Nikolas was accountable and responsible for his small misdeeds as well as his gigantic murderous scheme.

After the initial hugs and greetings, everyone sat down in chairs around the conference table, except for the two FBI agents. They remained standing by the door. Mrs. Antoniou noticed their sentry-like body language, and she turned to her husband. "Nikolas, who are these men?"

"They're my bodyguards," her husband lied. Stoker was not surprised how quickly Nikolas could manipulate situations for his benefit. "When you were kidnapped, my security people at the hotel insisted I surround myself with increased protection."

CHAPTER 27

Chicago, Illinois

The two FBI agents exchanged brief smiles. Ahmadi had instructed her men to allow certain lies to let him save face with his family. They had to keep Mrs. Antoniou and the children in the dark about Nikolas and his horrific crimes. The truth about their husband and father would sting soon enough.

Stoker was also watching the family, noticing the subtle interactions. Little things bothered him. So far, he was convinced Mrs. Antoniou and her children were just innocent, kind, and decent people. The family was clueless about the evil that lurked inside Nikolas. They had no idea his hotel and other businesses were near-silent mavens of terrorism and villainy.

Agent Ahmadi spoke. She directed her question to Mrs. Antoniou. "Will you please tell us what you remember about the afternoon you and your children were separated from your husband? What happened when you were kidnapped?"

"It was a whirlwind tour of Eastern Europe and the Middle East. We landed in Istanbul, Turkey and Nikolas led us on a two-day tour of amazing historical sites. Then we flew to Tehran to learn about the history of the Persian Empire and cap off the trip with two days of skiing at Dizin ski resort."

Stoker interrupted and asked the kids a question. "How was the skiing, guys?" Their faces lit up, and they both gave short enthusiastic answers. Stoker found this interesting. Until now all the kids had been more inhibited and quieter than he would expect, considering they were just reunited with their dad.

Stoker's subtle nod suggested she continue with her questioning. "Let's talk about what happened as you were returning from the ski resort to Tehran. You had a van transporting you and your luggage, correct?"

"Yes," continued Mrs. Antoniou. "We were just leaving the ski resort when a Mercedes SUV ran us off the road. The next thing we knew, three men were pointing guns at our car. They tore Nikolas out of the car, struck him a few times, and rushed him away. Then they ordered the children and me out of the car and into the SUV. They took us at gunpoint to a helicopter, tied up our hands and feet, and flew us to Saudi Arabia. They held us captive there until you rescued us a few days ago."

"While you were in captivity, I bet you had time to think. Did you remember anything important while you were in Saudi Arabia?"

"One thing jumped out at me when I woke up one morning," Mrs. Antoniou said. "There were two times in Iran when Nikolas seemed to understand Farsi. He may not have realized it, but he followed a ski resort employee's instruction spoken in Farsi. Another time, he nodded his head at our driver after he spoke in Farsi. I didn't realize it at the moment. But, when you're locked away, imprisoned, you start to recall a lot of details."

"Kids, do you have anything to add?" Ahmadi asked. Both kids shook their heads. They let their eyes travel around the room, but neither of them looked at their father. "You guys were so much more talkative yesterday," Ahmadi said. "Why so quiet today?"

After an uncomfortable pause, the oldest daughter spoke up. "I guess we told you everything, already."

Stoker asked, "How did you feel about this?"

They all shook their heads and said, "We don't know."

"What do you mean by that?"

"We have no idea why we were in captivity. We also wondered why our father could visit us? It seemed odd he could come and go, but we could not."

Stoker noticed the non-congruency of the family's statements and body language. The bonding with Nikolas was questionable in Stoker's mind. And, he made a mental note of this. "Thank you. I'll be talking with each of you again later."

Stoker, Rivera, and Ahmadi stepped out of the room and into the hallway. "What's your assessment, *amigo*?" Rivera asked Stoker.

"Let's just quickly look at this whole story. Nikolas came to the United States years ago. He marries an American wife. I believe there are questionable circumstances around the kidnapping of his family. It's awfully bizarre he could visit them while they were in captivity. Without giving you all the psychiatric terms, the father-child interactions are totally dysfunctional. I don't see or feel any bonding between them. I mean, look. There's no perceived grief, on Nikolas's part, about the son being killed. And, the circumstances around the son's death are not making sense in my brain."

"This all feels strange," Ahmadi said. "Has this all been planned? Did he contrive this storyline? I don't understand this, because he seems to change his emotions when he's with his family."

"Exactly," Stoker said. "His thoughts are not congruent with the portrayal of his emotions when he's with his family. And, he manipulates his emotions to change with each situation. It just means we cannot trust anything this SOB, Nikolas, says."

Rivera responded. "Let's face it. He's a psychopathic chess player! Let's keep this hot mess walkin' so we can see what he's really plottin'."

• • •

The cruise ship Tropical Solace made its final departure from Fort Lauderdale, Florida. But there were only a few passengers aboard—and this little band of passengers didn't consist of tourists. They only posed as such. During shore excursions, they had easy characters to portray. They were to act like tourists, eating, dancing, and taking in the sights. But back on the boat, they would be working.

For almost thirty years, this cruise ship had hosted hundreds of thousands of guests on their pleasure excursions in the Caribbean and Mexico. But now, she had reached the end of her serviceable life. Metal fatigue was haunting the great beams, decking, strakes, girders, and brackets of Tropical Solace. After this cruise, she would be on her way to a ship-breaking yard in Bangladesh, where she would be disassembled and her steel recycled.

As the vessel made its way to the first port of call in Mexico, this small group of passengers was much more subdued. No alcohol was served. The twenty people on board were all members of Hezbollah or the Iranian military. They had boarded using fake passports. When Tropical Solace docked in Cozumel, twenty people got off for a day of tourist fun. But that night, ten *additional* passengers—this time Yemenis—boarded the ship. These technicians possessed a specialized and deadly skill set. They would follow any orders their engineers and senior officers issued. But, they were still in the dark about their mission and how they would use their abilities, to a horrific end, over the next few days.

When any ship approaches Belize, it nears the second largest barrier reef in the world, the Belize Barrier Reef. Cruise ships can be harmful to this natural wonder. The reef has the potential to do crippling damage to cruise ships as well. Instead of coming into a port and tying up to a dock, cruise ships visiting Belize set anchor a few miles out to sea. Then smaller, more ecological friendly boats, or tenders, come and pick up groups of passengers and ferry them into port. When Tropical Solace set anchor in Belize, only twenty people boarded a single tender. Leaving Tropical Solace offshore, created the ideal environment for sneaking atrocious cargo aboard.

• • •

The news stories were getting more frantic. Hospitals were beyond capacity. Doctors, nurses, respiratory therapists, and other medical personnel were run ragged by the long hours and continuously urgent pace.

Members of the general public who did not understand the diseases started to over-react. Across the country, there was a run on home improvement stores to buy plastic. Some people assumed the pathogens where highly communicable, and they sealed off their homes refusing to go outside. Others naively purchased and wore surgical masks as they commuted, shopped, or circulated outside of their homes—for two illnesses that were virtually noncommunicable by breathing, coughing, or sneezing.

The society crippling problem with these illnesses was their duration. With even a minority of the population contracting one of the diseases, the hospital stays of thirty to sixty days filled up all hospital beds for long stays. Millions of people needed to get into the hospitals. However, very few were in any condition to leave.

Then there were the financial waves. These were not shockwaves. They were more like a series of tsunamis. Families scrambled to come up with deductibles and copays. Hospitals were submitting large claims to health insurance companies. Health insurance companies were drawing on their reserves. Many health plans filed claims with their reinsurance companies, the companies that insured the health insurers. These losses sent negative financial ripples throughout the world. Much of the reinsurance money came from Europe and Japan. The world was shocked to learn that Indian financiers were heavy investors in American reinsurance companies. A probable worldwide recession appeared suddenly on the near horizon. The major stock indices continued their long, protracted ramble downward. Precious metals skyrocketed.

• • •

He opened the door without knocking. Bo Jansen, whose aviator call sign was Bojangles, dropped his duffle bag on the ground before him. "Colonel Jansen reporting for duty." He had thick, black hair, which he wore a little long for someone with his military rank.

"Get your butt in here, Bojangles," Rivera said.

"I've taken countless orders from thousands of officers," Bojangles responded. He stood about six feet two inches tall and well-muscled for his age of fifty-five. "But, you are *not* going to dictate where I put my butt."

"Fine with me," Rivera taunted. "Stay out. I'll email you a sitrep and your orders."

Bojangles remained standing in the doorway. "I was enjoying a perfect summer in Boston, training for marathons, flying F-22s, and pounding out some really cool genetics research way above your pay grade. Now you've messed everything up."

"Don't blame me," Rivera said. "Blame an amoeba."

"Balamuthia mandrillaris," Bojangles responded as he stood unusually straight from his normal relaxed position. Then his face became somewhat intense. "Balamuthia mandrillaris. Found in freshwater and soil. Most of the time it causes a form of encephalitis that is amebic and granulomatous in nature. It's rare and has a very high morbidity rate, north of 90 percent. I recall case studies of two survivors, a four-year-old and a 64-year-old, who survived with a regimen of some pretty heavy-duty antibiotics, antimicrobials, and antifungals. The key to beating this pathogen is making a quick diagnosis and rapid treatment."

"You've become even more of a pain in the butt since you earned a Ph.D., *Doctor* Bojangles," Rivera said.

"What's going on?" Bojangles asked Rivera. "Why did you call in a genetics and stem cell specialist to deal with an amoeba?"

"It's your *totally awesome* IT skills we need," Rivera quipped.

"And, it helps that you know the world of biology so well. Because we've detected some scary stuff going on out there in the world of biowarfare," Stoker interjected.

Rivera stood and gestured toward Stoker. Let me introduce each of you. "Dr. Troy Stoker this is Bo 'Bojangles' Jansen. He's an F-22 pilot and geneticist. But, his ongoing hobby is information technology."

"Nice to meet you in person," Stoker said as he extended a handshake. "I'm Troy Stoker."

"Indeed, you are," Bojangles answered awkwardly. "According to the brief I read, you're the psychiatrist who infiltrated the governor's cabinet in South Dakota and broke up a huge meth ring."

"Believe me. It was not intentional. One of my patients happened to be in all the wrong places at all the wrong times. My infiltration was actually a set of circumstances. I just had to keep moving forward."

Rivera interrupted. "It was divine intervention. You were the man for the season, Troy."

Stoker changed the subject. "We really need you here. Our IT guru, Z, has contracted Balamuthia amoebic encephalitis."

Bojangles's expression turned grim. "Z? You mean that techie guy who grew up in the Northwest and studied electrical engineering at Stanford?"

"He is currently being treated with a cocktail of miltefosine, fluconazole, albendazole, and clarithromycin," Stoker said.

"As I recall, that's the last effective mixture of medicines they used on a patient who survived. That miltefosine's the new drug recently granted orphan drug status."

"Okay Mister Encyclopedia," Rivera said, "As always, your recall is still at one hundred percent correct."

"Z's such a brilliant guy," Bojangles said. "I remember

working with him in Maryland. My inner-ear tumor had just cost me my fighter pilot wings."

"Mister Bojangles had an acoustic neuroma. And he sure wasn't dancing then," Rivera said.

"Wow, you've sure made a great recovery," Stoker said

"Thank you. I did indeed recover fully."

"Tell him about your treatments in China," Rivera said.

"After recovering from the ear tumor, I looked into some other health-enhancing treatments in China. Treatments the FDA won't let us do here in America—yet. Some of the Chinese medicine might be more effective than people think."

"Treatment isn't the only thing Bojangles pursued in China. He did a bunch of post-doctoral work in genetics and stem cells. Of course, genetics is so database driven. And with all the modeling on computers, it just naturally led him to start in on a second Ph.D. in computer science.

"At MIT?" Stoker asked.

"Yes. It's an incredible campus. Brilliance and creativity abound."

"How's your hearing now?" Stoker asked.

"Oh, by the time I got back from China, it was superb. Let's just say it was the excellent, um, food and nutrition over there. To make a long story short, I got my wings back. And I'm thrilled to fly with a reserve F-22 squadron out of Virginia.

"Hey Bojangles, are you hungry?" Rivera asked. "You've been traveling all morning."

"I'm not hungry yet. But, I sure am itching for some exercise. Could I talk either of you into going for a run? I assume you've got someplace to get out and train around here?"

Stoker was always up for a run, swim, bike ride, or any form of exertion. With all the stress of the bio attack crisis, it was time to blow off some steam before they got back to the intensity. "I would love to show you a great excursion. Get ready for a section of the Lakefront Trail."

"Give me five minutes, and I'll be laced up and ready to go. Come on Rivera. Let's see what you've got. You can wear your Army boots if it makes you feel any tougher."

"I'm always tougher than the task at hand, Bojangles. I don't care if I have to run in boots or ballet slippers. I have a pretty consistent record of cleaning your clock on these distance runs."

"Yes, you do. I cannot argue with history."

Moments later the three warriors were running through the streets of Chicago toward Lake Michigan. Quickly the city gave way to the vast body of water flanked by a broad sidewalk that ran along the lakeshore. As the commanding officer, Rivera took the lead. Stoker deferred to Bojangles allowing his new fellow-warrior to run in second place. The much younger man, Stoker, had no trouble keeping up with Rivera and Bojangles. The run had been smooth so far.

After a few miles, Rivera began to struggle. And he dropped back and allowed Bojangles the lead position. To Stoker's surprise, Bojangles accelerated considerably. Rivera faded even faster. But Stoker's still had plenty of strength. He welcomed the new challenge, and he elected to remain right behind Bojangles. Stoker decided there was no reason for passing the older Bojangles. He would just stay behind him and enjoy the rest of the run.

Two miles later, Rivera had fallen almost 300 yards behind Stoker and Bojangles. Stoker was stunned when Bojangles quickened his pace yet again. Stoker matched him. But, he wondered if he could run at this pace for more than a mile or two.

Bojangles broke off the Lakefront Trail, started to run back toward downtown, and opened up into a brief sprint. Stoker had to let Bojangles pull away from him. There was no doubt in his mind his awkward new acquaintance would soon discover this strenuous pace was going to burn Stoker out. Indeed, a minute later Bojangles started to slow. Stoker began to close the gap. When Stoker got within fifty yards of his fellow runner, Bojangles accelerated slightly. He chose a new pace that was uncomfortable for Stoker.

It had been more than an hour that they'd been running hard. Stoker slowed his run to a very relaxed pace, and he watched Bojangles disappear into Chicago. Stoker decelerated to a walk to give Rivera an opportunity to catch up.

As Rivera approached, he was panting and struggling for breath. "I suspect Bojangles is going to tell us his new stamina is also from the amazing nutrition he experienced in China."

"Well, I hope he doesn't get lost on his way back," Stoker said. "A couple wrong turns, and he might end up in the wrong part of town."

"You don't have to worry about Bojangles," Rivera said. "He's already studied a map of Chicago. He's got this place memorized. He knows right where he's going. It's a thing with him. He's a walking Google map. If the power grid ever crashes or the Internet goes down, we'll have Bojangles to get us around."

"Let's get some water," Stoker said. They entered a small mom-and-pop shop, the kind of establishment that was so common in Chicago. Stoker purchased three bottles of water and handed one to Rivera. They each took long drinks from their bottles. Then they poured some water from the third bottle over their heads to cool off. "What just happened back there?" Stoker asked. This Bojangles guy is in some unnatural physical condition for a man his age."

"I have no idea," Rivera responded. "Today, he cleaned my clock. Something's different about Bojangles. I guess he's been doing some mega training?"

Stoker took another sip from his bottled water. "It's more than his training regimen, Rivera. Bojangles must still be eating what he referred to as 'the amazing Chinese food.'"

Stoker expected Rivera to laugh at his comment and the insinuation something unnatural was enhancing Bojangles's performance. But, Rivera didn't even smile. He just looked down the road and off into the distance. "When a geneticist and physiologist goes to China—a place where there is little regulation of medical experimentation—there is no telling what exactly that could mean. Who knows what kind of science and supplementations he's tried? I don't think he's going to say much, and he seems to be enjoying this newfound vigor." Rivera pointed down the road that led to the center of Chicago and the FBI field office. "Let's get back. Something tells me Bojangles will *now* be hungry."

"I need to call and get an update on Allie. Then, we need to find out how the debriefings are going with Nikolas's family."

• • •

When Stoker and Rivera got back to the FBI field office, they met with Special Agent Ahmadi about Nikolas's family. "Our forensic psychologists have learned a few things from the family so far," she said.

"Who did the family think was holding them hostage?" Stoker asked.

"They had no idea. The family didn't know they were in Saudi Arabia. They suspected they were somewhere in the Middle East. They eventually figured out their captors were speaking Arabic."

"So, what's next for the Antoniou family?" Stoker asked.

"Mrs. Antoniou fears for their safety. We've sequestered them in a special safe house until we've figured out the extent and scope of this attack. They'll lay low there while they process everything that's happened. We'll continue to work with them to see if Mrs. Antoniou can remember any other key details. The two surviving children appear to know nothing. They have no actionable intel."

"And what about Saudi Arabia?" Rivera asked. "Did their government know some Iranians were holding hostages in their country?"

Stoker knew the answer to this question. "No, our CIA boys have been poking around. Nobody in the Saudi Arabian government knew anything about it. I think the fact that we did *not* meet resistance entering or leaving the country confirms that. But, it was a brilliant place for the Iranians to hide their kidnaped victims. Nobody would expect them to hide them within an adversarial nation."

"In addition," Ahmadi interjected, "They were held in a pretty nondescript building owned by one of Nikolas's companies. We looked at the bank accounts of the two men Stoker and the special operators eliminated. The same company employed them as security guards and deposited regular pay into their bank accounts."

"Okay." Stoker's phone vibrated. "I think we're done here for now. Let's go put Nikolas through another little experiment."

CHAPTER 28

Chihuahua, Mexico

FBI Agent Ahmadi left the handcuffs on Nikolas's wrists. After all, it was a relatively short flight on a private Citation jet from Chicago to Chihuahua, Mexico. Nikolas was also blindfolded. He had no idea where they were going. When they landed, they put him in an SUV with Stoker sitting to his left and Rivera to his right. Ahmadi sat in the row behind Nikolas on purpose. They drove toward a safe house operated by some of Stoker's new CIA friends. They were kind enough to lend Stoker their humble abode for a few hours.

Stoker took off Nikolas's blindfold once they left the airport. Nikolas surveyed the streets of Chihuahua as he tried to hide his anxiety about this place that was so foreign to him. But there was no denying he was indeed in Mexico, and it was not a touristy part.

"This is where this whole bioterrorism ordeal started for me," Stoker said to Nikolas in a menacing voice. They passed through the streets of Chihuahua and Nikolas occasionally rubbed his nose with one of his handcuffed hands.

Rivera chimed in. "Welcome to Mexico, *amigo*. I'm thinking of introducing you to a few of the people who got some of your first doses of Campylobacter jejuni. Their families, too. I'm sure you'd be extremely popular with these folks. Let's invite them over to our place for a little fiesta, in your honor, Nikolas. You can be the honorary piñata."

"Mexico?" Nikolas asked. "Why would you bring me here? I would've been willing to tell you everything in Chicago."

"Well, let's just say we know the information will flow even faster here," Ahmadi said. "This place adds an extra incentive."

"We've rescued your family," Stoker said. "They're back safe on US soil."

"Thank you," Nikolas said softly, pretending to be deeply touched while glancing toward his feet.

"I'm sorry," Stoker continued. "Your oldest son was shot and killed as we were exiting the building and running toward the helicopter."

"Oh," Nikolas paused for a moment. "If it be God's will, God's will it shall be."

Stoker noticed how Nikolas showed little emotion, his lackluster response confirming his cold-hearted nature. While many people try to control their emotions when they learn devastating news, almost everyone had "tells." But, with Nikolas, Stoker noticed his tells were confusing. Subsequently, Stoker asked him a straightforward question. "So, Nikolas, how do you feel about your son being killed?

Nikolas didn't answer. He just looked down at his shoes.

"Listen," Stoker said. "I hate making this the hard way. But, I guess it's going to have to be that way. Let's find out what you think." Then he continued with his interrogation. "There are a lot of people suffering in the United States. Everyone's reeling right now. I'm sure you're gloating inside that hell hole of a mind of yours." Stoker pretended to think for a moment, and then he said in a facetious tone, "Hey, how about another quick flight. Let's go to Iraq, where they tend not to like you Iranians. We can get our good friends there to ask you some specific questions. The Iraqis will entice you toward free speech. An inalienable right."

Nikolas's eyes bulged, and the color drained from his face. "No, no, no! I don't need to go there. I'm telling you everything."

Ahmadi seized on Nikolas's fear. "Okay then. Right now, you're going to tell us everything—no games, from the beginning, nothing left out." She threw his Iranian passport onto his lap. "We located your boat in Athens. As you told us, your story began in Iran many years ago. We found the cargo hulls you used to bring over the bacteria and amoeba." Ahmadi scooted forward in her seat, scooted up behind him and spoke into his ear in Farsi. "You've not told us everything."

Ahmadi's dominant, aggressive behavior put the Iranian man in an awkward situation. Nikolas felt uncomfortable. He looked at Stoker and spoke. "Please remove this *jendeh* from my ear, or I will not say one word."

"Well," responded Ahmadi. "Was calling me a bitch an emotional response? This is progress! Things got more interesting as we scoured Hotel Esatto. We found this Greek passport in your office there." She tossed the Greek passport in front of him. "This is just the tip of the iceberg. We've searched your office in the hotel for documentation. We've confiscated all your cultures and lab equipment from the basement. There's plenty of evidence of the Campylobacter bacteria and the Balamuthia amoeba." Ahmadi stuck her nose into his ear. Nikolas's discomfort was through the roof. As an Iranian, Ahmadi knew how insulting and disrespectful her behavior was; and she chose to amplify it. "This *jendeh* knows there's more to your story. You've spent years here in America. You found a wife and won the green card lottery. You started a family. That's all fine and well." Ahmadi changed her tone from ridicule to a whisper. With soft words in his ear, she said, "You're one sick bastard to allow your family's kidnapping and house arrest. There's got to be more in your depraved history. At least tell me the whole story, even if you would be talking to a woman."

Before Nikolas could speak, Stoker jumped in. "Let's save it for the Chihuahua safe house. We want to record what you say."

The rest of the drive continued in silence. When the SUV pulled up to a large metal gate, the driver used a garage door opener to open the gate. The SUV passed through and parked in a garage. Stoker and Rivera got out of the SUV, and they brought Nikolas along with them into the safe house. They lead him into a crude interrogation room, but they elected not to turn on the cameras or recording devices. After Rivera, Ahmadi, and Stoker sat down at a table with Nikolas, Stoker calmly asked, "Are you comfortable?"

"Yes, thank you," Nikolas said.

Suddenly, Stoker pounded his fist on the table. "A long, slow, and painful powwow with the electric chair is way too good for shit like you. Two people who mean the world to me are attached to ventilators because of you. Thousands of people suffer."

"Dr. Stoker," Nikolas said with calm in his voice. "I've done horrible things in your country. I have anguished about my mandate for years," he lied. "I even worked to slow the pace of development on these two diseases. I never wanted to harm America. The coercion from the ayatollahs was so overwhelming, I had to act. They would've killed my family, and more."

Stoker noticed how Nikolas's response felt pre-meditated, almost scripted. The psychiatrist chose to minimize his response. He just listened. He was surprised this terrorist had already disclosed a blanket statement about doing horrible things to America. Nikolas acted as if he felt some contrition. He appeared sincere—another psychiatric confirmation to Stoker. *This is textbook psychopath 101,* he thought. *Remorse is not in his genetics, but good acting is.*

After a bit of awkward silence, Nikolas continued. "The big picture here was to use two pathogens, the Balamuthia amoeba and the Campylobacter bacteria, to bring America to its knees. The next few months are going to be very rough for your country."

Alarm bells went off in Stoker's head. Because Nikolas admitted his fault so freely, Stoker knew there were holes in his storyline. To be a terrific psychopathic liar, Nikolas had to share large portions of the truth, Stoker thought. *There must be more,* he told himself. "Go on," he said.

"The amoeba was a challenge. Balamuthia is uncommon. Once we found a source amoeba in North-western Iran, we had to replicate it. For years, we reproduced it in the Middle East. I brought over our batches of amoeba on the sailboat. American intelligence does not pay much attention to Greek recreational yachts sauntering into exclusive yacht clubs on the East Coast of the United States. We then disbursed billions of Balamuthia amoebas through mist systems at events in America. For instance, my company, CoolSolar, would go to concerts and events and provide a misting spray to cool the audiences."

"Did CoolSolar provide cooling services with your misters to Burning Man?"

"Yes."

"That's where you infected my friend," Stoker said," who now occupies a bed in an intensive care unit. So, you'll tell me everything, period. That's my friend. And, we've not even begun to talk about the other victim who's close to me." Stoker knew if he started to talk about Allie, as she suffered from Guillain-Barre syndrome, he would not be able to control himself.

"I will tell you everything. Burning Man was the first time we ever used our solar-powered mist machine along with a pathogen. In this case, it was the Balamuthia amoeba. We've also spread Balamuthia at other events with our misters. But, the largest population is all the tourists in Las Vegas. We had many mist machines in place there, and we estimate we've infected more than a million people at numerous locations along the Strip."

Stoker considered the magnitude of the horrific bio attack.

He fought a strong desire to give Nikolas a close elbow strike into his left temple. Then, Stoker reacted.

In the next moment, Stoker was leaping over the table. With a palm strike in the middle of Nikolas's chest, Stoker knocked him back off his chair and onto the floor. Then he jumped on top of Nikolas and pinned him down. "Tell it all! What about the Campylobacter jejuni? How did you make the bacteria so potent?" Neither Rivera nor Ahmadi tried to calm or restrain Stoker. They looked on with approval.

Nikolas was wild-eyed and terrified. "We genetically engineered a new strain." With Stoker's weight on his chest, he struggled to speak. "We increased the number of antigens likely to trigger Guillain-Barre syndrome. Through trials, we found out our bacteria increases the virulence of Guillain-Barre a hundredfold. With this strain, many more develop the Guillain-Barre syndrome."

"Yes, the trials in Mexico?"

Nikolas looked confused as he wondered why Stoker would ask an obvious question. After a few quick, panic-filled breaths he croaked out, "Yes. I thought that was a foregone conclusion."

"I was here, in Chihuahua. You certainly remember, yet again, a bunch of your men being shot up in the desert outside of town?"

Nikolas nodded his head rapidly.

"Just take a moment to reflect on how your wannabe terrorists were killed by a grenade."

Nikolas was speechless. The fear that he was pinned by a man with the skill set, track record, and justification to kill further gripped him with horror.

Stoker continued. "Let's reflect again on the plight of some of your lackeys. Your biologists *cum* terrorists training in the Mexican desert? The lab technician at *Hospital de Los Santos*? Your guys in *La Sotolería*? And, your guys who lost their trucks to grenades on a dirt road northeast of Chihuahua?" Now Nikolas's body was trembling uncontrollably. But, Stoker didn't care as he roared, "Yes! That was me! And now, here you are, attacking the United States of America." Stoker looked at Ahmadi as if to suggest she ask the next question. But, he remained on top of Nikolas pinning him to the concrete floor.

"The Campylobacter," she said. "Are there any more targets

in the U.S.?"

Nikolas was now in the throes of a full-blown panic attack. He could not control his frantic erratic breathing. But, he managed to push out raspy, whispered responses between short, poorly controlled breaths. "You've shut down my hundred plus people working in hotels and convention centers. Our attacks on NASCAR and NCAA football games are quashed. As are the sandwich shops, my hotel, and the mist machines. The empire I built over more than a decade, you dismantled in days. There are no more targets."

Rivera picked up his phone and called Bojangles as he stepped out of the interrogation room. Bojangles answered from the FBI field office in Chicago. Ahmadi followed Rivera, listening as he gave Bojangles the thirty-second summary of all they had learned from Nikolas, so far. "I need you and your hackers to follow the money," Rivera said.

"Yes, sir," said Bojangles. "We'll figure out as many transactions and trails as we can."

When the phone call ended, Ahmadi asked Rivera, "What's Mr. Bojangles doing?"

Rivera gave her an unexpected answer, "Hush my little. Watch the master."

They stepped back into the interrogation room, where Stoker no longer had Nikolas pinned. He had him sitting on a Spartan four-legged metal chair.

"What else?" Stoker asked Nikolas.

"That's all!" responded Nikolas.

"You mean that's all for the biological attacks. What about other attacks?"

"There are no other attacks."

Stoker frowned. "That's not true," he said in a quiet voice, almost a whisper. "Your government probably chose you for a few reasons. I'm sure they've praised you for your aptitude. You have a face that can pass for Greek. But, there's something else your government recognized—that I recognize. And, they would've withheld this information from you, for a good reason. You're a psychopath."

Rivera chimed in. "Oh, you're cool under pressure. You planned out every exact detail of this broad-reaching attack. You've rehearsed these answers a dozen times so you can keep us from finding out about the other attacks."

Stoker retook the lead by saying, "How do you treat people around you? When we went to rescue Rivera on your sailboat, you told us we were there to kill two men. There was no remorse in your voice. I suspect you had your son killed in Saudi Arabia, for most likely two reasons. Number one, to help foster more trust in us. And, number two, he might have known too much since he was your oldest son. He was working in the business, and he may have told us things you didn't want us to know. You married an American woman years ago in preparation for these attacks. I would say that qualifies as a bit unhealthy. Wouldn't you Dr. Rivera?"

"Perhaps, just a bit," Rivera answered sarcastically.

Nikolas stared blankly. Stoker got up in his face and grabbed his chin. Nikolas winced. "Ouch!"

"You know. We reserve some very appropriate colorful medical terminology for special people like you. You're a full-fledged psychopath. You know it. I know it. But, not everybody knows it. So now that I've made myself clear, it's countdown to check and mate."

"And, why does all of this matter?" Ahmadi asked and continued. "Because it comes down to deception. You've shared a lot of truth with us tonight. But, as a certified psychopath, you're using *select* truths as a smokescreen to hide other facts."

Stoker leaned in toward Nikolas, faced him with only four inches of distance between their noses, and looked the terrorist straight in the eye. Nikolas looked away, his eye movements glancing around the walls of the room. Stoker spoke. "You know, you really like to do things from afar," Stoker accused, "and watch people squirm. That's really what you like, isn't it? But, now, I'm in your face and in your brain. You're the one doing the squirming. But now, I'm the puppeteer, and you're the marionette. It's time for *you* to dance." Stoker poked him hard in the chest. "Hey! Am I getting you into that *discomfort* zone yet?"

Stoker grabbed Nikolas's chin. "Hey Nikolas," Stoker wrenched his chin to force Nikolas to look at him. "If you look away from me one more time, I'm going to start pulling your wings off— like you used to do to flies when you were a kid, as a young budding psychopath."

It was true. Nikolas had pulled wings off flies and tortured random dogs roving the neighborhood. When it was time to kill one of his sisters' chickens, he was more than up to the task. He had used fists, wits, threats, and blackmail to dominate his schoolmates.

"You see?" Stoker said. "I've got it. I've got you nailed. You like the control. You don't like being controlled like this—especially from someone four inches from your face."

It was true. Nikolas would've preferred physical pain to this emotional pain. Stoker had perfectly pushed all Nikolas's right buttons.

"You're hiding other information from us," Ahmadi said.

"There *is* something else," added Stoker. "What facts are you hiding in that twisted brain of yours?" Stoker was beating Nikolas at his own game. The psychiatrist knew Nikolas could neither feel psychological pain nor experience joy. "We want to know, what's driving you?"

"There's nothing else."

Stoker rapped his knuckles hard on Nikolas's forehead. "Knock knock."

Nikolas's face registered both surprise and pain. But, his tone of voice vacillated between victimhood and hostility. "What's that for?"

"Oops, it looks like nothing else is there. I'm just verifying it. If there's nothing else there, I'm just verifying the void."

Stoker thought, *That'll rattle him off balance a little bit.*

"I have no other tricks up my sleeve," Nikolas said. "Now please," he pleaded," go and use this information to save lives and reduce misery."

"The FBI and the medical community are already doing that," Ahmadi answered. "We need you to tell us the rest of your plot." Then she had a brilliant idea—an angle only an Iranian mind could think of. "Who's your bonyad director?"

Nikolas frowned as he froze. "This is where my transparency ends. If I told you about him, I would be dead within a week. My family would be, too."

"No, no, no," Ahmadi replied. "This is where your transparency *really* begins."

"I second the motion," Rivera said.

"Done!" Stoker said. "The motion's carried."

"Your bonyad must've been a very helpful source of

funding." Ahmadi turned to Stoker. "A bonyad is a type of charitable or not-for-profit organization in Iran. Some of the bonyads deviate from their noble intent. They start to champion causes and get into funding activities such as global terrorism, establishing a caliphate, and imposing Sharia Law on the rest of the world."

Stoker understood immediately. "If we knew who your bonyad director was, the United States intelligence community could target him. We could tie his activities to these two biological warfare attacks—as well as the other attacks you've been shrouding in your psychotic form of transparency and honesty. We just need to follow the money."

Nikolas sat with a stoic look on his face and said nothing.

"Who says you'll be dead in a week?" Stoker jumped up, grabbed Nikolas by the collar and picked him up like a rag doll, spun him around and slammed him into the wall. With one fluid motion, Stoker grabbed his right forearm and pulled it around Nikolas's back. The pop of Nikolas's shoulder dislocating echoed through the interrogation room, followed by his blood-curdling scream.

"Alireza Pour-Mohammadi!"

"What was that?" Stoker said as he kept him against the wall.

"He's a demon! Alireza Pour-Mohammadi."

Stoker looked back at Rivera. "Hey *amigo*, check out that name with Bojangles. Ask him to get us a profile. Tell him to get us as much financial data as he can dig up."

"That's right. When we follow the money we learn," Rivera said as he texted Bojangles.

> *Find all you can on bonyad director Alireza Pour-Mohammadi in Tehran, especially his money trail. Do your magic.*

Stoker turned back to Nikolas, who writhed in pain as he still had his face and body pinned against the wall. "You'd better be right about this."

After two minutes, Rivera's phone vibrated. He read the text from Bojangles and reported to the group. "Nikolas's info about his bonyad director checks out with Bojangles—so far. He's got a good start on a money trail, which includes a couple of decades of bank accounts and business transactions."

"That damn Bojangles, always gets the details right," Stoker said. "How does he do it?"

Then, with his muscular right arm and hand, he pulled Nikolas back toward him. He manipulated Nikolas's arm forward, placing his hand over his heart, and thrust his arm upward, forcing Nikolas's humerus bone back into his shoulder socket, reversing the dislocation. Nikolas's face concocted to a grimace and he let out a short scream.

"What's the rest of the story?" Stoker demanded again. "The part you're omitting?"

Nikolas's mind went wild. He'd already felt unbearable pain. And he could only imagine what else this Stoker would use, in this safe house in Mexico, to traumatize him into submission. But, he had trained for this moment.

In his youth, the Iranian intelligence machine had identified him. They had been screening promising students, and Nikolas profiled as a dyed-in-the-wool brazen psychopath. He was incapable of feeling sadness. And he felt no joy. His dominant emotion was a driving lust to dominate and control people. Even as a child, he had a knack for manipulating people. And the Iranian intelligence recruiters noticed how Nikolas flourished. He had an instinct and propensity toward verbal harshness, exploitation, and deception. But, they young psychopath wasn't the typical bully, who would back down from a confrontation. When provoked, he sometimes sidestepped the challenge. But, most of the time Nikolas fought with uncanny skill and instincts. His fists of fury were just a tool in his grander manipulative scheme. He would not be controlled—and never defeated.

Yet, Nikolas could feel physical pain. And, at this moment he was beyond the brink—the moment of his most profound physical pain. Now it was time for the lies. He had dozens of premeditated falsities he was ready to spew. The first lie to leave his mouth was a new story he had concocted when he first learned about this Dr. Stoker and his South Dakota roots.

"Do you remember the Hutterite chicken farms in your home state of South Dakota?

"The ones who lost their flocks to the avian flu?"

"Yes. That was not a phenomenon of nature. It was my man-made epidemic. That was our first trial run," Nikolas lied. Stoker knew it was a lie. The South Dakota Department of Health verified the source. "The avian version. It's a little like the trial run you stumbled into in Chihuahua."

"Are you saying you're going to unleash bird flu on the United States?"

"No, I'm saying I already have. Just days after we released the Balamuthia amoeba at Burning Man." Nikolas was lying about the avian flu, hoping to throw them off the trail of the truth. "Now that we introduced our Campylobacter jejuni and Balamuthia mandrillaris into the United States, we've turned our attention to Midwestern chicken farms. We're infecting chicken farms and wild bird populations through their water sources. Just wait. The headlines about Avian flu are only about a week away."

"They've kept me in the dark about anything else. All I know is it has something to do with a shipping container."

It was a weak deception, and Stoker frowned.

"How do they plan to use this shipping container?"

Nikolas channeled his torment and used the pain to contort his emotions to a pitiful and tearful state. "It will be some kind of biological attack. I don't know details," he said as he willed himself to break down emotionally. Between sobs, he continued his lie. "I don't know anything else. I don't even know which biological weapon they are planning to deploy."

"Let's confer in private," Stoker said to Ahmadi and Rivera, as he motioned toward the door.

Stoker, Rivera, and Ahmadi left the interrogation room.

Stoker looked at Ahmadi. "Another biological attack?"

"Using a shipping container?" Ahmadi said. "That could be land or sea-based?"

"Let's not get too focused on the shipping container. The shipping container is a lie. But, it's pointing to an element of truth. The truth being two things. One, he's lying about this. And, two, there is going to be another attack."

"He's definitely lying. But, how do you know he's lying?" Rivera asked.

"Listen Rivera. I know. We're being hustled about the shipping container. I'm from South Dakota, and I'm in constant contact with the Department of Health. This story about the chickens and avian flu is full of holes. I don't even want to go there. It's bullshit." Stoker furrowed his brow and held up his hand. "But when he spilled the beans on Alireza Pour-Mohammadi, his bonyad director, that was the truth."

• • •

Within an hour Bojangles uncovered an obscure bank account and a transaction for $49,000,000. "I found a wire to a boat broker in Indonesia," he said. "But, from there the trail goes cold. The broker's not answering my good old-fashioned phone call. But, we have a CIA operative in Indonesia about to pay the broker a visit."

"Good work Bojangles," Stoker said. "We need your help finding that boat. Get your butt in your F-22 and fly to Pensacola Naval Air Station. Use their fancy computers there to find a $49 million boat coming toward the United States. I want you to move as fast as you've ever moved before. I mean, pretend it's a footrace, and you're ditching me in the streets of Chicago."

"Roger that," Bojangles said. "I'm already running toward my plane. But, I'm a little surprised you're making suggestions—before I think them in my own mind."

"I'll get the president and joint chiefs on the phone," Stoker said. "We need to bring them up to speed, and they'll make sure you get priority in the skies."

Bojangles was gone, so Stoker called the direct number the president had given him. After a quick sitrep from Stoker and Rivera, the president issued orders to tighten up security and vigilance along the Eastern Seaboard and the Gulf of Mexico. And the president made sure Bojangles was welcomed with all access to Pensacola Naval Air Station.

"You know," Stoker said, "I'm going with my gut. You're going with your brain. I think we're both right. If we're going to find out the truth from Nikolas, we'd better—"

Rivera interrupted him. "Get him into an fMRI machine with Dr. Bocelli."

"Exactly," Stoker said. "Let's do it."

CHAPTER 29

Belizean Coast

Tropical Solace sat securely anchored off the coast of Belize. With the false passengers safely shuttled on a tender to Belize City for a day of supposed eating, drinking, and entertainment. A flatboat that looked like a smaller version of a barge approached Tropical Solace and anchored aft of the boat's stern. Crew members from Tropical Solace extended cables from the aft Lido Deck seven levels above. The crew of the small barge sent three disproportionately large anchors to the ocean floor before attaching a 270-foot long ramp to the cables and signaling for the men on the Tropical Solace Lido Deck to raise one end of the ramp to reach them seven decks above. Once the slope was set at approximately thirty degrees, a sixty-ton special transporter military vehicle pulled up to the front of the ramp. Its contents were enshrouded in military camouflage netting. The eight-axel Wanshan transporter fired up its engines and lumbered up the ramp to the Lido Deck.

Fifteen minutes later, the flatboat sailed away. The crew of Tropical Solace secured the transport vehicle and its payload to the deck with heavy chains. Then they covered the transporter and payload with the retractable rain cover roof. A plane or satellite observing from overhead would look down on Tropical Solace and see a normal looking cruise ship.

When the passengers returned from their day trip to Belize, Tropical Solace departed on a northward heading along its registered float plan. Twenty-five hours later, Tropical Solace approached the Gulf of Mexico.

• • •

Hospitals were so overwhelmed and ventilators so scarce that family members and friends of newly diagnosed Guillain-Barre syndrome victims were now using Ambu bags to hand-ventilate patients. Keeping someone breathing twenty-four hours per day was a lot of work. After a few minutes of squeezing an Ambu bag, most people's forearms started to burn. Friends and family teams were taking shifts. Four to six people would rotate, usually every fifteen minutes. Forearm muscles became fatigued in a short period of time. President Riddell mobilized military reservists and National Guard units to provide shifts of Ambu bagging. For a month, major league baseball, NFL, and, NBA practices and games were canceled. Teams went to hospitals to take shifts and help people breathe. The viral news clip of the week was an interview of last year's NFL MVP. "How did it go?" a news reporter asked the athlete as he walked out of the hospital late one night.

"That was a hell of a workout. With my forearms burning, it's the hardest workout I've had in years. But it's for a good cause. We'll be back to help patients again in a few hours."

More athletes from the ranks of professional and amateur athletics jumped in to help. Church groups, Boy Scouts, Girl Scouts, and many other service organizations galvanized to provide care to their fellow Americans.

Wealthy people found their attempts to bid high prices for plasma exchange and intravenous immune globulin were futile. Supplies were so scarce. You could not bid on something that just did not exist.

A wealthy man in Miami was grief-stricken when his daughter was diagnosed with Guillain-Barre syndrome. He sold his house at a fire sale price of $4,000,000. Then he proceeded to take out a full-page ad in the Miami Herald offering the $4,000,000 for plasma exchange and intravenous immune globulin. There were no takers.

Newly diagnosed Guillain-Barre syndrome victims would jump on airplanes to other countries, hoping to find ventilators there. For a week or two, some had success in Canada, France, Germany, Great Britain, Japan, Israel, Australia, Holland, Norway, Sweden, Denmark, and Finland. But sick Americans quickly utilized all excess ventilators in much of the industrialized world.

Ads began to appear in American newspapers from hospitals in India. While they did not promise access to ventilators, they promised to supply willing laborers to hand ventilate patients. Tens of thousands of Americans found themselves observing Halloween from hospital beds in Mumbai, New Delhi, and Bangalore. Other countries followed suit. In a dismal economy, one bright sector was international travel. Hundreds of thousands of Americans flew to nations they knew nothing about. But, these were not the ugly Americans. They were the grateful, humble Americans.

A month into the horrible epidemic, people started to notice something amazing. There were countless news stories about how well Americans were pulling together. America was figuring it out and getting it done, and the goodwill was palpable. The United States also had ample support from the international community. Even some countries that viewed America as an enemy reached out offering brotherhood during this time of crisis. The millions of Guillain-Barre syndrome deaths people had predicted from the lack of ventilators did not occur. As a matter of fact, deaths from Guillain-Barre syndrome were much lower than anticipated.

The amoeba, Balamuthia mandrillaris, lived up to much of its lethal reputation. But, the drug miltefosine proved to be very effective at killing Balamuthia mandrillaris when it was diagnosed early. And, the medical community was very assertive about early diagnosis. More than sixty percent of people who received the drug within a reasonable time fought off the amoeba. While approximately forty percent of its victims died, it was a vast improvement against a germ with a history of killing more than ninety-five percent of its victims. Nevertheless, there were still hundreds of thousands of Americans who died as a result of the amoebic infection. Virtually every American knew someone who met an untimely end from Balamuthia.

The United States was coming through this silent, bullet and bombless war, bruised but not broken.

CHAPTER 30

Chicago, Illinois

"What are you doing with me?" Nikolas asked. He was very nervous as he lay strapped to a cold hard table while sliding into an MRI tube. But, this was not just *any* MRI machine. It was the University of Chicago's functional MRI machine—one of only a handful in the world. Nikolas had no idea where he was or why he was there. Rivera and Ahmadi had brought him here in handcuffs and ankle irons. They had also blindfolded him during transport to keep him disoriented.

"Don't you worry," came the calm voice of Dr. Anthony Bocelli through a pair of headphones over Nikolas's ears. From a booth next to the fMRI machine, Dr. Bocelli spoke into a microphone that relayed his communication to Nikolas's earphones. "This will be painless."

Dr. Bocelli was one of the nation's top neuroscientists, who had flown to Chicago from the National Institutes of Mental Health in Bethesda, Maryland. Stoker and Rivera had worked with Bocelli months before to use fMRI to solve a high-profile crime in South Dakota. With one call from the president, Bocelli found himself on a private jet streaking toward Chicago.

"What is this machine?" Nikolas asked anxiously. "You must at least tell me what this machine is."

"I've got a deal for you," Bocelli said. "While I usually don't negotiate with terrorists, I'll at least offer you this. After you've told me the answers to my many questions, I'll tell you the answer to your question. I'll tell you all about this machine."

The fMRI's sounds made Nikolas very nervous. "You intend to torture me!" he yelled when he heard grinding and clicking. "This is against the Geneva Convention!"

"Nothing of the sort," Dr. Bocelli said. "I promise you. I've never tortured anyone. We are about to perform an exam, not cause you pain."

A few moments later, a high-pitched beeping sound joined the clicks and grinds circulating all around Nikolas from the machine that now encapsulated him. As the noise increased, so did his anxiety. He had no idea an fMRI machine was scanning his brain. Dr. Bocelli started to ask Nikolas questions. Much like the polygraph technician, Bocelli had to capture some baseline measures of truth and lies. He asked several questions while watching which areas of Nikolas's brain lit up when he told the truth, and when he spoke lies. Like most human beings, parts of Nikolas's prefrontal cortex, inferior parietal lobule, anterior insula, and the medial superior frontal cortex activated when he lied.

Bocelli asked the fourteenth question. "Have you ever cheated on your wife?"

Nikolas ignored the question out of anxiety. "Is this another polygraph test?"

Bocelli didn't answer Nikolas's question. He simply repeated, "Have you ever cheated on your wife?"

"No," Nikolas said.

Bocelli could see Nikolas was telling a lie as he watched the four key regions of his brain light up. He asked him another question. "Do you believe the true religion in Allah's sight is Islam?"

"Yes," came the response. But, this registered as a mild lie.

"Did you attend school in Greece?" he asked.

"Yes." It was a truthful answer.

"Did you attend school in England?"

"Yes." Again, the truth.

"Were you born in Iran?"

"Yes." A truth.

"Were you complicit in the death of your son?"

Nikolas's answer lacked any emotion. "Yes." The fMRI confirmed he was telling the truth. His psychopathy precluded him from feeling pain or regret about his own son's death.

"Do you know of any other imminent attacks on the United States or its allies?"

"No." The fMRI revealed his answer was almost certainly a lie.

"Does your bonyad have any other attacks planned?"

"I don't know." The response registered as a lie. Nikolas knew more than he was letting on.

"Has your director, Alireza Pour-Mohammadi, shared any other attack plans with you."

"No." Again, it was a lie.

"Are there any other terrorist groups involved in your plot?"

Nikolas paused, just a little, before answering the question. "No."

Stoker pointed at a section on the brain scan. "Look at how his insula lights up when he considers terrorist groups. He feels a level of reproach or disgust toward these other bad actors. Nikolas presumes to be much more sophisticated than these other rag-tag bastards, in his mind. Nikolas considers himself the alpha terrorist. He's a conduit that leads directly to the top in Iran."

Bocelli turned to Stoker and pointed to the screen. "Do you see this brain activity? That means he's not quite sure. It means I was not specific enough about the term 'terrorist group.'"

"So, we doubt he's deep in cahoots with the PLO, Hezbollah, or The People's Mujahedin," Stoker responded. "Because these groups are terrorist groups by a narrow definition. But, let's expand the definition. Ask him about nations that may be collaborating with Iran and his bonyad."

Bocelli pressed on the microphone again and directed another question to Nikolas. "Is your bonyad, and the nation of Iran, working with other nations to execute more attacks?"

"No," Nikolas responded. The data on the fMRI left almost no doubt Nikolas was lying.

"Are you working with Vietnam to perpetrate terror?"

"No." He told the truth about Vietnam.

"Are you working with Cuba?" Again, the answer was no. Bocelli continued to ask about many other countries. Stoker clenched his jaw. This protracted slow-rolling attack fueled his indignation. And, Nikolas still dared to attempt his manipulative charade. But, the fact he was obviously holding back information to buy time pissed off Stoker to no end. It wasn't the selfish, immature type of fury. It was the "million lives at stake" kind of outrage. Stoker could control his anger in any circumstance. But today, he would make the very deliberate decision to unleash his wrath for the greater good. And, he seethed as Bocelli continued to list many other nations. "Are you working with Russia to attack the United States?"

"No," Nikolas said. This time the fMRI machine registered an ambiguous response. Rivera saw it on the screen. "There's Nikolas's 'I don't know response' again," he said to Bocelli.

"Yes," responded the neuroscientist. "I'll circle back around again in a moment and ask him some related questions."

Coached by Rivera, Bocelli continued to ask Nikolas a barrage of questions. He asked about the weapons that would deliver the attacks, the timelines for the next attacks, the location of the attacks, the people who would carry out the attacks. Nikolas was an intelligent man. Based on the questions the doctors asked, he recognized that somehow, this medical machine that surrounded him, distinguished his lies from his truths. It was like a horrible game of twenty questions, repeated over and over again. Despite the answers he gave, Dr. Bocelli's interrogation would get more specific—closer to the truth. *How do they know?* Nikolas wondered. Then Dr. Bocelli asked a question about the Gulf of Mexico.

• • •

Bocelli spoke to Nikolas. This time it was not a question. "The machine you are in is a high-tech medical instrument called functional MRI. Among its many useful abilities, it can distinguish between lies and the truth with remarkable clarity."

Then Stoker's voice came through the microphone. "Let me tell you what we've learned here." Stoker took two minutes to summarize all their findings. He shared the specifics about the attacks from Asia, details about the cruise ship in the Gulf of Mexico. He even explained how Nikolas was not sure what was going on with Russia. But, Nikolas had a strong hunch Russia was involved. Then Stoker asked the final question. "Have we deduced your plan correctly?"

"No," Nikolas said. Again, the fMRI showed a distinct pattern of brain activity that proved Nikolas was lying.

"You know what else we found out?" Stoker asked. Then he answered his own question. "You're not a true follower. You don't really believe in Islam. Ironically, your personal disbelief is encouraging to me. I've had a chance to embrace your beautiful culture and language over the last six months. I've seen the majesty of Islam; and I cannot believe anyone—especially an educated man like you—who truly believes the Koran would become a terrorist. A warrior to defend Islam and homeland, perhaps. I can understand the fervor to see the Caliphate a reality. But a terrorist, halfway around the world? Never."

Nikolas's tone changed dramatically, and fierce anger flashed in his eyes. "This was never about Islam, jihad, or creating the Caliphate!" he lashed out. "This is only about power and hatred. I don't care that the West is decadent. I have relished in decadence. I love decadence. I loved my school years in Greece and England.

"But oh, how I hate the greed, corruption, and haughtiness of you Americans. I hate the brute force of your armies and how you insist on converting everyone to liberty. What an irony. Forced freedom. Well, let me tell you. Your compulsory liberty just equates to starvation."

• • •

In Iran, the Ministry of Intelligence was observing the situation in America. Their spies planted in the United States provided constant updates to military leaders, the Grand Ayatollah, and the Iranian Supreme Leader. They had lost contact with their operative, Nikolas. Chicago newspaper websites reported Hotel Esatto was now an active crime scene.

"He may have been arrested by the Americans," bonyad director Alireza Pour-Mohammadi reported in a rare face-to-face meeting with the Iranian President and head of the Ministry of Intelligence. "However, In my last conversation with Nikolas, he was defiant with me. Consequently, I do not know if he's been captured and arrested or if he has—of his own free will and choice—gone underground to elude us."

"Let us hope it's the latter," the president or Iran said. "If he wants to elude us, he has the intelligence and resources to stay in the wind for years. If he's elected the treacherous path—an unfaithful dog fleeing from its master—he could also feed the Americans large swaths of our next phase."

"It's not that simple with Nikolas. He's not choosing any side but his own. We selected Nikolas, all those years ago, because of his ruthlessness—his psychopathic tendencies. He only cares about dominating the people around him. He will only act in his self-interest, which probably means staying far away from the American authorities. I don't imagine them offering any sort of plea bargain with a man who has infected so many and may kill millions."

"On the other hand," the president of Iran responded, "if the Americans captured him, it might take a while to crack him. He's cagey, so pinning him down and getting much actionable intelligence out of him would be hard for quite some time, as long as it serves his interests."

Pour-Mohammadi took a risk and issued a contrarian opinion to his president. "I'm concerned. Even with the mild American interrogation techniques, I don't think it would take long for Nikolas to start talking. He's been living a very pampered life in his hotel. And, pain is one of the only feelings he understands. He's like a crazy divorcing Hollywood housewife, who will say or do anything to keep the house, stocks, bonds, and cash."

Then the president stroked his beard. "How close are we to the next phase?"

"The next hours of the western twenty-four-hour news cycle will be all about our careful planning and meticulous execution," Pour-Mohammadi said. "There just won't be many televisions left to watch it on."

• • •

"I am Colonel Jansen," he said introducing himself. "But, my call sign is Bojangles."

"I'm Commander Walker. I've been assigned—by the president—as your liaison. Welcome to the Pensacola Naval Air Station war room. We have orders to expedite your mission and give you anything you need."

Bojangles quickly looked around the expansive space. It was like many he had seen before, a massive war room with huge screens dominating the front of the area. Toward the back, technicians and analysts wearing naval uniforms worked on computers. The middle of the space contained a conference room table. "Thanks for your help. I'm here on special assignment from the president, and I'm hunting for a needle in a haystack. We have reason to believe an attack is imminent, and I want to look at the East Coast and the Gulf of Mexico. I'm looking for vessels displaying erratic behavior—anything that could be abnormal. It's going to be a larger boat—300 feet or more, bow to stern."

"What else can you tell me?" Commander Walker asked.

"I think there might be some unfriendlies trying to approach our shores with an intent to harm us. But, I don't know how they plan to attack."

"I see, Colonel. Thank you for the heads up. Let's find that rogue boat," Walker replied as he sat down at the conference table and gestured for Bojangles to join him. With a keyboard and mouse, he called up a map of the United States on the main screen. "Let's start with the Eastern seaboard." Zooming the map in on the East Coast, he asked, "What kind of vessel are you looking for?"

"One that would've recently sold for $49,000,000. A vessel substantial enough to bring in a payload of hell."

The map on the screen populated with thousands of icons, each representing an active boat. "Let's filter out U.S. military ships as well as yachts and pleasure boats less than 200 feet," Walker said. "I suspect none of those ships will pose a threat to the United States today."

"Perhaps it's an old cruise ship?"

"Look Colonel Bojangles. With all due respect, do you think Royal Caribbean is going to participate in a conspiracy to catalyze a world war?"

"No. I don't. I don't know exactly what we're looking for. But, I *do* expect this attack to come from a creative and twisted mind, somebody who would figure out a way to shock us with their strike. Spending $49,000,000 on a boat is extreme behavior. But, coming from terrorists, I wouldn't doubt it. The attack itself will also be on the magnitude of extreme.

"To state it another way, flying airplanes into buildings seemed preposterous on September tenth, two thousand and one. The next day, on September 11th, where did we stand on that supposedly preposterous idea?"

Convinced, Commander Walker started typing. "Okay. Let's also look at cruise ships." With a few more keystrokes the screen was filled with oil tankers, commercial fishing vessels, and boats full of shipping containers. "I'm running the analysis now."

"I agree."

The screen refreshed. "That's a lot fewer vessels," Bojangles said, "but we need to figure out some way to write a program to identify boats with unusual behavior."

"We can develop and test algorithms."

"How so?" Bojangles asked.

"On the fly," Walker said. Using programming, just as fast as we can write the queries and algorithms."

Bojangles smiled. "I love Pensacola already, Commander. What language is optimal for your system?"

"We like the clarity of C," Walker said. "We'll also use some SQL to query."

"Excellent," responded Bojangles. "Let's rock this."

"You're a pilot and colonel," Walker stated. "How do you know about programming?"

"I picked up a little here and there," Bojangles said, vastly understating his abilities. "Now who around here can show me the ropes on this system?"

"Try to keep up, Colonel," Walker said. "I've been developing military applications for more than two decades."

"Okay, let's see what you've got," replied Bojangles with kid-in-a-candy-shop enthusiasm. "Let's start by including any ships that have deviated from—"

A loud horn bellowed, and the large screen switched from the map of the boats to a different map zooming in on the Korean peninsula.

"We're getting an alert. It's got to be Kim Jung Un playing with matches again," Commander Walker said. "North Korea's scale-shattering leader thinks he's a world superpower. I bet he tosses another missile into the Pacific Ocean."

Overhead another announcement broke in. "We have a North Korean ICBM launch detection toward the United States. Repeat, we have a North Korean launch detection." After providing the coordinates of the launch site, the disembodied voice from NORAD started to provide velocity, acceleration, and trajectory figures before interrupting itself. "We have second and third ICBM launch detections, inbound for the United States. We repeat, we have second and third North Korean launch detections." The voice gave the launch site latitude and longitude. Then it said, "THADD missile defense system activated."

"This just became very real," Walker said. "We're going to try to shoot those ICBMs down with the AEGIS systems, from both sea and land."

Bojangles was less interested in the AEGIS missiles. He was in deep concentration as he absorbed the data streaming about the ICBMs' trajectories from the screens. "The first North Korean missile's going to re-enter the atmosphere bearing down on Los Angeles, and the second is headed toward Las Vegas. The third one is headed toward Seattle," Bojangles said.

"How do you know?" Walker asked.

"I did the math."

"Yeah, right," Walker said with ample disbelief in his voice.

Bojangles ignored his comment. The voice from NORAD updated the altitude, velocity, and trajectory of the missiles. Then it added, "Missile one re-entry estimated at 33° 50' 7" N / 117° 54' 49" W, near Anaheim, California. Missile two re-entry estimated at latitude 36° 6' 52" N and longitude 115° 10' 22" W, in the vicinity of Las Vegas. Missile three re-entry estimated at latitude 47° 36' 22" N, and longitude, near Seattle."

"How did you know?" Walker asked.

"It's just math," Bojangles replied looking up at the screen before him.

"Very complex math. The complexity a computer handles."

"Hey, I get lucky sometimes."

Bojangles and Walker watched one of the giant screens as a map rendered the location of the missiles arcing toward space.

"I do believe Kim Jung Un has the war he'd previously been begging for," Walker said.

The on-screen map continued to update the missiles' paths toward the United States. Other screens showed icons for hundreds of other planes, tanks, and missiles active on the Korean Peninsula. The NORAD voice spoke. "AEGIS missile away."

"Let's watch how this plays out," Bojangles said. The AEGIS system just fired an interceptor missile from the guided-missile destroyer USS Curtis Wilbur, off the coast of North Korea."

Within seconds, the AEGIS missile, as designed, intercepted and destroyed the Las Vegas-bound ICBM on its upward trajectory, just over North Korea.

"Go Navy!" exclaimed Walker. Cheers erupted from the technicians and analysts in the war room.

"Excellent shot," Bojangles said. "A bullet hitting a bullet. Now, let's see what happens with the two other inbound nukes. Just minutes to Armageddon."

"We have about twenty minutes," Walker said. "NORAD is preparing its response and the president is being briefed, as we speak."

A phone rang. Walker picked it up. "Yes, sir. Right away, sir." He slammed down the phone and picked up another one. "On the order of the president of the United States, execute Operation Boomerang." He slammed down the phone. "Now it's time to watch and wait for our defensive posture."

"What's Operation Boomerang?" Bojangles asked.

"It's a flexible plan that attempts to move many of our air assets out of harm's way. They fly away from the United States, then boomerang back once the threat diminishes."

Bojangles pointed at the screens. "The two active missiles remain true to their original trajectory. L.A. and Seattle."

"Are you still doing your math?"

"Yes."

"Well, hold onto your slide rule and protractor. The Navy may have a few more tricks up its sleeve."

The NORAD voice came through the overhead speakers providing an update on the missiles' positions, velocities, and trajectories.

"Hang on," Bojangles said as he closed his eyes in a moment of concentration. "The Seattle missile's veered off its projected course."

"What do you mean?"

"Look at the data stream. That ICBM's not going to reenter the atmosphere near Seattle anymore."

"How are you coming up with that?"

"The data shows an error in the navigation. The new re-entry point will be about 400 miles west of Seattle."

"You mean out in the ocean?"

"Yes! Hopefully."

"What do you mean, 'hopefully?'"

• • •

On the California coast, dome-shaped lids hinged open, and two ground-based interceptor missiles roared away from their silos at Vandenberg Air Force Base in California. Accelerating toward its 15,000 mile-per-hour kill speed, the interceptor missiles arched up into space over the Pacific Ocean. Two similar interceptor missiles left their silos at Fort Greely, Alaska.

From Pensacola Naval Air Station, Walker and Bojangles were watching the screens. An announcement from NORAD came overhead. "Vandenberg and Fort Greely ground-based interceptor missiles away."

"So, those are the other tricks up the Navy's sleeve?" Bojangles said to Walker.

"Like you," Walker responded, "I too, can predict the future. In the next few minutes, you'll hear NORAD announce those AEGIS missiles saving Los Angeles. I bet they still nail the Seattle missile, too."

On the large screen before them, Bojangles and Walker could see renderings of the interceptor missiles speeding toward the North Korean missiles.

"That makes sense. The military must protect those millions of people." Bojangles reached into his pocket and pulled out his phone. "I'm calling Troy Stoker." As he was about to dial, the voice from NORAD came over with a new announcement. "Updated estimates project missile one atmospheric re-entry at 33° 53' 52" N / 118° 3' 57" W, and impact just southeast of Los Angeles. Revised re-entry point for missile three is now at 380 miles due west of Seattle."

"In eight minutes, we'll know if the ground-based interceptors from Vandenberg and Fort Greely are successful."

"Good. That will give Troy Stoker just enough time to squeeze some critical intelligence out of a source."

"How come North Korea's only lobbing three missiles at us?" Walker asked. "Don't you think they would want to send more over to annihilate most of the United States?"

"No!" Bojangles replied. "Their supreme leader only needs

one or two. He doesn't need fireballs engulfing cities. These specific nuclear attacks will be silent. Humans won't even feel them."

Then it dawned on Walker. "No—this could be more horrendous than I thought. A brief surge of energy is going to fry all our electronics. I can't believe I didn't think of it."

In silence, they watched the screen as the missiles passed upward through fifty miles above the earth, and then 100. Bojangles reached Stoker. He immediately sprung a question on him. "What does that Nikolas scumbag know about three North Korean missile launches? The AEGIS system intercepted one as it lifted off near North Korea. The other two are projected to re-enter Earth's atmosphere in a few minutes. One 380 miles shy of Seattle, and the other one's on a trajectory for Orange County."

"Nikolas hasn't said a thing about missiles," Stoker said. "I thought they dismantled all of their nukes."

"A lot of people did," Bojangles said. "There are some of us, with the right clearances, who really knew what was going on. But, right now we need to make sure we're getting the right intel out of Nikolas. Because I don't think we are."

"He's still in the fMRI machine," Stoker said. "I'll yank him out, dislocate his other shoulder, and find out."

"Good. But, don't hang up. Keep me on speaker phone."

"No, I'll call you back," Stoker said. "Cell phones don't work next to fMRI machines." Then he ended the phone call.

The large screen showed the missiles passing beyond 300 miles above the earth. And, in a few short minutes, they had climbed to 500 miles above the Pacific Ocean.

"Now, those nukes are higher than the International Space Station," Bojangles said. "Seconds away from their apex in space."

About twenty heartbeats later, the missiles reached their highest point in space and turned their nosecones downward toward earth. Bojangles's phone rang, and he saw Stoker's name on caller ID.

"Are you there with that Nikolas guy?" Bojangles asked.

"Yes, he's right here. I've not used any persuasive techniques on him, yet."

"Colonel Bojangles," cried out the desperate voice of Nikolas Antoniou. "I know nothing of the North Korean attack." Bojangles heard a struggle ensue. "No, no, no," his yells crescendoed in volume and desperation. "Nothing!" Nikolas cried out. "I would tell you anything just to make this misery go away."

"Think about it really good," Bojangles said. "Can you link anything in your mind? We'll even listen to theories and long-shot ideas. How does this missile from North Korea relate to your bonyad director, Pour-Mohammadi?"

Commander Walker interrupted to capture Bojangles's attention. "We're just a few seconds away from the impact of the ground-based interceptor with a missile."

"That Nikolas guy's a useless information source so far, Troy. Dislocate his hips while you're at it," Bojangles said. "No need to hang up the phone or anything. I can hold while you do your work."

Stoker spoke up, "Look Bojangles. I'm not your commander or boss. But, I really want to encourage you to set aside everything occurring on the West Coast. I know I'm asking a lot. But, the civilized world, as we know it, really needs you to scour the Gulf of Mexico and East Coast. We need you to find any ships that may be threatening America."

"Bojangles immediately switched off his interest in the missiles flying toward the East Coast. "Okay Stoker, I'm with you on that."

"I think this guy is a master chess player," Stoker said. "And I just got a bad feeling about why there are only missiles going after the West Coast—so far."

"Exactly. The Gulf of Mexico," Bojangles said. "I'm on it."

Walker spoke up. "Ten seconds to ground-based interceptor impact on the Los Angeles-bound missile."

Bojangles stepped in front of Walker, interrupting his view of the many screens at the front of the room. "We need to ignore what's going on the West Coast and turn our attention toward scouring the Gulf of Mexico."

The NORAD voice counted down. "...three, two, one." The voice went silent for a moment. "Warhead not destroyed. I repeat. Warhead not destroyed."

"Don't worry," Bojangles said. "The AEGIS from the USS Bunker Hill is going to hit it. The data stream all lines up. Seventeen seconds to impact." He paused for effect and grabbed Walker by his shoulders. "We need to scour the Gulf of Mexico, and we need to do it now. The East Coast is much more hardened than our softer underbelly in the Gulf of Mexico. There's a huge threat there."

"Look Bojangles. I've got a war to run here."

"Really? How much can you do for the people of Seattle, here in Pensacola? Where is your responsibility? What happens if we're attacked from the Gulf on your watch?"

Walker balled up his fists at his side. "Do you want me to remove you from my war room?"

"No! I want you to defend the United States of America from an imminent threat. It will be no consolation prize if you kick me out, and I end up writing you up if we're attacked from the Gulf!"

When the second AEGIS intercept vehicle plowed into the Korean missile, the whole Pensacola war room team shouted in celebration. But, Walker and Bojangles did not participate in the spontaneous festivity. They were using the data about all the ships in the Gulf of Mexico to find those that might be an imminent threat to the United States.

"This one's interesting," Bojangles said. "It's a fishing trawler from Vietnam. It's approaching Veracruz, Mexico. Can we get a satellite on it?"

"Give me about thirty seconds." Walker typed away on a keyboard. "It's loading up now."

Bojangles and Walker watched one of the screens as a grainy image appeared and then snapped into focus. The two men examined the fishing boat from stem to stern. "I don't see anything unusual going on there," Bojangles said. "But, you're the squid. Boats are your specialty."

Walker smiled at the mild insult. "No, I see nothing out of the ordinary on the ship. I think we put the Vietnamese fishing trawler on a watch list and keep searching. We can check on it again a little later."

A voice from NORAD came through the overhead speakers. "We have a thermonuclear detonation. Repeat. We have a nuclear detonation. Approximately 395 miles west of Seattle at the height of 33 miles."

"No!" Bojangles said with a dawning sense of dread. "We don't know the warhead's kiloton yield. But, I bet the nuke generated an electromagnetic pulse that's knocked out power and electronics from Vancouver down to Portland."

In a microsecond, the nuclear blast from space cascaded an overwhelming pulse of electromagnetic energy toward earth. The people in the area didn't feel it. But, every electrical circuit within a 500-mile radius of the detonation point received an overwhelming pulse of energy. The EMP blew out almost every circuit it hit. Smaller circuits had no chance. Tablet devices, cell phones, automobile computers, airplane navigation systems, televisions, radios, laptops, and medical devices were turned to useless junk in the blink of an eye. The computers and electronics that controlled the electrical utilities, natural gas lines, and municipal water supplies in the Northwest were gone in an instant. Those services ceased in the blink of an eye. In a moment Vancouver, Seattle, Tacoma, Portland, and the communities surrounding them plunged into the 1850s.

"But, the EMP is preferable to an atomic fireball," Walker said. "We can have food and water to all of those people within the next seventy-two hours. It's a small consolation, but I'm relieved we won't be crawling amongst radioactive rubble throughout the whole Northwest."

Bojangles and Walker ignored the preliminary data coming in from NORAD. They set aside their concern about the electrical blackout tormenting the Northwest. Bojangles and Walker knew there were thousands of ventilated patients in the Northwest suffocating at this very moment, but they set their horror aside. It was time for them to head off the next attack, whatever it may be.

"Let's look at this ship that radioed in a new destination," Walker said as he pointed to an icon on his screen. "This one's an Aramco oil tanker."

"How often to oil tankers change their plans?"

"Not very often. Sometimes the capacity of the tanker and the supply of the derrick are not a match, so the powers that be change the plan."

They looked at the satellite footage. It was unremarkable. Walker radioed to the boat and learned a bean counter in Houston had done a calculation and recommended the rerouting.

Over the next sixty minutes, the men identified twenty other boats and examined them with satellites. Sometimes they contacted the ship or the company that owned the vessel in question.

"By my estimation," Bojangles commented, "we've ruled out any ships posing an immediate threat. What do you think?"

"I had just arrived at the same conclusion. Let's look a little further out. Using our same criteria, I see nine boats we should look at." Walker refreshed the screen, and nine icons sat there at different places within the Gulf of Mexico.

"What's the story with this Tropical Solace boat just passing by Cancun?" It's coming from Roatan, Honduras, and Belize." Bojangles said. "But, it doesn't fit the profile of your typical cruise ship. It's a smaller ship—like a cruise ship from twenty years ago."

"It just feels whacky," Walker confirmed. "Let's do our homework." After a few keystrokes, he said, "It's owned by a company I've never heard of out of Chicago."

"The mention of Chicago makes the hair on the back of my neck stand up," Bojangles said. "Chicago is the epicenter of this whole biological attack."

"Well, I'm relieved to see the uber-analytical Bojangles may actually have some intuition. Working with you can be a little like working with—"

"Mr. Spock?" Bojangles interrupted him and asked.

"Yes. I guess I'm not the first person to point out the parallel."

"No. But, you might be the first person who's ever helped me recognize my... my... intuition."

"You call the company in Chicago," Walker said. "See what their boat is up to. I'll get a satellite looking at this ship."

"Can you upload images of the ship to my F-22?" Bojangles asked.

"Absolutely," Walker responded. "I can send you a continuous video feed and send you coordinate updates every few seconds." Walker typed away like a madman. Then he picked up a phone and spoke to somebody of a much lower rank, ordering them to get a satellite trained on Tropical Solace. When Walker finished the call, he explained. "If your intuition is kicking in, Bojangles, let's get a pristine live satellite feed of Tropical Solace. You'll see a high-quality feed right on the screen, right there. He pointed at one of the many displays.

"Whoa!" exclaimed Walker. "Look at that. What are they building on Tropical Solace?" When he heard no response from Bojangles, Walker started to turn around and exclaim. "Don't you see what's—" But Bojangles was gone.

CHAPTER 31

Korean Peninsula

North Korea's attack plan had another major objective. Their new war's primary goal was a takeover of South Korea to rule the whole Korean Peninsula. Only in conjunction with Iran's grand plan, would the North Korean military have ever dreamed of striking like this. Iran created a prime set of circumstances with its biowarfare. And, North Korea quickly galvanized to intertwine their opportunistic agenda with that of Iran. North Korea's supreme leader recognized that he may never get a window of opportunity like this ever again. He hoped the EMP attack would cripple the United States. After all, America was already reeling from the Iranian-executed biological attacks. He saw it as an opportunity to check the alleged imperialistic potential of the United States that he feared so much.

The attacks on the United States were intended to cripple the country and preclude it from intervening in its takeover of South Korea. The moment North Korea launched the ICBMs at the United States, they commenced their aggressive invasion of South Korea.

They didn't nuke Seoul. They wanted to occupy it. Instead, they began firing conventional short-range missiles into South Korea. Most of their weapons were too impotent to reach Seoul. Only a few of the projectiles wreaked havoc and destruction in the city of 30 million. But, the barrage was short-lived.

The South Korean, Japanese, and American response to North Korea was swift. Even before the AEGIS system intercepted missiles in space or the EMP detonated west of Seattle, the three allies unleashed missiles from their battleships sitting off the Korean Peninsula. Then, they sent their fighter jets screaming toward North Korea. As the fighters approached, they fired hundreds of cruise missiles at North Korean missile launchers and other military targets. About seventy percent of North Korea's army troops had been positioned within sixty miles of the border between North and South Korea, and they sustained heavy losses from the rockets that poured into that hotspot.

New weapons, the CHAMP EMP drones, were deployed to unleash electromagnetic microwave signals and knock out the electronics in military command and control centers and disable all sorts of electric devices throughout Pyongyang—at least the ones not running on vacuum tubes or crude pre-integrated circuit electronics.

U.S. Submarines launched their Trident II missiles. The nuclear warheads came down as bunker-busting tactical nukes to obliterate tunnels that hid North Korean troops and mobile missile launching systems.

Munitions continued to pour in from the allies' battleships at sea. Redundant missiles pounded the known and suspected locations of North Korea's mobile nuclear missile launchers. For more than a year, classified American satellites had been keeping a real-time inventory of these launchers. The intelligence efforts paid off when the allies eliminated every nuclear missile threat during the first minutes of the war.

When the B-2 bombers arrived with their payloads of missiles and bombs, they finished off the few conventional artillery and missile launchers that still threatened Seoul.

But, there was one complete surprise for North Korea's leader. He had expected a nuclear response on Pyongyang, so he had ordered its millions of residents down into the deep subway system, which was also designed to double as a series of reinforced bunkers.

He could not have been more wrong. The United States did not strike Pyongyang with a nuclear device or any other ordinances. However, they did continue to fly the CHAMP EMP drones throughout Pyongyang releasing the magnetic pulses. Most of their electrical devices were fried. Beyond the EMP drone, the South Koreans bombed water, sewer, and electrical plants that served the city. The result was a besieged and anxious populace.

CHAPTER 32

Gulf of Mexico

"Troy, I'm traveling south on a heading of 178 degrees due south, and a velocity of 1,200 knots at 8,000 feet," Bojangles explained. "I'm in my F-22 on an intercept with a retired cruise ship—."

"Tropical Solace!" interrupted Stoker. "We learned Nikolas recently purchased the boat through a shell corporation."

"Yes. How did you find out?" Bojangles asked.

"Nikolas divulged it during his fMRI exam. Then, I found the paperwork. How did you know?"

"From Pensacola, we found its erratic behavior. Now it's traveling under the disguise of a cruise returning to Galveston. She's slipping into the Gulf of Mexico. The problem is, satellite images reveal a crew on the deck preparing something."

"Say again?" Stoker requested. "I did not copy your last statement."

"Check your phone, Troy. In about five seconds you'll be getting a message from a Commander Walker—a Navy guy. The picture is worth a thousand words." Stoker lifted his secure phone just as it vibrated. The message contained a satellite image of a typical cruise ship. Bojangles explained more. "In three minutes, I'm going to fly over Tropical Solace. I need to confirm what exactly is happening on that boat." A few seconds later, Bojangles yelled out. "Whoa, no way!"

"What's going on?" Stoker asked.

"I've got to deal with this right now," Bojangles said. "Pensacola just sent me an updated satellite image of Tropical Solace."

"What are you talking about?"

Bojangles ignored Stoker and toggled his communication over to Walker in Florida. "I want moment-by-moment updates on Tropical Solace. If anything changes on that ship, I want you to tell me about it."

"Don't worry Bojangles," Walker said. "We'll give you every

detail."

"Okay," came the pilot's reply. "I'm about to make visual contact."

. . .

As Tropical Solace slipped through the Yucatan Channel and into the Gulf of Mexico, the team of engineers hastily readied the equipment on the Wanshan special transporter military vehicle. "We're ready Captain," the lead engineer radioed to the ship's captain. He responded by opening up the ship's throttle and accelerating Tropical Solace to twenty-six knots. Every nautical mile counted. If he were detected by the United States Armed Forces, the captain wanted to be as close to the mainland as possible when he executed his mission. After ten minutes of acceptable operation, he accelerated the ship's engines again. The relatively empty boat quickened to thirty knots. And, she seemed willing to sustain the velocity.

All over the world, the United States Navy was on high alert. It had been mere minutes since much of Oregon and Washington had plunged into the Dark Ages by an EMP from North Korea.

Racing at Mach two plus, Bojangles broke through some clouds and visualized Tropical Solace. "Stoker, I have visual confirmation of a missile in the middle of the cruise ship standing upright. That baby's gonna liftoff. I'm engaging."

"Copy that, Mr. Bojangles. I was just calling to let you know that I'm pretty sure this is the fourth and final stage of that psychopath's plan."

"You know, your intuition is ahead of my logic. Yes, my feet run faster, and my clearance is higher than yours. But, you were right on, buddy."

. . .

"Sixty seconds!" the ship's captain exclaimed. The numbers

on a small digital readout continued to descend, one second at a time. "Congratulations, men. You are about to change the course of history and usher in God's will. The age of Sharia in the decadent West!"

They cheered and celebrated the moment. But, as the countdown clock approached the last twenty seconds, they cut their exuberance short. The men scrambled away from the missile launch platform into the interior of the ship.

· · ·

In his earpiece, Stoker started to hear a familiar song.

Well, you don't know what
We can find
Why don't you come with me little girl
On a magic carpet ride

Bojangles's voice spoke over the Steppenwolf song. "We have liftoff. I'm at 10,000 feet. I've gotta take care of business." Stoker continued to hear Magic Carpet Ride coming through the radio from Bojangles cockpit.

The missile shot into the air. Bojangles calculated the proper vector in his head and made a quick adjustment upward in his supersonic flight path. As he pulled through nine Gs, he almost fainted. "Stoker you bastard, you were right. And, tell my wife to name him Errol."

He never felt the impact, saw the ball of white light, or heard the horrible explosion. The sky lit up with a burst—a colossal spray of fire. As the debris fell from the sky, there wasn't much left of Bojangles's plane or the missile he knocked out of the air. Colonel Bojangles did not hesitate to make the ultimate sacrifice. There was no decision, just an unselfish muscle-memory reaction.

• • •

"Give me a sitrep, Bojangles!" Stoker was almost shouting into the radio. But Stoker knew. There would be no reply from Colonel Bo Jansen. His phone vibrated in his pocket, and he answered it immediately.

"Dr. Stoker, this is commander Michael Walker from Pensacola Naval Air Station. I was just tracking and communicating with Colonel Bojangles as he flew out over the Gulf of Mexico."

"I think we just lost a true American," Stoker said.

"We did. But, we gained a hero," replied Walker. "One of the most important in American history." Walker paused for a moment before speaking again. "I'm looking at satellite data. Bojangles's collision did not set off the nuclear warhead. But they're picking up plenty of disbursed radiation from the debris plume. Metaphorically speaking, it turned out to be like a bullet intercepting a bullet. Based on the first few seconds of the missile's trajectory, we calculate it was meant to explode in space, not re-enter earth's atmosphere."

"Another EMP," Stoker said.

"Almost certainly," Walker confirmed. "The burst would've exploded over Kansas and kicked the rest of the United States back to the 1800s. And, can I share something else with you?"

"What's that?" Stoker said.

"Bojangles had missiles on his F-22. But, he was smart enough to know he did not have time to arm and fire his missiles. His airplane was the only weapon in position to intercept the missile—at least during those key seconds."

"He did the math," Stoker said.

"He went out in a blaze of mathematical glory," Walker said.

"I'll suggest his family put that on his tombstone," Stoker replied. "I think he would've loved it."

"It's truly amazing how he was able to hit that missile going at supersonic speed."

"You know, he probably had the collision calculated to the last microsecond—how he was going to hit it," Stoker said.

CHAPTER 33

The United States East Coast

NORAD had been watching the Russian Tu-95 bomber for the last hour. The lethal craft was flying over the Atlantic on course for the northeastern United States. At 300 miles from the United States Air Defense Identification Zone, and 450 miles from New York City, the Air Force scrambled fighter jets.

The pilot had strict orders from Moscow to remain outside of American air space. "Decrease speed to 350 knots," he ordered. The six-man crew knew better than to ask questions, but their anxiety was palpable as they traveled toward the United States. The pilot was keeping all mission information to himself, as ordered.

A radio signal arrived from Moscow. After hearing the entirety of the message, the pilot reacted. "Increase speed to 400 knots and open the bomb bay doors." According to his instructions, they would have a narrow window of opportunity to run a risky mission taking them within miles of New York City. He'd also learned their flight operation was not a recognizance mission, flyby, or drill. This was a true offensive. The Russian bomber carried a lethal payload of bombs. But, it had also been retrofitted to launch air-to-surface nuclear-tipped cruise missiles.

At a point 250 miles from New York City, American F-16s showed up on the bomber's radar screen on a course destined to bring the Russian Bomber and American fighter jets into visual contact within a few short minutes.

Then the pilot heard the command. "*Otmenit!*" came the order in Russian from Moscow. "Abort!" The pilot listened to be sure he'd heard correctly. "We repeat, abort the mission. You have strict orders to turn around and return to base." Suddenly the Russian bomber closed its bay doors, slowed its velocity, and made a sweeping turn to the Northeast.

The Russian crew knew nothing of a brave American pilot, somewhere in the Gulf of Mexico, who had made the ultimate sacrifice. A collision between an F-22 and a nuclear missile arrested a chain reaction fated to dial back America and her technology to the

Nineteenth Century. He also closed a window of opportunity for the opportunistic Russian president to exact irreparable damage to a country he considered his enemy.

CHAPTER 34
Walter Reed National Military Medical Center
Bethesda, Maryland

Ever since Troy had arrived, Allie Stoker's condition improved rapidly. They'd been weaning her from her ventilator. Today, the doctors were ready to take her off the machine—a ventilator respiratory therapists would quickly clean, sterilize, and put to good use on another patient in dire need.

"Okay Mrs. Stoker," said the pulmonologist. "Just like we talked about. Take a deep breath and cough." The doctor gently pulled the tube from Allie's throat out through her mouth. Allie had an incredible tolerance for pain and discomfort. No distress graced her face. A look of serenity came over her after they put a simple oxygen mask over her mouth and nose.

She tried to talk, but her vocal cords didn't work quite yet.

"We know, Allie my love," Troy Stoker said. "The pain is nothing. You're just happy to be free of the machine."

Allie nodded, closed her eyes, and laid her head back on her pillow. The worst was behind her, and a ski trip to the Rocky Mountains was in her future. For now, she was surrounded by her parents, sister, and husband. She was grateful to be alive and on the mend.

That night, Allie was transferred out of the ICU and onto the medical floor. She was surrounded by soldiers who were patients, many of whom were also recovering from Guillain-Barre syndrome. The next day, Troy, her family, and Errol Rivera put her in a wheelchair. "Let's go visit Z," Stoker said. Troy wheeled Allie down a corridor and into a conference room. There, also in a wheelchair, sat Z with his girlfriend, Jessica.

"Hey, Z," Allie said. "Fancy meeting you here in Bethesda, Maryland. It looks like you've lost some weight."

"About thirty pounds," Z said. "Strange meeting you here, too. What do you have to do to get a beer around here?"

A voice from the doorway said, "Today, we're only serving

the wonderful fermented Mexican beverage, sotol."

Everyone turned toward the door. Allie and Z were shocked to see the president of the United States, James Riddell, walking into the room, flanked by Secret Service agents.

"Well, Mr. President, hello! And, I'll pass on the *soltol*," Z said. "What about you, Stoker?"

"No *soltol* for me today, Sir," Stoker replied to the president. "I'm also not in the mood for tangerine juice."

The president walked over to Allie and Z. "I can't tell you how happy it makes me to see both of you recovering." Then he pulled up a chair beside Allie and sat down to talk to her. "Mrs. Stoker, your husband is a hero. There's a long list of reasons he's a hero. Thanks to his efforts, we estimate he's prevented millions of people from going on ventilators. He helped millions of people infected with an amoeba called Balamuthia to get a medication they needed. And, he figured out who the mastermind of this whole bio-terror attack was. He captured him, interrogated him, and brought him to justice. Then, to top all that off, he helped identify a ship that was about to fire a final silent strike at the United States. Allie, I just want to thank you for having the wisdom to kick him out of the hospital a few weeks ago."

"You're welcome, Mr. President," Allie replied. "Call it women's intuition or whatever you want. I just had a strong impression Troy was a bit conflicted. It was either the terrorists or me. I had to set him straight. And, since I was in a coma during the last few weeks, I'll need everyone to fill me in on the details. The hospital sedated me a few hours after you addressed the nation."

Z chimed in. "I kind of checked out for a while, too. What did Allie and I miss?"

The president made a suggestion. "Dr. Stoker, why don't you tell the story. I may have a few pieces to add. But, there is nobody who knows the details of these attacks like you do."

For the next few minutes, Stoker filled Allie and Z in on events that had happened while they were in the hospital. Then he asked President Riddell if he had anything to add.

"Here are a few particulars. The CIA had a—well, let's just call it a chance meeting—with Alireza Pour-Mohammadi, the bonyad director who was Nikolas's boss. Operatives extracted some fascinating information out of him. In any case, this plot goes all the way to the top. Both the Iranian president and the grand ayatollah were complicit with the bio attacks and the EMP strategic coordination with North Korea. Subsequently, the Air Force took out every single Iranian nuclear facility. Our military destroyed much of their armed forces and crippled their government. I'm pleased to say collateral damage to the good people of Iran was minimal. The people of Iran are amazing, and we owe them all the protection and support we can give them. It's the leaders who are the cancer."

"What about North Korea?" Allie asked.

"We surprised them with how limited our strike was. We hit their weapons and military hard. But, we barely touched Pyongyang, and the populace there sure got out of hand quickly. We disabled their water and electricity. Within a few days, there was chaos. The Chinese army rolled into Pyongyang as peacekeepers and started handing out aid. Little did the North Koreans know, but a bunch of the food was from America. And, we just may have had a few CIA boys inserted with the Chinese peacekeepers.

"The international community praised us for our relative restraint. That paved the way for us to ask China for some negotiation and nation-building help. The Chinese president stepped in and scolded the North Korean leaders like children. China's going to take it from here. North Korea doesn't get much choice. They get to stay socialist. But, there will be a new North Korean regime that is going to interject business and industry in much the same way China does. Say what you will about China; but I'll take the pro-business communists of today, over the Chairman Mao ideologues of the past. Mutually assured destruction was and is a difficult pill to swallow. I feel a lot more enthusiasm for mutually assured trade and transactions."

"We've neutralized North Korea and Iran from any future nuclear or conventional war ambitions," Rivera interjected. "What do we know about Nikolas's organization, Mr. President?"

"I'll let newly appointed FBI Assistant Director Ahmadi answer that," the president said.

"We've arrested hundreds of Nikolas's terrorist combatants," Ahmadi explained. "While people working at Little Italy sandwich shops did *not* know they were harming people, many of the students Nikolas had seeded into hotel and banquet facilities knew they were infecting people. Some CoolSolar employees also knew. That Roya woman—the one I fought in Hotel Esatto's basement—has been a phenomenal source of information."

Rivera asked a question. "Did we ever find out why Nikolas's son was killed during the family extraction?"

"He knew too much," the President said. "He had grave suspicions of his father, and he'd overheard information about a boat, the Tropical Solace cruise ship. When the son started snooping around, Nikolas's bodyguards caught onto his curiosities. Having him in the United States, where the son could've continued to figure things out, would've been dangerous for the leaders of Iran."

"Sir, what about the EMP attacks?" Z asked the president.

"With just a few missiles and modest ten-kiloton nuclear warheads, this band of well-funded, organized, and fanatic Iranians almost exploded the warhead 100 miles above the center of the Continental United States. In league with North Korea, they sent three missiles up from the Korean Peninsula. Then they almost snuck the other one in on us from the cruise ship. They hoped at least one or two of the missiles would achieve their aim. With only two EMPs, Iran and North Korea would've destroyed the American power grid and fried most of our electronic devices. Televisions and radios would've been silenced. Phone calls would've ceased to exist. In hospitals, life-sustaining equipment would've failed. Within seconds, America would've been in chaos."

Rivera spoke up. "There could've been a lot of pandemonium. Within thirty days, ten percent of Americans would've died. Within ninety days, about half of the population would've perished. It would've been prime time for troops from Iran, North Korea, and a few other countries hostile to the United States to attempt a land invasion. They would've divided up geographic sections of the country amongst themselves like a butchered cow."

"Mr. Bojangles is the real hero," Stoker said. "He stopped the missile."

"You know," Rivera said, "the last moments of his life were adrenaline-fueled exuberance. If you're gonna go out, that's how you do it. I'm sure it was thrilling in the mind of that patriot, Bojangles. It wasn't even a decision for him. He just did what he had to do."

"Absolutely," the President said. "Congress and I will award him the Medal of Honor, posthumously. Yet, I think this medal does not even come close to what he did to save the United States."

"How do things look in the Northwest?" Jessica asked. "Z grew up in that area, and we have friends there."

"After their EMP, it's not pretty. But, we've been able to get food, basic medicine, and some limited electricity in place. There have been too many casualties, but it could've been even worse. We're able to feed almost everyone. But, there's not enough water for bathing and sewage. Hospitals and healthcare services are severely limited. We lost a lot of our Guillain-Barre syndrome patients on ventilators because the ventilators got knocked out by the EMP. We're also concerned they won't have heat during the winter. But, we're getting some natural gas and other energy services restored. We hope to have heat restored to most of the area by Christmas."

"Are you willing to share the small Russian episode with us, Mr. President?" Rivera asked. "My conspiracy theory friends think the Russians were involved."

"Your friends are only partly right," the president responded. "The Russians had only heard chatter about what North Korea and Iran were up to. They were waiting on the sidelines. But, when Colonel Bojangles blew up the missile, they closed the bomb bay doors on a plane that was on its way here to crash the party. Then they turned tail and ran home."

The president looked at his watch. "I need to get back to the White House. But, I have a little business to conduct before I leave. Dr. and Mrs. Stoker, I'm awarding you the Presidential Medal of Freedom." Rivera, Ahmadi, and Z gasped in unison. "Troy for your incredible courage, and Allie for the courage and sacrifice to kick your husband out into the chaos when we needed him the most." The president paused for a moment. "Also, when I find out everything you accomplished, Dr. Stoker, you also should be a shoo-in for the Nobel Peace Prize."

"Mr. President, sir," Stoker said. "I'm sorry. But there's no way Allie and I can come to the White House, participate in the public ceremony, and have our names shared with the nation. If you publicize *Espada Rápida* and me, you retire us and make us ineffectual. We'll be worth more to this country if nobody knows we are your weapons."

"I'll tell you what," the President said. "I'll tuck your awards and your story away. When the time is right to tell the world your story, the sitting president will already have my instructions. I only hope I'm alive to be at the ceremony."

"That makes a few of us," Allie said. "I've been hoping for Troy's safety ever since my husband started to run around with Rivera."

THE END

THE AUTHORS

Dr. Francis Bandettini is a private practice psychiatrist and co-author of the Troy Stoker, M.D. psychiatry thriller novels. He graduated from the University of Wisconsin-Madison with a degree in the molecular biology honors program and earned his medical degree at Des Moines University. Dr. Bandettini completed his psychiatry residency at the University of South Dakota School of Medicine where he subsequently joined the faculty as an assistant clinical professor of psychiatry. He is a retired Captain from the United States Army and South Dakota National Guard. He lives with his wife in the greater Sioux Falls area.

Matt Nilsen is a co-author of the Troy Stoker, M.D. psychiatry thriller series. He completed his undergraduate business degree at the University of Utah. Matt also earned a Master of Health Administration degree from the Medical College of Virginia, Virginia Commonwealth University. His career has allowed him to work in clinics and hospitals all over the United States. He and his family currently live in Yuma, Arizona where he practices the Spanish language and works in hospital community relations.

53194400R00181

Made in the USA
Lexington, KY
25 September 2019